CAPTURED IN DEATH

CAPTURED IN DEATH

A KENZIE KIRSCH MEDICAL THRILLER
BOOK TEN

P.D. WORKMAN

ISBN: 9781774686355 (KDP Paperback)
ISBN: 9781774686379 (KDP Hardcover)
ISBN: 9781774686348 (Large Print)
ISBN: 9781774686362 (Lulu Paperback)
ISBN: 9781774686331 (ePub)
ISBN: 9781774686386 (Accessible Audio)

ALSO BY P.D. WORKMAN

MYSTERY/SUSPENSE:

Zachary Goldman Mysteries
Private Investigator
She Wore Mourning
His Hands Were Quiet
She Was Dying Anyway
He Was Walking Alone
They Thought He was Safe
He Was Not There
Her Work Was Everything
She Told a Lie
He Never Forgot
She Was At Risk
He Drowned in Memory
Their Walls Were Empty
They Came for Him
They Sought Vengeance
She Was Their Target
His Fear Was Real
She Was Out of Reach (Coming Soon)
He Was Deceived (Coming Soon)
She Once Vanished (Coming Soon)

Kenzie Kirsch Medical Thrillers

Unlawful Harvest

Doctored Death

Dosed to Death

Gentle Angel

Rushin' Death

Posed for Death

Death of a Corpse

Endowed with Death

Shattered to Death

Captured in Death

Parks Pat Mysteries

Police Procedural Set in Canada

Out with the Sunset

Long Climb to the Top

Dark Water Under the Bridge

Immersed in the View

Skimming Over the Lake

Hazard of the Hills

Knows the Hills

Spanning the Creek

Sanctuary in the Stream

Echos of the Engine (Coming Soon)

Bench with a View (Coming Soon)

Beneath the Icy Depths (Coming Soon)

AND MORE AT PDWORKMAN.COM

For friends who speak up
Even when speaking up is impossible

1

It wasn't the way Kenzie's cases normally came to her.

As an assistant to the medical examiner, she was used to bodies being brought in by van, laid out on the table and cleaned, ready for her to begin her postmortem. She would have some scene notes to peruse or, if she had gone out to the scene herself, she would have dictated the notes. Maybe she would be by herself, or maybe with Dr. Cook, who was substituting for Dr. Wiltshire while his broken hand was healing.

A very different scenario from the one she currently found herself in, sitting in the visiting area of the psych ward with Rhys sitting across from and Zachary next to her. Kenzie pulled her eyes away from the photograph on the phone she held in her hand to the serious Black teen who had handed it to her and was waiting for her to say something.

"Rhys, this needs to go to the police. They need to investigate. Do you even know who this is?"

Rhys, non-speaking as usual, spread his hands apart, palms up, in a gesture of helplessness. *Don't know.*

Zachary leaned in to look at the picture again, his face close to Kenzie's so she could smell his shaving cream. He usually sported a three or four-day growth of beard, which made him look like a home-

1

less person or, at least, someone down on their luck. Someone people didn't want to make eye contact with and would forget as soon as they walked away. As a private investigator, he didn't want people to remember him. But today, he happened to be clean-shaven. His dark eyes were intense as he stared at the photograph. He ran a hand over his close-cropped dark hair.

"We don't even know if it is real," he pointed out. "It could be... stage makeup."

Kenzie didn't have to look again at the grayish skin or the bullet hole in the man's forehead to know that this was no makeup job. She had seen enough corpses in the course of her work to recognize one when she saw it, even in a picture.

"He's dead," she told Zachary with certainty. "It's real."

Rhys nodded his agreement. His dark skin kept him from looking pale, but his expression was pinched and worried. His frown deeper than usual. He had been through an ordeal, a mental collapse apparently triggered by this very picture, followed by a reaction to the drug used in the experimental treatment program he had been placed in, and then finally sedated to let him catch up on the sleep he needed and get back on track again.

It had been over a week since Stanley Green had found him wandering in the street in a fugue state. And if that fugue state had been triggered by viewing this picture, then the man in the picture had been dead for over a week and still hadn't shown up in the morgue.

Maybe he never would. Maybe his body had been dumped somewhere no one would find it.

Rhys held out his hand for his phone. Kenzie shook her head, not giving it back to him. "This is evidence. The police will want to look at the photograph's metadata and any other evidence on your phone. Where you got it from." Kenzie raised her eyebrows, asking again for Rhys to tell her where he had gotten the picture. How did a teenager end up with the picture of a murdered man on his phone? Who had sent it to him and why?

Rhys looked frustrated. Maybe he wanted to text her something on his messaging app. He relied on his phone for communication. He couldn't tell his story to her in gestures and facial expressions. Some things could be communicated that way, but he needed something more.

Kenzie slid her own phone across the table to him. "Send messages to Zachary's phone," she prompted.

Rhys picked up her phone with long, slender fingers and operated it quickly. He found the messaging app he wanted, swiped and tapped rapidly with his thumbs, and the first message popped up on Zachary's phone in a few seconds. Zachary held it so that he and Kenzie could see it at the same time, their heads close together.

Rhys had sent a picture of a dog, a recurring theme in his messages. This one was a cartoon picture of a basset hound dressed in a Sherlock Holmes deerstalker hat and peering into a magnifying glass.

Kenzie nodded. "I know you want me to look into it. To find out what I can. And I will... but this is a police matter. They will have to figure out where the picture came from and who it is. Until I actually see the body, there's not much that I can tell just by looking at a picture."

Rhys pointed at the picture of the dead man, rolling his eyes. What other information did Kenzie need than the fact that the man had been shot in the head? Wasn't that enough to determine cause and manner of death? It was glaringly obvious.

Then what was he expecting her to find out in her investigation? Was she supposed to be able to tell from the photograph who did it? Why?

"Okay, yes," she said as patiently as she could. "I can see that he was shot. Cause of death. I can't issue a medical examiner's report based on a photo. I don't know who it is or the circumstances surrounding his death. I mean, I do issue reports on John Does, but it still needs to go through the official channels for me to do that. I need human remains. Who did you get this from?"

He shrugged and made the ASL sign for "friend," both index fingers hooked together. A well-known sign, even though he did not generally use ASL to communicate, but relied on his own gestures and the phone pictures and short texts to get his message across.

P.D. WORKMAN

"A friend from school?" Zachary asked.

Rhys nodded.

"And do you know where *he* got it from?"

Rhys shrugged. He had already communicated to them that it was something that had been circulating the school. His friend had gotten it from another friend, who had gotten it from another friend.

"What are they saying about it?" Kenzie asked. "They're not just sending it around by itself with no explanation."

He pointed at the phone and made a gun shape with his hand, complete with a jerk showing the gun had been fired.

"What?" Zachary asked. "'Here is a picture of a man who was shot.' That's it?"

Rhys nodded. Kenzie wanted to search through his phone to see who it had come from and exactly what the attached text had said. But she didn't want to touch anything that the police would want to look at. It had probably been sent through an app where the message self-destructed, and all of that information was gone. But maybe the police techs could pull off information that had been deleted but not overwritten.

There was just one thing that she needed to do. If Rhys wanted her to investigate the man's death, she needed a copy of the picture. She didn't know what she could do for Rhys, but he needed to see that she was doing everything she could. He had trusted them with this information that he hadn't shown anyone else, and he was counting on her being able to make everything right.

She didn't know if she could do that, but she would do everything she could for him.

2

I 'm going to send this to your phone," she told Zachary.

It might make more sense to forward it to her own phone. She would need it there eventually. But Rhys didn't need it popping up in his face again while he was holding her phone in his hands. It had been traumatic enough the first time.

And she would probably get Zachary to look at the photo's metadata to see if he could tell her anything about its origin.

Zachary nodded his agreement. Kenzie sent it to him, then slid Rhys's phone into her pocket. It would need to go to the police as evidence. Kenzie would get Rhys another phone. His grandmother, Vera, could probably not afford it. Kenzie didn't think she had much disposable income. But Kenzie didn't want Rhys to be left without a means to communicate beyond gestures.

"This whole thing," Kenzie motioned to the phone in her pocket. "I'm so sorry you had to deal with it. It must be really difficult after what happened to your grandpa."

Rhys nodded. His eyes dropped to the phone in his hand, but he didn't type anything immediately.

Until the drug therapy that Rhys had reacted to, they had all assumed that what had happened to Grandpa Clarence when Rhys was just five was long forgotten, or at least very murky in Rhys's memory. But the MDMA had made Rhys voluble, overcoming his usual mutism, and he had related the images to them over and over again.

His grandfather murdered before his eyes. Shot in the head, like the man in the picture.

It wasn't that Rhys was afraid that the same murderer might have come back, that she had killed a second time and he might be in danger.

Because Rhys knew who the murderer was. He had always known, and he had lived with her for years after Grandpa Clarence's death. Because it had been his aunt Robin. She had since passed. so they all knew that it wasn't the same killer. Just the same cause of death.

Kenzie saw Rhys's lips moving. The same mantra repeated over and over again. Even though he didn't voice the words, she still recognized them.

Stop it. Just stop it.

Robin's words, the night she had killed her father.

"I know," Kenzie said softly. She leaned forward and put her hand over Rhys's briefly, unsure how he would respond to the physical contact. "This is terrible for you. Are you having a lot of flashbacks?"

After remaining unfocused for a few long seconds, Rhys's gaze finally returned to Kenzie's face. He cocked his head slightly as if he knew that Kenzie had said something but wasn't sure what it was or what she meant.

"I asked if you're having flashbacks," Kenzie said slowly, "If you keep remembering what you saw and felt the night that your grandpa was killed, there are things that you can do to try to reduce the impact of the flashbacks, to… get back to the present."

He held out one hand, palm out, inviting her to go on, eyebrows raised curiously.

"One method that helps Zachary is called anchoring." Kenzie looked at Zachary.

He nodded but didn't explain. His flashbacks were better than they had been, but he wasn't over them. The fire that had destroyed his childhood home and precipitated the rift in his family was still ever-present in his mind. Even if he wasn't having flashbacks, he was still aware of it. And although he could stand to be around a lit candle or small campfire now without being thrown back to that experience, other things still triggered flashbacks for him.

"You concentrate on your senses," she told Rhys, since Zachary didn't seem inclined to explain. "You name five things that you see, five things that you hear, five things that you smell or feel. Focusing on those things, on your senses and surroundings, helps minimize the flashback and anchor you to the present."

Rhys nodded slowly. He couldn't name the things he saw out loud and probably couldn't type them on his phone when he was in the throes of a flashback, but he could still focus on them and hopefully get himself out of a flashback faster.

"Maybe you could tell Vera about anchoring, too," Zachary suggested. "She can help talk Rhys through it."

Kenzie nodded. "*You* should probably talk to her rather than me."

Kenzie wasn't exactly in Vera's good books these days. Kenzie had been vocal about Rhys not going to Persons, the private psychiatric facility that had done the experimental drug protocol, for treatment. Kenzie had tried to tell Vera that it was too dangerous, that what they were doing there was not ethical, and that MDMA therapy was too risky for Rhys.

But Vera had been desperate. After years of not hearing Rhys's voice more than just a word or two here and there, and then his falling into the fugue state where he was completely uncommunicative, not even acknowledging that they were speaking to him, let alone trying to respond, she had been willing to risk anything for the miracle cure Persons had dangled in front of her.

Kenzie had been right. The fact did not endear her to Vera. Kenzie was sure Vera would feel awkward and embarrassed that she had gone ahead and done what Kenzie had warned her about and that the result had been negative, just as Kenzie had feared it would be. Kenzie being right about the therapy would be harder for Vera to forgive than being wrong would have been.

Zachary looked at Kenzie for a few seconds, reading this in her face, and eventually nodded. "I'll talk to her about anchoring," he agreed. "Walk her through how to do it." He looked at Rhys. "It does help. It doesn't make them go away completely, but it helps you to... not drown in the flashbacks."

Rhys gave a thumbs-up. He was all for anything that might help.

Kenzie wondered how he felt about the treatment that Vera had put him through. Did he understand that she had just been trying to help him? Did he resent being treated like an animal or a child with no understanding, with no choice in how she decided he should be treated? He hadn't been able to talk to her at the time, hadn't been able to understand or to express his wishes one way or the other, but that understanding wouldn't necessarily change his feelings about what had happened.

Feelings were not always logical. Kenzie sometimes found herself feeling completely opposite from what she wanted to sometimes. No matter how much she tried to talk herself into feeling a certain way, she couldn't control her primitive brain.

"So..." Kenzie took a deep breath and let it go.

They had asked him whether he wanted to talk about Grandpa Clarence and what he remembered. He had shown them the picture of the stranger and asked Kenzie to look into it. Kenzie didn't know how much success she would have in her assignment.

Rhys was looking tired and strained around the eyes. It was bound to be taking a lot of effort for him to act as normal as possible and socialize with them. He had been through a lot in the last couple of weeks, and it would take time for him to recover.

"So, I guess we should probably be going," Kenzie said, standing up and looking at Zachary to encourage him to do the same. "You're looking pretty tired," she told Rhys. "I don't want to wear you out. I'll talk to the police and get started on this... and one of us will bring you a new phone by the end of the day so you can use it to communicate. I don't know how long it will be before you get this one back. I assume they'll need it for a day or two to get all the information they need."

Rhys shrugged, looking unconcerned about whether he got the

phone back or not. Kenzie supposed that if he got a new phone in the deal, he wouldn't be too upset about it, as long as he could still log back in to all of his accounts and not lose any information.

3

Kenzie and Zachary were quiet while they took the elevator back to the main floor and walked out to Zachary's car. Kenzie rubbed her temples. As much as she would like to pretend that she was back to full health, she couldn't deny that she was still having headaches, which she assumed were the result of her mild concussion.

Or maybe it was just this new headache that Rhys had handed her. How was she going to get anywhere on it?

"Who are you going to talk to?" Zachary asked, putting a slightly different spin on it.

Kenzie knew her share of homicide detectives. She could pick who she wanted to take it to and who would give it the most time and attention. Someone who was more likely to believe Rhys, a mentally ill teenager, and not to just brush the case off or say that since no one had found a body, it was obviously a faked photograph, and she could forget about it and just go about her normal business. And so could Rhys.

But how would Rhys go on as usual when the memories of his Grandpa Clarence's murder and the picture of the murdered man that had arrived on his phone stacked up to cause him even more mental distress than he had felt over the previous decade? How was he going to put his grandpa's murder behind him, relegating it to the past when this new face brought it all back again?

She had worked with Detective Elena Garcia on a couple of cases, but Garcia was more likely to be impatient and to roll her eyes at the paucity of the information. She would need a lot more concrete evidence before she would take something like that on. Tuttle and Baker had worked with Kenzie on the Wade homicides, and she considered them seriously before shaking her head. She was sure they had already taken enough flak for having to arrest the congressman's wife. They probably didn't need to take on anything controversial in the wake of that case.

Kenzie shook her head, thinking about it.

"What about Campbell?" Zachary suggested.

Kenzie considered him. He had come to her aid when her father had been missing, helping her sort that mess out and deal with the threats and unexpected developments involving the Russians. He wasn't strictly a homicide detective, but he was a good man to go to with a case that needed to be handled somewhat differently from the straightforward homicide cases Kenzie was used to dealing with.

"Yeah. He might be a good person," she agreed.

"He doesn't jump to conclusions," Zachary offered. "He listens."

"Do you think he'll believe it? That this is real?"

Zachary chewed on his lip. "I think he would consider it. He wouldn't automatically brush it off."

"Yeah."

They reached the car and Zachary disarmed the alarm and unlocked the doors.

"What do you think of the picture?" he asked.

"What do I think? I think someone needs to take it seriously. I don't know who this guy is or when or where he was killed, but someone needs to make sure that we find out."

"You think it's legitimate. That it is someone who was shot and killed."

"Yes." Kenzie looked at him. "You don't think so?"

"I reserve judgment. I don't know."

"You think it's a prank?" Kenzie's voice rose slightly, though she tried to keep it under control.

"I think you know a dead body when you see one."

"And I say it is a dead body."

Zachary nodded. He started the engine and pulled out of the parking space. "Then it is."

"Do you really believe that?"

"Yes." He said it firmly. No waffling. Not that he believed it if she believed it. If Kenzie were looking for an argument, she wouldn't get one from him.

The rest of the discussion on the way to the police station was whether Zachary should also go in with Kenzie. Would they be taken more seriously if both of them showed up, believing this was a real case that Campbell needed to look into? Or would Campbell wonder why Zachary needed to be there to prop up Kenzie's story?

Zachary didn't have any evidence independent of what Rhys had given Kenzie. She had the phone and the picture, and Rhys's brief explanation of where it had come from.

Ultimately, they decided it would be best if Zachary dropped Kenzie off. She worked in the basement of the police department so, when she was finished talking to Campbell, she could just go downstairs and work the rest of the day. Meanwhile, Zachary could go home and analyze the copy of the photo Kenzie had forwarded to him and see if he could find out anything about its origins.

Sergeant Joshua Campbell was at his desk and able to see Kenzie right away. She had been worried that he wouldn't be around, and then she would have to decide whether to leave a message, put it off, or pick someone else to talk to about it.

"Dr. Kirsch," Campbell greeted, standing up when she walked in and extending a hand. "It's great to see you. What can we do for you today?"

"Well... I'm in kind of a quandary," Kenzie admitted, sitting down in the guest chair in front of his desk and thinking about it. She had been trying to script out how the meeting would go ever since they had left the hospital, but she had been unable to come up with anything that made her happy. Of course, it would be great if he just agreed that it was a case that needed to be looked into and that it was an actual, legitimate murder and not some hoax. But she couldn't see a clear path toward getting him to agree with her on that point.

"I'm happy to help you out any way I can," Campbell offered with a smile. "Can I get you some coffee?"

"No, no. I'll get one when I get down to work."

"How's Zachary?" Campbell's eyes wandered to his computer, maybe checking the date to see how close they were to Christmas. "Is everything okay with him?"

"Yes, so far."

Campbell was aware of Zachary's seasonal depression and the suicidal thoughts that had landed him in the psych ward the previous year.

"He's on a different cocktail this year and I'm hoping it will work better," Kenzie told him.

"Good. Glad to hear it. So you aren't here about anything to do with him."

"No. This is... a new case. Maybe a case. Something I'm hoping you can investigate."

Campbell raised an eyebrow, waiting for Kenzie to get on with it.

Kenzie pulled Rhys's phone out of her pocket. She brought the picture up on the screen again and handed it to him.

Campbell looked at the picture for a few long seconds before focusing on Kenzie.

"Is this a threat? Did someone send it to you?"

"No. It was sent to a friend of ours. Rhys Salter. From what we can understand, it's circulating throughout his school. One of those... horror pictures that people gawk at. Like a bad car crash. Shock value. Curiosity. Have a look and pass it on to your friends."

Campbell blinked at her. Kenzie wasn't sure why he looked so confused. She shook her head, waiting for his response.

"Rhys Salter?" Campbell repeated.

"Yes. It was received by him. This is his phone."

"Is he related to Robin Salter, the woman who was murdered?"

"Oh." Kenzie nodded. She had forgotten that he had been involved in the case while Zachary had been investigating it. "Yes, this is Gloria's son. Robin's nephew."

"The mute boy."

"Selectively mute," Kenzie amended. "Yes. But he does have other ways to communicate, and he gave us this. Wanted us to pursue it."

Campbell pondered this. The picture on the phone disappeared as the screen shut off, and he pressed the button to bring it up again.

"This man appears to have been killed in the same way as Rhys's grandfather."

"Yes."

"And you don't find that odd?"

Kenzie shook her head, frowning. "No. What do you mean? What's odd about it? It is disturbing, for sure, but I don't know that I would call it odd."

"I'm thinking that perhaps... this boy has unresolved issues where his grandfather's murder is concerned. Maybe he sought out a picture of a man who was killed in the same way because he is trying to understand his feelings about what happened. Or trying to play it out in his mind again in order to try to control the outcome this time. You hear all the time about adult criminals who are trying to reenact something that happened to them as children in order to be in control of it. Because they had so little control as children."

4

Y ou're not saying that you think Rhys killed someone because of what he witnessed." Kenzie's anger flared at the sugges- tion. "This boy has been through enough trauma without someone accusing him of being a killer."

"No, no," Campbell made a dampening movement with his hands, patting downward. "I'm not saying that he killed someone. I'm saying he might be trying to accept his feelings about the original murder. This could be his attempt to gain control or to examine those feelings from another perspective."

"No," Kenzie shook her head. "All it will take is one of us going to the school and finding out whether this picture has really been circulating the students like Rhys says it has been. But I can tell you, I believe him one hundred percent. I believe this picture was sent to him by someone else, out of the blue, and that it greatly disturbed him. He went into a fugue state. He's been hospitalized since he got this picture; it bothered him so much and brought back all those old feelings. This is *not* something that Rhys did himself."

"Okay, okay. It was a question that had to be asked. And even if it is circulating the school, that doesn't prove he didn't start it. He might have been the first one to send it around. He could control multiple fake accounts to keep it circulating. You don't know."

"I don't believe that. This is something that was sent to him and caused a great emotional shock. And he wants to know who it is and what happened. *That* is what he wants to resolve. He already knows who killed his grandfather. He doesn't need to resolve that."

"He may still be having a lot of emotional disturbance due to his grandfather's murder. He *is* still mute, isn't he?"

"He's… well, mostly, yes."

"So it hasn't been resolved."

"Not in that way. But there is no way to tell if he will ever be able to talk normally, even if he has fully accepted and integrated what happened to his grandfather. Sometimes those scars are just too deep."

Campbell nodded, looking at the picture. "So you are coming to me to… investigate this crime…?" He tapped the side of the phone.

"Well, yes. I can't really open an investigation from the medical examiner's office because I don't have a body. But maybe this is enough evidence for *you* to open a file and conduct some preliminary investigation…"

Campbell swiveled slightly to face his computer and typed a query. He scrolled through the screen, shaking his head.

"This doesn't appear to be a local death. Nothing on our system indicates that we have opened an investigation into a man who was shot in the head in the last few days."

"It would be longer ago than that."

"How long?"

"Closer to two weeks. Maybe longer, if the picture didn't start to circulate immediately."

"At two weeks, it should be on your table by now. If there was such a crime."

"Unless the body was dumped somewhere and just hasn't been discovered yet."

"I'm not sure how we're supposed to do anything if that is the case. But there's also nothing to indicate that this is a local murder. It could be hundreds of miles away. It could have been five years ago. It could be staged."

"It's not staged."

But Kenzie couldn't deny that he could be right about it not happening two weeks before. Or being local. She had assumed that the murder happened just before the picture started circulating at the school. Still, she had seen a number of stories make their rounds on social media every few years, showing up with a few details changed so that it was suddenly brand new again. Everyone was agog, not realizing it had happened five, ten, or even twenty years before.

"What about facial recognition?" she suggested. "If we could identify who the man is, we could narrow down the time and place. Find out whether it really is something that happened recently."

Campbell sighed. "I can get the techies to run it, see if they get any hits. I don't know whether the resolution is high enough or whether we have enough of his face to get a hit. The portrayals you see on TV of facial recognition are highly exaggerated. You need a full-frontal view, no profiles, with all of the landmarks visible. And only a fraction of felons are actually in the database yet. There are a lot of databases that are not accessible to us."

"It's *almost* straight on."

"Almost. That's why I said I'd see if they can get any hits off of it. But don't hold your breath. It isn't as easy as you see on TV. It's a very sophisticated technology, and it doesn't do as well in the wild as it does in controlled tests and fiction."

"So you'll open a file on it?"

"I'll need to open a file to log the evidence and have it examined," Campbell said, touching the phone again. "But I'm not opening it as a homicide. Only as 'disturbing peace by use of telephone.' Someone sending this disturbing picture to a minor, especially one who has previously witnessed a similar murder in his own family, could well be seen as an attempt to 'terrify, threaten, harass, or annoy.' "

Kenzie nodded her agreement. "Especially when you consider the outcome."

"Right. In the meantime..."

Kenzie waited for his question. "Yes...?"

"I assume you kept a copy of this."

Kenzie shrugged, her cheeks getting warm. "Well... yes."

"You might see if Zachary can trace the origin of the picture. If it has been circulating the internet for a few years, or if it is from a movie set, he may be able to identify it and confirm that it is not actually a current, local murder that needs to be solved."

"I already have him looking at it," Kenzie said. "I hadn't thought about finding out if it is already on the net somewhere, but I did ask him to check the metadata to see if it leads us anywhere."

"I'm sure he'll go the whole way. Photography is his thing. If he could do that, I would appreciate it. My techs' time is precious. I don't like to waste it on a wild goose chase. If he can narrow down whether it is really something that we need to look into… I would appreciate that."

"Sure. I'm sure he would be happy to loop you in."

"Good. I haven't talked to him for a while. We could do coffee and catch up."

5

After the talk with Campbell, Kenzie headed downstairs to the morgue. It was a late start, but she had warned Dr. Cook ahead of time. She and Zachary had needed to go see Rhys, and Kenzie had put in a lot of hours at the morgue lately. It wouldn't hurt them for her to take a couple of hours off. Better for her mental health than overworking herself for two weeks straight. Had it been that long since she'd had a break?

Kenzie sat down at her desk and dialed Zachary to tell him about her meeting with Campbell. As she checked her email and digitally filed a number of reports that had come in overnight, she filled him in on the details. Zachary agreed to do as Campbell had said and to do some image searches to see if he could find out where the picture had originated.

"He says you guys should get together for coffee," Kenzie said. "So if you can find anything, you should follow up. Maybe he has some other stuff they want to contract out. Or maybe he just wants to catch up with you."

"It has been a while," Zachary admitted, sounding far away. "I'll follow up."

"Good. And can you email me the photo? I want to have Dr. Cook take a look at it, too."

"Yeah? Okay. I can do that." She heard him typing rapidly. "There you go, on its way to you. Thanks for talking to Campbell. I'm glad he decided to look into it."

"Well, as a phone harassment case, not as a homicide. But I don't really care, as long as he can start pulling together some information to find out who the guy is and what happened to him."

"Well, we know what happened to him."

"Well… before that. And after that. Who did it, and why, and what happened to the body? Because Campbell says that nothing has shown up on their radar. No body."

"Maybe he's right and it's something that happened in Russia. Or ten years ago. We just assumed that it was something that had just happened, but…"

"Anything in the metadata?"

"Not much. From the looks of it, it was a screen capture somewhere along the way. The original metadata isn't still attached. Someone received it, grabbed a screenshot, and then forwarded that screenshot to someone else. And so on. Probably more than once. But if I can find other copies of it on the internet, I might be able to find something with the original metadata still attached. Or other information that could help us."

Kenzie sighed. "I suppose it was too much to expect someone to leave all the information attached to the photo. Geotags, dates, what kind of camera it was taken with. That would have been nice, wouldn't it?"

"No such luck," Zachary said, sounding a little too cheerful about it. "But I'll see if I can find other copies online. Maybe I'll have better luck that way."

Kenzie had the photo on her screen when Dr. Cook walked up to her desk to touch base on how they were going to be spending the day.

"Morning, Dr. Kirsch," he greeted, and his eyes slid over to her screen. He frowned. "I didn't get a call out today. What case is that?"

"Oh… actually, it isn't a case yet. The police are looking into it, but…"

"If there is a dead man and the police are looking into it, then why hasn't the medical examiner's office been called?"

"Because actually… we don't know where the photo came from. It could be nothing. It could be something that happened years ago or in another part of the world altogether. But it could also… be something that happened here a couple of weeks ago."

"I would think we would have the body on the table by now if it happened a couple of weeks ago."

"Maybe. I mean… if it was left out on the street where someone could find it. But if it was disposed of somewhere else… out in the Vermont woods… I mean, there are a lot of wild areas it could be hidden and not found for years."

"That has been known to happen," he admitted. "So… you're freelancing now? Off finding your own bodies?"

"Well… it sort of fell into my lap." Kenzie's cheeks were warm. "That is… I have a friend who received this on his phone and wanted me to look into it. See whether it was legitimate or not. I don't know anything yet. I haven't had enough time to investigate it. And… we have other cases to work on, legitimate ones. Where the bodies are on our tables."

"Yeah." He didn't move on to their legitimate cases. "But nothing so urgent that we can't take a few minutes to examine an intriguing photograph. See what we can discern from it." He leaned on the high counter of her reception desk, looking at the photograph thoughtfully.

Kenzie turned her attention back to her screen. "Everyone's first reaction is that it can't be real. That it is just stage makeup or something. But…" Kenzie grimaced. "I've seen my share of dead bodies. More than most people. And that looks like a real dead body to me. The dead bodies on TV, with all of the makeup and special effects they have at their disposal, never look the same. They look like live people who are pretending to be dead. Or else like gruesome zombies too bloody and gory to be real."

Dr. Cook nodded his agreement.

Kenzie was suddenly uncomfortable with how close he was leaning to her. Cook was good-looking, with dark, longish hair and brilliant blue eyes, looking like a movie star who had wandered off some set and, while Kenzie had gotten used to being around him most of the time, he was a bit too close for comfort and she was a little bit too aware of his good looks. She leaned away from him, pushing her chair to the side slightly.

"Do you want me to send it to you?"

"No, this is fine." He seemed oblivious to her discomfort. "So we're looking at a small caliber bullet fired close to the head. Execution style."

Kenzie nodded. "A 22 round, maybe. Small entrance wound, not a lot of bleeding, no exit wound that we can see on the photograph, but obviously we can't see the back of his head."

"But there isn't a pool of blood under his head. And only a little bleeding from the forehead. So, I think it is probably still inside. Bounced around inside his skull until it lost velocity."

"Right," Kenzie agreed. In the enclosed space of the skull, a 22 could do a lot of damage as it ricocheted inside the skull.

"I don't see any other signs of violence on the body, but we can't see the whole thing. No way to tell if he was armed or had been in an altercation."

"It's not likely he shot himself."

"No," Cook agreed. "Few suicides go for the forehead. That's more likely to be in the mouth or under the chin, like you see in the movies."

Kenzie's skin crawled. She paused, waiting for the goosebumps and the knot in her gut to fade. She didn't like talking about suicide. She had investigated plenty of suicides, but few of them were by gunshot. It was a particularly violent and messy way to go. She couldn't help thinking about Zachary whenever she was talking about suicide. He had not attempted suicide in the time that they had known each other, but she knew he had when he was younger. Sometimes cutting and sometimes pills. Maybe other methods she didn't know about.

The previous year had been a difficult one, and Zachary had

struggled with suicidal thoughts enough that he had admitted himself to the psych ward in order to keep himself safe and get back on track. It had been a scary time. In the days before he had admitted himself, he had taken the sharp knives from the butcher block in the kitchen and put them away out of sight so that he wouldn't be tempted by them. She had been afraid whenever she left him alone, worrying about how he would be while she was gone.

She shook off the dark thoughts and tried to focus her attention back on the photography.

"You okay?" Dr. Cook asked.

"Yeah, just… a bad feeling. It's nothing." She didn't want to get into any detail with him, but she also didn't want to deny her emotions. She didn't want to fall into morbid thoughts. She could stay removed from the situation and view it from a clinical perspective.

The victim was not anyone she knew. She cataloged what she could tell or guess from the picture. A long-haired blond man. Probably in his late twenties or early thirties. While his face didn't show a lot of extra weight, his stomach did strain against his waistband and shirt, as if he'd bought clothes a size too small or recently put on weight. He was not well-dressed. Not someone she could immediately identify as homeless, but he didn't look like he was comfortably situated. On the skids.

He looked like an aging street punk. Gone to seed. Someone who had spent too much time drinking or doping, or both. Not a crackhead, but not clean.

"How about the background?" Cook suggested. "When they examine pictures of hostages or child pornography, they always look at the background to see if they can find something that will help them to pinpoint the location."

Kenzie didn't find the background very helpful. The guy was lying on the pavement. There was no city skyline behind him, no store or business name they could pick up. Just a man lying on the street. She looked at Cook to see if he had discerned anything else from it.

"Well…" Cook looked for something to say. "It looks much easier on TV. There is always a historic building they can trace or some kind of mountain range or train station that they can use to triangulate the location."

Kenzie nodded. "It looks like half-light. Early morning or evening. Do you think it is a street, sidewalk, or back alley?"

They both studied it, trying to guess from the aggregate and any other indicators exactly what the surface was.

"Not a sidewalk," Cook said. "And no lines or curbs. It doesn't make much sense that he would be executed in the middle of the street where everyone could see. So… a back alley. That would be my guess."

That narrowed the possible locations down by about half, but still wasn't anywhere near the amount of information they would need to positively identify the location.

"I guess this wasn't terribly helpful," Cook admitted. "An interesting exercise, but I guess we'll have to rely on the cops to figure out who it is and where and when."

Kenzie nodded. "Yeah. I guess I'm not very good at a virtual autopsy."

"It's a little easier when you actually get to see the scene and get the body on your table. Not much we can test or investigate in this case."

Kenzie agreed. She closed the photo window. Dr. Cook stepped back. "Well, then, back to our regular programming," he announced with a smile.

6

It was late in the day when Kenzie stopped by the hospital to give Rhys the new phone she had picked up for him.

She had tried to balance the wishes of Rhys and his grandmother. Rhys would, of course, want the latest and greatest thing in cell phones. Whatever was the most popular or the newest release—something with all the bells, whistles, and latest features.

Vera, on the other hand, might be embarrassed if Kenzie got something too expensive, showing her up, making her feel like she couldn't provide for her grandson. So, Kenzie had bought a middle-of-the-road model. All of the features she thought that Rhys would really need, access to the streaming data he would need to be able to communicate most efficiently, with enough storage for him to be able to keep pictures and maybe install an actual AAC app to communicate with.

Rhys seemed unwilling or unable to use any alternative communication system. Kenzie wasn't sure whether it was because he was afraid he would look different or fail, or because his brain just would not fit into the confines of how the rest of the world felt he should be able to communicate. But he could not seem to be able to implement a language system that would let him tell them in detail what had happened the night Grandpa Clarence had been murdered. Robin's order to "Just be quiet" seemed to have taken such a hold on Rhys that he couldn't do anything but obey, no matter what communication methods might be available.

Vera was still at the hospital, which Kenzie hadn't anticipated. She had thought it would be late enough for Vera to be at home getting ready for bed. She smiled and warmly shook Kenzie's hand, but Kenzie sensed a lingering reserve.

"How nice of you to come."

"Thanks." Kenzie also shook hands with Rhys, and he looked at her with bright, expectant eyes. He knew why she had come back. Kenzie chuckled. She pulled out the phone she had set up for Rhys and handed it to him. Rhys beamed. He pressed the home button and started tapping and swiping to explore the new device and what he could do with it.

Vera was frowning at Kenzie. "Is your phone not working? He's very good at fixing them."

Kenzie looked at Rhys, who was too enthralled by the phone to pay any attention to the conversation. He had apparently not told Vera about the picture or why Kenzie had taken his phone away. She probably thought it was still locked away, as the psych ward did not normally permit the patients to use their phones, having run into some behavioral issues with other patients. When Rhys had let them know that he needed to show her something on his phone, Kenzie had insisted that Rhys be allowed to use it, as it was one of his only means of communication.

"Uh, no. This is Rhys's new phone." Kenzie tried to think of how to tell Vera what Rhys had shown them.

Vera was looking at her, shaking her head, trying to understand what was happening.

"It was... well, you know that something triggered Rhys's breakdown a couple of weeks ago," she said quietly.

Vera nodded. Of course she knew that. It had been the focus of her life from the moment Stanley Green called her to tell her he had found Rhys wandering the streets, unable to communicate with him.

"Well, Zachary and I were talking to Rhys about what had

happened, and it turns out that there was a picture on his phone, one that was sent by a friend."

Vera's jaw dropped, shocked and horrified. "Was it... pornographic? I've warned him. I've told him that's what kids these days do, and he just can't get involved in that. He could be prosecuted if he ever participated in forwarding pictures like that." She glared at Rhys as he played with his phone.

"No," Kenzie said. "A picture was being forwarded around the school, but it wasn't pornography. It was... a picture of a murdered man." She said it baldly, getting the pertinent information out as quickly as possible. She didn't want there to be any question of what kind of picture she was talking about. It wasn't the time to be vague or use kind euphemisms. Vera needed to know what she was dealing with.

"A... murdered man!" Vera grasped Rhys's arm tightly and pulled him toward her.

Rhys was forced to look up from his phone to see what was going on. He looked at Vera's face, put his other hand over hers, and then looked at Kenzie for an explanation.

"Yes," Kenzie said, keeping her focus on Vera. "It was a picture of a man who had been shot, and it was very upsetting to Rhys. It brought back... a lot of old stuff." She couldn't bring herself to say Clarence's name or to allude more directly to his murder. "It was overwhelming to him. But now that he's feeling better," she put on a lighter, happier tone, "He would like us to find out who it is and what exactly happened to him. To make sure that it is handled properly."

That was probably a tactless thing to say. Kenzie hadn't planned her explanation out very well. Would Vera assume Kenzie meant they hadn't handled Clarence's death properly? Of course, they had not. They had covered up what had happened and Robin had never been brought to justice. Rhys had lived with the unpunished murderer for years. Now, Rhys wanted another killer brought to justice. Kenzie didn't know if she could find the killer or help see him convicted. But she would try. She would do everything within her power to identify the victim and his killer.

Vera looked at Rhys, licking her lips, swallowing hard. "Rhys…" Her tone was a mixture of horror and accusation.

"He hasn't done anything wrong," Kenzie told Vera. "He was just one recipient of the photograph, and he has asked for help."

"Well, we can't… we can't get involved in this. That kind of thing, it would just be too hard on Rhys. We don't want to get involved."

"I've already taken his phone to the police. I'm sorry if you think that was… that I was taking liberties and should have left it to you. It seemed like the right thing to do. So… they have his phone, and I brought this new one for him to use."

Rhys nodded. He let go of Vera's hand and picked it up to show her, pointing to the bright, crystal-clear screen and the icons and widgets he was already playing with.

Vera tried to smile, but she was clearly upset. "You just went ahead and did this without even talking to me?"

"I… yes. Rhys asked for my help, and I just went ahead and did it. I didn't think about anything else… I guess I thought he would tell you about it and that you would want me to do the same thing."

"He can't be involved in this." Vera shook her head and rubbed her eyes. "The police are going to want to talk to him and he's going to get dragged into something ugly. Something that has nothing to do with him. He should have just deleted the picture and forgotten about it."

Rhys looked at his grandmother reproachfully with that peculiar, sad-eyed frown that always reminded Kenzie of a basset hound. Kenzie didn't want to take sides or interfere with their relationship. Still, she had already done so, and they had the evidence from history that hiding things, burying them and trying to forget them, had done Rhys no good in the past. He had only been harmed by this strategy before.

"Vera… I don't think that would work or do any good for Rhys. He needs to… he wants to help. To feel like he has done something for this man."

"We don't even know him. You have no idea who he is!" Vera glared at Rhys. "You don't even know him from Adam, do you?"

Rhys shrugged and spread his hands out, agreeing with her. He had no clue who the dead man was. But why should that stop him?

"This is all a big mistake," Vera said. "Some joke email. A kids' prank. The police will write it off, warn us not to bother them with silly stuff like this in the future, and we can go on as before."

"They're going to look into it," Kenzie told her. "They are not labeling it a homicide. They don't know yet what it is. Nobody is in trouble for anything."

Vera shook her head grimly. "Well, you can expect that trouble is going to come looking for you."

7

Kenzie wasn't feeling great after the meeting with Vera. It was Friday night, date night. She and Zachary were supposed to be out exploring Vermont and their relationship with each other, enjoying themselves and relaxing.

But she didn't feel very relaxed. They had decided to go to a classic car show in Burlington. Kenzie didn't know a whole lot about cars, but she loved her "baby," a cherry red convertible— though the cooling weather meant that they were taking Zachary's more practical, nondescript surveillance car more often. Zachary didn't know much about cars either, so they were on equal footing, both interested in what looked shiny and retro without getting bogged down with engine configurations, exhaust pipes, or all-original-parts.

She tried to be cheerful and get into it. But despite the rows of beautiful cars, the food vendors, and the people offering various car services, she was still down in the dumps.

They sat down at a table with soft drinks and small servings of fries and mini donuts, fragrant with grease, yeast, and vanilla, and ate slowly, savoring the treat and the special time together. But Kenzie found her mind constantly distracted by Vera's reaction to Kenzie stepping in and taking over Rhys's phone and deciding what was best for him without any thought that his guardian might have a different opinion.

Kenzie's life experience had been very different from Rhys's or even Vera's. A white girl, growing up in a wealthy, privileged home, her biggest challenges had been related to her sister Amanda's illness. Rhys and Vera had to deal with prejudices against Blacks, especially in law enforcement and the legal system. They grew up fearing random police attention and unfair prison terms. Vera also dealt with the terror of Rhys not being able to speak to the police, being taken as a problem: having an attitude and being unable to explain himself verbally. The family's reaction to Clarence's murder had not been to seek justice, but to keep it quiet. To cover it up and turn away police suspicions.

Considering Campbell's reaction to finding out that Rhys was the boy who had been in possession of the picture of the man with a bullet in his head, Vera was right to believe that the police would think the worst of Rhys. That they would automatically see him as a troublemaker, either a criminal or an attention-seeker, rather than as a troubled boy who had been traumatized by what he had witnessed and then received on his phone. They did not see him as vulnerable and broken, but as a potential threat to public peace. Campbell was one of the good ones. Kenzie could only imagine what those who were *really* prejudiced would think.

She initially flinched when Zachary put his hand over hers. But she relaxed and looked at his face and forced a smile in response to his concerned expression.

"Are you okay?" Zachary asked. "You must be tired. It's been a long day, and with the concussion…"

"The concussion isn't a problem," Kenzie said. "I don't think I'm having any more symptoms. It was just very mild. But… I am tired."

"We'll head for home once we finish eating."

"Yeah, that would be good. I'll need some time to unwind before we go to bed."

He nodded. His eyes still searched her face, maybe sensing that there was more to it than just tiredness. But that was up to Kenzie to explain. He had already asked her if she was okay. He wouldn't push too hard for more than she had offered. He wouldn't dig down deeper unless it was really obvious that something was bothering her and, hopefully, she'd not given that much away.

"It's just Vera," Kenzie told him. "She was really not happy with me going ahead and taking Rhys's phone and the picture to the police."

Zachary nodded slowly. "I don't see how we could have done anything else. But… I guess I can see where she's coming from. He's her grandson; she's the boss and the one making decisions for him. And it is kind of… the second strike."

Kenzie winced. "Because I was against the MDMA therapy."

"Yeah. So that's twice when you've 'known better' than her what was best for Rhys."

"I suppose so. She was pretty upset."

"How was Rhys?"

Kenzie thought about it. If it was Rhys that she was trying to help, then she should probably focus on his reaction rather than Vera's. Vera was his caregiver for now but, in a few years, Rhys would be making his own decisions, and he was old enough now to defy Vera, riding across town when he was supposed to be at school, showing up at Stanley Green's late at night when he was supposed to be in bed. Vera might think that she knew what was best for Rhys, but how had Rhys felt about it?

Rhys had seemed happy. He had certainly liked getting the new phone, but that wasn't all there was to it. He had not bowed under Vera's opinion that taking the case to the police had been the wrong thing to do. He had still maintained that was what he wanted done. And she thought he seemed lighter for having passed that burden on to Kenzie. He no longer had to shoulder it alone and to figure out what to do and how to get justice for the murdered man. Instead, he could leave it to Kenzie and the police to sort out, and he could go back to being a kid.

Or at least, not as much. She suspected he would still think a lot about the dead man. And still have flashbacks to Grandpa Clarence's murder. Nightmares too. But at least he had taken one step, a constructive step to resolving the situation he found himself in once more. He wouldn't stand by and be a silent witness this time. His voice might have been silenced, but his brain and his body weren't, and he could still shout his story out to anyone who would listen.

Kenzie nodded her head slowly. "Rhys was okay with it. Happy, I think. Happier than before."

"I felt when we left there this morning that it was a relief for him to talk to us about it and to get you looking into it."

"I guess so. It's hard to hold things in." Kenzie closed her eyes and passed her hand over her lids, tired. "Even though it was really hard to talk to you and Dr. B about the... about the Russians..." She still had a hard time saying the word *kidnapping*. "I really did feel better about getting it out in the open and not having to keep it a secret anymore."

Zachary nodded. He ate a fry and stared away from Kenzie, ostensibly looking at a row of shiny Fords. But Kenzie knew he wasn't looking at them.

How many secrets was Zachary still hiding, trying to stuff down things that had happened in his life that he'd been forced to be quiet about? And how many times had something happened, like the assault by Archuro, and Zachary had done his best to forget it because it was so traumatic? She hoped that, somehow, he would be able to talk about more of those things.

8

---

*Z*achary confirmed the fact that he couldn't find any copies of the photograph of the dead man that had been in circulation prior to two weeks before, when Rhys had received it on his phone.

Once the picture had started circulating the school, there were a few instances where it had popped up on the internet in places that should have been secure, but were not to someone who knew the secrets of getting into such places. And it appeared more frequently on the deep web, where it couldn't be easily deleted or blocked by the content scrubbers searching for offensive material.

But none of the copies were more than two weeks old. And the picture seemed to have originated locally, though it had been distributed to some far-flung parts of the world very quickly.

"So, I think I should talk to some of the teachers and kids at the school and see if I can find out some more about it," Kenzie told Zachary over breakfast. "It may be that a few well-placed questions will crack this open, and we will be able to find out who that man was and where the message came from pretty quickly."

Zachary grimaced. "I don't think it will be as quick as you think. Kids aren't necessarily going to want to talk to you. They like their secrets. You're an adult, and not a trusted one."

"But I have to try, right? The only way I'm going to find out who forwarded it to whom is by asking. They still have the choice of whether to answer me or not. But I only need one or two people who will answer my questions."

"One or two people who know something," he clarified.

"Well, yes." Kenzie was slightly deflated. It wouldn't do to have a hundred students telling her they had no idea who the man was or why they had been sent the picture. She needed one or two people who knew what was going on.

"I know the principal over there," Zachary offered.

"At Rhys's school?"

"Yeah."

Kenzie sat up. "That would be great. How do you know him?"

"Her. I talked to her when I was looking for Madison. Principal Lakes. I'm sure she'll cooperate if you mention my name."

"Because you helped Madison?"

"Well, as far as they are concerned, Madison was fatally injured in a shootout on the highway, so I didn't do much to help her. But I also... broke a case regarding Principal Lakes's predecessor."

"*A case regarding* her predecessor?"

"Yeah. It turned out that she was... seeing some of her students socially."

It took a minute for his meaning to sink in. Kenzie's brows rose. "She was a pedophile?"

Zachary nodded.

"And you were the one who figured it out?"

"I can't take all of the credit. It was her husband who figured she was seeing someone behind his back. And the police who made the arrest."

"But you're the one who caught her with a student."

Zachary nodded.

Kenzie vaguely remembered something in the news a couple of years before about a principal dating a student. But she didn't think she had known at the time that Zachary had been the one to break it. It had been early in their relationship. Maybe just around the time she had met him.

"Well, I guess you're in the new principal's good books, then," she agreed. "Unless, of course, she has a similar leaning."

"No," Zachary shook his head quickly, getting red-faced, "She told me why she was having to rebuild everyone's trust after Principal Montgomery was arrested. She would have known better than to do anything like that, even if she did have... leanings." His face got redder still.

"Do you want to come with me, then?" Kenzie offered. "If I talk to the school on Monday, do you want to ride along and break the ice for me?"

He looked proud of himself. And well he should. Principal Lakes had good reason to be impressed with him after he both exposed a pedophile working in the school system and rescued a girl who was being trafficked. She had no way of knowing that Madison's story hadn't ended on the tragic note she thought it had. And she didn't know that Zachary had rescued Luke at the same time. And again, once more since then, had proven that Luke was not guilty of the murder he had been accused of.

Zachary had done a lot of good over the last few years. And maybe he could help Kenzie solve this case, too.

"Sure," Zachary agreed. "I'll make some time for it. Besides, you shouldn't be driving yet, anyway. You'll need someone to take you over there."

"My head is fine." At some point, he would have to let her start driving again. She was going to have to insist. But she needed him at the school, so she would let him drive her one more time before insisting on his letting her return to normal

---

Saturday and Sunday were more relaxing. Now that the deaths at the private psychiatric facility were off of her plate and Rhys was back in the public hospital where he was safe, she could take some time to rest and regenerate. She put in a couple of hours of work on Saturday and nothing on Sunday. She knew she had a slight backlog of bodies to catch up on when she returned to the office. But it would only take her and Dr. Cook a few days. There was nothing too controversial or unexpected. Unless something turned up in the postmortem examinations that gave her cause for concern, she should be able to deal with them quickly enough.

So, Monday morning, she and Zachary headed over to Rhys's school to see what they could find out about the picture's origin. Zachary had messaged the principal over the weekend so that she knew they were coming, though she didn't know any details about what was going on yet. As expected, Zachary was an angel in her eyes, and she went out of her way to clear her schedule to see them.

Principal Lakes was a young woman. She was the type of young professional that always made Kenzie feel like she had wasted the first part of her life when others, like the principal, were building their careers early, hitting it hard and getting ahead before Kenzie had even figured out what she wanted to do with her life. It wasn't the money. She knew that principals did not make a lot. It was just the feeling that she had been left behind in the dust while the movers and the shakers had taken up their positions.

"Dr. Kirsch, it's very nice to meet you," Principal Lakes greeted, shaking her hand firmly, but not too hard. Just the right professional touch. "Why don't we all have a seat, and you can tell me what you're here about today?"

She gestured to the couch and chairs grouped at the end of her office opposite her desk, where a coffee carafe, mugs, and milk and sugar were waiting.

Principal Lakes gave Zachary a quick hug before letting him sit, making him blush. Kenzie enjoyed his discomfort.

They all sat down and helped themselves to the coffee. Principal Lakes asked Zachary how he was doing, and he answered her questions politely and professionally.

"So." Principal Lakes wrapped her hands around her mug. "What can I help you with today? I guess this has something to do with Rhys?"

Zachary looked at Kenzie, indicating it was time for her to take over.

Kenzie took a deep breath and let it out slowly to calm herself.

9

W̲e found out from Rhys that there is a photograph circulating amongst the students, which is disturbing and impacted him quite significantly."

Principal Lakes shook her head. "Selfies? Nudes? We have talked to students about that before. I thought they were doing very well. But of course, that is from an administrator's perspective, and I don't see everything that happens on their phones. I do try to be aware of it, and we have frequent discussions about what is appropriate or not appropriate to have on their phones."

"No," Kenzie said. "Not selfies." She brought the picture up on her phone and handed it to Principal Lakes. She stared at it, frowning.

"What is this?"

"It appears to be a dead man. A man who was shot."

"This can't be real. It's probably off of some television show or movie."

"I will be very relieved if it turns out to be," Kenzie said. "But it is very realistic. As someone who deals regularly with dead bodies, I can tell you that. I don't believe it is from a movie. I think it is real."

"But where would students get such a thing? I suppose it's off of the internet—some crime scene photo. People have ways of repurposing material and using it to achieve their own goals. Maybe a student thought this looked disgusting and wanted to cause drama and upset people. Or maybe it was originally sent by a student interested in forensics or pathology, like you," Principal Lakes nodded to Kenzie. "It could be quite innocent, initially."

"We would like to figure out where it came from. To trace it back to its origin."

"Do you think that the students have done something criminal here? I don't see how they could be charged for this."

Kenzie thought about Campbell opening it as a phone harassment case. There were certainly things that students could be charged with for forwarding explicit or terroristic material to their friends. Even if they didn't intend any harm. But she wasn't about to tell Principal Lakes that her students could be arrested and charged for what they had unwittingly done.

"We just want to find out where the picture originated, to help us identify who he is and what happened to him."

"And you will not charge any students in this matter."

"I'm not a cop. I'm not charging anyone with anything."

"And you're a private investigator," Lakes looked at Zachary for confirmation. "So you're not laying any charges either."

"No, ma'am."

"Well, this is something that bears looking into." She meditated for a moment, considering the matter. "My first guess would be that it was a picture that someone found online, like I said. If it wasn't that, my next suspects would be the drama club."

Kenzie raised her brows. She had difficulty believing that a group of students could pull off something that looked so realistic with amateur makeup skills. But then, sometimes an amateur job could look more realistic than a professional one. Amateurs had certainly fooled experts with pictures in the past. And a group of dedicated hobbyists might have the ingenuity to pull off something like that. She remembered back when she was in school; students had been using oatmeal and food coloring to make fairly convincing zombies. Who had come up with the idea of oatmeal? Not likely a professional.

"If it was created by a group of kids," Zachary said slowly, "then wouldn't the apparent victim be a kid?"

Principal Lakes looked at him, lips pursed. "They could have talked an adult into being their test subject. We have the auto mechanics students working on people's cars and the hairdressing students cutting hair for other students or adults. It's not unusual to recruit an adult for help with practical application."

Zachary looked unconvinced. "We can talk to the drama club, but I suspect they would have used another student. This guy doesn't look old enough to be someone's parent. If it were a teacher, you would recognize him. They didn't just recruit some random guy off the street."

The principal looked at the photo again, for a bit longer this time, deep frown lines between her brows, clearly trying to figure out if she could identify the "victim."

"If you could let us talk to the drama club kids," Kenzie said, "that would be helpful. And if you could identify who some of Rhys's friends are, so we can talk to them about what they might know about the picture and its origins, that would also be great."

She should have asked Rhys for the names of his friends. That would have sped things up a little. She could just say who she wanted rather than rely on the principal to know who Rhys hung out with the most. But Rhys had been tiring and not as communicative at the end of their discussion. And Kenzie hadn't wanted to ask him anything about the picture in front of Vera. She knew when to keep her mouth shut.

"I can call a few people down to the office to talk to you," Principal Lakes offered slowly. "But this is not an official interview. This is just you, as a friend to Rhys, trying to help him with a personal problem. I don't want there to be any suggestion that the police are involved or that these interviews are being done on their behalf."

Kenzie and Zachary nodded. The police would probably have the very same request. They wouldn't want Kenzie and Zachary holding themselves out as police agents either.

"That's exactly what we want," Kenzie agreed. "We're just doing whatever we can to help Rhys. He's... had a pretty rough time."

"That boy," Lakes sighed. "I only know a little of what he's been through, but I know he's really had a tough life. I wish there was more that we could do to help him."

10

A pparently, drama kids slept in. Principal Lakes only managed to find a couple who had shown up for their morning classes on time. She rolled her eyes and shook her head at Kenzie.

"Free spirits. If I had skipped classes, my parents would have killed me. Or at least grounded me and pulled me out of drama club until I started behaving myself. These kids tend to be very bright. They keep their marks up okay despite missing classes and hanging out to smoke weed or work on their next production. Yes, I know they are smoking. There's not much we can do about it if they are off school property. It isn't like their parents don't know."

Kenzie couldn't imagine how her parents would have reacted if she had thought she could get away with skipping classes and smoking weed. Step one would have been grounding and visits to a therapist to work through her issues. They would probably have blamed it all on the difficulty of dealing with Amanda's condition. Step two, if that failed, would have been to ship her off to some foreign girls' school with strict security. Somewhere they could ensure that she wasn't involved in anything illicit and would not have the chance to escape until she was finished earning her high school diploma.

Walter and Lisa would not have put up with any nonsense. She was sure of that.

The first boy was named Graham. He was a sleepy-eyed youth wearing a knit hat even when he had come in from the cold and had a pair of sunglasses hooked over the collar of his t-shirt. Apparently, he was rebelling against the idea of rebelling by not wearing appropriately warm clothing in the nippy Vermont air. Instead, he was so cool that he could pull off wearing it indoors. Kenzie saw Principal Lakes's eyes take in the hat, consider making a fuss over it, and decide this wasn't a hill she was willing to die on. She just shook her head slightly and introduced Graham to Kenzie, explaining that she had some questions that might help out another student.

Graham gave her a sleepy smile as he sat with her at the table in the small meeting room. It was a nice room, not just a cheap round table and tubular chairs, but a sturdy wooden table, solid rather than laminated particle board, and padded swivel chairs that poofed and squished when Kenzie sat down. Pretty comfortable. Maybe where the principal, her vice principals, and upper-level staff sat down to sort things out with a weekly meeting.

Graham looked Kenzie over, smiling, and ignored Zachary. "So..." he leaned forward, giving her a better look at his acne scars, "how can I help you, beautiful?"

Kenzie laughed. She was a bit old for him. But he was a charmer. "Well, thank you. I'm glad to find you in such a helpful mood. I gather your friends all slept in this morning."

He chuckled. "We had a busy weekend. It's hard to get up Monday morning."

Kenzie didn't want to spend too much time on the preliminaries. She held her phone up for him to look at the picture. "I'm wondering if you know anything about this?"

Graham's eyes took in the body, looking unsurprised. Not shocked that she would have such a thing on her phone. "Yeah. I've seen that. It's not bad, huh? A little putty and corn syrup blood..."

"I'm with the medical examiner's office." Kenzie put the phone down on the table where they could both still see it. "This is not fake."

43

He shrugged. "You can't tell by looking at a picture."

"Look at the color of his skin. There's no red blood circulating through it."

"A little makeup." He leaned over to look at it more closely. "Probably a green base layer, with natural flesh tone and a little blue mixed together applied on top."

"So, is this your work?"

"Mine?" He sat back again. "No. I didn't do it. I'm just guessing. Telling you how I would have done it. I don't know whose work this is. It's good, but I could do better."

"You said that you had seen it before. Do you know where it came from? Principal Lakes said it was probably something pulled off of the internet. Maybe something from a movie."

He shook his head and chewed on his lip, thinking about it. "I haven't seen it online anywhere. Only being sent around the school. Don't know who did it. But that's not Hollywood."

"Oh?" Kenzie was amused at the assertion. As if he had seen everything that Hollywood had produced. "How do you know that?"

"Look at the asphalt." Graham leaned forward again and zoomed in on a patch of pavement beside the body. "Look at all of those cracks. That's from winter weather. Water getting down into little fissures and freezing and expanding. Pushing it apart. You don't see that in Hollywood. No ice."

"You know your concrete, do you?" Kenzie looked closely at the cracks, wondering if Graham could be right. He certainly made it sound like he knew what he was talking about.

"Asphalt," Graham corrected. "Not concrete."

"What's the difference?"

"Bitumen." He looked into her eyes, serious and engaged. "The sticky black stuff that holds it together. Concrete is different. Like sidewalks." At Kenzie's unspoken question, he sat back again, folding his arms across his chest. "My dad is in road construction. What do you think I do every summer?"

Kenzie laughed. "I see. So you do know your, uh, paving materials."

"Aggregates. Yeah, I do. Someday, if I put my mind to it, I could be the king of concrete," he said in a snobbish tone. He motioned to the phone. "This could all be mine."

She liked the cheeky kid. "How wonderful."

Graham snorted.

"So, where do you think this came from?" Kenzie asked.

He shrugged with one shoulder. "Like I said, Vermont, or somewhere with winter weather. And I don't think it came from TV. The lighting is bad."

"TV can't have bad lighting?"

"No director worth his salt would accept that. You need a second light source. Something to even it out. A fill light and diffusion panel." He cocked his head, considering. "I mean, they could be going for the unfinished look, like in Blair Witch Project, something that is supposed to look amateur. This doesn't look like it was done by a cinematographer."

"Do you think it could be real?"

He cocked his head in the other direction and considered, fiddling with the edge of his hat. "Well, I suppose it could be," he said eventually, grudgingly. "But I don't know. Does that bullet hole look authentic? I would go for something a little bigger. Build up the edges a bit to make it look deeper. This just looks... like it was slapped on."

"Well, I have seen a few real bullet holes in my time."

"And you don't think that's too small?" He peered at it again.

"I think it is a small caliber bullet."

"But it doesn't look like it would do any damage. This guy might still be walking around after being drilled by something like that."

"As long as they have enough penetrating force to get through the front of the skull, it doesn't matter if they come out through the back or not. They do a lot more damage by bouncing around inside."

"Oh." He nodded. "Cool."

Kenzie shook her head. "Not cool. So can you remember when you saw it the first time?"

"Uh..." he stared off into space for a bit. "Say... a couple of weeks, probably. I don't think I could tell you the exact day. But it hasn't been that long."

"And you don't have any idea where it came from? Who sent it to you?"

"I don't remember." He smiled and patted the pocket his phone was in. "And they self-destruct, so don't ask me to look it up for you."

"That's convenient."

"How else are we supposed to defend ourselves against parents and teachers who search our phones? If there's nothing for them to find, there's nothing to get upset about."

"And they won't get upset about a program that deletes a message after it is sent?"

"Teachers don't get upset about it. Parents might, but what are they going to do? Tell you that you can't message with your friends anymore?" He scoffed at this. "They can't stop you. They try, and you pick up a burner. Keep one phone for the 'rents and one for…" He motioned to Kenzie's phone on the table. "Stuff they wouldn't want to see."

"And that keeps everyone happy."

"You got it."

"Who else is in your drama club?"

He raised his brows. "Most of them aren't here right now. Principal can give you the information if she wants to. But I don't know you from Adam." He glanced over at Zachary, who he had been ignoring, but had not forgotten. "Or Eve," he amended.

"Do you know Rhys Salter?"

"Rhys?" He seemed to think about it for a moment. "Oh, the Black kid? Silent Salt? Yeah, I know who he is."

"But you don't know him personally?"

"No. He doesn't hang around with the drama kids." He gave a little laugh. "He could be a mime, I suppose. I'll bet he'd be good at that."

"He can communicate, even if he can't speak."

"Sure." He shrugged. "I know he can. That's why I said he'd be a good mime. But he doesn't run with my crew. Sorry."

"Do you know who would have sent him that picture?"

"One of *his* friends, I guess. Wouldn't make any sense for me or any of the drama geeks to send it. What do *we* know about him? I know we've been in the same school for years, but Rhys doesn't mix much. I don't really know much about him except that…" Graham trailed off. His eyes dropped to the photo on the phone.

Kenzie waited, not offering anything. She glanced at Zachary, who listened with interest but let her take charge of things. She had thought that he would be more involved, but suspected he was holding himself back from participating because Rhys had asked Kenzie to look into it, not him. So far, she thought she was doing a pretty good job of it. And she knew Zachary would help when she asked for it.

Graham scratched the back of his head under the hat, frowning slightly. "Didn't his grandfather get killed?" he asked. "Shot in the head or something?"

Kenzie nodded.

Graham shook his head. "That's messed up. Who would send that to him? That's like… making cripple jokes to an amputee. That's just wrong, man."

"It was pretty upsetting to him," Kenzie agreed. "But we don't know that he was being targeted. The photo was making its rounds through the school, so it isn't like he is the only one who got it."

"Yeah. It was making its way around," Graham agreed. "I got it a few times."

"But it didn't make its way to any social networks or discussion groups?"

"I dunno. Most of us, we don't hang out on the old-people social platforms. We might have accounts there that we post to now and then to keep them happy, but we've got our own places. Private servers. That kind of thing."

"Did any of the other drama kids make it in this morning?"

"A couple. But why are you looking at us? I mean, like I told you, we don't really know Old Salt. Talking to us isn't going to get you very far."

"Principal Lakes thought it was a good starting point. She thought that maybe the drama club had staged the picture. That it was some kind of prank you guys had pulled off. Or a picture you grabbed from the internet to get attention."

"Nah. None of us did that. I would have done a better job of it. Even if that *is* real… I could make something that looked *more* real. And more scary. This guy… he kind of looks soft. He doesn't look like someone who would get shot in the head. You want someone who is a real tough guy. Big and beefy, tattoos, bald. Mouth bleeding. Black eye, or at least a bruise under one of them. More blood. Bigger hole. Better lighting. I could really make it *pop*."

"Okay, I'm convinced," Kenzie said, holding her hands up. "The Concrete King wins."

Graham grinned at her. He stretched and settled his knit cap on his head. "I should probably be getting to class. It isn't like the teachers will hold the lessons for me. And the reason I'm here so early ain't because my parents are happy with my recent performance."

"Well, I appreciate you taking the time to talk to me. It was very… enlightening."

11

P rincipal Lakes escorted in a boy who seemed too small to be in high school. He had blond hair that was just a little too long to be called short and too short to really be called long. It curved around his face, making it appear more round. He looked about ten years old.

"This is Hugh. He is a friend of Rhys's."

Kenzie nodded to him. She was afraid she might appear too intimidating to the small boy if she stood up to shake his hand or greet him, so she stayed where she was. "Hi, Hugh. Thanks for coming to talk to us."

He looked at Principal Lakes, who gave him a small push of encouragement and then withdrew, pulling the door shut behind her. Hugh looked at the chairs and climbed up into one of them. The big, formal chair made him look even smaller, like a munchkin.

"Hi."

"Hi. I'm Kenzie Kirsch, and I guess Principal Lakes already told you I'm here to help Rhys."

"Don't know how you can help him when he's not here."

"Well, he can't be here right now, but we can. How long have you known Rhys?"

"I don't know. It's been, like, forever," The small boy made a motion to indicate something that had happened far in the past. Amusing, since he seemed like he couldn't have known Rhys for more than a minute. He was *so* young.

"And you guys are pretty good friends?"

"Well… we have some classes together. And sometimes… we eat lunch together. Stuff like that. I mean… it doesn't seem like much. We're just school friends. We don't hang out together outside of that." He rubbed his chin. "My parents don't like me to go anywhere else."

"You never went to Rhys's house?"

"Especially not to Rhys's house. Not when someone had been killed there." He shrugged dramatically. "I know it's silly, because it isn't like there was still a murderer lurking around there, but my folks are a little…"

"Overprotective?"

Kenzie didn't actually think they were being unreasonable. Despite what Hugh said, the murderer had still lived with Rhys for many years. She wasn't there anymore, but it hadn't been a random break-in like the Salters had told everyone. Kenzie didn't think that Hugh would ever have been in any danger there, but Rhys had been exposed to his grandfather's murderer daily, and no one knew what had gone on between them. Had she continued to threaten and terrorize Rhys for all those years? Or had she ignored him and pretended that the murder had never happened?

"Yeah, they're overprotective," Hugh agreed. "I've been sick a lot, and they worry about everything. Thinking that it might put me in danger."

Kenzie was disappointed that Principal Lakes hadn't managed to come up with someone a little bit closer than Hugh, who was "just a school friend."

"So… I guess you're wondering why we want to talk to you. It's about… this." Kenzie displayed the picture on her phone for an instant. She didn't want to leave it on too long and risk traumatizing the boy with something so graphic. His overprotective parents would not be thrilled with her for that.

Hugh's quick eyes caught the picture, cataloged it, and recalled it. His eyes widened.

"What's that?" he asked, pretending not to know.

"You already know what it is. I'm sure everyone around the school has a pretty good idea what it is."

Hugh looked down at the table and then out the window, but not back toward Kenzie's face.

"Some stuff gets forwarded between people, back and forth," he said eventually. "That doesn't mean I saw it or had anything to do with it."

"No. It doesn't. But we're trying to figure out where it came from originally. It's important to figure out what happened and whether this is a legitimate picture."

He rolled his eyes. "It's not real."

"How do you know?"

His eyes flicked back toward Kenzie's phone, which was turned off.

"Never trust anything without a source. It's fake news. It's just some picture someone photoshopped. Not *real*. I told Rhys it wasn't real."

"Did you?"

Hugh nodded. "He was freaking out over it. I told him it was nothing. That he should just delete it and forget about it if it bothered him."

"What did he say to that?"

Hugh crossed his hands in a big X sign, and pushed it away from him. A gesture that Kenzie had seen Rhys make. *No. Definitely not.*

Kenzie nodded, chuckling a little that she could actually see and hear Rhys in her head, telling her no.

"So he didn't think ignoring it was the right thing to do."

"No." Hugh looked at Kenzie as though she were a child that he had tried to explain something elementary to. "Rhys isn't the kind of guy who would look the other way."

"Did that ever get him into trouble?" Zachary inserted.

Kenzie looked at him, surprised, but stayed silent, letting Hugh answer the question.

"Sometimes it did," Hugh admitted. "He'd get smacked around by the bigger guys. Or get in trouble with a teacher for talking back."

He shook his head. "Kind of funny, when he hardly ever says a word."

"But he can make himself understood," Zachary said.

"Yeah." Hugh smiled. "He can."

"Who smacked him around?" Kenzie asked.

Hugh looked wary. "Just guys. Rhys took care of himself. Don't mess things up for him."

"How bad was it?"

"They all knew he was kind of a teacher's pet. The staff all felt sorry for 'that poor Salter boy.' So anyone who wanted to rough him up had to be pretty careful. And not go overboard. He fared better than some of us."

He apparently read Kenzie's face and quirked a smile at her. "And yeah, they feel protective of me because I'm so tiny, too, so I don't do so bad."

"Do you think one of those people who beat up on him might have sent him the picture to intentionally upset him?"

Hugh shook his head slowly as he considered it. "No... I don't think any of them are that inventive. Or that bright."

Zachary snickered. Hugh looked at him, spreading his hands wide as he asked the question. "I mean, you know how it is, right? These bullies are either meatheads, or they're these all-stars who are killing it in academics as well as sports, but still never had an original thought. They might be able to answer textbook questions but, as far as coming up with something inventive like torturing Rhys by sending him pictures of dead bodies...?" Hugh shook his head. "No way."

"I thought you didn't believe this was a real dead body," Kenzie said.

"Well... I don't know. I doubt it. Who would be sending out pictures of real dead bodies?"

"Just one, as far as I know. Were there more?"

"No, no. Just that one. But I saw it a few times. It was one of those posts that no matter how many times you slap it down and delete it, people keep forwarding it to you again."

"And Rhys too?" Zachary asked.

"Yeah. I guess. We all did."

"That would be pretty hard to deal with," Zachary reflected. "He couldn't just delete it and forget about it even if he wanted to. Because every time he tried, it just landed in his inbox again."

"And if each time, it causes flashbacks and distress…" Kenzie said. She didn't need Zachary or any psychology textbook to tell her it wasn't going to do much good for his mental health.

"He was getting worse, wasn't he?" Zachary asked Hugh. "Even his grandma knew that he was having more trouble at school. Getting into fights, getting upset with the resource room teacher. They were worried about him before he broke down."

"He probably should have just deleted the app. Or set up a new account," Hugh admitted. "I thought it would stop, or he'd get over it. If I knew he was gonna go off the rails like that…"

"What would you have done?" Kenzie asked.

"I dunno. I'm just a kid," Hugh pointed out. "He should have, like… gone to his therapist. Told his grandma. Gone to someone who could help him. What was *I* supposed to do?"

"I'm not blaming you," Kenzie told him gently. "And he did go to a family friend to try to get help. But maybe he got the picture again before getting there, and it pushed him over the edge."

"Is he okay now?" Hugh asked, his eyes wide. "No one will tell us what's been going on with him, when he'll be home again, or anything."

"He's doing better, but still not ready to go home. It's been pretty difficult for him." She didn't tell him about the residential care facility, about how he had reacted to the drug therapy. It would be up to Rhys how much he wanted to reveal to his friends about what had happened.

"Can we go see him?" Hugh asked. "He came to see me in the hospital before. If I can go and talk to him…"

"I don't know. I'll ask him and his grandmother about putting you on the visitor list, and then I'll let you know. I'm not sure he's ready for more visitors yet. He might need some more time."

Hugh looked down. "It was pretty bad, wasn't it?"

"Yes."

"I should have done something. I should have talked him into seeing someone or called his grandma. She would have helped, if she had known."

"You did what you could by being his friend," Zachary reassured him. "It wasn't your responsibility to push him into treatment. He had to decide that for himself. Or... for this to happen so that they could admit him." Zachary met Kenzie's eyes. "It can be really hard when you're doing everything you can for someone you love, but they're not ready to do what you think they should."

Hugh gave a heartfelt sigh. "You're right about that."

Kenzie nodded her agreement.

12

A s Hugh stood up to leave, he paused, looking at Kenzie one more time. "You should talk to Ayla."

Kenzie nodded. "Okay. Who is she? A girlfriend?"

Hugh looked at her, frowning, and shook his head. "Just a friend," he said firmly. "Rhys doesn't have any girlfriends."

Kenzie was not surprised by this. She knew that Rhys was interested in Luke, or at least had been in the past. She didn't know if he was also interested in girls. He had been interested in Madison when she had gone missing, but maybe that had just been friendship. Zachary would have a better idea. It had been his case, nothing to do with her. Other than when she'd had to help him clean things up.

She glanced over at Zachary and decided that it was best not to ask whether Rhys had a boyfriend, or whether he was interested in both genders. She didn't want to disclose anything if he wasn't "out" to Hugh.

"Ayla," Hugh repeated. "You should talk to her."

Principal Lakes confirmed that Ayla was one of the kids she planned to have Kenzie and Zachary talk to and that she was present. She checked the girl's schedule and had her called to the office. In a few minutes, Ayla showed up, a shy Black girl with her hair pulled into a large bun. She looked at Kenzie and Zachary suspiciously, not too keen to talk to them.

"It's about Rhys," Lakes explained to her. "They're trying to help him out. You know that he's... sick in the hospital, right?"

Ayla chewed on her thumbnail. "He's not sick."

"Well, what would you call it, then?" Principal Lakes challenged. "Whether it is physical or emotional, he is not well. He is in the hospital, and Dr. Kirsch and Zachary are trying to help him."

Ayla folded her arms across her chest. Looking thoroughly uncomfortable and blocked off. "I don't know anything. He just didn't come to school one day. And someone said he was in the hospital. That's all I know."

"Could we talk to you for just a few minutes anyway?" Kenzie coaxed. "We won't take too much of your time, and you might know something that can help us."

Kenzie didn't want to discuss the photo in the main office where people could overhear. Once behind closed doors, she could explain it to Ayla and see if she knew anything more than the other kids did about where the photo came from or who had sent it to Rhys.

They all waited. Finally, Ayla rolled her eyes and consented to go into the meeting room to talk to Kenzie and Zachary. Kenzie reintroduced herself and tried to connect with the girl, assuring her that they didn't believe she had done anything wrong. They simply wanted to see if she had any information that could help with Rhys's case.

"I don't know what's going on with Rhys," Ayla said stubbornly. "We're friends, but he didn't tell me personal stuff. Like about his illness or anything. We just hung out together sometimes." She shrugged. "When you're, like, two of the only Black kids in the school, you stick out like a sore thumb. People think that you belong together. I don't think we're that much alike in anything but our skin color. Maybe our grandmas. But I can't tell you what was going on with him before he had his... breakdown."

"Did you notice that something was going on with him? That he was getting in trouble, having fights, distressed about something?"

"Yeah, I know he was fighting. So what?"

"Did you know why? What was going on with him?"

"He was a Black teenager. They get in fights. Especially in a school like this, surrounded by…" She made a surrendering gesture as if she didn't know what to call the other students. "These people."

"White? Privileged? Jerks?" Kenzie offered.

"All of the above. Yeah. So it was unusual, but it wasn't, you know? Everybody is going to blow sooner or later. You can't just… keep dealing with it all the time."

"We think that the reason for Rhys's behavior and the breakdown, was this." Kenzie showed her the picture briefly, as she had with Hugh, turning it off again right away.

"That picture? That was disgusting. I don't know why everyone shared it and acted like it was such a big deal. Why do I want that on my phone?"

"Do you know who was circulating it?"

"Everyone. I got it more than once."

"Who do you think started it? And was it targeted at Rhys?"

"Why would it be…" Ayla trailed off. "Because of his grandpa, you mean? Well, I guess… but it wasn't like they looked anything like each other."

"What do you mean?" Zachary asked.

"I mean, his grandpa was an old Black man. Nothing like this weirdo white guy all gone to seed. They don't look anything alike. Why would it bother Rhys?"

"Because both men were shot in the forehead. We know that it bothered Rhys, gave him flashbacks to his grandfather's murder."

"Yeah?" Ayla looked thoughtful. "I don't know why it would. They don't look anything like each other."

"They don't have to. Flashbacks can be triggered by just one thing. A smell. A color. A bullet in the forehead. It doesn't matter if the rest of the circumstances are the same or not."

"Oh. Okay, then…"

"Do you know who started sending the picture around? Was it the boys who were bullying him? The jocks? One of the kids that he got in a fight with before the breakdown?"

"No, I don't think so. Why would any of them have that? Something like that, it probably came from the losers."

Kenzie raised her brows and blinked.

She shouldn't be surprised. She'd heard enough kids called losers at school. It just surprised her that a minority, someone on the outside, would use the term so casually.

"What losers would that be?"

"Kids who are on their way to dropping out. They're only at school half the time, if that, they're doing drugs or drunk all the time, they're failing, don't have anyone to keep them on the straight and narrow." Ayla shrugged. "The losers."

"Do you have anyone in particular in mind?"

"I don't know them personally," Ayla said. "Why would I hang with that crowd? I don't do drugs. I'm not a loser."

"You must know some of the kids who do. You must have certain kids in mind."

"I don't know them," Ayla insisted. "They hang out back behind the bleachers. Or at the convenience store across the street. Smoking and doing their sh—doing whatever they want. You ask me, those are the kids who started this going around."

"Why them? What makes you think it could be them?" Zachary asked.

"It's just the kind of thing that they would do. Starting rumors, excitement, looking for negative attention. How do I know why? I just know that they are the kind of people who want to disrupt things. To make people feel bad."

Zachary accepted this. Kenzie nodded. At least it was somewhere to start. Maybe Ayla just had an instinct and didn't really know where it came from. Or maybe there was more to it and she had seen the photo being forwarded by members of that group.

"Anyone in particular in that group?" Kenzie prodded.

Ayla opened her mouth to answer, then closed it and shook her head. "I think... no, I don't know. I have no idea. I don't run with that group at all."

"Does Rhys know any of them? Would one of them have sent it to him because they were friends? Or because they thought it would bother him?"

"I don't know." Ayla chewed on her thumbnail again. "He didn't hang out in any of those places. But sometimes… Rhys knew things. He kind of… fades into the background and he hears things. People know he won't repeat anything they say, so they don't worry about him being around."

"So he might have heard something. One of them might have said something around him."

"Maybe. He cared about things, you know? Cares. Like… people who fly under the radar. Who aren't very popular, just living on the edge… That could get him in trouble."

It already had, Kenzie knew. He was the one who had put Zachary on to Madison's case when she had gone missing. Others had brushed it off, but Rhys had not been willing to. And he had pictures on his phone that had been instrumental in figuring out what was going on with her and, eventually, in finding her.

Sometimes, knowing things got people into trouble.

13

S hould we see if we can make contact?" Zachary asked Kenzie, making it sound like he was talking about getting in touch with extraterrestrials rather than a group of kids.

"I suppose they won't necessarily cooperate with Principal Lakes in coming to talk to us," Kenzie said, thinking about the dynamics.

"If they're even in the school. It is Monday morning, and that crowd tends not to be early."

"You think we should wander over to the bleachers or the convenience store? See if they're around?"

Kenzie wasn't sure if they would be found at either of those places. If they were hung over after a weekend of partying, they might still be home in bed. She looked at her watch. She had told Dr. Cook that she would be late getting in, but she should try to get to the medical examiner's office before long.

"Chances are, their parents at least got them out of bed and kicked them out of the house this morning," Zachary said, seeming to read her mind. "And they won't be inclined to run this early in the morning."

Kenzie chuckled. "You think they would try to run away from us? I doubt it. We can't exactly make them talk to us. They would know that."

"If someone has a guilty conscience, they're not going to stay around to find out who we are and if we are with the cops."

She conceded the point. But would they think they had anything to be guilty about if all they had done was to forward a creepy picture to a friend? She supposed there were other things that they might be guilty of that she had no idea about.

"Sure. Which do you think is the most likely place to get them?" Zachary had a better insight into their minds than Kenzie. She hadn't exactly been part of the popular cheerleader crowd in high school, but she hadn't been one to hang out with the goth kids smoking out behind the school, either. Zachary had been more on the fringes. Maybe not one of the kids Ayla would classify as a "loser," but not part of any of the clubs or cliques, either.

"Convenience store," Zachary said with certainty. "If they've got coffee…"

Kenzie wouldn't mind getting another coffee herself. It seemed like it had been a long time since her cup at breakfast. "Convenience store it is," she agreed.

They stopped to thank Principal Lakes for her cooperation in their investigation. They didn't tell her that they were going to look for the loser kids to interview them. It was outside of school. They didn't need her permission and she didn't need to know about it.

"I hope it was helpful," Lakes said, looking doubtful about the possibility. "I'll keep my ears open and see if I can find out anything about that photo or who might have started forwarding it around. I wish there was more I could do for Rhys. Will you tell him that I said hello?"

"We'll pass it on," Kenzie agreed. "I'm sure he'd be comforted to know that you were thinking about him."

"I've always been concerned about Rhys and trying to make his school experience positive. You know, as a principal, you tend to attach to certain kids, those who have particular needs. I wish there was more I could do for Rhys."

They said their goodbyes and, rather than walking to Zachary's car, headed across the street toward the convenience store for a cup of coffee.

"My perception of principals as an adult is really different than it was as a kid," Zachary confessed as they walked, pondering what they had heard that morning.

"Yeah? I guess mine is too. They were an authority figure when I was a kid. If you had to go to the principal's office or got singled out for some kind of attention, that was a really bad thing. If a principal had a special interest in you, like Principal Lakes has in Rhys, that would not be seen as a positive thing."

Zachary nodded. "I remember some of the principals I banged heads with… they were really hard cases. Or that's how I saw them. Looking back, I suppose they were just trying to keep order in their school and keep everyone safe. Trying to keep an eye on the troublemaker."

"I'm sure they didn't see you as a troublemaker," Kenzie protested. The Zachary that she knew was a quiet, thoughtful, caring man. He got attached too easily and had problems letting go of the people who had been a part of his life—certainly not a fighter or rabble-rouser.

"Don't kid yourself," Zachary laughed. "A foster kid who had burned the house down and destroyed his family? Big red flag right there. Spent half my time in institutions rather than families. No friends. Impulsive. Couldn't sit still or read or focus on the work. I was every teacher's nightmare. I practically lived in the principal's office at some schools."

"But those things are all misperceptions. You weren't a bad kid. You'd been through some terrible experiences. You had disabilities. If they had focused on helping you instead of seeing you as a bad kid…"

"I'm sure some of them were trying to help me. Probably most of them were. But I didn't see that. I saw them as a threat. Dangerous. Adults who would punish and hurt me." He shook his head. "I don't remember any principals hitting me. Looking back, I can see the compassion. But I couldn't then. Adults were not to be trusted."

They entered the convenience store, filled "to go" cups, and stood in line waiting to pay, not talking, just thinking over what had been said. Kenzie wondered about the "loser" kids. How many of them were struggling like Zachary had, with learning disabilities and early trauma that had put them at odds with the rest of the world? Kids who had not learned to trust and *couldn't* behave the way they were expected to even if they tried.

And why try, when they knew they were bound to fail anyway?

They left the convenience store and stood sipping their coffees, looking around at the various other people coming from and going to the store. Zachary nodded toward a group of kids who were ostensibly waiting for the bus but, since school was in, they obviously should have been heading into the school rather than going anywhere else. They had undoubtedly been told before that they weren't allowed to loiter around the door and the parking lot of the convenience store, so they instead stood around an area where people were expected to stand around. They just weren't actually interested in getting on the bus.

Kenzie nodded in agreement. Zachary led the way, wandering closer to the bus stop, ignoring the kids initially.

The kids quieted and watched them; then, as they decided Kenzie and Zachary were no threat and were just waiting for the bus, their conversations picked up again. Kenzie eavesdropped on their discussions, which were mainly school gossip and celebrity news.

One of the oldest boys kept eyeing them and eventually turned to them, confronting them directly. "Who the hell are you? I haven't seen you around here before. What are you doing, hanging around here and listening in on our conversations?"

Kenzie wasn't sure how to respond. Deny that she was listening? Suggest she had just as much right to be there as anyone else?

Zachary's response was to pull his coat closer, as if he were cold, and to look around him suspiciously. That immediately had the kids checking for other watchers as well. They drew closer together and the boy's voice dropped lower and quieter.

"Never seen you here before," he repeated.

Zachary nodded. He looked around again, very obviously. He nodded at the school across the street. "You guys attend there?"

"Depends what you mean by attend," one of the girls said. She had dyed black hair and several nose rings and other piercings.

The other kids laughed appreciatively at her response.

"Young guy I know goes there," Zachary said. "Sometimes," he added, tilting his head toward the girl to refer to her joke.

They chuckled at this. "Who?" the boy who had confronted them asked. "And why would you be talking to us about it? You some kind of pedo?"

"Rhys."

Kenzie expected him to use Rhys's full name and explain why they were there, but Zachary didn't. He was spare with his words, which seemed to keep the kids on the hook rather than immediately running him off because they didn't like extra observers around.

"Rhys," the boy repeated, looking at Zachary. "Skinny Black kid?"

Zachary nodded. "Doesn't talk a lot," he contributed.

This brought an explosive laugh from the boy and snickers from the other kids. "Doesn't talk a lot!" the boy repeated loudly. "Kid never says a word!"

Zachary nodded his agreement.

The laughter died down, and they waited for him to say why he was there, listening to them, talking to them, but he didn't offer any further explanation. The kids stood around looking at each other, asking questions with their eyes until the leader again pursued it with Zachary.

"Rhys ain't been around lately. I heard he was sick."

Zachary nodded his agreement. He shifted, sliding his hand out of his pocket with his phone. They watched him warily, but phones were normal. Phones were not guns or something sinister. They all had phones practically grafted into their hands. Zachary had the picture ready. He turned the phone screen on, flashed the picture of the dead man, and turned it off again.

The students shifted and looked at each other uncomfortably. Zachary slid the phone back into his pocket.

"Anyone else seen that? I'm guessing you have. I'm guessing it's been on all of your phones sometime in the last couple of weeks."

There were nods and shrugs, no one admitting it directly or offering any more information, but no one denying it.

"Who's she?" one of the girls asked, indicating Kenzie.

"She's a friend of Rhys's, too," Zachary informed them. "He asked her for help."

"What kinda help? We don't know the guy. Sure, we seen him around the school, but that isn't the same as knowing him. None of us can help you. Or her. Or Rhys."

14

T hat picture's been going around for a couple of weeks," Zachary said. "The same as Rhys has been away for a couple of weeks."

"You saying that one has something to do with the other?" another of the boys demanded. He was shorter than the others, but still taller than Zachary. He was heavyset and powerful-looking. Someone who lifted weights or did other heavy work. He could mash either one of them without a second thought.

Zachary nodded. He sipped his coffee. His brief answers and silences seemed to get to the group, who wanted to know what he was all about and why he was talking to them. There were more comments being tossed back and forth between them as they tried to figure out what was going on with this strange man and woman who came to ask them questions and then didn't ask questions or give any information.

Zachary looked around again. "This probably isn't the best place to talk."

"This is fine. Ain't no one here but us and you."

"They might have…" Zachary bent over as if to look under the bus bench and then around him again. Acting paranoid. Kenzie had seen him paranoid before, really paranoid, and recognized that this was just an act.

"What? Bugged our bus stop? Come on, man. I heard that Salter was in the psych ward. Is that where you came from? You some loony tune that he talked into helping him with some crazy mission? This is safe. This is our place, and no one has bugged it."

"That's some kind of crazy, man," another boy contributed.

"This guy," Zachary tapped the phone in his pocket. "You ever seen him before? You know who he is?"

There were head shakes around the group. They were elbowing each other now. Making quiet and not-so-quiet jokes about Zachary's sanity. About him coming there on some mission for some crazy kid about some unknown guy no one had ever seen before, who got himself shot in the head.

"It's a picture," the young man who had initially confronted them said with exasperation. "Just a picture of some dead dude."

"Some *really* dead dude."

He shook his head, "You're either dead or not dead. You don't get any deader."

"No, I mean… not fake dead. Not a costume or a prank. Not makeup or Photoshop. Actually dead dead."

Until now, everybody immediately protested that the photo was fake, but the young man was the exception.

"Yeah, probably. Looks dead enough for me. So what? Why do you care?"

"Rhys."

"Why does Rhys care? I mean, really. Unless he's the one who killed him, why give it a second thought? It's some stranger, right? No one knows. It's a shocking picture. That's why you send it around. No way to tell who the guy is or what happened to him, so you make up a story. How you knew the guy or saw him after he was whacked. Or he's your cousin or something. You tell everyone you saw the guy. The dead dude. You touched him or you took his picture."

"But the picture has already been circulating around the school, so people know it wasn't you," Zachary countered.

"They don't know. Not if they don't know where it came from first."

"So that's it? You just send it around so that you can brag that you know the guy or saw it happen? No one will believe you."

"Doesn't matter if they believe it or not. It's just something to do."

"So you don't know him. You don't really know anything. All you got is a picture."

The boy nodded his agreement. "Yeah. You got it. All I got is a picture. I don't know this dude. I don't care what happened to him. It's just like... a meme. Something to share."

"Do you know who shared it first? Who started it going around the school?"

"Could be Rhys himself. How do I know?"

"You didn't start it. Do you know who sent it to you?"

The kids looked back and forth at each other. There had been a temperature shift. Kenzie found it hard to define, but something had happened. They had gone from laughing at Zachary and his paranoia and being unconcerned about the two strangers who had shown up in their territory, to suddenly guarded, wanting to get them out of there. And Kenzie had no idea what had changed.

"Look," a girl said. She was medium height, a little heavy, with straight brown hair and a wide, flat nose. She wore a t-shirt with a jacket, and jeans with a red bandana tied around the thigh. "You should stay out of stuff that isn't any of your business. This guy, whoever killed him, he wouldn't want you poking your nose into it and asking a lot of questions. You should just stay out of it; forget you ever saw anything. Tell Rhys to forget he ever saw anything." Her dark eyes were serious. "You don't want to get involved."

Kenzie breathed in slowly and let her breath out again. Did they know? It was the first sign that someone knew something about what was actually going on. Where the photo came from, who it was. There wouldn't be any danger from an anonymous person. From someone killed on the other side of the world months or years ago. There would only be danger if it were current and local.

"It actually is my business," she said, venturing to speak for herself to these teens at last. "I am with the medical examiner's office, and poking my nose into suspicious deaths is exactly what I do."

The girl stared at her, mouth hanging open in shock for a minute before she realized and closed it.

"If you know something about who this is and what happened to him, I want to know about it," Kenzie said. "If you know where that picture was taken… who it was that started circulating it… those are things I need to know about."

"You're like those CSI folks?" the boy asked, speaking over the dark-haired girl before she could respond. "You collect and run all that evidence from the crime scene?"

"No, most of that has usually been done by the time I get the body. Sometimes, I'm at the scene before the crime scene techs, examine the body, and release the crime scene to them. But usually, I'm at the medical examiner's office and do post-mortem examinations when they are brought in."

"Cool." He seemed impressed by this. "Anyone who works with dead bodies is chill in my books."

"She *has* to keep chill," Zachary told him. "Have you ever been in the morgue? It's like working in a meat locker."

The boy snorted, then covered his mouth, hiding an unexpected smile. "Dude."

Kenzie rolled her eyes. She was used to Zachary's terrible jokes about the morgue and the bodies she worked on.

"Look," she addressed the group of youth in a confidential tone, leaning forward. The others drew in closer, whether intentionally or unconsciously drawn in by her tone. "I don't know who might actually know something about this body—who he is, where he came from, what happened to him—but if you do know something, you can reach me through the medical examiner's office. I'd really like to know what you know." She kept her hands out of her pockets and didn't pull out any business cards for them. They wouldn't take them, and if they did, they would just throw them away the minute she walked away. But they were internet savvy; they could certainly find the number for the medical examiner's office with a quick search.

The teens looked at each other, and no one offered anything.

They were circling the wagons, drawing closer to each other to protect anyone who might be vulnerable. They knew something; Kenzie was sure of that now. But she wasn't going to get it out of them, and certainly, they wouldn't give it up to the police if they ever became involved.

Zachary touched Kenzie on the shoulder and made a small shuffling motion to indicate they were done and it was time to leave. Kenzie nodded. She looked at the kids again, meeting as many of their eyes as she could, and then followed Zachary's lead to walk away from them.

15

T hey know something," Kenzie told Zachary as they got into the car and prepared to head over to the medical examiner's office.

"Yeah," he agreed. He looked solemn and thoughtful.

"Do you think they know who the guy is? Or just where the photo came from?"

"I don't know." Zachary shook his head slowly as he considered. "It was hard to get a good read on everyone at the same time. Very cautious… but I don't know who they are protecting, or why."

"What changed?"

"What changed?" Zachary repeated, frowning.

"Something changed there near the end. Before they decided to shut us out."

"Mmm." He nodded his agreement. "I think that maybe, up until then, they didn't realize that someone in the group was involved. I don't think it was until then that they all realized it was anything but a meme being forwarded around because they thought it was something cool. But then… they suddenly realized that someone knew something or was involved somehow. And then they wanted us out."

Kenzie nodded. It made sense to her. She just wished she had been quick enough to catch the shift and see who had known something. She hoped that whichever one it was would call or email her at the medical examiner's office, but she expected that was probably a lost cause. Zachary had already spoken his thoughts earlier. He hadn't trusted any adults. Those teens sharing with each other out by the bus stop would never trust an adult—certainly not a stranger who had never done anything for them.

Kenzie was at her desk working through her email filing and responses when Dr. Wiltshire called. She looked at the Caller ID and picked it up, glad for the chance to talk to him. She had Dr. Cook there as a substitute to help provide Kenzie with any extra manpower she needed when Dr. Wiltshire was on disability leave, waiting for his broken hand to heal. But there were some things that the young, handsome substitute just could not help Kenzie with.

"Doctor," she greeted cheerfully. "How are you doing?"

"Healing slowly. You should see all the lovely colors it has been turning to."

Kenzie could well imagine. The external fixator device holding Dr. Wiltshire's bones in place while they knit together left his hand much more visible than a regular cast would have, so she had been able to see, each time he came in, the black and blue bruises, gradually turning to green and yellow. A little more gruesome than the leaves changing color on the trees, marking the passing of the year, but just as colorful.

"And how is the pain? And your head?"

"Getting gradually better," he said,. "As I need to take fewer painkillers, the brain fog is clearing, leaving me with more workable time. I know it will be a while before my hand is healed enough to work, but I am glad to at least be getting my brain back."

"Yeah." Kenzie was sympathetic to Dr. Wiltshire's plight. At least when she wasn't inconvenienced by his absence. Those times when she needed him to be there for her, she could get quite irritable about the lengthy waiting process for herself rather than him. "Before we get into anything else, I'm wondering if you remember a case from some years back…"

"With this head, I can't promise you anything. But… tell me what you can, and I'll try to remember."

"It was a man who was shot in the head during a supposed burglary. He died instantly and the case was closed."

Dr. Wiltshire didn't volunteer anything, so Kenzie kept going, trying to give him enough information that he would remember it, without tainting his memories.

"An older man, Black, right in the forehead. Sitting at his dinner table."

"Ahh," Dr. Wiltshire's voice held promise. "Yes, yes. I do remember that one. Felt bad for the family. No one was expecting such a thing. It was a good neighborhood. Quiet town. Home invasions simply aren't our speed here."

"But it wasn't a home invasion."

"Not as we have come to define them, no. The police thought that the homeowner and burglars had startled each other. He didn't know there was anyone in the house, so he was just sitting at his table eating. And they didn't think he was home so, when they saw him, they were taken off guard and reacted reflexively. They probably wouldn't have done it if they had been thinking things through. They could have just left again without being caught."

"It turned out it wasn't a robbery," Kenzie said. "It was just staged to look that way. As it turned out, it was actually his daughter who did it. You reopened *her* death when Zachary got involved in it."

"Salter," Dr. Wiltshire recalled.

"That's right."

"The daughter did it? Was that proven?"

"The family admitted to covering it up but, by that time, the daughter was dead, so there wasn't really any point in gathering the evidence to prove it."

"So… why are you asking me about this case now? What bearing does that have on anything? If he was murdered, and the murderer is dead, why are you bringing it up now?"

"There was a grandson, a witness to the murder."

73

"The son of the woman who killed him?"

"No. Grandson through another daughter."

"Okay. I seem to remember something about that when the Salter woman's case was reopened. He was missing, wasn't he?"

"They both were, for a while. So... he's having some trouble now."

"Is it any wonder?"

Kenzie gave a little laugh. "No. This is just my roundabout way of saying... there has been another death. Apparently unrelated. But he was a... witness of sorts. Saw a picture of it, and it triggered a breakdown. Because... on the surface, it was the same as his grandfather's death."

"Shot."

"Yes. Same type of thing. Execution style. Shot to the head."

"And you are asking, in your roundabout way, about the previous murder because..."

"I'm wondering... what you remember about it. Trying to figure out if there are any other connections that I have missed, aside from it being a shot to the head."

"Do you expect there to be?"

"No. I don't think that one had anything to do with the other. It's just that... I think I should know all of the similarities between the two if I am going to help Rhys to work through it."

"I see. Well, I'm afraid I don't remember much more than we have already discussed."

"Was there anything unusual about the death? Anything notable about the face? I'm grasping at straws here... there probably isn't anything else that ties the two together."

"Any similarities between the victims? An older Black man?"

"Uh, no. Young white man. In the street, not in his house. I haven't looked at the pictures of Clarence, but I don't imagine there are a lot of similarities between them physically."

"Pictures should still be on the system. You should be able to access the old autopsy file still. It was ten years ago, but we're still on the same system."

Kenzie hadn't even thought to look. She had just thought about the physical box being shoved away in a warehouse somewhere, along with rows and rows of similar packages. It hadn't even occurred to her that it would still be on the computer.

"Oh, that's great. I'll look it up." Kenzie was already tapping the keys to bring it up on a search for Clarence Salter. There was an immediate hit. Kenzie clicked on it and immediately saw the main picture on the file, a headshot of Clarence in death. Lying on the autopsy table. Small caliber bullet through the forehead. While the victims looked nothing alike, the similarities between the mode of death were striking. It was not surprising that Rhys had been so upset by receiving the photo of the unknown dead man.

And had received it over and over again, several times. It must have seemed like a nightmare, having that image show up on his phone repeatedly, triggering flashback after flashback.

"Poor Rhys," she murmured.

"You found it?" Dr. Wiltshire asked.

"Yeah. Thanks. I'll read through the file and see if there were any other similarities between them."

"Who is the second victim?"

"We don't actually know who he is yet."

"A John Doe?"

"I can't even open a case yet. We don't have the body. Just a picture."

"Well, you can't autopsy that."

"No," Kenzie agreed. "Dr. Cook and I went over as much as we could… but you really can't tell very much from the photo."

16

Kenzie looked up at the sound of footsteps approaching down the long, tiled hallway from the elevator. From the man's bearing, he was a cop, maybe with military training, so she was not concerned by his approach. She nodded when he reached her.

"How can I help you?"

He was not in uniform. A plain-faced young man. They seemed to be putting them through the academy younger and younger, the older she got. There had been a time when all policemen were older than she was. But that time was long past.

"I'm Detective Saul, ma'am," he introduced himself, holding out a large hand to shake.

Kenzie stood up so that he wasn't towering over her and shook his hand briefly. "Detective." He was young to have achieved that title already. "Good for you. What can I do for you?"

"Well, actually, I'm here to report to you. Sergeant Campbell brought me in on the phone harassment case. And I thought I would fill you in on what we have discovered so far."

It took just a split second for Kenzie to remember that the phone harassment case was actually Rhys Salter's dead guy photo. She nodded her head eagerly.

"I'm glad that he's got someone looking into it. I don't suppose… that you've been able to find much out." No one at the school had mentioned anything about being contacted by the cops, so she had wondered whether they even had anyone looking into it and making inquiries, or if the new file was only populated with the details she had provided him. The picture, Rhys's phone, and Rhys's name and details.

"Not much we can do," Detective Saul acknowledged. "Not insofar as actually finding a body, which I gather from Campbell is what you are hoping for."

Kenzie shrugged. "No geo coordinates, unfortunately."

"No," he agreed with a slight frown. "Nothing like that."

"And no real clues in the picture. Other than the asphalt he is laying on, which I am told is consistent with Vermont asphalt, not Hollywood asphalt."

His brows climbed his forehead. "You have an asphalt expert on staff?"

"Just a consultant," Kenzie said with a laugh.

"We have been trying to track the progress of the photograph through the various platforms or programs it was transferred through since it first appeared in the school."

"Have you had much luck with that?"

"Unfortunately, the most popular messaging apps that teens use are the ones that delete the message and any attachments after they are read."

Kenzie nodded. "Which makes it kind of hard to track what hands—or phones—it has gone through."

"Exactly. I am told there aren't any signs of it before it started circulating through the school. Which means that it likely originated with someone at the school."

"You mean that one of them *took* the picture?"

Up until that point, Kenzie had been assuming that someone at the school had received it from someone outside of the school and then circulated it to his friends. She hadn't considered the possibility that it had actually been taken by one of the students.

"We don't know for sure. In fact, we can't even be sure that it was a real picture and not something created in a graphics program. But... it is a possibility that it is, in fact, a local death, and was taken by a student."

"Do you... know who that might be? Who started circulating it?"

She thought about the kids at the bus stop. Protecting each other. Protecting the person who had taken the picture. Had the person who took the picture been the killer? It seemed unlikely that anyone else would just happen to stumble over a body and take a picture of it. And start circulating it to their friends or other students. On the other hand, why would they kill someone and then start circulating the picture to their friends? That didn't make much more sense.

Kenzie supposed that such things did happen. People were arrested all the time for a crime that they had committed and posted about in an online public forum.

Saul looked at her, his eyes discerning. "Do *you* know who it might be?"

"No... we talked to some of the kids this morning, but I don't know... if any of them took it, or why they would."

"If I could get their names from you, I can talk to them and push a little more. See what I can find out."

"I don't actually know any names. They were just standing at the bus stop."

"You didn't get any names when you knew that they might know something?"

"Well, no. I didn't find anything concrete. I'm hoping one of them will come forward about what they know, but... I don't know how likely that is."

"Not very likely without any names."

"They didn't tell me anything. I just got a feeling they knew something about where the picture had come from."

Saul looked at her, his lips pressed tightly together in a thin, straight line. Clearly, not impressed with her investigative efforts. "Well... that's too bad. I hope we'll be able to track down the photo's origin. If it is legitimate. Sometimes, these things are just pranks, you know. Kids trying to get people upset or to get attention."

"I don't get that feeling in this case. I mean... if they wanted attention for it, wouldn't they be talking about it instead of covering it up?"

"Maybe. But they might only be looking for attention from a certain person or small group. They might not have intended it to get out to the public."

Kenzie supposed that was true.

"If you find anything out, be sure to give me a call," Saul told her. He took out a business card and snapped it down onto her desk. "That's my direct line. If there is *anything* on this case, give me a call to talk it over. We want to be kept in the loop. In fact, you should not be investigating it yourself. Leave that to us. You stick to bodies."

"If I had his body, I would."

Saul chuckled. "Leave it to us. If these pictures are of someone who was really killed, we'll figure it out soon enough. I'm sure you have enough other cases on your plate already. Or rather, on your table." He laughed at his joke.

Kenzie nodded. As soon as she finished her computer work, she had a couple of bodies to roll out and start working on.

"All right." Saul smiled. "Be sure to call me if you hear anything from your contacts." He patted her desk before walking away.

17

Kenzie worked late, since she had missed so much of the morning following up with the interviews at the school. When she got home, it was long past dinner time. Zachary had already warmed up a microwave dinner and Kenzie had settled for a sandwich from the vending machine down the hall. Kenzie showered off the sweat and stresses of the day and settled down on the couch to at least have some relaxed time with Zachary. Kenzie wasn't in any mood for discussion. She was ready to skip straight to mindless TV drivel.

When Kenzie's phone vibrated, she wanted to ignore it but knew she could not. She needed to at least make sure it was not a call-out to a scene of death that she had to attend. She pulled it out of her pocket to look at the screen and sighed.

Not a call out. But not a call that she could ignore, either. Lisa Cole Kirsch. Kenzie rolled her eyes at Zachary and swiped to answer the call.

"Hi, Mom."

"MacKenzie. It's nice to hear your voice, dear. It's been a little while since we last spoke."

"Yeah, sorry about that," Kenzie lied. "I've been busy."

"You have to be careful not to get too wrapped up in your work.

That is a challenge your father has always had. He gets so embroiled in his work that he forgets to spend time with loved ones."

"I know. We've talked about that before. He and I. That's one of the dangers of doing the work you love. You get so into the work that you forget to balance it out with other things."

"Exactly," Lisa agreed. "And I don't want to see that happen to you and for you and Zachary to grow apart."

"Well, right now, I'm sitting in front of the TV with him, getting ready to watch a movie."

"Watching a movie is not exactly a relationship-building activity," Lisa's voice was disapproving. "You need to do something other than sit in front of the TV together. You need to talk with each other. Go out places. Don't fall into the trap of thinking that TV is all you need to be entertained and have a happy relationship."

"I know that, Mom. We do other things. But today has been a long day. We were out together this morning. Tonight, I just need to unwind and have some time *not* to think of anything."

"Of course. I'm sorry, I shouldn't be interfering."

Kenzie hated it when her parents interfered or asked personal questions, and then said they shouldn't, still expecting her to answer their questions despite the apologies.

"How *are* you and Dad?" Kenzie asked, turning the conversation to her mother instead.

"Oh, well, the same as usual, I suppose. We are both busy with our own things. He will be coming to dinner next Sunday, if you would like to join us…"

Kenzie cleared her throat and thought about her schedule. "Usually, Zachary and I like to see the Petersons on a Sunday if we have the time. Not every week, but we haven't been there for a few because of the cases I have been working. It's a lot harder right now with Dr. Wiltshire being away."

"I thought that you had someone subbing in now."

"I do… but with Dr. Wiltshire, he did stuff independently and had me fill in where he needed to. With Dr. Cook, it's sort of the other way around. I do everything I can, and he fills in on the stuff I can't get to. And I don't really give him the run of the office. I know that technically, if he's subbing for Dr. Wiltshire, he is my superior. But really, it is my office, my responsibility, and I want to make sure that he doesn't... mess anything up."

"Good thing you are not a control freak," Lisa teased.

"I know, I know. I need to let him do more and trust him to get stuff done the right way, even if it means giving up control. But..." She trailed off.

"So, dinner on Sunday...?"

"I'll have to see."

"I think we should at least get equal time with Zachary's parents. It's the first time that I've asked you to dinner. We want to get to know Zachary better and to spend some quality time with our daughter."

Secretly, Kenzie was still mad at her parents for interfering with Rhys's treatment plan and not informing her. She didn't want to meet with them or to spend some nice social time together. She didn't even want to talk on the phone with them. It was an effort to act as if nothing had happened and be civil.

"I hear what you're saying," she said neutrally. "But it will depend on what other commitments we have made. I'll get back to you."

"MacKenzie..."

It wasn't a whine, but the tentative beginning of something else. And Kenzie didn't want to talk to her about something else. She wanted to hang up now and watch the movie with Zachary. He was watching her with a concerned expression, wondering what was happening.

"What, Mother?"

"I'm sorry... for that business with your young friend. You know that my intentions were good. We just happened to pick a program that did not work for him. We had no way of knowing that he would react to the drug. You do see that, don't you?"

"You should have talked to me about it."

"I couldn't when you might have a conflict of interest. We wanted to help you and your friend with something he needed, to surprise you later when you were no longer working on any cases at that facility. We thought it lined up perfectly and would be a real help for Rhys."

"Well, it wasn't, and I would have told you that if you had bothered to ask. But you didn't. You just went in there anonymously, interfered with the treatment of someone we love, and ended up causing harm that I could have warned you about if you had asked me instead of going off on your own and thinking you knew what was best for him! You're not a doctor."

Lisa was silent.

"I'm sorry, Mom," Kenzie realized as she said it that she was doing just what she had just observed that her parents did, apologizing for something she was not sorry about. "I know that I'm probably being unfair to you. But what you did caused real damage. And could have killed him. Saying that your intentions were good is... just not good enough."

"No," Lisa agreed quietly. "We should have done our due diligence. And maybe we should have waited until you had cleared your cases there and could go over a treatment plan with you. But it sounded so good, and you said that his condition was serious and that he needed treatment as soon as possible."

Kenzie held her tongue. They would just keep going around in circles over the same material again and again. There was no point in rehashing it when both had a valid argument. Kenzie was convinced she was right and Lisa should not have interfered.

"I'll let you know about Sunday," she told Lisa firmly.

"Thank you. I would appreciate knowing as soon as you are able to decide."

"Have a good night. We'll talk later."

Kenzie didn't wait to see if Lisa would terminate the call and pressed the red button to end it herself.

Zachary's finger hovered over the remote, not starting the movie. "What was that about? Your mother wants us to come for dinner?"

"Yes. She thinks she ought to get equal time with Lorne and Pat. That we should split between them instead of always going to the Petersons'."

"Well, she might have a point there," Zachary conceded. "I don't want to neglect your mom and dad and your relationship with them. I've said before that we should spend time with them if we can. But I didn't think she was really interested in things like family dinner."

"She's not. She's never suggested it until now. So why should I be concerned with giving her equal time? Your family has spent much more time and effort getting to know us. My parents are always occupied with their own social events."

"If they're opening up to other possibilities now, then maybe we should take it onboard and try to give them some time too."

"We had to leave right in the middle of Pat's breakfast last time. We need to make that up to him. That's more important than dropping everything and running because my mom decided to play hostess and invite us over for once."

"Maybe you could offer a different date instead? The next weekend? Or give us a weekend at home and then see if she's available the following weekend?"

"Yeah. Maybe something like that. I'm just not inclined to jump through hoops for her. She said that Dad is coming this Sunday. That's why she wanted all of us."

"Maybe he could come in a couple of weeks."

"Yeah. I agree. If it's that important to them, they should be making some effort to work with our schedule, not force us to theirs. To hers."

"I don't know if anyone is trying to *force* anything."

Kenzie sighed. "You have your parental issues, and I have mine."

He smiled at that. Kenzie knew that her parental issues were minor compared to his. The abuse, neglect, and abandonment he had been through made her arguments with her parents occasionally stepping on her toes seem small and petty. She should be happy that she still had parents in her life. That they were good people at their core. That she could rely on them.

"Maybe you should bring it up with Dr. Boyle at couple's therapy," Zachary suggested.

"I think I need a whole different therapist to deal with all of that," she joked.

"Well, you could, you know," Zachary pointed out seriously.

"Yeah. I know. But I really don't think it's anything I need therapy for. It's just normal parent-child dynamics and me trying to assert my independence while they're trying to keep me a dependent child."

Zachary shrugged, backing off of it. He knew what it was like to have someone pushing therapy at him when he wasn't ready for it or didn't think it was necessary. She had been on the other side of the table enough times to recognize that he was trying to be helpful in his suggestion, not to irritate or tease her. But it wasn't something that she needed. She could handle her parents without a third party mediating.

18

Kenzie noted the police department transfer number on the caller ID of her desk phone and pressed the button to take the call. The dispatcher greeted her warmly.

"Looks like we've got a body dump for you, Dr. Kirsch."

"Well, things have been pretty quiet around here. I guess we needed a little excitement. What are the details?"

"Body found in a dumpster." The dispatcher gave her the location details. "From the sounds of it, this one is pretty ripe. You'll want a mask."

"Ripe because of what else is in the dumpster or ripe because of decomp?"

"Decomp. The reporting LEO said that it was not a fresh kill. And there were… certain familiar noises in the background of the call indicating that it was not a particularly pleasant scene."

Kenzie chuckled. Few death scenes were pleasant. And even fewer dump sites. It sounded like at least one of the law enforcement officers at the scene had lost his lunch over it. As the dispatcher had suggested, Kenzie had better make sure she had all of her gear with her, including a mask. It wouldn't completely block the smell, but it would help a little. Once the body was in the morgue, she could turn on the big exhaust fans that would clear most of the decomp smell while she was working. The rest she would get used to, as she always did.

She put in a call to Carlos to let him know she would need help with transportation. He promised to have the van ready to go in fifteen minutes. She texted George to tell him that she would need him to help in autopsy and also gave him a heads-up about the state of the body. She looked over the remaining emails and paperwork she had to deal with, and decided none of it took precedence over the new body. She locked her computer, tidied her desk, and went to Dr. Cook's office to talk to him.

She knocked on his open door and entered the room, not speaking until she was sure he was not on his phone. It was difficult to tell, sometimes, with his Bluetooth earpiece.

"I've got a call-out," she told him. "Something ripe that will need to be handled fairly quickly. Are you free this afternoon?"

"Oh, yes, please."

Kenzie laughed. "Just what you were hoping for, right? I'll let you know more when I see the scene. Dispatcher said it was a dump, so I'm not sure how much we will know about the cause of death or the actual scene of death."

"If we're lucky, maybe it was a bum who smelled particularly rancid even before he died."

Kenzie grinned. She waved at him and left to deal with the new victim.

Zachary had finally relented and let Kenzie drive herself in her own car, deciding that she was well enough and not dealing with any more concussion symptoms. So, rather than waiting for Carlos, she headed to the dump site ahead of him. Roxboro was not the big city and it did not take long to get there. It was obvious she had arrived at the right place from the police vehicles with flashing lights left on and the yellow tape strung around the scene.

She parked her car well away from the other vehicles, not wanting it to get scratched or clipped with their coming and going. Carlos would need room to drive the ME's van up. She got out of the car and locked it securely behind her. One of the uniformed officers on crowd control stopped her as she walked up to the tape.

"Crime scene, ma'am. You'll have to wait—"

"ME's office," Kenzie told him, pulling out her ID and showing it to him.

"Oh." He looked at her for a minute as if he couldn't quite believe it. Probably because of the little red convertible. Most MEs didn't ride around town in something so flashy. But Kenzie would get as much use as she could out of it before winter hit full force, making it impractical for longer trips. She could still use it for the short drives to and from the office, but for anything that was too far, it wasn't easy to keep the car warm enough for comfort during the winter months.

"So...?" Kenzie motioned to the dump site.

The officer nodded. "Oh, yeah. Go ahead."

He lifted the tape for her to duck under. Kenzie stopped at the edge of the perimeter to pull on coveralls, put booties on over top of her shoes, a hair net and cap over her curls, and gloves. Ready to go, she picked up her bag and headed for the knot of people surrounding the dumpster and chatting with each other.

"Dr. Kirsch," one of the figures turned to her and she could make out the shape of Detective Cameron under the protective gear.

"I would shake," Kenzie offered, then shrugged. She obviously couldn't touch him and not contaminate anything. "What have you got for me?"

"I'm not sure how much they've told you, but this one is pretty nasty. Been here a while. I guess this bin doesn't get checked very often. I don't know how often it is supposed to be collected, but it looks like it's been a few weeks, at least."

"Pleasant."

Kenzie walked over to the dumpster. A step stool had been set up so she could get up to the right level to look down at the pile of rotting trash and a putrefying corpse that, as the others had already said, had been there for an extended time.

She looked at the longish blond hair, the size and shape of him, and the damage to the middle of his forehead. She felt suddenly dizzy and unstable on the top step of the stool and held on to the edge of the dumpster, contaminating her gloves. Detective Cameron was at her elbow and guided her back down the steps.

"You okay, Dr. Kirsch?"

Kenzie stood there, frozen, for a few seconds, reviewing everything in her mind. She had not been expecting to find him there. And yet, she had. She had been waiting for him to show up.

She stripped off her gloves, unzipped her coveralls, and reached deep into her pocket to pull out her phone.

"You get a call?"

Kenzie shook her head. She woke and unlocked her phone, then tapped through her photos until she found the one she wanted. She turned the phone around and showed it to Cameron. He stared.

"You think that's the same guy?"

Kenzie nodded. "Looks like it to me."

Cameron took the phone from her and walked up the step stool without touching anything to steady himself. He held the phone out in front of him and looked down at the corpse, viewing the images side by side. He nodded and stepped back down to hand Kenzie her phone.

"There you are. Yup. I'd say we've got your man. But how exactly did you have his picture before getting here? And who is he?"

"I don't have a name for him yet. Maybe now that we have fingerprints, we can get an ID."

"And you already have his picture because…"

"Because it's been circulating the local high school for the past few weeks."

"Ah. And someone contacted you to determine whether it was a real body or a hoax."

"More or less," Kenzie agreed. "I'm glad he finally showed up. While he was still identifiable as being the same person."

"Well, I'd never be able to tell by the face, but the hair and clothing are the same and the bullet hole is in the right place."

Kenzie nodded. She took a deep breath and headed back toward the dumpster, doing up her coveralls and pulling out a fresh pair of gloves.

"You okay to go up there again?" Cameron asked solicitously.

"Sure, I'm fine. It just gave me a turn when I saw him and realized who it was. That's all."

He nodded understandingly. "I can see why that would be a little startling!"

The second time looking down at the John Doe who had finally surfaced, Kenzie was able to look around appraisingly, looking for anything that had been dumped along with the body.

"There is a tarp. He was probably carried on top of or inside it. Make sure the tech guys get that."

"Right."

"You're going to have to sift through the contents for the gun. It might have been disposed of here at the same time."

She didn't see anything else that was relevant to the murder. She knew it was a dump site and was unlikely to provide many clues about where the man had come from or what had happened to him before and after he was shot. She didn't expect to get much from the body itself. However, she might get lucky and be able to get some trace evidence from his clothing that would be a clue as to where he had lain in the street, the vehicle he had been transported in, or something about the person who had transported him from one location to the other.

If she were really *really* lucky, maybe the dead man would have skin cells under his fingernails.

19

Kenzie had a little time when she returned to the office to check for any emails or messages left while she had been gone and to fill Dr. Cook in on the basics of the body dump. She had helped Carlos load the liquifying remains into the van. He and George would offload, and George would do the initial work to take pictures of the remains, remove and catalog the clothes, and prepare what was left for autopsy.

"This is the body you were looking for?" Dr. Cook asked.

"Uh… yes. The one who we had a picture of."

"So I guess it was not a prank."

"I guess not," Kenzie agreed. She decided she'd better call Sergeant Campbell and tell him the same thing. His phone harassment case could now be transitioned to a homicide, and the preliminary work that Detective Saul had done in tracking the origin of the photo could be used for the basis of when the man had been killed and who was there to take a picture of the body at the time. They had a head start on that, despite the age of the corpse.

She and Dr. Cook went to the autopsy and dressed and scrubbed, getting ready to begin as George finished separating the clothes from the decomposing flesh. Kenzie was glad for the good ventilation and the modern equipment that allowed her to quickly raise and lower the autopsy tables, make a recording by tapping the floor button with her foot, or give the computer instructions using voice commands and keywords. All of that made it so much simpler than it would have been ten or twenty years before when everything had to be done by hand, having to stop the autopsy in order to do anything else.

Once everything was ready, she tapped the floor button and began recording the John Doe's file number, the date and time, and her and Dr. Cook's names. She began with the gross examination—an appropriate appellation given the state the body was in—carefully describing everything she saw. While she knew that the man had been dead for over two weeks, she could not rely solely on her knowledge about the timing of the picture being circulated around the school to date the man's death. He obviously hadn't been killed after that date, but he could have been killed before. The decomposition and insect activity would give them a timeline. From her initial observations, two weeks was a pretty good estimate.

The body was bloated and red. As Cameron had observed, the face was unrecognizable. Without the photo on her phone, she would have had to order a forensic reconstruction done in order to visualize the face. There had been plenty of insect activity, with very little flesh left where the bugs had been active. The clothing had protected the body to some degree, and it was more intact than Kenzie would have hoped. Even so, there was very little to autopsy.

She had paused for long enough in her narration for Dr. Cook to speak up. "Would you like me to collect the fingernails and test them for a secondary DNA source?"

"Uh, yeah, that would be good." Kenzie waited for him to do so, looking at the body and trying to figure out what else would be constructive. She wasn't sure any organs would be intact if she opened him up. She worried that she wouldn't even be able to shift the body to look at the back and front without damaging it significantly. George and Carlo had done very well to get it onto the table intact. She hadn't thought they would be able to get him out of the dumpster in one piece.

"You're not going to be able to do much to manipulate it," Cook advised. "I don't think it's going to hold together. Maybe check each limb individually, but not the torso. We'll see what's left on the table in the end."

Kenzie nodded. For the recording, she described the appearance of the head wound, describing it as it was rather than as she had seen it in the photo. Since John Doe's death, it had become enlarged, harder to identify as a small-caliber bullet wound. But she had a better view of the hole in the skull and might be able to identify the size of the bullet and other factors from that.

She carefully picked up each of the limbs, describing any markings or tattoos still visible. The hands were in pretty bad shape, in an advanced state of decomposition, but Kenzie thought she might be able to get fingerprints from a couple of them. Maybe only partial prints, but it was possible they could still be helpful in identifying him. She examined each finger in turn and, with Dr. Cook's help, rolled each one that had any intact skin left that they might be able to pull a print from. In the end, only a couple looked like anything more than blotches on the screen. But with those two partials, it was possible that they would be able to get an ID.

She logged the weight of the remains, even though she knew it was far lower than the man would have weighed in life. Height was still reasonably accurate.

"Okay." She looked at Dr. Cook and then back down at the man again. "Do we do anything else? I'm not sure what a full autopsy would reveal at this point. The organs are liquifying."

"Some samples for tox screens. X-rays. While you know that he died from a bullet to the head—as far as we can tell—we want to build a picture of anything else we could before that point. Was he drunk? Was he in a fight? Those things could inform the ruling."

"Sure."

She proceeded on that basis. It was fascinating, and somewhat poignant to see how a body started to return to nature within a couple of weeks. Before long, if they did nothing to halt the process of decomposition, nothing recognizable would remain of their John Doe but the bones.

The X-rays didn't show any recent breaks. There were a few old, healed fractures, the recalcified areas brighter white on the X-ray.

Nothing significant that Kenzie could see. He had not lived a seden-
tary life. But she couldn't classify which breaks were accidents, which
were from fights, and which might have resulted from abuse. He
might just have been unlucky.

Unlucky enough to get a hole in his head.

They worked efficiently to collect tissues and fluids needed for
tests.

"We should retrieve the bullet, I guess," Kenzie suggested.

Dr. Cook agreed. They took an X-ray to determine the position of
the bullet so that they wouldn't have to dig around looking for it.
Kenzie took films from several different angles so that the police
would have as much information as possible about the murder
weapon and how the man had been killed.

"A .22," Kenzie observed as she put the bullet into a shallow dish
and gently washed and dried it off before bagging it as evidence.
"Like we thought from the photo. It isn't too badly deformed. Maybe
they'll be able to match the ballistics to a known weapon."

"With any luck. If we get both—DNA and ballistics—there
might not be anything left for the police to figure out."

Kenzie smiled. It would be rare to luck out with that much physical evidence. But one never knew.

20

Zachary had been at his therapist's while Kenzie was doing her autopsy, so he was tired when he got home and ready for ice cream and a relaxing evening. Kenzie told him about finding the John Doe, hesitant to suggest they go see Rhys and give him the news. But she didn't have to ask.

"We should go to the hospital," Zachary said immediately. "I know it doesn't *really* make any difference that the body has turned up… it doesn't prove anything except that he was really dead, and it wasn't just a Photoshop job. But I think he should know. It's important to him."

"Are you sure you're up to it? I can go alone if you aren't. He'll understand you're tired today and will come the next time."

"I'm seeing him at his worst. It doesn't really matter if I'm a little tired."

"If you're sure. I don't think he would mind."

"I'm going," he said firmly.

"Okay. We'll have a bite to eat, and then we can go."

She saw Zachary looking longingly toward the freezer. "You can have ice cream after dinner. Not for dinner."

"Sometimes we have ice cream for dinner."

"Not today."

Zachary grunted. He opened the freezer anyway but reached for a frozen dinner instead of ice cream. He took it out, then put it back away. Then he went to the cupboard and grabbed a can of Chicken and Stars soup.

It might not be what she would have picked out for supper, but it was better than the ice cream. If he needed the familiar comfort food after his session, that was his choice. How many times did Kenzie pick salad over something carb-filled, creamy, and satisfying? Not as often as she should.

They worked around each other in the kitchen, making separate meals. Zachary might go for the childhood favorite, but it wasn't high on Kenzie's list.

"So he was shot?" Zachary asked, introducing the subject of the autopsy.

Kenzie smiled and nodded. That much Zachary knew already. "Yes, .22 caliber. We got the bullet for ballistics. That's about all of the hard evidence that we have at this point. We'll see if anything shows up in any other tests. We're checking for DNA, in case the victim and the shooter had close contact. But there was no sign that he had been in a fight, so I'm not confident he got close enough to touch or scratch the gunman."

"But it was fired from close by?"

"No skin charring that I could see, so not a contact wound. But I would still guess that it was pretty close."

"Anything else at the scene?"

"Well, we don't have the murder scene. Only a dump site. The police are checking the dumpster for anything that might be related."

"Lucky them."

Kenzie nodded. "At least I get a morgue with good exhaust fans for the autopsy. I'm afraid they don't get the same for the garbage dive."

"At least it isn't one hundred degrees out."

"There's that. I still don't imagine they'll be too happy about it. Dirty, smelly business. Especially when you have a corpse marinating on top of everything. But if the gun or anything else is in the bin, they need to find it."

"You don't have any other trace evidence or avenues of investigation?"

"I'll go through the clothes with a fine-toothed comb tomorrow. You never know, we might find hairs, fingerprints, who knows what."

"Yeah. You never know. It might be right there under your nose."

They ate their dinner without ceremony. Kenzie didn't want to take any longer than she had to, knowing they both wanted to get home as soon as possible after the hospital visit. When they signed in at the hospital to visit Rhys, they found Vera there. Kenzie shouldn't have been surprised. She knew that Vera spent a lot of time at the hospital with Rhys. He didn't likely have anyone else visiting him. But she had imagined that they would have Rhys to themselves again and be able to update him on the John Doe.

Rhys was in the visitor area at a table with Vera. He jumped to his feet when he saw Zachary and Kenzie coming. He immediately shook hands with Zachary, clasping tightly and slapping him on the shoulder. He looked at Kenzie and leaned in for a hug. Kenzie put her arms around his shoulders and squeezed him tightly before releasing him.

"Hey, Rhys, how are you doing?"

He was recovering from his ordeal, his eyes looking less hollow than they had. His mood seemed lighter. Maybe they had him on a new medication. Or maybe it was not having to look at that oppressive image on his phone any longer. It must have bothered him to have to keep looking at the picture as it was forwarded to him repeatedly. She assumed he had logged in to all his social networks on the new phone. Hopefully, everyone had seen the picture and grown bored with it, and it was no longer making its rounds.

"Vera," Zachary greeted, and put his hand out to shake. Vera gave him a smile that still seemed a little forced, but she took his hand and then clasped it with her other hand so that his was sandwiched between both of hers.

"Hello, Zachary, Kenzie. It's nice of you to come see Rhys."

"I hope we're not interrupting," Kenzie ventured, giving Vera the opportunity to tell them that it was not a good time and they should leave.

"No, no. We run out of things to say after a while."

Rhys laughed silently at this, drawing a chuckle out of Zachary. Vera patted her hair, looking embarrassed.

"Well, of course, that's never stopped us before," she said good-humoredly.

They all sat back down around the table. Kenzie saw that Rhys had his phone in his pocket and was glad they were letting him hold on to it, at least while he had a visitor there, so that he could communicate more easily.

"You're looking better," Zachary commented, looking Rhys over. "You're feeling a bit better?"

Rhys nodded his agreement. He looked at Kenzie and raised his brows. Kenzie understood that he wanted to know how she had fared on investigating the picture of the John Doe, but wasn't sure she wanted to jump directly into the subject, especially with Vera there. She glanced over at Vera, wondering if she had any thoughts of going home now that Rhys had other visitors. She would probably be going home anyway so that she could go to bed.

"Rhys will be coming home soon," Vera contributed. "It will be nice to have him back again. It has been hard having him away for so long." She patted Rhys's arm affectionately. He put his hand over hers briefly.

"That's great news. I'm glad you're doing so much better," Kenzie told Rhys.

He gave a small smile and nodded. He pulled his phone out of his pocket and navigated to his messaging app. Her own phone buzzed and displayed a picture of Snoopy lying on top of his red doghouse, looking happy and comfortable. *Home.*

"Will it be hard to get caught up with school?"

Rhys rolled his eyes at this. He slumped in his seat and let his head fall back in mock exhaustion.

"He'll probably need some help," Vera said, "but we'll get him back on track."

"That's good."

"We met a couple of your friends," Zachary told Rhys.

Rhys turned his face to Zachary, raising his brows in inquiry.

"Hugh and Ayla," Zachary told him. "We were asking them when that picture had started circulating around the school."

"They seem nice," Kenzie contributed.

Rhys nodded his agreement. He didn't seem overwhelmingly positive about Zachary and Kenzie having met his friends. Maybe he hadn't thought that they would need to go to his friends when making inquiries about the dead man. Maybe he had thought that Kenzie would just be able to go to the morgue and look through unclaimed bodies to find the man and give Rhys a rundown on who he was and what had happened to him. Or that she would be able to tell him that the body had been claimed and he was back with his people, at rest. Maybe the killer had already been caught and was behind bars. All of that would be good and would let him know that everything was okay without ever having to talk to anyone at the school.

He raised his brows at Kenzie, wanting to know what she had found out.

Kenzie looked at Vera, but she wasn't leaving.

"So, we looked into the picture you got on your phone," Kenzie started awkwardly. "That's why we were talking to your friends and some of the other kids at the school. When I looked into recent deaths, I couldn't find anything that matched the picture. No one was even sure whether it was local or recent. A lot of people thought that it might have been a prank."

Rhys's jaw set, and he shook his head adamantly.

"No, I know it was real," Kenzie agreed. "I just ran into some opposition with people not believing it."

He nodded, and, after a moment, pointed at his own chest. Kenzie studied him, trying to interpret the gesture. "Did you run into that too? Where people didn't believe it was a legitimate picture? That it was just some kind of joke or hoax?"

He nodded. Kenzie wondered who he had shown it to. Had it just been in discussions with friends, or had he gone to someone at the school and tried to convince them to look into it? Maybe to the school resource officer? If he had, word had not gotten back to the principal. Lakes had never seen the picture before Kenzie had shown it to her. Or at least, not that she was admitting. But would she admit it if she realized that it was the picture that caused Rhys's breakdown? She wouldn't want to admit that she hadn't taken Rhys seriously or that she had ignored something that she knew was circulating among the student body.

Kenzie nodded her understanding. "So I ran into the same thing, even though I'm an adult and work with the medical examiner. Someone who knows a thing or two about dead bodies."

Hopefully, it would make Rhys feel better to know that it hadn't just been him. It hadn't been just because he was a kid, or a minority, or had communication difficulties. Even Kenzie, the expert, had run into the same challenges.

She shifted in her chair, trying to get comfortable in the hard seat that was clearly not designed with comfort in mind.

"I did get the police to open an investigation into the picture," Kenzie told Rhys. "Not a homicide investigation, but an investigation into phone harassment, the picture being circulated around the school to upset people. It was the only thing he could do without a body or even a missing person report on the victim."

"I'm sure it was just a kid's prank," Vera said. "Why would anyone be passing around pictures of a real dead body? That's just... inappropriate."

Rhys shook his head, frown lines between his brows.

Kenzie put her hand on Rhys's arm to try to keep his attention on her. "Then today, they found the body."

21

W hat?" Vera's voice was weak. This was not what she had wanted to hear.

"No one could even confirm until today that this was even a real person or a real death," Kenzie said. "Even though it looked real, it's true that it could have been some kind of makeup job or Photoshop manipulation. They can do a lot of things to make it look realistic. But as Rhys thought, it wasn't just a hoax. It wasn't just a meme being passed around school to disgust or upset people."

Rhys nodded his agreement. His eyes were riveted on Kenzie.

"But it was real," Kenzie said. "All of it. The man, the bullet wound in his head. A picture being taken of him after his death. I had him on my table this afternoon."

She could see Rhys breathing heavily.

"Are you okay, Rhys? Is this too much?"

He made a calming gesture with his hands.

"You're okay?"

A nod.

"You're sure? If it's making you feel extra anxious or panicky, you could get a sedative or spend some time talking to your therapist."

He moved his hands in a horizontal line. *No.*

Kenzie held his gaze for a moment to make sure that he wasn't getting too upset. He nodded encouragingly.

"The police have opened a homicide file now. I did the autopsy this afternoon. As much as I could do with the shape the body was in."

She probably shouldn't go into too much detail about the state of the man's remains.

"They will be trying to identify him. Now that we have some data, his DNA and fingerprints, hopefully, they will be able to figure out who he is, and we will be one step closer to finding out what happened to him."

Rhys nodded.

"I'm sorry that it took so long for the body to be found," Kenzie said. "It might have been easier on you if they had been able to confirm right away that he was deceased and opened an investigation into it. Knowing that it was circulating the school would have informed their investigation, helped them to sort out the origin of the photo sooner."

He cocked his head, questioning.

"They don't know who took the picture or started it circulating yet," Kenzie told him. "But they're working on it. It will be a higher priority now that it is a homicide rather than just phone harassment."

Rhys tapped something into his phone, and Kenzie looked down at hers when it buzzed. It was a gif of a spinning globe. Kenzie let Zachary see it and tried to think of what Rhys was trying to say. Zachary pursed his lips.

"Where did you find it?" he suggested.

They both looked at Rhys, who nodded and pointed to Zachary to confirm the question.

"It had been left in a dumpster," Kenzie told him. "One that wasn't emptied regularly. So it was longer than it should have been before someone found it."

Rhys pinched his nose.

"Oh, yes," Kenzie agreed with a laugh. "It was not a pleasant experience for the police, I'll tell you that."

He pointed to Kenzie, eyebrows up.

"Or to me. Well, no, but I've got good ventilation in the morgue, so it wasn't too bad. And I'm used to it to a certain degree. My job stinks."

They all chuckled over this.

"Well," Vera's huff clearly indicated she was attempting to change the subject. "I'm glad that Rhys can finally put his mind at ease about this whole situation. I don't know what happened or how that picture ended up on his phone, but now that he knows it is being taken care of, he can put it out of his mind and look to the future. What we need to focus on now is Rhys getting out of here soon and the outpatient treatment he will be following. The hospital has recommended a couple of therapists."

"Good," Zachary approved. He looked at Rhys. "I really didn't want to be in therapy, but it has helped me a lot. And it has helped Kenzie and me; we've done couple's therapy to help with that. You might want to do some family therapy with Vera as well as individual therapy. It could help you to communicate better."

Rhys rolled his eyes.

"I know it's not fun," Zachary emphasized. "I know you don't feel like doing it. But it does make a difference."

Rhys made a motion to his back, which Kenzie assumed was a reference to the past and the therapy he had done previously.

"Even if you had a bunch of therapy in the past," Zachary said. "It can still be useful."

Rhys shrugged.

"You're lucky they're going to fund the therapy," Vera told Rhys. "So we can afford it. We can afford to get someone good, not just whoever we can get with my benefits."

Kenzie looked at Vera, her throat tightening. "Who is funding it?" she asked, even though, of course, it was none of her business.

"The anonymous donor," Vera said. "The one who was paying for the experimental therapy at Persons. They said that since it didn't work out, since he reacted to the drug, they would fund something else. Whatever therapy we chose."

Kenzie happened to know who the anonymous donor was. The Kirsch family foundation. She was irritated to learn that they were still funding Rhys without even telling her about it. After the last debacle, she thought they were going to tell her whenever they did something that impacted her family and close friends. They had kept the experimental treatment a secret from her because of a potential conflict of interest, but there was no reason to keep the ongoing funding from her. Unless they thought she would be upset about it for some reason.

If they were letting Vera and Rhys choose what kind of therapy they thought would be best instead of funneling Rhys into a particular program, which Kenzie had told Vera was too risky, then the only reason she had to be angry about it was because they were doing it behind her back. Again.

She shook her head. Vera stared at her, frowning, trying to figure out what Kenzie was expressing her disapproval of.

"You just said he needed therapy. Why would you be opposed to an anonymous donor funding it?"

"Sorry," Kenzie said, trying to lighten her voice. "I was just thinking of something else. I didn't mean to scowl at you." She pasted a smile on her face. "That's great. I'm glad that money will not be a deterrent and you can get Rhys whatever treatment the two of you decide is best."

"It won't be that drug therapy," Vera told her in a tentative voice.

"No, I know that. I think it would be too risky after what happened the first time. Even if they lowered the dose, he might still react to it, and we don't want to do what could be irreparable damage."

Vera nodded her agreement, looking relieved.

Vera had been pretty insistent about Persons and their therapy before. She had stood up to Kenzie and ended up being wrong. She was probably worried that Kenzie would think she was making a bad choice again and didn't want to draw her disappointment.

"Will you be glad to be out of here and back at school?" Kenzie asked, turning her attention back to Rhys.

He made a face and shook his head.

"You don't want to go back to school?"

He nodded.

"You'll be glad to see your friends again, won't you? That will be nice."

He nodded, but didn't seem too excited about it. Kenzie remembered Hugh saying they were just school friends and didn't see each other outside of school. And Ayla didn't seem that close to him, even though Hugh suggested they talk to her. If those were Rhys's two best friends, and he didn't even see them outside of school hours, she could see why he wasn't too excited about going back to see them. He might be lonely at the hospital, but he would be lonely at home with just Vera to keep him company and lonely at school with just one or two friends to hang out with.

"Did you ever think of getting into one of the clubs?" Zachary asked.

Rhys looked at him and widened his eyes. *What clubs?*

Zachary shrugged. "I don't know. I always thought being in the photography or yearbook club would be fun. I couldn't ever be in any clubs or extracurricular activities, but I thought those might be cool. You wouldn't have to talk a lot for them."

Rhys nodded, but didn't look that interested. Maybe he wasn't interested in photography or they didn't have a photography club. Kenzie didn't know what Rhys was interested in.

"If there are any clubs you are interested in, we could help out with them," Kenzie said. "If there is some equipment you need to buy."

Vera looked at Rhys, but he just shook his head and didn't indicate any interest. "I think our Rhys is just a homebody," she said. "That's where he wants to be the most."

22

S orry I couldn't get down yesterday to watch the autopsy," Campbell told Kenzie when he arrived at her desk. "I meant to get down for it, but too much was happening. A bunch of noise upstairs about other issues, and then finding a DB in the dumpster that somehow the medical examiner knew about before the police did kind of set some people's nerves on edge. As much as I explain that I can't be walking around to all the dumpsters in town looking for new bodies, they don't seem to understand that it is all just up to chance."

Kenzie smiled and shook her head. "I guess you're going to have to up your game. Make a list of high-priority dumpsters. Have them checked every day. Any time there is a body part, no matter how small, you make sure it is reported to you immediately…"

He grinned, "That's how new policies come to be," he agreed. "So, the autopsy?"

"You didn't really miss anything. Nothing that you would probably want to see, anyway." She grimaced. "The body was so old it was half liquid. It's a wonder it didn't burst when we took it out of the dumpster or during transport. There wasn't a lot that I could do with him. I got some fingernails, a couple of fingerprints, sent some DNA off to the lab for analysis and searched CODIS, but other than that…

there was nothing remarkable. We couldn't tell much more from the body than we could from the picture. In some ways, the picture is more helpful. Oh, and I did get the slug that was in his head. That's been sent to ballistics in case they can identify the gun it came from, but I'm not that hopeful."

"Identifying features? Tattoos?"

"I took pictures of what I could. But anywhere his skin was still intact, the colors were not great. Someone who knew him well might be able to identify them."

"And nothing to indicate there might be another cause of death?"

"Shot to the head seems most likely. I am also getting a tox screen, just in case there are any complicating factors. If he was drunk or drugged, if he was poisoned. It isn't comprehensive, but we do what we can. If you tell me to look for another substance, I can do that."

"Nothing at this point. We need to identify the guy before we can find out much more about what happened to him."

Kenzie nodded. "We've got a few avenues for identification. Hopefully, one of them works out."

"Until then, what happens to the remains?"

"We've taken a few slides and samples to be held for future tests. If he is not claimed in the next few days, we'd best send them for cremation. His cremains can be held for any relatives who pop up much more easily than the soupy mess we've got in there now. Getting gradually soupier."

Campbell wrinkled his nose. "Thank you for that image."

"Like I say, you should be glad you didn't watch the autopsy. I don't think you would have enjoyed it quite as much as our less... aromatic patients."

Campbell laughed. "Dr. Kirsch, you are a ghoul."

"If you hadn't figured it out by now, you're not the investigator I thought you were."

Kenzie had thought that Campbell might stick around to be there while she examined John Doe's clothing in detail. But after hearing her summary of the autopsy, he apparently decided that he'd heard enough and retreated to his office.

Kenzie took each item of clothing one at a time, laying them all out on the autopsy table. She didn't usually spend so much time on the clothes but, given the state the body was in, she hoped to glean a few more details from the clothing, which was in better shape. A bloodstain on the shirt could indicate an injury that she hadn't been able to see on the body due to its advanced state of decomposition and predation. Or it could indicate an injury to his attacker and another DNA profile to be analyzed.

Other trace evidence might give her a better idea of where he had been when he was killed. It was unlikely that they could narrow it down to one site or a handful of places as they always could on TV, but it would give them a better idea of where to look—and who knew? Maybe they would be able to find the death scene and additional evidence. Unlike in *Bones*, she didn't have a botanist or entomologist on staff but, if she identified something of interest, she could track down an expert to tell her about it and whether it was significant.

She stretched the t-shirt out and smoothed the wrinkles the best she could. She took a couple of pictures of it, front and back, looking for any stains or tears or trace evidence that might be important. There were a few long, blond hairs on his collar that she assumed were the victim's own, but she carefully preserved them and marked the exhibits so that they could be analyzed and compared with the his hair, just in case they were from his girlfriend or assailant. She turned the shirt over and photographed and examined the back as well. Neither side presented much of interest. Kenzie bagged it separately and moved on to the jeans.

Nothing identified what stores the victim shopped at. He hadn't been buying designer clothes or jewelry. If Kenzie were to guess, she would say that he'd either had the clothes for a long time or he had gotten them at a thrift store or mission. Cheap, old, and worn.

The knees of the jeans were worn, but not torn. He had probably not been kneeling on the pavement—or asphalt—before he was shot. There was no motor oil, no particularly special soil that she could analyze to find out where he had been lately. Using tweezers, she pulled everything she could find out of the pockets. A couple of nearly unreadable receipts. Some loose change.

The jean jacket was similar to the pants. Nothing remarkable. Nothing that looked out of place.

That left her with a belt, socks, shoes, and bandana. No identifying phone or wallet. No weapons. Kenzie photographed and examined each piece. She looked closely at the belt, hoping it would have a unique buckle or something else that the victim had purchased as a special treat or been given as a gift by a family member or close friend. But it looked like a belt she could have purchased off the shelf in any department store. Not a collector's piece. No inscribed belt buckle. Just a generic, off-the-shelf belt.

23

I'm just not sure what you're doing here."

Kenzie paused as she stepped out of the morgue and heard raised voices. She cocked her head. Dr. Cook and...?

"This is my office. I have every right to be here," Dr. Wiltshire shot back.

"Of course, it's your office," Dr. Cook replied, his voice still louder than necessary. "But why are you here now? Today? I have everything under control. You are supposed to be off. Healing. Until your hand has healed, there isn't anything for you to do here."

"I want to keep on top of the new cases. See what's going on. See if Kenzie needs anything."

"That's why I'm here."

"I know her better than you do."

Kenzie rolled her eyes. They were fighting over her? Over the morgue? Acting territorial over dead bodies? She put the bagged and tagged clothing where it belonged and followed the voices to the boardroom, where both men stood while engaging in what sounded like a heated discussion, but was really quite ridiculous. Neither one had a leg to stand on. It was Dr. Wiltshire's office. Dr. Cook was legitimately there as his substitute. Either one could be there, doing whatever duties they were able to perform.

CAPTURED IN DEATH

"What's going on?" Kenzie asked, to get their attention. It was already evident what was going on.

"Kenzie," Dr. Wiltshire turned toward her. His red face got a little redder. He smiled at her, forced and frozen looking. "I just thought I would check in. See how everything is going."

Kenzie nodded. "We're doing pretty well. Keeping up, for the most part."

Dr. Wiltshire nodded. "Good…"

"Dr. Cook has been very competent," Kenzie said, looking at him and giving a nod of acknowledgment. "It's been very good to have someone else here to lean on while you're healing."

Dr. Cook looked like he wanted to say something aggrieved, like "I'm the good guy here," but he restrained himself, nodding back to Kenzie. "Dr. Kirsch and I have been able to stay on top of things so far. She is also very competent."

Kenzie chuckled to herself. Wasn't it great that they could all get along?

The two men still had the puffed-up appearance of tomcats confronting each other over their territory. She hoped that her words would soothe the savage beasts and put a stop to the cater-wauling.

"Did you want to go over this new John Doe with me?" she invited Dr. Wiltshire. "We've done the autopsy—what little we could do with the advanced state of decomposition—and I've just finished going over the clothing. I could use your guidance on anything else we should do before incinerating what is left."

Dr. Wiltshire nodded and looked authoritative. "Certainly. Of course. You want to do it here?" He motioned to the boardroom table. He knew, of course, that Dr. Cook was already established in his office. He couldn't really kick him out just to assert his dominance when Dr. Cook was legitimately there to substitute and keep things running smoothly during Dr. Wiltshire's recovery.

Kenzie nodded. She went to the computer attached to the AV equipment in order to navigate to the files so they could blow up the pictures and imaging on the big screen.

"I'll leave you to it, then," Dr. Cook said stiffly. "Anything I

111

should know about on the examination of the clothing, Dr.—uh—Kenzie?"

While he had refused to call her by her first name before, he had apparently changed his mind now that he'd heard Dr. Wiltshire calling her Kenzie.

"No, nothing significant. I wish I could say that we have more than we do."

"It's understandable. We can't force the issue. It is whatever it is."

Kenzie nodded her agreement. Dr. Cook retreated to the office and Dr. Wiltshire sat down at the table. Kenzie shook her head and did not ask, "What was that all about?"

She already knew Dr. Cook had been listening to rumors about Dr. Wiltshire losing his money gambling and possibly having his hand broken by some enforcer trying to persuade him to pay up. If he was going to listen to nonsense like that, it wasn't particularly surprising that he would end up in a showdown with Dr. Wiltshire when they met in person.

Kenzie was sure Dr. Wiltshire was not a gambler and his hand had just been hurt in an accident. He had suggested at one point that he might have broken it while golfing. But he'd been too embarrassed about the circumstances to explain it in any detail to Kenzie. Maybe it had been golfing, and maybe it had been something else. But some kind of mob enforcer? Kenzie couldn't see it.

"First, the picture that started to circulate before the body was found," Kenzie announced, pulling up the photo of their John Doe. The picture she had seen many times on her phone and was now looking at on the big screen. Amazing that such a substantial person, looking like he had been dead only for minutes, could be changed so quickly to the fragile, dissolving body that had been discovered in the dumpster, and then fell to pieces under Kenzie's knife. But it only took days for the decomposition process to really kick in, moving from the just-dead corpse to something almost unrecognizable.

Dr. Wiltshire gazed at the picture for a moment, his eyes flickering to each detail, trying to catalog it and gather all of the information he could from this postmortem picture.

"Right," he agreed. "And have the police had any success in determining the origin of this picture?"

"Not yet. I should have asked Campbell if they had found anything else when he was here earlier, but I didn't. I just figured if there was anything new, he would have told me. The timeframe is about two weeks. That's all. It was being circulated at a local school, but they don't know who the first person was to start sending it to their friends there."

"How does a high school student get a picture of a dead body like that? Not one that has been on movies or in the news, but just fresh, when there has been no police involvement?"

Kenzie didn't like to think about it. When she pictured Rhys or one of the students she had talked to about the picture being in a position to either see the murdered man and snap a photo, or to be sent the picture by the actual killer or someone else on the inside, she felt sick. They were supposed to be at school, sheltered, getting an education that would serve them well in the real world. They should not be around murdered men or people who happened to have photos of recently murdered men.

"I wish I could tell you. I think I know the group that started distributing it, but not the one person that sent it to that group to start with. They're... well, disadvantaged, I guess. Not drop-outs, but close to it. On the edge."

Dr. Wiltshire nodded. He didn't pursue it and ask for more details about the "loser" kids that Hugh had pointed her toward. He wasn't one for conducting personal interviews. He preferred to let the evidence speak for itself, and, where the evidence could not speak, to remain silent.

Kenzie brought up a couple of photos showing the body first in the dumpster where it had been found, and then on the autopsy table, prepped and ready to be processed. Dr. Wiltshire didn't flinch. He had seen plenty of bodies in advanced decomposition in his day.

"About two weeks into decomp," Kenzie advised. "Quite advanced."

"Well, you got him here in one piece. That was pretty good work."

Kenzie nodded. She ran through the high points of the autopsy and what tests they had done or requested. Then she brought up the pictures of the clothing she had just taken.

"See anything significant?" she asked. "I hate to just toss the clothes in a bag and say that there wasn't anything noteworthy. But other than a few hair follicles, there wasn't really much to find."

"Some cases, you just don't have enough evidence," Dr. Wiltshire agreed. "Unfortunate, but in real life, unlike a TV drama, cases go unsolved. John Does may never be identified. As many tools as we have at our disposal, it is still not possible to solve every crime."

They both stared at the screen, searching for any small clue that would give them a "Eureka" moment and push the case forward.

"Maybe the police will find something. Or the fingerprints or DNA will give us an identity."

Kenzie shook her head. "I'd really like to know what he was doing here to get himself shot in the head."

24

A t home that evening, Kenzie repeated her frustration at being unable to find out anything else about the man who had been killed, even his identity. She had hoped they would get results back from the fingerprints, but they might not have been clear enough, half decomposed as they were, for any kind of match. A DNA result could take weeks or months. Campbell had said that they did not want to show his face on TV or the media until they had exhausted all other means of identification. Doing so would result in a flood of calls, most of which would be nonsense and a waste of resources. It was clear that no one was looking for the man. There was no matching missing person report in Vermont or the surrounding states. They had even checked for matches across the border in Canada and come up dry.

"And everything he was wearing was generic?" Zachary asked. "Nothing that identified where he might have come from or if he was even local?"

"No. Brands you could get at any department store. Nothing new. Nothing traceable."

She brought up the pictures of the clothes on her phone and let Zachary flip through them to see if they jogged anything for him.

Zachary stopped, and Kenzie reached to take the phone back

from him. He didn't hand it over, but turned it around and showed her the picture of the bandana.

Kenzie nodded. She had seen bikers use them as do-rags, teens using them as masks, and a number of other decorative uses. "Yeah, so? You see a lot of those around. They're trendy with the kids."

"You don't remember seeing anyone else with one of these recently?"

Kenzie shook her head slowly. But Zachary's words triggered half a recollection. Something tickled at the back of her brain, and she struggled to bring it forward into conscious thought. *Had* she seen one recently? She must have, if Zachary said that she had. And he had been with her at the time, so that narrowed down where she might have seen it. She closed her eyes and ran her fingers through her hair, trying to dredge it up.

"No?" Zachary asked.

Kenzie shook her head and opened her eyes. "No. Where?"

"At the school."

It flashed into her mind. "The losers."

"One of them."

Kenzie had seen one tied around her thigh. She'd thought it an eighties fashion throwback. "One of the girls. I remember." She shrugged. "So they must be getting popular again."

"Were they the same color?"

Kenzie rolled her eyes. "Yes… I would say both were that same shade of red."

Zachary nodded slowly, handing her phone back to her. "Gang colors."

"What?" Kenzie shook her head. "No. Gangs don't even wear colors anymore. They dress just like anyone else to make it harder for the police to identify them."

"The bigger gangs, sure. But some of the little ones that float around and aren't into big money laundering or drug trafficking operations. Some of them do."

Kenzie stared down at the picture of the bandana. "And you think this identifies John Doe as a gang member. And that girl at the school."

"That's what they're for. To make it easier for members to identify each other. Or to identify rivals who infringe on their territory."

They were at the school the next morning to talk to Principal Lakes.

Kenzie knew that they needed to pass what they knew on to Detective Saul so that he would be able to trace the victim's identity, any rival gangs, and all of the details needed to solve the case. But she wanted to talk to the girl with the bandana first, to see if she had been the one to start circulating the photograph. That was the part of the investigation that Kenzie felt she needed to follow up on personally. That was what had affected Rhys, and what she had agreed to follow up on for him. Where that photo had come from.

Obviously, she couldn't do anything for John Doe now. It wasn't a matter of protecting him. They would try to bring his killer to justice, but she wanted to understand why the girl had started passing around the photo. Was it some kind of brag or trophy? Had she wanted to upset Rhys or other students in general? Did she realize the kind of damage that she had done just by sending out the photo, even if she'd had nothing to do with the execution? Even if she hadn't even seen what happened or taken the picture herself.

People experienced disconnect with the internet and other methods of social communication. They were separated from the consequences of their actions. They did cruel things to others because they could hide behind a screen name, avatar, or anonymous phone number, and no one would know who they were. And they would never know what harm they had done.

Kenzie did her best to describe the girl to Principal Lakes, with Zachary providing a few additional details that she had missed. Lakes nodded slowly.

"That sounds like Emily Cross." She sighed. "She's had a few problems this year. I wish I could say that she couldn't be involved in anything like this, but unfortunately… some kids go astray and there isn't much you can do to reach them…"

Kenzie tapped the name into her phone. "If we could get her

contact information… We'll check out the bus stop where they were hanging out before, but she might not be there this time. I might need to reach her at home or on her phone."

"We can't really give out students' personal information."

"This is for the medical examiner's office. And it is related to a police investigation into a homicide."

"I know that." Lakes was hesitant. "But the police would come to me with a warrant, not just a verbal request. I can comply with a warrant and not get in any trouble for it. But giving the information out to just anyone…"

Zachary gave her a charming smile. "This isn't just anyone. You know me. I've protected your students before. We're trying to protect Rhys and others like him. We just want to talk to Emily about what happened and the consequences of sharing a photo like that."

Kenzie could see that Lakes wanted to give in. But she was still hesitant. "If it was the police…"

"I'm sure they'll be around later. You're not giving away anything you shouldn't. You're just… releasing it a bit early. So that we can talk to Emily before the police talk to her and she clams up. You know she's not going to talk once the police get involved. I think we can do some good here."

"Well… I think what I'll do is write down the information that the police will need. And I'll give it to them when they come for it. I can't give it to you. But I'll just step out and see whether she has shown up for her first-period class. If she has, I'll have her called to the office so you can talk to her."

Kenzie watched Lakes tap a search into her computer and then write down Emily's name and her personal contact information very neatly on a memo page from the block near her pen holder. "I'll just be a moment," she told Kenzie and stepped out of her office, shutting the door behind her.

Before Kenzie could move, Zachary was out of his seat and positioned his phone in front of the note. He snapped a picture and sat back down. He assumed a casual stance, looking as if he were just scrolling through the social networks on his phone, waiting for the principal's return. It couldn't have taken more than three seconds.

Kenzie opened her mouth to say something to him when her phone buzzed. She looked down at it in time to see the message come from him, with an image attached. Now, she was part of the conspiracy. She had Emily's covertly obtained contact information as well. She stared at Zachary.

"I can't believe you could move that fast."

Zachary grinned. "It's all about taking the opportunities when they pop up."

Lakes gave them plenty of time before she returned with a cup of coffee. She set it down on her desk and smiled at them as she sat in her chair.

"Emily is not in her first-period class, unfortunately. I'm sorry about that. But I can't say I'm surprised. She has been truant quite a lot lately. She's barely hanging on by a thread. She'll be expelled before long."

"Do you know what's going on with her?" Kenzie asked. "Is she involved in something that's keeping her away from school?"

Of course, she already knew this, but she was curious how much the school knew of what was happening and how deep Emily's involvement with the gang was. Was she just flirting with danger, or was she deeply involved with the gang and the violence they perpetrated?

"Unfortunately, it's pretty hard to know what is happening with all the kids. We've tried to talk to her. I've talked to her, her teachers have, her guidance counselor has." Lakes sighed. "But she just doesn't want the help. She doesn't want to talk to anyone about what is going on with her. I assumed there are issues at home. Maybe drugs. A lot of the kids in the group that she is hanging out with are involved in drugs. Not heavily, but… enough to get them into trouble."

"Gangs?"

"Gangs? No, not that I know of. There are some groups and cliques, but I think I would know if there was any gang involvement. It's a pretty safe neighborhood. We haven't had to worry about that."

Maybe Emily was an exception. Or maybe Zachary was wrong and she had just been making a fashion statement. Emily might have just purchased the bandana at a department store and had no idea that it was the same color as the symbol being used by a gang in the area. Or she could be imitating the gang, knowing they used the red bandana. Just wanting to look tough or like she belonged to something.

"Well…" Kenzie looked at Zachary. "Shall we see if we can find her?"

Zachary nodded his agreement. "Thanks for your help," he told Lakes. "I understand why you couldn't give us the information we were looking for. Just pass it on to the police when they get around to making their inquiries…"

Lakes smiled and nodded. "I will. Nice to see you again, Zachary."

25

They left the school and headed toward the convenience store.

"Coffee?" Zachary suggested.

"Haven't you already had enough?" Kenzie asked with a laugh. He'd had at least two cups before leaving the house that morning and another supplied by the school while they had been waiting for Lakes to get out of her early morning staff meeting.

"I could always have another."

"I would be so wired if I had that much."

He shrugged. "It just makes me more focused. Mild stimulant."

"Well, you'll be super focused if you have another one."

He shrugged, and they headed directly to the bus stop instead of going to the convenience store first. There were a few kids at the bus stop. Fewer than there had been earlier in the week. They looked at Zachary and Kenzie, faces tightening, not as open to talking to them as they had been the last time.

"What are you guys doing here again?" the older boy they had talked to before demanded.

"Following up," Kenzie said in what she hoped was a casual, soothing voice. Like they just needed to confirm something that they already knew. She looked over the faces of the kids there, disappointed to find that Emily was not there. She wasn't at the school. She wasn't out with her friends. Maybe she was still home, in bed asleep. If she were hanging out with a gang, she might have been out with them late at night or in the early morning hours. Lakes said she had been truant a lot.

"We ain't interested in following up with you," the boy said in a tough voice. Kenzie shrugged it off. Of course he was going to pretend to be a tough guy. That didn't mean he was or she should respond to him as if he were.

"Where's Emily?"

The kids exchanged concerned looks with each other. They didn't like Kenzie looking for her, asking for her by name.

"Is she okay?" Zachary asked.

They kept close together as a group, huddled together, watching and listening to each other, communicating more by expression and body language than the whispers that passed between them.

The boy gave Zachary a measuring look. "Why? What do you mean?"

"I just want to make sure… that nothing happened to her. With all of this stuff going on… I wanted to make sure that she is safe."

"What stuff? Why wouldn't she be?"

Zachary didn't say anything. Kenzie waited to see if he were going to contribute something else, but he didn't. He just looked at her, then looked back at the boy again.

The boy looked at his friends, frowning.

"How long has it been since you saw her?" Kenzie asked.

"She's been around," he said with a shrug.

"Devon," one of the girls murmured, a bit of a whine in her voice.

"Shush," he told her. "Keep it to yourself."

But the others were starting to get antsy about the situation as well.

"She hasn't been at school," one of them pointed out.

"In how long?" Kenzie asked. "We saw her here on Tuesday. Have you seen her since then?"

"Why are you guys here stirring everything up?" Devon

demanded. "It ain't any of your business what Emily or any of us are doing. Who cares? You live in a different world."

Kenzie had to admit that was true. But there was a certain point where their lives intersected. Two points now.

"It actually is my business," she said. "Especially now that we have the body."

"You have the body?" one of the girls screeched. "What body? Emily?"

"Would she be here asking after Emily if she had Emily's body on ice?" Devon asked. "Think about it, stupid."

"Well, what is she asking about, then? Em is in trouble? Are you telling me that picture was actually real? I mean, we were just laughing at it, saying how unreal it looked. That it could be really real. It was just another one of her stories."

He shook his head and made a "zip it" gesture. "Shut up, Clarissa."

But Clarissa looked at Kenzie appealingly. "What happened to her? Where is she? You know something about what is going on?"

"If you'll tell me what you know, we can sort this out a lot faster. I don't want Emily to come to harm, so if you guys could help out so that we can make sure nothing happens to her…"

"Why would something happen to her?"

"She's a witness," one of the others pointed out, her voice low, trying to keep Kenzie and Zachary from being able to make out what she was saying. "Right? How do you take a picture of a body like that without someone seeing you? And if they catch you taking a picture, or they know that you've been spreading it around, what do you think they're going to do? Just laugh it off? Someone has already killed at least once. You think Emily planned to be the next one?"

"Do you know the name of the man in the picture?" Kenzie asked. "If Emily was the one who showed it to you or sent it to you, did she tell you his name? Even just his first name or an alias? It would be really helpful to be able to identify him."

"I don't know what you're talking about."

"She never told you the name of the man in the picture?"

There were a few headshakes, but no one answered aloud. Devon, the apparent leader of the group, was trying to keep everyone quiet and keep them from saying too much. But they were not listening to him. They would not have made a very good gang. Kenzie assumed that they were just a group of friends and there was no hierarchal structure that would put Devon over anyone else's head.

"What is the name of the gang she is in?"

"Emily isn't in a gang," Devon scoffed.

"We know she's in a gang," Zachary said dismissively. "The same one as the dead man was in. He was killed and that puts her in danger too. What was he involved in? Why was he taken out? If the two of them were close…"

It was interesting to watch the dynamics between the members of the group. Zachary clearly knew how to talk to them and communicate with them better than Kenzie did. He had been closer to the street, closer to gangs and teen dropouts and the grittier aspects of the street than Kenzie ever had been. She had been raised in a privileged home, had everything she needed, had never had to worry about being suspended or expelled, drugs, or gang involvement. She had no idea how to talk to these kids other than just being direct in her questions and answers. Zachary led them in different directions, pretended to know things that he didn't, and held back instead of giving them everything he knew.

"Whatever Emily was involved with, that's her own business," Devon declared. "Doesn't have anything to do with me. With us." He motioned to the rest of the kids in the group. "We're not in any gangs. We're just hanging out. Having a smoke and talking. Nothing illegal about that."

Forget the part about it being illegal for minors to buy cigarettes or be truant from school.

They weren't concerned with those kinds of things. Murder was on a whole different plane from any minor complaints about how they were spending their time.

The other kids, particularly the girls, objected to his declaration that Emily's concerns were not theirs. They took care of each other. Watched each other's backs.

"And how is she watching our backs?" Devon demanded. "If she's involved with someone getting killed, or some other stupid gang stuff, and she brings that back to us, you think anyone is going to care that we weren't involved in it? We're going to get painted with the same brush. I don't know about you, but I don't want to end up with a bullet in *my* forehead."

They quieted, thinking about this. Still looking at each other, exchanging glances back and forth while they weighed what Devon had said. Deciding whether to follow his lead or go out on a limb on their own, risking his wrath and unsure how the rest of the group would take it.

The girl, Clarissa, finally spoke up again, addressing Kenzie. "I don't know where Emily is. Haven't seen her for a couple of days. I don't know how long, for sure. I lose track of the days unless it's the weekend."

"Have you talked to her?" Kenzie asked. "Messaged her? Or has she been completely silent since then?"

They looked at each other. Clarissa played with a stud in her lip, looking uncertain.

"I don't know."

"Can you call her? See if she answers?"

She rolled her eyes at this suggestion. "We don't call each other. Who wants to talk on the phone? We message. Or whatever."

Kenzie choked back her own reaction at this. Today's kids behaved differently from the way she had, growing up in the world of landlines and no internet, talking forever on a cordless phone with her friends. Lisa eventually got Kenzie her own line, so the main house line would be available when Lisa wanted it.

But kids who had grown up with devices in their pockets and instant messaging preferred that over actually speaking to each other voice to voice. If they did talk, it was probably in a video or gaming group.

"Could you message her right now?"

Out of the corner of her eye, Kenzie saw Zachary give her a quick shake of the head. He was right, of course. Kenzie should try to get to Emily before anyone could tell her that some stranger was looking for her. If Emily knew people were looking for her, she would stay out of sight.

"She didn't want to talk to you guys then," Clarissa said. "Why would she want to talk to you now?"

"Maybe she wants to get her story out there before everyone knows about the dead man. Maybe she needs some protection. Or maybe she just wants to get it off of her chest. Maybe she has been posting about what she saw because she was traumatized by it."

"Traumatized?" Devon snorted. "She was proud of herself. Acting all big and important for having taken that picture."

So she *had* been the one to take the picture, not just an early recipient. Kenzie thought about that, wondering what all of the implications were. How had she been there? Who knew she had been there? Why had she taken the picture? Why had she shared it? Kenzie couldn't understand why Emily had acted the way that she had. There didn't seem to be any logic to it.

But then, people often behaved in illogical ways. Even when Kenzie knew that something she was doing was illogical, that didn't stop her from doing it. She considered herself a logical, reasoning person, but she still did things she knew didn't make sense. She made an emotional decision. A split-second reflex. A compulsion. Magical thinking. There were a lot of reasons for behaving illogically.

26

D o you think anyone will be home at Emily's house?" Kenzie asked Zachary as they walked back away from the kids to get into the car.

"Who knows what her schedule is like? Some people work during the day, some don't. Since you're out right now, we may as well check and find out. Or maybe Emily herself will answer the door. Then we would at least know that she is home and safe." He shook his head. "I hate to think of her out with the gang somewhere after someone in the gang turns up dead and she takes a picture of him. That's not... that doesn't show a good sense of self-preservation."

Kenzie chuckled. "That's different from how I would have put it, but you're absolutely right. I have no idea how she is mixed up with this gang or what she is doing, but it doesn't strike me as particularly wise to be disseminating pictures of a dead gang member so indiscriminately."

"No. I don't think so. There's a code in these groups. You start sharing gang business around in other places, and you break the code. I wouldn't want to be in her place."

"She's so young. You really think she's a member of a gang?"

"She's not that young. Teens are prime recruits for gangs. And when you're dealing with family memberships, kids of established gang members, they can easily be brought up while they're still in single digits. Eight or nine years old. Start running courier for the gang, standing as lookout, anything like that. They're born into it."

Kenzie couldn't even picture it. Gang members as young as that? But surely they wouldn't be considered full members. Wouldn't be expected to keep all of the gang's rules.

They were driving Zachary's car. He put the address he had photographed into the GPS and started driving without waiting for directions. He obviously knew what area of town it was in even if he didn't know the exact street or house.

"How much do you know about gangs like this?" Kenzie asked.

"Not a lot. I don't know what kind of gang it is, whether they are a local chapter of a bigger gang or it is a small juvenile gang that is just a bunch of friends who got together and play at being tough guys. I don't know if they have something to prove. Whether Emily is a full gang member or has to perform some challenge to be initiated into the gang. I don't know why your John Doe was killed."

There were a lot of questions to be answered. There wasn't any one gang template that would fit over the situation and give them all of the answers they were looking for.

The GPS started giving instructions, which Zachary followed until they got to the address. It wasn't far away. Roxboro wasn't a big town, and Emily had to be close enough to the school to attend there.

It was an older neighborhood. Houses that had been there for a long while and had not withstood the test of time very gracefully. Many had long grass and unkempt yards, paint peeling off of the house, maybe an abandoned, rusty car sitting in the middle of the driveway or yard, sometimes up on blocks, sometimes with a missing tire, propped up by a jack.

"Nice," Kenzie said, shaking her head.

She immediately regretted it. Who was she to judge these people by how much time or money they had to maintain their homes? They clearly didn't have much of anything and did the best they could with the little they had. Was she better than they were just because she made more money, having come from a family that made more money and allowed her to get the education she had in order to pursue an interest in medicine?

"Sorry," she said to Zachary, shaking her head at the inappropriateness of her judgment.

He shrugged. She was sure he had probably heard much worse judgments his whole life, at least all of his growing-up years, which had been very lean. He had been on the other side.

They stepped carefully up the slightly wobbly steps to the house and rang the doorbell. Kenzie couldn't hear the bell ringing inside the house, so she followed up with a firm knock on the door, which should rouse anyone within.

They waited for a few minutes, looking around, watching the rest of the neighborhood, while the neighborhood watched them. Even though it was the middle of the workday for many people and the middle of the school day for the kids, there were a good number of people out and about, sitting on front porches, working on cars, and taking the dogs for a walk.

Eventually, they could hear footsteps inside, and the door handle turned. A woman opened the door and looked at them. Her skin was whiter than Emily's, her face narrower and more finely-boned. Emily didn't look enough like her for Kenzie to be sure that they were biologically related.

"Hi. We're looking for Emily Cross?" Kenzie asked.

"She's not here. It's a school day. She's at school."

"We just came from there. I was hoping she would be here."

"Who are you?" The woman leaned forward and looked Kenzie up and down. She glanced at Zachary, but discounted him as unimportant and continued to speak to Kenzie. "You her probation officer or something? You're not from the school."

"Is she on probation?"

The woman looked at her suspiciously. "Who are you?"

"I'm... with law enforcement, but I'm not her probation officer. I didn't realize she was on probation."

Mrs. Cross shrugged as if it didn't make any difference. And Kenzie didn't suppose it did. She hadn't said anything to the mother that would give her any cause for concern or explain why Kenzie was there or should know that Emily was on probation.

"She's not at the school. If she's not here, then where do you think she is?"

"I don't know. She'll show up sooner or later."

"When was the last time you saw her?"

The woman rubbed her forehead. She shook her head. "I don't know. It's been a crazy week. We have been on opposite shifts, so I don't really see her."

Kenzie couldn't imagine not even knowing where her teenager was for a week. Not even knowing when the last time she had seen her was.

"That must be difficult," she said sympathetically. "And tough for Emily. So... is there a friend she might be with? A boyfriend?"

"Em doesn't have a boyfriend," Mrs. Cross said immediately, shaking her head. She was awfully sure about it for someone who didn't even know when the last time she saw her daughter was.

"Oh, Okay. You don't know where else she might be hanging out?"

The woman scratched the back of her neck. "I don't know. Who did you say you were?"

"I'm with the medical examiner's office," Kenzie finally admitted. "Someone that Emily knows was killed recently, and I wanted to make sure that she is okay."

27

Mrs. Cross blinked, frowning, trying to make sense of what Kenzie was telling her. She shook her head and stepped back from the door, motioning for them to enter.

"You'd better come in."

Kenzie entered and Zachary followed her in, his head turning back and forth as he looked around the house. Kenzie realized she should probably be more aware of her surroundings, her "head on a swivel," as the cops liked to say. But she was too focused on the woman in front of her, leading her into the untidy front room that smelled of stale smoke, where a TV was playing too quietly to make out the words.

Mrs. Cross motioned for them to seat themselves, and the two of them tried to shift things around to make a place where they could sit comfortably.

"Who died?" Mrs. Cross demanded, "What are you talking about? A friend from school?"

Kenzie shifted uncomfortably, not sure what to say. She didn't want to show Emily's mother the picture of the man to see if she could identify him. Emily had probably never introduced him to her family, if they were in a gang together. There was no point in showing the dead body to Mrs. Cross, something that would just upset her. But she also wanted the woman to understand how concerned they were for Emily's welfare and to find out what she knew and why she had done what she had.

"A man that Emily knew... from the neighborhood," she said after a period of consideration. "He was killed... violently. I don't know if Emily was around when it happened, but it seems likely. She definitely knew about it." Kenzie stopped short of revealing that they knew Emily had seen John Doe's dead body. That might be revealing too much.

"A man?"

"A... young man. But... older than Emily."

"Who?"

"I don't know his name. I was hoping that Emily could help me with that."

"You don't know his name? How do you know that she knows him?"

"From her phone. You know kids... and their apps."

She thought that the reference had been too oblique, but Mrs. Cross rolled her eyes as if this were something she complained about often. Maybe it was. Kenzie didn't have to deal with teens and their phones in her line of work. She only knew what she did from absorbing it from the culture around her.

"Yeah, I know," Mrs. Cross agreed. "Why don't you ask her friends where she is? Have them look on *their* magical apps and tell us where she is right now."

"We didn't find her friends terribly helpful," Zachary inserted dryly.

Mrs. Cross snorted. "I would guess not."

"You're not impressed with her friends?" Kenzie asked with a laugh.

"You know... once upon a time, she was a very nice, sweet girl. I remember when she was a toddler, she just charmed the pants off of everyone. Even when she started school, the teachers all loved her, and she was so helpful. I think she thought she was one of the teachers, not one of the students, because she was always trying to do

things with the grown-ups and talked about the kids her age like
they were little kids she was taking care of instead of friends her own
age."

Mrs. Cross stared off into the distance, then rubbed her eyes as if
she were looking through a fog.

"She was such a nice little girl. But she didn't stay that way. When
she was ten, eleven, she wanted to be off on her own. Leave her alone.
Don't talk to her. Don't ask her about her friends or school or
anything. And then the rest started creeping in… the hair stuff. Piercings that I certainly had not approved. Tattoos. Clothes that were…
not little girl clothes. I would have been happy if she had just worn
jeans and a t-shirt. But she had to be… too grown up. For a while, I
thought things were better. She was in one of the early-morning clubs
at school, and it was like she was happy again." She sighed. "I wonder
whatever happened to that little girl sometimes. Whatever happened
to my little girl?"

"That must be difficult. I know mothers and daughters can have
complicated relationships."

"I just wish… that I *had* a relationship with her. I really don't.
We're like… two people who live in the same house. That's all. We
don't talk. We don't eat together. I don't know when the last time was
that we went out shopping together. I used to take her shopping for
school clothes at the beginning of each school year. Kids don't really
do that anymore. Start school with new outfits. I guess it's… gauche.
Not cool."

"She's had a lot of truants this year?" Kenzie suggested.

"Yeah, sure. It isn't like I can force her to go to school. Even
before I was working shift, I couldn't. It isn't like I could physically
force her into the car. If I told her she had to go, she would just tell
me no. What am I going to do? Take something away from her?
Ground her? There wasn't anything to take away from her. She barely
had anything. The way we live… paycheck to paycheck… there aren't
any extras. And grounding her? How can I keep her here when I'm
not here?"

"That would be pretty difficult," Kenzie admitted.

"They won't let you chain them up," Zachary added.

This made Mrs. Cross chuckle. "It would be so much easier if you could."

"Well…" Kenzie sighed. "I guess there isn't really anything else I have to ask you. If you don't know where Emily is, you don't know where she is. Do you think she would answer the phone if you called her?"

"She never does."

"If you texted her?"

"Maybe." Mrs. Cross pulled her phone out and tapped the screen several times.

"I wouldn't ask her where she is," Zachary advised. "That will just put her off and warn her that someone is looking for her. Is there something you would normally text her out of the blue? That you're just checking in to see how she is? You want to take her out to dinner? Can't find your tablet?"

"My hair dryer." Mrs. Cross shook her head in disbelief. "She is always taking it and leaving it somewhere else. And the girl never actually looks like she's done her hair. She looks like she just rolled out of bed. So what does she need a hair dryer for?"

"To dry her fingernails?" Kenzie suggested.

"Maybe so." Mrs. Cross pondered this. She tapped her phone and sent a text off to her daughter. "I don't know if she'll answer. Sometimes she just ignores me."

She scrolled up through her conversations.

"She texted me Wednesday."

"And she sounded okay?"

The woman shrugged. "Seemed like it. I guess so. It was just… routine stuff. You know. Sort of roommate stuff, since we're hardly mother and daughter anymore."

Kenzie nodded, not sure what to say to this. They all sat there waiting for the beep that would indicate Emily had texted her mother back. Mrs. Cross sat looking at the phone. Nothing happened. Eventually, she looked around the room.

"I really need to clean this place up. I don't think she's going to answer me. Maybe she went to the school after you were looking for her. She's not allowed to use her phone during classes."

"That's probably it," Zachary agreed.

Kenzie nodded. She didn't think that any of them actually believed it, but she didn't want to do anything to make Mrs. Cross feel worse. It was bad enough that she didn't know where her daughter was, hadn't seen her in days, and had no idea where she could be or who she might be with. She wasn't going to be in a very happy mood when they left her to her own thoughts.

"Thank you for your help," Kenzie told her. "I'm sorry we couldn't answer more of your questions. Do you think that you could ask Emily to call me when you see her next?" Kenzie got out one of her business cards and handed it to Mrs. Cross. "I'd really appreciate it."

"Sure, of course," Mrs. Cross agreed.

But Kenzie left wondering if Mrs. Cross would ever see her daughter again.

28

There wasn't much more that Kenzie and Zachary could do. Kenzie needed to get to the office to continue with her regular work. The medical examiner's office did make inquiries to assist in their postmortem examinations and reports, but actual detective work was sort of outside of her purview. There was only so much she could do without raising eyebrows.

"Sorry we weren't able to get anywhere," Zachary told her.

"No, it's fine. I didn't know if we would be able to find anything. I should just leave it to the police and their investigation, but I thought that since Emily was one of the kids at the school, and we were trying to help out Rhys, I might be able to get somewhere with it. I'll just let Campbell and Detective Saul know what we found out and let them look into it."

"Do you want me to do any more investigating? Checking into Emily's background? Investigating gangs in the area?"

"No, it's fine. You've got your own cases to work on. The police are already on it, so we shouldn't be duplicating their efforts and getting in their way."

Zachary held Kenzie's gaze for a moment, trying to read her. She hated it when he tried to interpret what she was saying instead of just listening to what she said. Yes, there were times when she said she was fine with something when she was not, but he should still listen to what she said, until she was ready to tell him otherwise.

"Really," Kenzie assured him. "The police will take care of it. I don't want you to waste resources on it. You have enough to do."

In truth, she had no idea how many cases he had and how much of his time was spoken for. But he seemed to have plenty to keep him busy and she didn't know whether he would be able to get any further on the case anyway. And she didn't want to be accused of hiring a private investigator or involving a related party without authorization.

"Okay," Zachary agreed finally. "I'll drop you at the office and pick you up later. Are we going out tonight?"

Kenzie tried to remember what they had lined up for date night. The previous week had been the car show. She thought that tonight was just a walk in the park. It would be chilly and the sun would go down early, so she would need to get out of work in good time. Or failing that, choose another activity.

"Yes. For sure. If I don't get out in time to go to the park…"

"You're already going into the office late, so it probably wouldn't be a good idea to leave early. Why don't we plan something else tonight? A movie. Something we can start late that won't take any special planning or a lot of effort."

"Yeah, that sounds good. If you're looking for something to do today when you break for lunch, see what's showing. Otherwise, we'll look at the listings when I get home."

"Or just go over there and look at the posters and pick something on the fly."

"Oooh, that's living dangerously." Kenzie grinned. "That sounds great, actually. I think a movie is a good idea."

Zachary smiled and gave her a quick kiss before she exited the car.

Campbell said he would come down to talk to Kenzie when he was free, so she could get started on her regular work and not lose time waiting for him upstairs. It was nearly lunchtime before he came down to find her.

"We have some progress on your John Doe," Campbell told her as he stood by her desk. "First thing we got any results back on was ballistics."

Kenzie had not been confident that they could match the bullet to anything, so this was good news.

"The gun has a history?"

"Been used before in an armed robbery. A shot fired into the ceiling, not into a person," Campbell reassured her.

"Was it a gang?"

He raised his brows and looked at her. "Was it a gang," he repeated slowly. "Do you know something about gang involvement in this case?"

"It was Zachary who made the connection," Kenzie said. "I was frustrated not to be able to get anywhere on the identification, and I showed him the clothing. We were trying to figure out if there was anything identifiable, anything that we could trace back to a particular source that would tell us something about the victim or his identity."

Campbell nodded. "And Zachary's got a good eye," he acknowledged. "What did he see?"

"There was a bandana. I didn't think anything of it, but he thought it might be a gang identifier. Gang colors."

"Not too much of a stretch," Campbell admitted. "Although most of the gangs don't use identifiable colors anymore. They prefer to stay under the radar. Wear them to funerals or other public events where they want to show their solidarity but, most of the time, they keep them under wraps to make it harder for the police or the casual observer to identify them as gang members. Keep the heat off."

"Zachary said that some of the smaller local gangs still use them."

"Yep. He's right. Especially ad hoc neighborhood gangs. They want to be visible. Want people to know that it is their territory, and that there are gang members around. Be able to quickly identify rival gang members and allegiances when they are fighting over city blocks."

"Even here in Roxboro?"

"No town is too small for one or two gangs. That might be all they can support, but one or two—you really need two; a single gang can't survive in a vacuum—yeah. Even if it is just a few members. They like to swagger around, bully citizens. Pretend they're tough and independent. James Dean syndrome."

Kenzie chuckled at the reference to the cultural icon from *Rebel Without a Cause*. The kids today probably had no idea who James Dean was, but they still needed something to rebel against. Still needed to fight for dominance. In a poor neighborhood like the one Emily lived in, it was vital to have something to fight against and fight for.

"So do you know which gang uses red bandanas around here?"

"Yeah, there are a couple of small gangs, and I know one of them wears red. I'll get details from someone who knows the situation a bit better. And in answer to your question, the robbery wasn't necessarily a gang action, but I wouldn't be surprised to find that it was perpetrated by gang members or was used to fund gang activities."

"But they weren't wearing colors when they did it?"

"That would make things a bit too easy for the detectives investigating it. They're not completely stupid, these kids."

"We think that the girl who started circulating the picture of the murdered man was a member of the same gang."

"Oh?"

"She was wearing the bandana when we saw her the first time. We thought—or I thought—it was just a fashion statement. Zachary was the one who put the two bandanas together to come up with the theory that they are both members of the same gang. We went back to the school to talk to her today to see if we could get the name of the John Doe from her. But she was gone. The group of friends she hangs out with, who are not all gang members, said that she hadn't been around much since we talked to them."

"What day was that?"

"It was Tuesday that we talked to them before. And then this morning. They weren't sure if they had seen her since then."

"Do you have a name? We'll look into it. Drop by her house and talk to her folks. See what's been going on with her."

"We actually…. dropped by there this morning already. Her mom was home; doesn't know when she saw her daughter last."

"Is she a missing person?"

"I wouldn't say so. Not that her mom has reported missing, anyway. She said that they don't see much of each other. Mom works shift. The girl—Emily Cross is her name—has missed a lot of school. Sounds like she doesn't get there very often. I have the address and phone number. I'll text them to you,"

"You got them from her friends?" Campbell raised an eyebrow in disbelief.

"Well… let's just say that we managed to get them when we went by the school to talk to her friends."

Campbell coughed into his fist, laughing. "Okay, let's go with that," he agreed. "Zachary was with you?"

"How did you guess?"

"Well, the first clue is saying 'we' but, even without that, I would still have guessed. He has a remarkable talent for getting information out of people."

"He knows some people over there. Apparently, he got the previous principal busted."

"Ah, yes. That was a nasty case that did not endear the school administrators to the parents and community."

Kenzie thought of how Zachary had not only gotten the information from Principal Lakes, but had also managed to draw out the "loser" kids that Emily hung out with, holding back information and making them ask him about it, instead of the other way around. He knew people.

"He's a talented private investigator," she agreed.

"So, with all of that, I suppose I don't need to tell you the dead man's identity."

"Do you know who he is?" Kenzie asked eagerly. "We didn't manage to get a name. He's older than the school kids and, if they knew who he was, they weren't telling. Emily's mom said that Emily didn't have any boyfriends and she doesn't know who her friends are."

"Always nice to have such involved parents," Campbell said dryly.

"I don't think it's entirely her fault. I think she would like to do more. But it is tough when she's not home at the same time. Single parenting. Shift work. Teenagers. It's a pretty difficult scenario."

Campbell nodded. "Thank goodness for my own parents and their stability," he said simply.

"Were you ever a rebellious teen?"

"When we played cops and robbers, I was always the cop."

"Ah." Kenzie nodded. "So you didn't struggle to figure out what direction you wanted to go. This was always your end game."

"Pretty much, yeah. So I was careful not to do anything as a teenager that might disqualify me from being able to serve as a law enforcement officer. That helped to keep me on the straight and narrow. No drugs. No arrests."

"And you have a name for our John Doe?" Kenzie brought the conversation back to the critical revelation. She hated having unidentified bodies in the morgue. Every body had a name. Every body should be identified. She didn't like anyone going to potter's field without a name. Even if they went unclaimed, they shouldn't go unidentified.

29

Your victim's name is Trevor Mercer."

Kenzie immediately wrote it down on the pad next to her and pulled up the file on the computer to substitute Trevor Mercer for John Doe.

"Great! How was he identified?"

"Fingerprints. Not a great match. Not enough index points to be sure of the ID, but enough to get a pop on the system to check it out. Comparing the initial picture to his driver's license. Showing his next of kin a sanitized photo. They're going to give us DNA and dental records to verify."

"Perfect," Kenzie nodded. With all of those things, they could be sure they had the right man, even with the advanced state of decomposition. She had retrieved enough DNA for the lab to profile, and his dental work was entirely intact. No baseball bat or bullet to the teeth. She had already done the X-rays needed for the comparison, once they tracked down the last dentist that Mercer had gone to.

"So who was he?" she asked. "He must have a record if you got a hit on fingerprints."

"Just low-level stuff, no felonies. And he was only ever arrested or convicted in Ohio."

"Ohio! Well, he was a little way from home. Is that where his family is?"

"Yes. He got in some trouble as a teen. Got himself out of there, ran away to New York. Ended up in Vermont." Campbell shrugged, spreading his hands apart. "Don't ask me how or why. So we're trying to track his movements now in Vermont, but there isn't a lot. He stayed below the radar."

"Maybe he had a cousin or friend in Vermont."

"Probably. There is not a big draw for criminals to come from New York to Vermont. Retired couples, maybe. People who want to run B&Bs or take over a family maple operation. But criminals?"

Kenzie nodded her agreement. She saw enough crime, working for the medical examiner's office, but it was mostly local. Some cartels from other countries. But it wasn't somewhere that usually drew much interest from petty criminals in nearby states. Unless they were trying to escape something. Start over again.

"And do you know if he was in the gang? The one you were talking about that wears red?"

"I will be looking into it. The bandana is a good lead. It's hard to know who is in what gangs when the criminals don't advertise it."

"He wasn't the owner of the gun?"

"Not originally. But it has gone through several hands since it was registered, and it is pretty hard to say whether he ever owned it or not. These guys tend not to register the transfers."

"Well, someone should talk to them about that," Kenzie teased.

"Yes. I'm sure if they realized it was their civic duty, they wouldn't be so negligent."

Kenzie laughed. "Well, I hope this helps you figure out what happened to him. I'm very relieved to have a name. I don't like them to be unidentified."

"I'm sure his family will be grateful to know what happened to him, too. Maybe not happy about what happened to him or about the state of the remains when we found him, but at least they won't have to spend decades wondering whatever happened to them."

Kenzie reported Campbell's findings to Zachary when she took a break for lunch. He listened to the details and was happy to hear that Campbell had agreed that Emily and Mercer were members of the same gang and would follow up about it.

"We're getting closer," he said, pleased. "Or rather, you're getting closer. The police are getting closer. They'll be able to figure out where he was and what happened to him if they keep digging. The main work—identifying him and the connection between him and Rhys's school—has been done."

"I hope that they can work it all out. I still don't understand why Emily would circulate his picture to her friends and acquaintances at school."

"Maybe it was… some kind of memorial. Making sure that he wouldn't be forgotten. The more people she got it to, the more of a 'legend' he would become. He would leave a footprint. A legacy. Instead of being a nameless, faceless guy the local gang had just offed, he became… a face they would remember, anyway."

"Still nameless."

"As far as we know. Maybe when she started to circulate it, it included his name. But later in the process, the name wasn't forwarded to Rhys, or the message that contained his name was erased, but Rhys managed to save the photograph. But even nameless, he would still be remembered."

Kenzie nodded in agreement. "And for someone like Rhys… that picture is imprinted on his memory forever. He will never forget it."

"Oh, *Rhys.*"

Kenzie could tell from the tone of his voice that he had just remembered something.

"Yes? Rhys what?"

"He was discharged today. He's back home."

"Oh!" Kenzie felt some of the tension go out of her. She hadn't been aware that she had been holding herself so stiff. "That's good to hear. I'm very glad about that."

"Yeah. It's always better to be at home than the psych ward. When you're feeling well enough to be home, I mean."

"Of course. I knew what you meant. Sometimes the hospital is a necessity. I'm glad that he's recovered enough that he and Vera and the doctors all feel like he can be home now."

"Me too. I might go over to see him this afternoon. Take him a burger or something and just chill at home where he is comfortable."

"That sounds good. You should."

"I think I will," Zachary agreed. "I'm not being very productive today. I keep starting on other things, but I don't get anywhere. Keep thinking about Emily and Rhys."

Kenzie could understand that. She was feeling somewhat distracted herself. At least the Mercer case was actually something she was supposed to be working on, so she could obsess over it and still be considered to be doing her work.

"I'll see you tonight. We'll do the movie thing, maybe go out for supper, and you can tell me how Rhys is."

30

They had a good evening. Kenzie was glad to get away from work and to try to put all of her files to the side for a while. She worked hard at the office and, when she left, it was time to hang up her scalpel and spend time with Zachary or do other things she needed to. She wanted to be fully present in those other things, not with half of her brain working on her medical examiner work, while the other half tried to keep up with her social or personal life.

She remembered how much Walter had focused on his work when she was a child. There was no escaping it. When the Senate was in session, he was away all the time, dealing with bills that should pass and those that shouldn't, wining and dining politicians, developing his strategies and constantly obsessed with achieving his ends. On those rare occasions he was home and spent time with his family, he always brought up his work, what he was doing, what frustrations he was dealing with. Everything there was to know about whatever cause he was working on. Sometimes, it was exciting, and Kenzie was interested in seeing how he worked things out, fascinated with the complex processes he worked through, with how much knowledge he had to have to perform his job. He made everything seem exciting and important.

But over the years, she had learned that everything was not exciting and important. Bills that were defeated kept popping up again and again in later sessions, under other names and sponsors. Bills that passed did not change the world as Walter had promised they would. The world moved slowly. The frenetic pace at which Walter had tried to get everything done didn't mean anything. The pace did not continue once a bill was passed. It was in someone else's bailiwick then, and changes happened slowly and gradually. What passed in one session might become too bloated and bogged down to go anywhere. Or it might be reversed again in the next session.

She didn't want to be like her father. She wanted to give the people in her life enough of her time and intention to know they were important and brought her joy.

So she deliberately put all work concerns aside for the night and just enjoyed her time with Zachary.

They had a good visit, watched an action movie that both of them liked, and spent a little quiet time before bed to unwind and make sure that they were ready for sleep.

Kenzie woke up with a start. Someone was shaking her arm and, as she awoke she realized her phone was ringing. Not the loud ring tone of a call-out, but the muted buzzing of her phone vibrating against the side table.

Kenzie grunted and tried to say something coherent to Zachary, the person who had obviously been shaking her. She fumbled with her phone, pulled it off of the charge cord, and held it up to her ear while trying to swipe the slider on.

"Hello?"

"Is this… the medical examiner? It's Clarissa."

Kenzie blinked hard, trying to wake herself up and make the connections.

"Clarissa?" she repeated.

"You said call you about Emily and anything we knew about her."

Kenzie sat up in bed, trying to make sense of the girl's voice on the other end of the call.

"Clarissa… about Emily."

"Yes," the girl said impatiently. "You said to call you."

"Yeah. I'm glad you did. You just caught me off guard. I'm sorry. I'm just getting my thoughts in order now."

"Emily knew him. The guy who died. Who was shot."

"Yes, I know she did. And she was the one who took his picture and started circulating it around, too, wasn't she?"

"Maybe. I guess so."

"They were both in the same gang together?"

"I don't know if it is a gang," Clarissa temporized.

"Well, it isn't a social club."

Clarissa laughed weakly at that. "Well... I don't know. A lot of these guys call themselves clubs now, instead of gangs."

"I don't care what they call themselves. As long as we can figure out how Emily and Trevor Mercer were involved with each other and sort out what went wrong."

"You know his name?"

"Yes. Maybe you were hoping that you would be the one to tell me that. If you were, then thank you for at least calling to tell me that part. But there are a lot of other details that are still missing from the picture."

"Trevor... she didn't even call him that. She called him by his last name. Mercer."

"Did she talk about him a lot?"

"I don't know. Sometimes she talked about him. Sometimes, she didn't want to talk about anything to do with the gang. She just pretended that they didn't even exist."

"Was she involved in... the criminal aspects of the gang? Or was it just another family to hang out with?"

"I guess they were like a family," Clarissa agreed. Kenzie rubbed her eyes, trying to remember what she knew about Clarissa and what the girl looked like. She had been one of the crowd. White face, blond, kind of tangled hair, if Kenzie were remembering the right girl. Young looking. But they all looked young. She couldn't believe how young the teenagers looked now that she was older.

When she was that age, she had figured she was no different from an adult. She'd been mature, but that didn't mean she made all the right choices. Clarissa was racking up her mistakes. Skipping school.

Doing whatever the "losers" who hung out together did. She knew her friend was involved in a gang, even if she wasn't herself. She had known about the dead man and yet had lied to Kenzie and Zachary when they had asked if she knew who he was and who had started circulating the picture. Everything she had done had shown that she wasn't ready for adult responsibility yet.

Then again, not all adults were ready for it, either.

Kenzie drew in a long breath and let it out. "So you called me, Clarissa. What did you want to tell me? Other than Mercer's name and the fact that they were in a gang together. Because I already knew all of that."

"You didn't know it earlier," Clarissa sounded pouty.

"No. But things can move fast in an investigation. That's why you should tell us everything you know when we first ask, so we can get out ahead of the ball instead of playing catch-up the whole time."

"Yeah… well, Emily wouldn't want me to be telling you all of this stuff. But I figured… I don't want her to get hurt. I'm worried. She's not answering any messages. I thought… she would be back. We could talk. She could tell me what I should or shouldn't say. I could tell her to talk to you about it, because you could help her. But… I don't know what's happened."

"When was the last time you heard from her?"

"I'm not sure. Wednesday or Thursday."

"Did she tell you what was going on? Anything about why Mercer was killed? Why she was sharing his picture with everyone?"

"No. She said…" Clarissa paused, trying to gather her thoughts. "She said that she had to stay clear of the cops, that it wasn't safe. So I knew she didn't want to talk to you guys."

"What did she think the police were going to do? Did she see Mercer killed?"

"I don't know. Yes. She was really freaked out. She said that every-thing had gone wrong. She wanted to get out. She wanted to find some way to be safe."

"She wanted to get out of the gang? Out of town? What?"

"I don't know."

"Were she and Mercer friends? Or just both in the same gang?"

"They're family, those guys."

"And I know that. She needed some structure and support. She didn't feel like she was getting it at home. Her mom was always out and didn't have the time for her. And I guess she wasn't getting all of the support she needed from you guys at school, either, if she felt the need to join the gang."

"We couldn't all get together outside of school time," Clarissa said defensively. "Some of us got parents at home. Curfews. Bed checks at night. We can't all get out at night or whenever we want to."

"So…" Kenzie persisted. "How close was Emily to Mercer?"

"They were… you know… getting together. They liked each other."

"They were intimate?" Kenzie clarified.

Clarissa snorted. "Whatever you want to call it. Yeah. Some stuff was going on. But they weren't… like… exclusive. Boyfriend and girl-friend or anything."

"If she liked him, why didn't she report to the police when he was killed? Why did she send those photos to other kids instead of letting the police know that something had happened to him? Doesn't she want whoever killed him to be punished for it? And then she doesn't have to be afraid. The person who killed him will be behind bars, and she will be safe."

"No, no. She said that she couldn't. I don't know all the details, but she said she couldn't talk to any police about it."

Kenzie knew that the police spent all kinds of money on programs to introduce kids and cops to each other so that they could develop good, trusting relationships and so, when something happened to a kid, he didn't feel like he had to be afraid of the cops. He would know he could go to them with his problem and they would help him. There were resource officers in the school and the community. The police went to community events, let kids sit in the police cars or police helicopter. All so the kids didn't think they had something to fear from the police.

And did it do any good? Kids got to be Emily's age, and they didn't trust any adults, especially those who wore uniforms.

"Well…" Kenzie rubbed her eyes. "I appreciate you calling to let me know some of these details. It is really helpful. I want to help Emily, and that's pretty hard if she won't have anything to do with me. If she'll come to me, I can introduce her to the policeman who is in charge of the case. He's really nice. I've been involved in other cases with him. He's always been very helpful and calm and good to work with. I think that once she knew him… she would feel differently."

"Yeah. I don't think she's going to take that advice."

"If you see or hear from her, please tell her that. I'm a woman and not a cop, and I think she could approach me without worrying that I would turn her into a suspect. I'm a nice person. You know Rhys Salter? You ask him. He can tell you that I'm a good person and I've helped him out before. My boyfriend and I have both helped him."

"Oh yeah, Salter. Well, he won't talk to me, will he?" Clarissa laughed.

"He can still communicate. He can tell you that we are trustworthy."

"Even if you are, I know the police *aren't*. So that's not going to happen."

Kenzie shook her head. "Okay, Clarissa. You do whatever you think is best. Let Emily get into trouble because she won't listen to good advice and turn in a killer."

She waited momentarily to see if Clarissa had anything to say to that, and then ended the call.

31

That sounded interesting," Zachary commented.

Kenzie lay back down and felt for the side table to lay her phone down again. Her head was throbbing, and she hated how she felt after being dragged out of a sound sleep and having to talk on the phone and sound coherent. Would she be able to get back to sleep now that she'd woken up?

"I don't know why she bothered to call me," Kenzie groaned. "She didn't have any new information. Certainly nothing that she needed to wake me up for."

"But she didn't know what you already knew."

"Not really. But there's no reason she couldn't have waited until morning. It's just rude to wake people up in the middle of the night."

Zachary put one arm around Kenzie, snuggling her close against him. "She probably did it on purpose."

"To make me mad? To show her power over me?"

"Maybe. Or maybe because she wanted to catch you off balance. To make sure you didn't have a way to call the police or figure out where she was."

"I don't need to know where she is right now. She's probably at home. She was talking about curfews and bed checks. And I know where she'll be tomorrow. Or rather, on Monday. So I don't need to know where she is tonight."

"Unless she was with Emily."

Kenzie opened her eyes and stared into the soft, velvety darkness. "What?"

"If she was with Emily tonight, and that was why she called you, then she wouldn't want you to be able to trace her there. So she calls you at night, out of a deep sleep, so you won't be able to put the police on to her until it's too late."

"Do you think that's what she was doing?"

"I don't know. Just one possibility. She could also have called you because she couldn't sleep. Maybe she was worried about Emily and couldn't settle in until she'd called you to talk about it."

"Yeah."

"Either way... there's not much you can do about it. If Emily doesn't want to be found, Clarissa isn't going to tell you how to find her."

"How did you know that?"

"It was obvious from your side of the conversation that she wasn't giving it up. Emily is in hiding. She doesn't want to be found."

"She said the last time she talked to Emily was Wednesday or Thursday."

"Maybe. Or maybe they are together. She may not tell you the truth."

"Of course not," Kenzie agreed. Even though she knew this was true, she still always expected people to tell her the truth, or some version of it, to start with. She had to remind herself that even she herself didn't tell the truth, or the whole truth, all the time. "Do you think they are together? That Emily is okay?"

"I think Clarissa would be more worried if she thought that Emily was in real danger. It didn't sound from your conversation like she feared Emily being discovered or killed at any moment."

"No. She wasn't acting like that."

"Then whether they are together or not, Clarissa doesn't necessarily believe she is in any real danger."

"She's just repeating what Emily said. And she thinks Emily is being paranoid."

She felt Zachary nod. He readjusted his grip on her. "Yeah. probably."

"Emily doesn't think it is safe to talk to the police either."

"Most kids don't."

"Yeah. That's what I was just thinking. And I don't even know why that is, because most kids do not have experiences where the police have been violent toward them or have treated them unfairly. Most kids haven't even had any contact with the police, and they still have this… rift."

"Yep," Zachary agreed. He breathed into her hair. "We should probably be quiet; let you settle down to sleep again."

"What about you?"

"Don't worry about me."

He wouldn't go back to sleep, she knew. But Kenzie staying awake wouldn't make any difference to his sleep. There wasn't anything she could do to make him relax and go back to sleep.

There was a message on Kenzie's work voicemail from Detective Saul, asking her to call him back about developments on the case. He didn't know that Clarissa had called Kenzie, of course, but maybe he suspected she had more information than she had given Sergeant Campbell. Campbell had only wanted the general structure of what Kenzie knew. Maybe Saul wanted to dig down deeper. Kenzie felt like they should be getting somewhere with the investigation but that they were not moving fast enough.

She often felt that way, though. The timelines seen on TV versus what happened in real life were very different. A case was not solved in a day or two. There was a lot of investigation and case building to do before they had enough information to lay charges. As Zachary had indicated, they couldn't just take Clarissa or anyone else at their word. The police needed evidence to verify Clarissa's story. Where her phone GPS said she had been. Whether she'd been exchanging calls with Emily or a burner phone. Whether what she said about Emily's and Mercer's relationship was true.

She called Saul back and, getting his voicemail, left him a message to follow up with her when he was ready. They could put their heads together and review what each knew.

Saul showed up while Kenzie was working on another autopsy. He stood in the observation room until she noticed him.

"Oh, hi." Kenzie looked back down at the body she was finishing up with. "I didn't know you were there. How long have you been standing there?"

"Just a few minutes. I didn't want to startle you."

Kenzie appreciated it, but thought it was more than a little creepy to have him standing there watching her silently when she didn't even know he was there. It was common courtesy for a cop to announce himself when he entered the room if she were already in the middle of a procedure.

"Uh, next time, just say hi. I'd rather know you were there waiting for me."

He shrugged.

"I'm just about finished with this post. Do you mind waiting another five minutes? Then we can grab the conference room and run through everything."

"Sure. No problem. Who are you working on now?"

Kenzie filled him in on the details. "Natural death. Just unattended. Guy had a massive coronary. Everyone knew he was a ticking time bomb. He'd probably been told that half a dozen times himself. Looks like he had regular medical appointments when it would have been brought up."

"No rare poisons? Family members waiting to inherit? Business rivals?"

"Nope. From all indications, just died in his sleep. Well, he probably woke up for a few seconds or minutes before he died, but there isn't anything to suggest foul play."

"I guess they can't all be so interesting."

"No, a lot of the postmortems we do are just boring old natural deaths or accidents. There isn't usually a big mystery or conspiracy around them."

32

Kenzie finished all that she was going to do and stripped off her gloves. George would clean up and close the incisions. Kenzie was out of Saul's line of sight for a couple of minutes while she pulled off the rest of her protective clothing. Then she motioned for him to follow her and took him to one of the smaller meeting rooms. They both sat down.

"So, what can you tell me so far about Mercer?" Saul inquired. "I guess I already know cause and manner of death. But you have also been making other inquiries."

"Yes. As you know from Sergeant Campbell, Mercer was in a gang before he died. And one of the kids that we talked to the other day was in the same gang. They both had a red bandana, which I guess they used to show that they were members of the gang when they wanted it to be known."

"So you have a witness."

"I'm not sure yet what she witnessed, and what she might have just happened across lately. I don't have her story yet. The girl's name is Emily Cross. She's only sixteen, and I guess she and Mercer were involved despite the difference in their ages."

"Emily Cross."

"Yeah. I tried to follow up with her home address, but she wasn't there. Her mom isn't sure when she was last home. She could be staying with a friend somewhere."

"Or the gang."

"Right." Kenzie nodded. "I guess you could watch the gang to see if she is with any of them."

"Do you have the names of her friends at school?"

"Not really. The principal might be able to help you. I know a couple of first names, but that's all. She could give you full names and contact information. I couldn't exactly get a warrant for that information, but you could."

She didn't tell Saul how she had gotten Emily's home address, and he didn't ask her.

"Right," Saul agreed. "We'll be sure to follow up with them. And her friend that you know, the one who started all of this."

"Rhys."

"Yes. I should talk to him directly. Do you suppose they would let me into the psych ward to do an interview?" Saul made a face. "I suppose I'm going to have to explain in court why I think a psych patient's testimony is reliable."

"He is out of the hospital. He was released yesterday."

"Oh. So I could see him at home or at the school."

"I don't know if he'll be at school on Monday," Kenzie said. "He might still need some more time before he is ready to go back. But he'll be at home today and tomorrow."

"Good. And he lives with his parents?"

"With his grandmother. She has raised him, either by herself or with her husband or daughter—the boy's mother—since he was born. It's just the two of them right now."

"What happened to the mother?"

Kenzie shrugged as if she didn't know or it was unimportant. Saul really didn't need to know those details. If Kenzie just glossed over them, he probably wouldn't pursue it. Kids were left alone or with grandparents for a lot of reasons.

"But…" she approached the topic delicately, "as far as talking to him goes, did Sergeant Campbell tell you about him?"

"What about him?"

"Uh, that he is selectively mute?"

"He's a mute?"

"He speaks occasionally, but usually only a word or two at a time."

"Does he use sign language, then? I need an interpreter?"

"No. He uses some gestures, but not sign language. And he uses his phone messaging app."

"Oh, of course. It's all texting with kids these days."

"Well..." Kenzie tried to give him a sense of what he would be dealing with, worried that he was getting the wrong impression. "He doesn't text full sentences."

"I know." He waved a hand at her. "No punctuation. I've seen the ways kids text. No periods and half the time no vowels. But I can figure it out."

"No, what I mean is, he will just use a word or two, and pictures or gifs. It's kind of like... trying to solve a word puzzle."

"Charades?"

"Well, there are some similarities for sure," Kenzie admitted. "It's a mixed bag. His grandma will be able to help you to figure out what he means. But she is *not* happy about him being involved with all of this. You might run into some problems with her. She wasn't happy with Rhys coming to me about it and taking his phone, making a police report without her. And I guess I kind of overstepped my bounds there. I just acted because Rhys asked me to. I didn't stop to get permission from Vera."

"Has Campbell talked to her?"

"Not as far as I know. But he's not telling me about every step of the investigation. He... he knows Rhys and Vera from a previous case. So he might have decided not to bother because of the difficulty in communicating with Rhys. He has the phone, and Rhys didn't know where the pictures originated. They were circulating around the school; Rhys didn't know Emily directly."

"Do you know that for sure?"

"Uh... well, I guess not for sure. I haven't talked to him since we identified Emily as the source. Maybe he does know her, but they were not close friends. The kids that Emily hangs out with knew who Rhys was, but it didn't sound like any of them knew him personally."

Saul nodded. He pulled out his notepad and made a few notations so that he would remember this information later. Emily Cross. Rhys Salter. Probably something about their family situations and Rhys being selectively mute.

"Okay. That is helpful. I can definitely follow up on that. And you don't know any of Emily's close friends?"

"No." Kenzie wondered about Clarissa and whether she ought to tell Campbell and Saul about her. Clarissa hadn't provided any additional information, and whether Emily was staying with her was up for speculation. Kenzie hadn't heard anything on the call the previous night that would indicate that Emily had been with Clarissa. Kenzie didn't know Clarissa's last name or where she lived. Saul would need to get that information from the school anyway. "The principal is your best bet. There was a boy named Devon and a girl named Clarissa. And other kids. They are… not always at the school. They tend to be truant a good deal. So you may be able to find them there, and maybe not."

Saul jotted down the names. "Good."

"Was there anything else on Rhys's phone?" Kenzie asked.

He glanced at her, startled by the question. Maybe she wasn't supposed to be asking him any questions about the case. He was in charge of the investigation into the phone, now the homicide. It wasn't Kenzie's place to be asking about what he had found.

"Anything else?" he asked. "Like what?"

"I just didn't know whether you would be able to get anything else. Maybe there were other pictures he had saved. Or conversations in his messaging app. I don't know. I don't think he knows Emily directly but, if he does, then he might have other relevant information."

"Yeah, we're looking into all of that. The electronic forensics guys." He made a gesture to indicate that they were all working on it upstairs.

Kenzie supposed that, like everything else, this took longer in real life than it did in a one-hour cop show on TV. And there was likely a backlog. Would there be any kind of rush on it now that it had turned out to be an actual murder case? Or would they assume that since the murder had already occurred that there was no reason to hurry the results along?

In the meantime, Rhys had his new phone, so Kenzie didn't have to worry about his being unable to communicate. But she might ask him again whether he knew anything else that he hadn't told her. And whether Rhys knew Emily. When he had gone to Zachary about the trouble that Madison had been in when she had been involved with human traffickers, he had known a lot more about her and the people around her than anyone else. People tended to discount Rhys. The fact that he was mute meant that he was not likely to repeat anything that he had heard, so they just ignored him.

But Rhys had ways of communicating what he knew. And maybe it was time to find out if he knew more than he had initially revealed about the picture of the body and where it had come from. He might have known all along that it had originated with Emily and was just trying to keep her out of harm's way. Emily was concerned about the police giving her trouble, and maybe Rhys was too. Maybe she had talked him out of helping out in any other way, so that the only thing he could think of to do was to show the medical examiner the dead body.

33

When Kenzie returned to her desk, she found an envelope from the archives storage company. She sat down and grabbed the scissors to slit it open. Out of the plastic packet she pulled an old file, dusty, the color of the folder having degraded over time, two-toned where the info tab had been exposed to light, but the rest of the folder had been squashed up against its neighbors.

Salter, Clarence

Rhys's grandfather. The murder that he had been witness to very early in his life. Five years old. He had been the only one in the house with Grandpa Clarence and the killer. And the killer had been his own aunt.

But the people who had compiled this file had not known those details. They just knew the physical description of the victim, a bare bones description of the scene, and how he had died. When Kenzie started to skim through the description, she only found a couple of lines about Rhys. According to what the medical examiner had been told, he had been in the house, asleep. The police investigation had suggested that Grandpa Clarence had been killed in a burglary gone bad. The burglars had not known that there was anyone in the house. Maybe they had rung the doorbell or knocked on the door before breaking in, but Clarence, hard of hearing, hadn't heard them.

He had been sitting in his kitchen at the table, eating a bowl of spaghetti. The burglars had stepped in and pulled the trigger, driving a bullet straight into his forehead, killing him instantly.

In Clarence's case, it had not been a .22 caliber round, but a steel-cased .45, and it had not stopped inside his skull, but had continued on a downward trajectory, through his brain stem and out the back of his skull—as close to being killed instantly as anyone could hope for. If he had looked up in time to see the woman standing in front of him, he might have had a second or two to recognize that she was holding a gun on him and, when she had pulled the trigger, his consciousness had ended.

Not a bad death for Clarence.

Not so great for the five-year-old who had been in the house. The Salters had insisted that Rhys had slept through it and that the trauma he had experienced had just been because he had suddenly lost the grandpa he idolized without understanding what had happened to him.

But as Zachary and Kenzie had discovered, that had been a lie.

When Vera and Gloria had gotten home that day, they had known immediately what had happened. Robin's violence had been escalating before the murder. Her rage over minor irritants had led to a number of incidents already. However, at that point, her family had been more concerned about hiding what was happening than about getting her proper treatment. Or maybe that was unfair, and it had not progressed to the point where they could have her admitted involuntarily for assessment. Or maybe she had been assessed and released, and the doctors did not consider her a danger to anyone.

But they had definitely covered up the murder. They said it was a burglary, that no one but Clarence and sleeping Rhys had been home. They had moved home electronics into a pile so that it looked like a break-in had been in progress. They said they had found Rhys still asleep in his bed. Vera and Gloria had never changed their story or told anyone what had really happened.

But when Zachary had been helping Madison and Luke to escape from the human trafficking cartel, and Luke had been skimmed across the head by a bullet, it had been painfully obvious that Rhys had seen his grandfather after he had been shot, if not actually witnessed the shooting. He had immediately devolved into repeating the words he had said over and over again after Clarence's death— Robin's familiar warning, "Stop it! Just stop that!"

Kenzie had thought that was probably the only evidence they would ever have that Rhys had seen Clarence's face after he was killed. None of the Salters were willing to talk about it.

But after his MDMA therapy, Rhys's mouth had again been opened. He had been unable to stop talking and obsessing over the memories. And Kenzie had learned a lot more about that day as the words spilled out like they never had before, and maybe never would again. It had been disjointed, never the whole picture

or sequence at once. Maybe he had only been able to take it in in fractured bits. Or maybe his brain had broken it apart to store the memories separately because it was too overwhelming and terrible to have to see and hear the whole thing as a coherent whole. Or maybe the therapies over the years had helped him access some parts but not others.

Maybe it was the MDMA itself and that was how hallucinogenics always worked. Kenzie had never studied hallucinogenic therapy in detail.

As Kenzie read through the clinical autopsy report, Rhys's words echoed in her brain, and she pictured the horrific event.

At the scene survey, subject was found to be still seated at the kitchen table where he had been shot.

Grampa eating 'getti. Grampa eating red 'getti.

Attacker entered the kitchen from the living room area after apparently breaking in and gathering electronics to be stolen from the home. On discovering that the homeowner was, in fact, present, the intruder shot the victim in the forehead as he sat.

Grampa, no! Put away! Be a good girl.

The bullet traveled on a downward trajectory, through the brain stem, causing immediate death.

The noise! Loud! Grampa sit. Red 'getti. Red 'getti.

Victim had been eating spaghetti and meatballs with red sauce. Forward blood spatter on table and dishes noted, photographed, and measured, as well as exit wound spatter. No voids, no discrepancies.

Grampa eating 'getti.

Rhys had cried. It was not often that a teenage male would dare show tears to the world, and Kenzie didn't know if he had cried as a five-year-old when Vera and Gloria had arrived home. But under the influence of the MDMA, he had cried in horrified gasps, the tears pouring down his face.

Grampa! Grampa!

And then a switch from his frantic sobs to Robin's repeated,

Stop it! Just stop it!

Several times, as he told the story, Rhys collapsed onto the bed and lay in a fetal position after recounting the gunshot, curled up, hands over his head, shaking in terror. When it became too much, he would switch off and talk about the spiders he saw crawling on the walls or repeating other nonsensical phrases, convinced that they meant something, or that Kenzie and Zachary would understand if he just kept repeating them.

It was heartbreaking. Kenzie could picture the little boy he had been, just five years old, terrified by the gunshot. His Grandpa Clarence, previously a central figure in his life, sitting motionless in the chair where he had just been eating, a spaghetti-red hole in his head, red spatter across the table, unresponsive to Rhys's screams as Robin picked him up and put him back to bed, where he had supposedly been when his mother and grandmother returned home.

The police had taken Vera and the others at their word and written it up as a murder during a burglary. The burglars were never caught. They hadn't taken anything from the scene, but had fled after firing on the old man. They had left no fingerprints, no hair or other trace evidence that could be used to find them. Clarence was the only one who had seen them, and he couldn't tell anyone.

34

Kenzie paged through the pictures, and then finally closed the file. Would it do anyone any good to bring the real story to light now? Would anyone other than Vera and Rhys care what had really happened? They already knew. It would be part of their family history forever, no matter how hard they worked to hide it. The killer could never be prosecuted because she was dead. The file could be closed, which might help the police stats a little. But being such a cold case, who would even look at the statistics?

It was a tragic case. She hadn't really learned anything from the file that she hadn't known from Rhys's own mouth. Maybe the technical stuff, like the bullet going through the brain stem. But anything that was important, she had already known.

But she felt like she had needed to see it, needed to read through the dry narrative to pull together all of the pieces of the puzzle into a coherent whole.

She tidied up her desk and put things away. It was a Saturday, so she had no particular schedule she needed to follow. She didn't officially have to be at the morgue at all. She just liked to spend a little extra time getting caught up on the bits she couldn't get done during the week.

"Dr. Kirsch," Nathan, one of the regular security guards in the parking garage, raised a hand to wave at her. "Have a great weekend!"

"Thank you, Nathan. You too. You got some time off after this?"

"I'm working tomorrow. I'll take my weekend Monday and Tuesday."

"Well, enjoy your weekend then."

He nodded, smiling at her. "I sure will."

He watched her walk to her car and get in, then nodded as she drove off.

Kenzie drove to the Salter home. She had a few things she wanted to talk to Rhys about. She didn't think that Saul would be able to get anything out of him. If Rhys didn't want to talk to him, if he didn't think that Emily would want him to talk to Saul, he would just shut down. He wouldn't respond to any questions, and there wouldn't be anything that Saul could do about it. Even if Rhys had been subpoenaed to give testimony in a case, they couldn't force him to. He had a well-documented psychological condition that prevented him from being able to communicate through any conventional means.

Kenzie wasn't sure that Rhys's usual means of communication would even be taken as sworn testimony if he were willing to try. He could give a yes or no head shake to a question, with an unbiased third party interpreting his answers for the court clerk, but how would they interpret dog gifs, photos, and gestures without codified meanings? Would a word or two typed into a messaging app be enough for a judge to agree that his meaning had been clear?

But he would do his best to communicate with Kenzie. He had a bit of a crush on her and never refused to see or talk to her. Kenzie rang the doorbell and was a little surprised when it was answered by Zachary. He laughed at her expression.

"I did say that I might stop by to see Rhys," he reminded her. "Did you forget that?"

"It seems like days ago," Kenzie confessed. "Yeah. It completely slipped my mind."

"So you don't want to see me."

"Well…" Kenzie walked in the door. "I always want to see you, but I came to see Rhys."

"Hello, Kenzie," Vera greeted, getting up from the couch. "I want to thank you for helping Rhys out with this. I know I wasn't too positive about it before, but even if it isn't what I want, I am still grateful to you for helping Rhys."

Kenzie gave her a brief hug. "Of course. I'll always help Rhys whenever I can."

"He's in his room," Zachary said. "I just came out to open the door for you because Vera saw you pull up."

It did help to have a recognizable vehicle! Kenzie glanced out the window at her little red convertible and smiled. She walked with Zachary to Rhys's bedroom. He stood up from his bed to give her a hug.

"Hey, it's good to see you. I'll bet you're glad to be home," Kenzie told him.

He released her from the hug and nodded vigorously. When she thought about all he had been through the last few weeks… no kid should have to go through what he had recently. And as a child. He had been lucky to be raised by loving grandparents, which was probably the only reason that he had managed to get through the traumatic experiences he had. And even with that, he had not escaped unscathed. Kenzie wished she could take back the choices that his family had made both before and after Clarence's death. They had been too afraid of the system to stop the abuses within the family.

They all looked for places to sit down. Zachary had claimed the swivel chair at Rhys's study desk. Rhys sat on the bed. There was no other chair and not a clear place to sit on the floor. Though she was sure that Rhys and Vera would not have let her sit on the floor anyway.

"Why don't we go out to the living room?" she suggested. "It would be more comfortable."

Zachary looked at Rhys, who shook his head. He motioned for Kenzie to sit on the end of the bed, patting it like he was trying to call a cat or dog to jump up. Kenzie sat down. Rhys probably wanted his room's privacy so Vera didn't have to overhear what they discussed. As much as Vera loved Rhys and was grateful that Kenzie had agreed to help him, she still did not like the police interfering with their lives.

She would probably not even let Detective Saul come over to interview Rhys. She would tell him no, that she didn't want Rhys talking to law enforcement about anything.

"So, what have you guys been talking about?" Kenzie asked Zachary, hoping to ease into the conversation gradually.

"Mostly... how he's feeling about going back to school. If there is anyone he's interested in. What he likes best about school..."

Kenzie rolled her eyes. "Well, I guess I have school questions too. I hope you haven't talked him out."

Rhys made an expansive gesture to Kenzie, inviting her questions.

Kenzie sighed, trying to decide where to start. "I want to ask you questions, but I don't want to upset you, and some of these things might be upsetting."

He nodded seriously.

"I don't want you to think I'm accusing you or anyone else of doing something wrong. Okay? I don't know much about what happened, and I need you to tell me more about it."

Rhys nodded again. He pointed at Kenzie. *Take it away.*

"Was it Emily who sent you the picture? Or someone else?"

He rocked his hand back and forth uncertainly.

"You don't know who sent it? Why not? Was it sent anonymously?"

He shook his head. He ticked off his fingers as if enumerating a list of points.

"It was sent to you several times," Zachary said. "I remember you said that. You kept deleting it, and it kept coming back again."

Rhys pointed at him in agreement.

"Okay, you got it several times. Did you get it from Emily?"

Rhys pursed his lips, then nodded.

"The first time you got it, was it from her?"

Rhys shook his head slowly and shrugged. *Not sure.*

"Right. You got it several times, and it gets muddled after a while. But you know that one of the times you got it, it was from Emily."

He nodded.

"Did she send any message with it? Or was she just sending out the picture without any text?"

Rhys shrugged. Kenzie thought he was being intentionally evasive. "Were you and Emily friends?"

He shook his head.

"You didn't hang out with those kids at all."

He shook his head again.

"But you knew who she was?"

Rhys nodded. He made a circular motion with his finger pointing up. Kenzie hazarded a guess. "Everybody knew who she was."

He grinned and pointed at her. *You got it.*

Kenzie had a feeling that Emily was a person who liked attention. She did what she could to get it. Had that been the only reason for sending around the picture of Mercer? She couldn't get past the fact that they had been close. It didn't make sense that she would circulate his death picture just because she hoped it would go viral. Kenzie didn't think that was her motivation.

"And did everybody know that she was the one who started circulating the picture?"

Rhys shook his head. He pointed to himself and made a slashing movement with his hand.

"You didn't?"

He nodded his agreement.

"You got it from her, but you didn't know that she was the one who had started it. You thought she was just one of the people forwarding it around."

Rhys agreed.

"Did you find out that she was the one who took the picture?"

Rhys stared back at her.

"Was Emily the one who took the picture?"

He shrugged. He frowned and shook his head. *Don't know, don't think so.*

"Did you talk to her about the picture at all?"

A shrug.

"Did you talk to her, message her, ask her if she was okay?"

Rhys pointed and nodded at the last suggestion.

"You asked her if she was okay?"

He nodded again.

"What did she say?"

Rhys frowned and shook his head.

"You don't remember?" Kenzie asked.

He shook his head. He pointed to the space beside him and shook his head, still frowning.

"Emily said she was not okay?"

A nod.

"Did she ask for your help? Is that why you wanted me to get involved once you were feeling better?"

He shook his head.

"She didn't want help?"

Another shake.

Kenzie had only seen Emily briefly, but she tried to call up a picture of the girl in her mind. To imagine that they were talking to each other. She tried to call on all of the information her mother had given about her, to get a sense of the girl's background and personality. Emily was independent. She hung out with a gang. She was separate from her mother at home, more like roommates operating on different shifts than mother and daughter. She was not going to school often and, when she did, she was hanging around with the wrong crowd. She had a boyfriend, even if she wasn't calling him that. She thought she was grown up. That she could do everything on her own without her mother's help or anyone else's.

"Did you know the man in the picture was her boyfriend?"

Rhys shook his head.

"Did you know that the both of them were in a gang?"

His eyebrows shot up.

Kenzie nodded. "Yes. In a gang. I suspect that's where she hung out when she wasn't at school. She wasn't at home very often."

Rhys nodded.

"Had you ever walked her home? Did you know where she lived?"

Negative. Kenzie wasn't sure she believed they didn't really know each other or ever talk, but she didn't think Rhys had anything to do with her disappearance or the gang.

35

D o you think that Emily could have been the one to shoot him?" Kenzie asked finally. She had to ask. It had been niggling away at the back of her mind ever since she had found out that Emily and Mercer were in the gang together and had been getting to know each other even more intimately.

Intimate partner violence was a frequent cause of the violent deaths that Kenzie saw come through her autopsy. Knives, guns, fists, stairs, everything she could think of. Emily wasn't exempted by her age. And Mercer had been older than she was. Bigger and stronger. If he had come after her and she'd had to defend herself...

But if she had killed him in self-defense, she could have gone to the police. She could have told them about it. And why circulate his picture if she had killed him in self-defense?

What if it had been an initiation? Her ticket into a full-blooded member of the gang? Kenzie had heard that gangs didn't actually require murders to get in. That sort of initiation was a thing of the past. But she didn't believe it. Maybe the number of gangs that had demanded it had been exaggerated, so people thought that was the only way to get into any gang. But there were still those that required some kind of evidence that an inductee was willing to do whatever it took to get into the gang of their choice.

Rhys's eyes were wide. He shook his head. He made a large X with both hands and pushed them away from him in an adamant "No!"

"Do you know for sure she didn't do it?"

He repeated the gesture.

"Do you know who did? Or you just don't think that she could do something like that?"

There was a stubborn set to Rhys's jaw. He didn't answer.

Kenzie studied him for a minute, then nodded. "Did you have any other pictures or messages on your phone from Emily?"

He shook his head.

"Did you delete everything?"

He hesitated, then shrugged.

Everything except for that one picture, Kenzie thought. He had kept that to show to her. He had deleted it several times, but it kept coming back until he couldn't handle it anymore.

Zachary had sat back and remained quiet throughout most of the conversation, but spoke up now. "Did you upload anything to the cloud before deleting it from the phone?"

Rhys raised his brows. He shrugged.

"What did you keep?" Kenzie asked.

Rhys rolled his eyes up toward the ceiling and didn't answer.

"More pictures?"

Still no answer.

"Pictures of Mercer, the dead man?"

He shook his head.

"Pictures of Emily?"

He shrugged, looking away from her.

"Download them," Zachary ordered. "Let's have a look."

Rhys spread his hands out wide. *Why?*

"You don't know. There might be other clues in those photos that you didn't recognize."

Rhys didn't pick up his phone or make any move to do so.

"Rhys… do you know where Emily is?" Kenzie asked.

He shook his head.

"I would really like to talk to her, but she hasn't been back to her house or school the last few days. And of course now it is the week-end, so she won't be back to school before Monday. If you know where she's hanging out, it would be helpful…"

Rhys made a show of pointing to his closet, then shaking his head. He bent over as if to look under his bed and then shook his head. He shrugged.

"I'm not saying that you've got her hidden somewhere, or even that she's hiding. Maybe you could message her and let her know that we would like to talk with her."

Rhys shook his head.

"You wanted me to help, Rhys. How am I supposed to help you if you don't let me? I need to talk to Emily. You know I'm not going to do anything to hurt her. I promise I'm not asking just so I can turn her over to the police. I want to make sure she's okay and find out what she knows about Mercer's death." Kenzie shook her head. "You can't just start circulating pictures of a dead man and expect not to have to answer questions."

Zachary chuckled. "I think that's pretty sound advice," he agreed.

36

R hys was being pretty stubborn. He didn't want to download the pictures of Emily, and he didn't want to send her a message, yet he still expected Kenzie's help.

"You wanted me to look into Mercer's death," Kenzie coaxed. "His death reminded you of your grandpa's death and you didn't want another murder to go unsolved. You wanted to make sure that this man got justice."

Rhys looked down at his hands, fiddling with his phone. He nodded slightly.

"You saw what happened to your grandpa. That was really hard on you. You still see it all the time."

He looked up at her, surprised. He probably didn't remember much of what he had said when he'd had the MDMA therapy, but Kenzie had been struck by how many times he had gone back to Clarence's death. He repeated phrases and bits of what he had seen over and over again, and she didn't think that was just because of the drugs. She believed that was how Rhys's brain always worked, stuck in a loop, constantly obsessing over how Clarence had died, seeing his face again and again. Or maybe constantly. Maybe it never went away, even for a second.

"You didn't want to be stuck with Mercer's face in your head all the time too. Or it kept bringing back the pictures of Clarence. It was just too much. And you needed someone to help you with that."

Rhys pointed to Kenzie, agreeing.

"Yeah. You know I'm always playing with dead bodies," Kenzie joked, trying to lighten the mood. "So I can handle it. I can figure out who he is and what happened to him and make sure that his killer is brought to justice. So that Mercer can be at rest. So that you can let him go."

Rhys squeezed his eyes shut. Maybe Kenzie was making things worse by talking about it.

"I'm sorry. I just want to help. Let's find a way to help Emily and to help the police find out who it was that killed Mercer. I believe you that it wasn't Emily. You know her, right?"

Rhys looked at Kenzie again. He nodded his head vigorously.

"You understand other people a lot better than most of us do." Kenzie shrugged. "Maybe it's the nonverbal communication thing. You can read their body language and facial expressions better. You can see things that are going on under the surface. Beyond what everyone else sees."

The same was true of Zachary, but for different reasons. He had grown up in such a hostile environment, never knowing who he could trust, moving from one home to another after the fire when he was ten. He had to learn to read the people around him for survival. He wasn't a kid who could ever behave the way he was expected to. As hard as he tried, he could never be the perfectly behaved kid who wouldn't make waves and could please his foster parents or caregivers. Therefore, he had to know when to duck.

Rhys eyed Zachary and Kenzie, and finally reached for his laptop computer rather than his phone. The sticker declaring it the property of his school was big and bold, but starting to wear off. He opened it and touched the fingerprint recognition pad to unlock it. No need to type in a password. With the laptop screen facing Rhys rather than Kenzie, she could only see his fingers skating over the trackpad. She couldn't tell what he was doing with it. It was a few minutes before he turned the computer around so they could look at the pictures on the screen. Zachary left the office chair and sat on the bed with Kenzie.

His weight depressed the mattress, making Kenzie fall against him. She snuggled into position and he put an arm around her while they both looked at the first picture Rhys had pulled up on the laptop.

Kenzie saw the girl they had been looking for. Emily, whom she had only seen briefly, mixed in with the crowd of "loser" kids, trying to blend in and fly under the radar. Straight dark hair, flat nose, piercings. She wore blue jeans and an autumn jacket left unzipped. Fake leather with a warm lining and collar. Recent. She wouldn't have worn that in the summer.

She was glancing toward the camera, unsmiling. Nervous? Was she aware that her picture was being taken, or had Rhys been covert, not giving away what he had been doing?

"She's pretty," Kenzie said, not sure what else to say. But Emily really wasn't. She was plain and looked like she'd been sleeping rough for a few days. Kenzie searched for anything in the picture that she could use. Something that would tell her where Emily was or what had happened that day. Or why Emily would circulate the picture of her dead boyfriend.

Rhys nodded. After a few seconds, he turned the computer around and swiped the trackpad to view the next picture. He turned it back to them.

Emily with her group of school friends. Not a "me and the gang" picture where she was laughing with them and enjoying the halcyon days of her youth. Not one that she would look back at in twenty or thirty years as she fondly remembered the kids she used to hang out with in those years before taking on the responsibilities of adulthood. They smoked or hung out together, few of them actually looking at each other. Emily's dark eyes stared off into the distance. She looked lost, alone in the crowd, and hurting. Kenzie's heart squeezed. What had this girl been through in her life that others had no idea of? All the secret hurts and troubles were there on the surface, visible but unreadable.

"She looks so alone," Zachary murmured, echoing what Kenzie was thinking. Alone in the crowd.

Rhys nodded his agreement. Maybe that was what had stood out to him. How alone she was, just like Rhys.

Zachary pointed at the bandana, tied around Emily's leg like it had been the day they had seen her. "She wears the gang colors at school. That means there are either other members of her gang or the rival gang in the school. Probably both. But she's not hanging out with them. She's probably a new member."

"You don't think that shooting Mercer was her initiation, do you?"

Zachary shook his head. "Killing a member of your own gang wouldn't be an initiation. Unless he was known to be dirty. And even then, that would most likely be left to a more senior gang member so that a recruit couldn't mess it up."

That made sense. The gang wouldn't want to eliminate its own members. It had been a ridiculous thought.

"But you think she was new to the gang."

He nodded. "Yeah. Which would explain why she's hanging out with other kids at school instead of the gang. She hadn't made the transition from one 'family' to the other."

"And the guy in the gang that she liked the best didn't go to the school. Mercer was quite a bit older than her. In his twenties. If she joined the gang to be with him, or he had suggested that she do it, she might not actually like anyone else in the gang."

Zachary nodded. "You don't join a gang because you like all of its members. You join it for protection. You might like one person, or one person might have taken you under his wing or recruited you. But there are probably people associated with the gang that you really don't like and have to put up with anyway."

Rhys pointed at Zachary, eyebrows raised questioningly. Zachary shook his head.

"I was never in one. There were times when I considered it… but I was never in one place for long. Becoming a gang member would mean running away, and I always hoped… that I would find a family I belonged with. I saw what happened to the kids who ran away and ended up on the street. I might have envied them for a while, but things never turned out well. They had more freedom, but freedom to do what?"

Rhys and Kenzie both nodded. Zachary was lucky that he hadn't made that choice. It would have been even harder for him to climb out of poverty and homelessness, addiction, and violence, than it had been to pull himself up by his bootstraps and set himself up as a private investigator as he had.

They looked at a couple of other pictures of Emily. She wasn't smiling in any of them. They could usually spot the red bandana tied around her neck or hair, around an arm or leg. They were all school pictures taken by Rhys, so nothing showed her with Mercer, the rest of the gang, or her mother. Just candid shots of Emily by herself or hanging out with her group of friends, smoking or staring off into the distance.

37

See if you can set up a meeting with her," Kenzie urged. "Either with you or with me, whichever one you think she'll agree to more easily. She needs to tell her story. Just like you needed to talk about what happened to your Grandpa Clarence, she needs to be able to tell someone what happened. Why else do you think she was forwarding pictures of him to everyone?"

Rhys looked at Kenzie for a minute, thinking about it.

Kenzie might have overstepped her bounds. Did she really know what Rhys needed? What Emily needed? Was she just being manipulative, saying what she thought had the best chance of convincing Rhys to do what she wanted him to?

Eventually, Rhys picked up his phone. He tapped it a few times and frowned, trying to decide what to write to Emily. Or what picture to send her. He finally moved again, tapping out a couple of words and sending the message to her with an electronic *whoosh*.

He looked at Kenzie and Zachary, taking a deep breath and letting it out in a sigh. None of them knew if Emily would respond to Rhys. She might not trust him. She might be busy with other things or have switched phones. People did unpredictable things and, with a stressor like her boyfriend being shot and killed, probably in front of her, who knew what she might have done?

Was she in hiding or simply not going to school? It could certainly be "too much" for her while dealing with other things. Would her friends at school know where to find her? Would the police be able to pick up her trail?

Rhys's phone vibrated and he looked down at it. He glanced at Kenzie and then down at the phone again. Kenzie watched him think things through, find a gif to send back, and enter another word. Then they were waiting again.

It always fascinated Kenzie how Rhys used language. It wasn't just that he couldn't speak aloud whenever he wanted to. He could only use any form of communication in a limited way. A few words or a picture or gesture to express what he wanted to. She wondered if he thought in sentences or only in pictures or some other way, and had to translate each thought into something he could communicate with the people around him.

She leaned against Zachary, comfortable with his closeness, patiently waiting for Rhys to have his conversation with Emily and, hopefully, convince her to come out of hiding to meet with him.

Rhys looked at her several times, but seemed satisfied each time that she was not hovering, not angry that the process was taking time. How could Kenzie think that it wouldn't take time? Emily would need to ask a lot of questions before she was ready to meet with a stranger, or even with Rhys. She had been traumatized by the loss of her boyfriend. She probably didn't know who she could trust.

Kenzie's phone vibrated, and she slid it out of her pocket to have a look at it. It wasn't Rhys, texting her on the side to let her know how things were going, but Lisa.

Dinner tomorrow?

Kenzie almost groaned aloud. She had forgotten that Lisa and Walter wanted her and Zachary to come over for family dinner in Burlington, instead of going down to see Lorne and Pat. She held the phone so that Zachary could see it over her shoulder.

"Do you want to?" he murmured.

"No."

"Do you want me to talk you out of it? Or you want to use me as an excuse?"

"We had already planned to go see the Petersons, hadn't we?"

"You said your parents don't usually manage to get the same time off."

"I know," Kenzie grumbled. "But they're not going to get equal time. They might think they're going to, but there is no way they'll be free every couple of weeks. It will be twice a year, maybe."

"That sounds manageable."

Kenzie grunted an acknowledgment, thinking about it. She didn't like to give in to Lisa, just out of general principles. Hadn't she just been thinking about how she hadn't been a rebellious teen but had always tried to be responsible and to do what her parents wanted her to? Maybe she hadn't been rebellious as a teen, but she was certainly feeling her oats now, wishing her parents would recognize that she was an adult and lived an independent life, no longer tied to them.

What was the difference? Was it just because she was older and her brain had matured? Or because she was with Zachary now? Maybe there was something about starting her own little family unit that had set off her rebelliousness.

Or maybe she had been rebellious for years and just not recognized it in herself. Pretended that it wasn't really there.

Rhys grunted and nudged Kenzie with his toe. She looked at him.

He tapped his wrist, the universal sign for *what time?*

"What time can I meet with Emily? Any time. I'll make time."

His eyes dropped to his phone again.

Kenzie looked at her own phone. "I'm just going to tell Lisa I can't do it this weekend. Maybe they'll leave me alone then. If they don't, then we can find a time that works better."

"You wanted to spend more quality time with your parents. To do more with them."

"I thought you were supposed to be talking me out of it."

"I offered. You didn't answer, which I think means that I'm *not* supposed to talk you out of it."

"Hmm."

He was right, of course. Both in assuming that she didn't actually want him to talk her out of it and that she had promised to start spending more quality time with her parents. And a weekend dinner was perfect. Not too long. No pressure. Not a holiday or an assignment. Just dinner.

Another message popped up on her phone while she was looking at it.

Burlington tomorrow

She thought it was just her mother pressing her again, then realized that the message had actually come from Rhys, sitting across from her, looking at her to see whether that was good.

"In Burlington?" Kenzie frowned at Rhys. "Is that where she is?"

Rhys pointed at his phone screen and raised his brows questioningly.

"Yes, of course I'll meet her in Burlington tomorrow." Kenzie laughed. "It looks like I'm going to be there anyway. What time?"

He splayed his fingers. *Five.*

"Okay. Tell her yes and find out where I'm supposed to meet her. Or give her my number and she can text me the details." She looked at Zachary. "I guess she decided to get out of town for a while."

He nodded. "Probably a good idea. Roxboro is a small town, especially if you're in a gang. There is only a limited number of places you can go. It's too easy to find people."

"Even on the street?"

"Especially on the street. People see your movements. Report on you. You don't know who might have seen you. It's everybody's business where you have been and where you are going. When I went back to Clintock trying to find Robbie Elder, you wouldn't believe how fast word was out about who I was looking for, who I had met with, all of that. People were watching me before I managed to figure anything out."

"But you were well-known there."

"I hadn't been back for years. And Emily is well-known here. Especially if she was involved with someone in the gang. Someone who got killed. You can bet there are plenty of stories floating around about how he got killed and what her involvement was."

"Do you think she was involved?"

"No... not in the way you are thinking. I don't think she did it.

But she was involved with him, and she was involved in his death, which you know, because she had a picture of it."

"Right. We just don't know what that involvement was."

Kenzie's phone buzzed again, this time with a pin on a map. She looked at it and nodded. "Okay. I'll meet her there," she relayed back to Rhys. "Let her know I'll be there. And maybe Zachary too, since we'll be going to Burlington together for dinner with my family. You can vouch for Zachary. Tell her that he isn't going to bother her or get in anyone's way."

Rhys looked at Zachary for a minute before nodding his agreement. Was he worried that Zachary would scare Emily off? That it would turn into another high-risk case like Madison's? Or was he remembering how Zachary had helped him in the past? Found him and Bridget when she had been kidnapped. He knew that Zachary was reliable and would help out a teenager in need without question.

He lowered his head and started another message to Emily. Kenzie worried about whether she would understand everything Rhys said—or didn't say. She worried that Emily would get something wrong, and she and Kenzie wouldn't meet, or something about Kenzie would set Emily off and she would be angry or afraid.

She just wanted everything to go smoothly.

38

K enzie checked the time on her phone again. She caught Zachary looking at her.

"What time do you think we should leave?" she asked. "Should we be in Burlington before the meeting in case she calls back to say she wants to move it up?"

"I don't think she'll do that. She knows that you're coming from Roxboro. She knows that switching the time would mean you couldn't meet with her. It's possible that she will, but if she does, she's doing it to sabotage the meeting. Not because you weren't there in good time."

"What time do you think we should leave?"

He just smiled. "I don't think I've ever seen you so anxious about a meeting before."

"Well, is it any wonder? I'm not usually meeting with witnesses. Or volatile teenagers. Or gang members."

He laughed. "You'll do fine. You've talked to her before. You know she's not scary."

"She's not scary? Who are you kidding? Teenagers are terrifying."

"She didn't do anything to hurt or aggravate you before when you met her. She actually stayed pretty quiet. She didn't mock or bully you or pretend that she was so tough. Her mom seemed to think that she was a pretty good kid. I know she's been rebellious and hanging out with a gang, but her mom didn't talk about how violent she has been lately, or volatile, or using drugs. She sounds like she's lonely. Looking for help."

"But even kids looking for help can be pretty... angry."

Zachary nodded, conceding the point. Kenzie wondered what he had been like as a teenager. She knew he had been depressed, alone, and abused, but how had he shown that to the outside world? Had he been withdrawn? Angry? Swinging from one extreme to the other? From what he and Lorne had said, he had been a pretty good kid, just hyperactive and unable to control his impulses. He hadn't been the kid that you had to worry might bully or beat up other kids in the family. He hadn't been the one who would stand up to an authority figure, challenging or even attacking them. But were their recollections accurate or rose-colored after years of denial?

"She's going to be okay," Zachary assured her. "Emily is just looking for someone who will help her."

"Okay." She would have to rely on his assurances. He read people. He knew kids. He knew what it was like to be in the position Emily was in now, not knowing who to trust or how to get help. "I'm sure you're right. It's going to be fine."

He looked at the time on his phone. "We can leave in an hour or so if you like. We'll stop for ice cream when we get there and ruin our appetites."

Kenzie laughed. At least they would have a few hours to burn off the ice cream before dinner. Like many of those in their social set, Walter and Lisa ate dinner later than Zachary and Kenzie normally did. So an afternoon snack was probably not a bad idea. Maybe the ice cream would help her to de-stress.

"Sounds good," she agreed.

It was a good thing she didn't have to wait too much longer, because she was unable to get any work done in that time. She couldn't concentrate on anything. Whenever she tried to settle into something, her head was somewhere else. She kept thinking about

Rhys and his grandfather's death. About Emily and her boyfriend's death. Parallel paths. Things that others in their social groups probably couldn't relate to. Had Emily known anything about Rhys's history? Enough to recognize a kindred spirit? Was it just coincidental? Or had Rhys sought her out to tell her about it? Kenzie still wasn't convinced that Rhys hadn't known who Mercer was or that Emily was the person who started circulating the pictures before Kenzie had made those discoveries. But she didn't have any evidence to back the feeling up.

They took Zachary's car to Burlington. It was easier on gas, warmer in the crisp fall weather, and less noticeable on the street. They didn't want to attract attention when meeting with Emily. Kenzie let Zachary drive, but regretted it. He loved driving, so she didn't like to take that away from him, especially when it was his car. But she found herself at loose ends and wished she had something to keep her hands and mind occupied instead of just staring out the window, wishing they were there, and she didn't have to wait any longer.

They stopped for ice cream, as promised, but were only halfway through eating it when Kenzie's phone buzzed, and she saw it was Emily.

Where are you?

They weren't expected at the meeting location for another hour, so Kenzie wasn't sure why Emily was already texting her and demanding to know her location.

Having ice cream, she texted back. *Meeting you in an hour.*

Meet sooner?

Kenzie showed the phone to Zachary and raised her brows. He had been sure that Emily wouldn't do this. She wouldn't be playing games with them, trying to disrupt the scheduled meeting. But...

Maybe. When and where?

Emily proposed meeting in fifteen minutes at a different mall. Kenzie calculated the driving time in her head, along with how long it would take them to get to her car, and to walk from the car to the location inside the mall.

Can't make it in under twenty.

20 min then

"Okay, I guess we're on the move," Kenzie said.

"We can walk and eat."

They were finished eating their ice creams by the time they reached the car.

"You know where it is?" Kenzie asked. She had grown up in Burlington and he had not.

"Yeah, I'm good."

He drove faster than she would have and arrived within ten minutes. They looked around for any sign of Emily as they got out of the car, but didn't see her. They walked briskly into the mall and found the location she had designated for the meeting. They were there ahead of schedule.

"Not bad," Kenzie told Zachary. At least they were not late. Emily probably would be. Kenzie had an idea she knew how it would go down. Emily would not arrive right away. She would be watching them from a distance, maybe looking down from the second story. Making sure that they didn't have any police or other watchers with them, and that they weren't talking to other people on comms. All of the stuff that she had seen on TV.

But Kenzie and Zachary were not TV show cops or spies. They were just a couple of people there to see if they could help Emily sort things out in her life and maybe help bring her boyfriend's killer to justice. There weren't going to be any fireworks, no police descending into the mall from helicopters. There were no undercover cops pushing baby carriages or cleaning up trash. Just Kenzie and Zachary.

Kenzie's phone vibrated. She looked at it.

Meet me by the fountain

Kenzie looked around. The fountain was new since she had hung out there as a teenager. They checked the nearest directory and walked to the fountain. They moved slowly, like window shoppers or tourists rather than law enforcement officers trying to meet with a material witness.

They circled the large fountain. Kenzie checked her pockets and tossed a couple of pennies in, launching them toward a frog's wide open mouth and missing by a mile. Zachary laughed, but he didn't show off his own prowess.

"I was never any good at sports," he told her.

Kenzie wasn't sure that throwing money into a fountain counted as a sport.

"Hey."

39

K enzie turned and saw Emily sitting on a bench, hunched over inside her coat, a cap pulled down low over her face. Pretty hard to recognize if they didn't know who they were looking for.

"Hi," Kenzie greeted, giving Emily a warm smile that she hoped would help to calm her. "I'm glad you agreed to meet with me. How are you?"

Emily shrugged. She indicated the space on the bench next to her. Large enough for only one person. Kenzie sat down. Zachary withdrew a short distance away. He could still see them and hear them if voices were raised, but probably wouldn't hear anything that was said in a normal speaking voice or lower. Especially with the white noise of the fountain covering it.

"Your mom was worried about you," Kenzie tried. "She didn't know where you were. Are you staying here in Burlington, or is it just a place to meet?"

"It's where we're meeting." Emily looked around restlessly. Her hands were in her pockets. Kenzie hoped that she didn't have a weapon on her. Even if she had only brought something for self-defense, Kenzie still didn't want to sit within arm's reach.

"Is this where you've been since Tuesday when we came by the school?"

"It doesn't matter where I've been," Emily snapped.

Kenzie took the hint and stopped asking questions. She waited for Emily to take control of the conversation.

"Rhys said that you're the medical examiner," Emily stated. "You, like, cut all the dead people."

Kenzie thought about that for a minute. She didn't need to correct the inaccuracies, but tried to analyze what Emily needed to hear.

That she was an expert.

That she was trustworthy.

That she wasn't there to arrest Emily or drag her in for questioning on the death of her boyfriend.

"Yes, I work at the medical examiner's office, doing autopsies and making other inquiries to find out what happened to the people who end up on my table."

"And... you got Trevor now?"

"Yes. I'm sorry I didn't have him any earlier, but his body was not discovered for quite some time."

"They dumped him somewhere. I didn't know where."

Kenzie nodded. She didn't fill Emily in on the details. She didn't need to know he'd been left in a dumpster or the state of the remains when he was finally discovered.

"So you know it wasn't just made up, now," Emily said. "It wasn't just... a prop or a prank. It was *real*." Tears sprang to her eyes.

Kenzie reached over to pat Emily's leg to comfort her, but Emily jerked away.

"I know," Kenzie agreed soothingly. "I know that you weren't just trying to get attention. I don't know why you were circulating his picture to everyone, but I don't think it was because you were trying to... sensationalize what happened."

"No," Emily agreed in a small voice.

"Do you want to talk to me about what happened?"

"I don't want to... but I want you to know about Trev. So I guess I have to."

Kenzie nodded and waited.

"He didn't deserve to die." Emily swore. "I can't believe that I saw it, right in front of my own eyes. It was like a play or something, not like it really happened in real life. You know how many times I've seen people killed like that on TV or in GTA or something? You don't think about what it would be like to see it happen in real life."

"No. They say that violent shows and games desensitize us to death and violence. But I'm not sure that's the case."

"We always joke around about number of kills and being a criminal in first person shooter games and stuff, how it makes us tough or macho or something. But seeing it happen in real life... it wasn't anything like one of those games."

Kenzie had to school herself not to reach out and touch Emily. The girl wasn't looking for physical comfort. She had another agenda. Or she had agreed to follow Kenzie's agenda, since she was the one who had set up the meeting.

"So... how did it happen? Was there a fight?"

Kenzie was pretty sure it hadn't been a fight. It had been deliberate. Execution style. But she wanted to get Emily talking about it. Let her tell her story.

"No. It just... it was like it came out of nowhere, and my brain still doesn't understand what happened. I was with the gang. Or, we had been." Emily rubbed her forehead, wincing and frowning. "Then... it was Trev and me, and he was talking about that stupid cop. I just... I thought it would all blow over again, and him and me would spend some time..." She shrugged. "I just wanted to be with him. Didn't want all of the politics."

"What stupid cop?" Kenzie tried to get up to speed on what Emily was talking about.

"That stupid cop who was always making trouble. Like, if he caught you with a boosted car, then he wouldn't bust you if you... traded up for it. Like... if you were peddling coke, he wanted his cut of it if he was going to let it go. He was always here and there, stickin' his nose into everything. And since he got guys to trade information, he always knew something that was going on, and would use that to get more leverage..."

"A dirty cop? He was taking bribes for not making arrests?"

"Not bribes," Emily protested, though that was certainly how the police department would have seen it. "He was *taking* it. He wasn't saying, like, if you pay me, I'll look the other way. He would walk in, take what he wanted, and say you couldn't report him for it because he had something on you. You couldn't complain. All you could do was take it."

"So more like blackmail than a bribe."

"Yeah… maybe. I don't know what the hell to call it. Who cares? He was in it to squeeze everything he could from the gang members. Or other people in the neighborhood. Guns, drugs, girls, stolen stuff. It didn't matter. He didn't want to do the work to get it legitimately. Just to take it from somebody else."

"How long had this been going on?"

"Months. I don't know. As long as I was hanging around with them. You just had to watch out for this guy. Make sure he didn't see you doing anything. Didn't look at you and decide he wanted something you had."

Kenzie nodded, making a noise for Emily to go on.

"Trev was going on about him again, how he was screwing everything up and someone needed to kill him. Just shoot him in the head and get it over with." Emily swallowed hard and kept going.

"I was trying to get him to settle down. Like, no one was doing anything to him and he could just enjoy himself… enjoy being with me, and not worry about anything else. He'd wrecked enough other good times by obsessing over this cop and everything he was doing. Just… have a little time together," Emily said it in a coaxing voice, as Kenzie was sure that she had that night.

"But he wouldn't pay any attention to me. I tried to take him away from there so we could go somewhere private. Another flop or someplace private. He was acting drunk, all jelly legs and stumbling around in the street, but he hadn't had that much to drink."

"Maybe his drink had been spiked?"

"I don't know. I was with him, so I don't see how it could have been. But he was all… agitated. Yelling about the stupid bent cop and how he was ruining everything. He grabbed me and shook me, and it scared me. I didn't even know if he could see me anymore, or if he was seeing someone else. He wasn't talking to me. I'm not sure what was going on. He hadn't used. Hadn't for days."

"If he hadn't used, maybe he was in withdrawal. People can hallucinate in withdrawal. Get very agitated. Lots of mood swings and paranoia and not understanding that people are trying to help them."

"I don't know, maybe." Emily pulled her elbows in, hands still in her jacket pockets, holding her arms against herself like she was cold. Hunching down inside the jacket to hide from the world. "He was all sweaty and his eyes were funny. You would have thought he was on drugs, but it wasn't that."

Kenzie frowned, nodding. "And the whole time, he was complaining about the dirty cop."

"Yeah. I mean, I hated the guy too, but I didn't want to spend all of my time thinking about him, looking over my shoulder to make sure I wasn't being watched."

"Who was this cop?"

"I don't know his name. Trev called him…" Emily looked away from Kenzie for a moment, rubbing her forehead and laughing weakly. "He called him Deputy Donut. I don't know his real name. I always stayed away from him as much as I could. He didn't wear a uniform, so I never saw his name badge or anything. It was always just Deputy Donut. Not to his face; he woulda killed anyone who called him that to his face. But they liked dissing him when he wasn't around."

"And he was with the gang unit? Not a patrol officer, if he didn't wear a uniform."

"I don't know. I never asked anything about who he was or what department he worked with. Why would I? I didn't want anything to do with the guy."

"Why was Trevor so upset about him that night? What had he done?"

"I dunno if he had done anything new, or if it was just… overflowing from the rest of the times he'd caused Trev trouble. He was really angry, but I kind of thought he was just amped up about something else. It was all the usual stuff. Deputy Donut thinking that he could get away with whatever he liked. Ripping us off."

"Had he taken something that day?"

"I don't know. How would I know?" Emily protested, frustrated with Kenzie's questions. "I was at school during the day. I went over, thinking Trevor and I could have some time together. You know, hang out, enjoy each other's company. Instead, we'd had to do stuff with the gang, and then when everyone broke up to go their different directions, and I thought we could finally have some alone time, then Trev was going off the rails about Deputy Donut and how he'd ripped him off, and he was going to do something to get even."

"What?"

"I don't know. I don't think he, like, had a plan. He was just spouting off. Just because he said he was going to do something, that doesn't mean he was. He said a lot of things."

"Okay. And then what happened?"

40

Emily bent over, burying her face in both hands, elbows braced against her knees. This was clearly the crisis point. She had avoided going any further in her narrative because she didn't like where it ended up.

Kenzie was quiet, giving Emily a chance to regain her composure.

Emily swore. "I could really use a drink. Do you have anything? I need something to take the edge off."

"No. Sorry."

Emily lifted her head. "Pills? You're a doctor. You must be able to get some benzos or something, right?"

"I don't have anything. Try taking some deep breaths. Count them out, nice and long."

"I don't want to breathe," Emily muttered.

Kenzie caught Zachary's amused glance toward them. He could obviously hear some of what was being said and sympathized with Emily's irritation at being told just to breathe. Zachary probably had meds on him Emily would appreciate getting her hands on. Some nice strong anti-anxiety pills, for one thing. Zachary didn't like to take them most of the time, but they were helpful in heading off a panic attack if he took them in time.

"You're going to be okay," Kenzie reassured Emily. "Why don't you tell me what happened? Just take your time. Then we'll figure out what to do."

She sniffled and cleared her throat. "Then Deputy Donut shows up. The worst timing ever. He starts taunting Trevor and hitting on me. Saying he can take whatever he wants. You know, like he could have me too. He'd... some of the girls... you gave him what he wanted. What else were you gonna do? Get thrown in jail over some stupid, trumped-up charge? End up at the mercy of the COs and other inmates anyway? At least with Donut, it's over fast and you can go on with your life and forget about it." Emily shook her head, closing her eyes.

"So Trevor thought the cop was going to assault you?"

"I don't know. I guess so. I don't know if he would have. It seemed like what he really cared about was getting Trevor's goat. I don't know if he heard all of what Trevor was saying about him and wanted to get back at him. I just don't know what he was after."

"And then...?" Kenzie didn't want to lead Emily, but she wanted to hear the rest. This was what she had come for. And Emily wanted to get it off of her chest. Kenzie was sure Emily would not have come if she didn't want to tell her story.

"It was just... like... a standoff between them. An argument."

"Did it get physical?"

Emily shook her head. "Stupid Deputy Donut pulled a gun and pointed it at Trevor's head. Told him that if he didn't do what he was told and quit bellyaching about it, he was going to get his head blown off. Trevor laughed. He could barely stand. Looked like he was going to pass out any minute. He said Donut couldn't push him around, couldn't make him do anything he didn't want to. What was he gonna do, arrest him? For talking?"

"And what did he say about that?"

"He pulled the trigger. Just like that, no more arguing. Trevor said that he wouldn't, that he couldn't do anything, and he pulled the trigger. And..." Emily choked up. "Trev just went down."

Kenzie didn't have any trouble picturing it. She had seen the photo. Mercer lying there on the pavement with a bullet hole in his forehead. She shook her head in horror.

"How did you react? What did you do? That must have been terrifying."

"I just... I don't even know. Maybe I screamed, maybe not. I think I said something to him. Swore, tried to hit him or take the gun away. I wasn't... I didn't know what I was doing. Didn't know what to do. He kept telling me to settle down. Slapped me." Emily shook her head. "Like, maybe that works on TV, but I can tell you in real life, someone slapping me across the face just makes me want to take them on. You don't slap me."

Kenzie nodded.

"He said... he said he would take care of everything. I just had to stay quiet. If I didn't want to get popped too, I'd better keep my mouth shut. He could make both of us disappear, and people would think we had just run off together. No one would even look for us."

"So you listened to him."

"What was I supposed to do?" Emily demanded.

"You did what you had to to survive."

"He went to get... I don't know, a tarp or something. I didn't understand what he was doing. That's when I took the pictures." Emily swallowed. She looked around her as if she'd never seen the mall before, hadn't even known where she was. Eyes wide and startled to find herself there.

Kenzie supposed she had been so deep in the recollection that it was disorienting to return to the present.

"If he did something to me too... I didn't want anyone to think we had just run off together. I wanted everyone to know we were dead, not running off to New York to start over or something like that."

"So you sent the picture out to all your friends."

Emily nodded. "I wanted... I don't know what I wanted. I was just going on instinct. I got outta there. Went home to bed." She turned wondering eyes to Kenzie. "I don't know how I could just go to sleep! I shouldn't have even been able to sleep. Not after seeing that."

"People shut down after something like that," Kenzie reassured her. "It doesn't mean that you weren't upset by what happened.

Devastated. It's just your brain's way of dealing with something overwhelming. It wasn't because you didn't feel anything; it was because you felt too much. Too much emotion, danger, stress, not knowing what to do next. That's why you slept."

"I slept all weekend. Not just like... sleeping in in the morning and getting up late. But I just slept right through. I'd wake up to go to the bathroom, maybe check my messages for a minute, and then crawl back into bed and... go back to sleep again."

Kenzie nodded understandingly. "And he didn't come to your house? Did he know your name or where you lived?"

"No, I don't think so. I don't know if he even knew my name. Trev just called me Em or Babe most of the time. And I would tag with the letter M. So he wouldn't have known it was short for Emily."

"And the rest of the gang, they didn't know that either?"

"No. It was just me and Trevor. He's the reason that I..." She shrugged uncomfortably. "I got into the gang stuff with him because that was what he was into. But I wasn't in it before that."

41

Kenzie thought through the story. It would need to be verified, of course. She needed to call Sergeant Campbell and Detective Saul to tell them of the developments. They would not be happy to find out they had a dirty cop in their ranks. And not someone who had stopped at harassing the young gang members. He hadn't broken the law just by stealing drugs and guns from them. Or by coercing the girls to do what he told them to. He had murdered one of them, apparently in cold blood.

Who was he? Was he working for someone else? Was he even part of the Roxboro police department, or some other city, state, federal, or private organization? People sometimes mistakenly classified everyone who looked remotely like law enforcement as being cops when they were not. If "Deputy Donut" was not in uniform, Emily probably only knew he was a cop from what others in the gang said.

"What did this guy look like?" Kenzie asked. "Could you identify him? Do other people in the gang know his real name?"

Emily wiped her eyes. "I don't know. He was a cop. White guy, middle-aged, not some young rookie. Dark hair and eyes. I guess I'd recognize his picture." She sniffled. "I don't know his name, but some of the others might. But I don't know if I'm going back there."

"Does your mom know where you are? Are you staying with a friend?"

"I haven't told her. I'll let her know… sometime. When things have blown over."

"Where are you staying? A friend? A shelter?"

Emily shook her head. "I don't want anyone to be able to find me."

"But I'll need to be able to get ahold of you after I talk to the cops and make sure that everything is safe. If I bring you some pictures to look at, how will I find you?"

"Send them to my phone."

Kenzie supposed that having Emily's phone number gave her a way to communicate with the girl and for the police to trace her location, so she didn't push it further. She didn't want to scare Emily away. It was a big deal for her to be talking to Kenzie and knowing that Kenzie was going to go to the police when her boyfriend had been killed by a crooked cop.

"If he was working with gangs, then he was probably anti-gang unit or narco squad or something like that," she suggested to Emily.

"Yeah, I guess so. I don't know. I never asked. They knew who he was, but he wasn't any beat cop." She wiped at her nose with her sleeve. "What else would he be?"

"If he's federal, he could be DEA. Or something else."

"Long as I never have to see him again, I don't care what kind of cop he is."

Kenzie nodded. She tried putting a hand on Emily's shoulder and, this time, the girl didn't jerk away. Maybe she had become comfortable enough with Kenzie that she didn't fear her anymore. Or maybe telling the story had just left her so exhausted that she didn't have the energy to protect herself. Kenzie rubbed her back gently.

"You must be so tired. You were really brave to come here to talk to me today."

"Rhys said you're okay."

"Rhys is a pretty special guy himself. You would think that with all of his problems, he would be focused on himself, but he always seems to be watching and worrying about other people."

Emily gave a little laugh. "Yeah. Pretty amazing."

"How well do you know him?"

Emily sniffled and rolled her neck, probably stiff after sitting hunched over. "I've gone to school with him since we were little kids. But I don't really know him. Just… you know, always going to the same school, you know who people are. Especially if they're like him. You know, special needs."

"He has a lot of challenges," Kenzie acknowledged.

"I've been paired with him for group work because they mostly mainstream him. He does some resource room work but, mostly, he's in the regular classes."

"How do group projects go?"

She shook her head. "He's good at little cartoon pictures and lettering on posters. Finding pictures of stuff and research on the internet. But he doesn't write stuff out and he can't help with an oral presentation. Except, like, advance slides or use the pointer."

At least she'd been able to find things for Rhys to do. Kenzie had often wondered what things were like for Rhys at school.

She didn't imagine that everyone accommodated him quite so well. There would be those who just ignored him and didn't involve him in a project at all or who complained to their parents about being paired with him.

"So that's why you had Rhys's number? Because you'd worked with him on group collaborations before?"

Emily hesitated, then nodded. "Yeah. Because of that."

"Yeah? So you texted about what you needed to do for the project…"

She shrugged.

"Why would you send him the picture of Trevor? Didn't you know anything about his history?"

Emily blinked at Kenzie. "What do you mean?"

"You don't know what happened to him when he was little?"

Emily shook her head. "I told you I've known him since we were little. What are you talking about?"

"About his grandfather being murdered."

She continued to shake her head. "No, I don't know anything about that."

"He was shot in the head."

Emily's mouth dropped open. She stared at Kenzie. "What? Are you kidding me?"

"No joke," Kenzie said, shaking her head. "His grandfather was killed the same way as Trevor Mercer. When you sent him the picture… and he kept getting it from others as well… he was very upset about it. He ended up in the hospital for a while."

"Because of those pictures?" Emily swore and shook her head. "I never meant to do anything that would hurt him. He's a nice guy, I wouldn't do that."

"I don't imagine he was the only one upset by you broadcasting a picture of a murdered man to their phones. A lot of people would find that upsetting."

Emily was immediately defensive, her voice rising. "Well it was upsetting to me to see it and to think that Donut might make me disappear too, so excuse me for trying to make sure that someone would know the truth!"

"Why didn't you call for help? If you were afraid to call the police because of the dirty cop, why not call your mom? Or another trusted adult? A news reporter? There are better ways to get help."

Emily just looked at Kenzie and shook her head. She had no trust in adults. It shouldn't have surprised Kenzie that the only way she could think of to help herself, in the panic of the moment, had been to reach out to her friends, and that the medium had been a texted picture, their usual means of communication.

Kenzie just wished Rhys hadn't been one of the recipients.

She put up her hands to indicate that she was backing off. "I'm sorry. I guess I'm just feeling protective of Rhys. You did what you could to protect yourself. And you're still doing what you can to keep yourself safe. When you are in mortal peril, that's the only thing you can think about."

Emily pushed some of her long hair back over her ear, frowning at Kenzie. "Are you making fun of me?"

"No. I'm serious. When your life is in danger, you don't think about anyone else or about the long-term consequences of your actions. You just try to survive."

Emily didn't say anything, obviously wondering where Kenzie got this bit of wisdom. Kenzie shrugged. She didn't tell Emily anything from her personal experience. It really wasn't the time, and she didn't share those things easily.

42

Kenzie wished she didn't have somewhere to go after the meeting with Emily. She wanted to get back to Roxboro. She wanted to talk to Campbell or Saul about what she had found out; make sure they would follow up on it all and be able to identify Emily's "Deputy Donut."

But she had agreed with Lisa and Walter to come over for family dinner after the meeting with Emily. That meant it really didn't matter how tired or unsociable she felt; she still had to be at the house as she had promised.

"I don't know why they didn't pick a restaurant," Kenzie told Zachary as they wound their way down the long drive that approached the house. "It would have been easier. No cooking or catering involved. It would be a lot easier to cancel at the last minute if I didn't know she'd gone to all of the effort to do it herself."

"Maybe that's why."

"What?"

"Maybe she knew it would be harder for you to cancel at the last minute if she did the work herself."

Kenzie shook her head. "That's really devious."

"Not like your mother?"

"Totally like her," Kenzie contradicted.

Zachary laughed. Kenzie stared out the window. She should have realized herself that it was part of the plan to get her to the house and to make sure she stayed for a while to visit. If it had just been a restaurant reservation, it would have been a lot easier for Kenzie to just say that she was too tired from the day's events and go home.

The house was beautiful as they approached. Even though Kenzie hadn't been there much over the past few years, it still felt like coming home to see the bright, warm lights of the house at the end of the long drive.

"It looks like a fairy-tale castle," Zachary said.

Maybe not quite that grand, but it *was* pretty. Clean lines, lots of small lights that twinkled in the dark and lit it evenly across all of the above-ground levels. It was more of a chalet than a castle, but she could see Zachary's point. It wasn't like any place he had ever lived.

"It is pretty," she agreed. "Just park over there."

He pulled in against the curb where Kenzie pointed.

"Stay there," he told Kenzie, putting his hand on her leg for an instant. He was out of the car and quickly circled to her door before she could figure out why he had told her to stay put. He pulled the door open and offered his hand.

Kenzie took Zachary's hand, her face flushing, and stood up. He held on to her hand and they walked together to the front door. Kenzie knew her mother was probably watching out the window and would have seen Zachary's chivalrous gesture from inside. Which was why he had done it. To show them that he was a gentleman and knew how to take care of their daughter.

It was doubly impressive because he had not been raised that way. Kenzie didn't imagine any foster family training the boys to open the doors for the girls. No one would take the time for that. The girls would be expected to open the doors for themselves just like anyone else. Chivalry was not something taught in public schools, either.

The front door opened as they approached. Walter stood there, beaming at them, and ushered them inside. Lisa crossed the entrance hall to greet them, Lola walking politely at her side, not running and barking as she had the previous year. Lisa had obviously been working on her training.

"MacKenzie, my dear. It is lovely to see you," Lisa greeted, giving her a perfunctory hug and bussing both cheeks. She did the same with Zachary, who managed not to look too awkward at the greeting.

"The house looks great, Mom," Kenzie told her.

"Thank you. I hope you will enjoy your time here."

"Of course we will."

"Shall we begin with drinks?" Walter suggested, leading the way to the study, where a fire was already burning in the grate. "Have a seat. Make yourself comfortable. Wine for you, MacKenzie? As I remember, Zachary, you're not much of a drinker. Would you like to start with a cognac, or do you prefer Coke? Soda and lime?"

Zachary looked at Kenzie, his eyes questioning. Kenzie nodded. "Whatever you prefer. It doesn't matter."

"No pressure," Walter assured him. "We have a full range of beverages. If you would prefer a fruit juice, coffee, tea?"

"Well, Coke sounds good."

"I'll have a glass of wine with dinner," Kenzie said. "Just a sparkling water right now."

Walter acted as the bartender, getting everyone what they wanted. Lisa sat down on the couch with Lola at her feet, and motioned for her daughter and Zachary to sit down wherever they liked.

"Well, this is nice. We should have done this a lot earlier. How long have the two of you been seeing each other now?" Lisa asked.

Kenzie cleared her throat. "Well, it's been a couple of years, at least."

"Yes, we certainly should have done this before now. I am going to try to have something more often in the future. There's no reason we can't make time to do something as a family. We make time for everything else!"

Kenzie had to admit that, as much as she would like to say she was too busy with work and other engagements to have dinner with her family, she still had to eat, and it wasn't that much of a sacrifice to have a meal with them every few months. She shouldn't be so resistant to the idea.

"So, how is everything going?" Walter asked. "With your work? Any interesting cases for either one of you?"

"Well, neither of us can really talk about our cases," Kenzie said. "We can't give away anything confidential."

"Of course not," Walter agreed. "But there are probably still a few interesting tidbits that you could share, without any… identifying features."

"Some insurance work," Zachary said with a shrug. "Surveillance, reconstruction, checking backgrounds, that kind of thing. Skip traces. It's all pretty routine right now, nothing really big."

"But we don't really want those big cases too often," Kenzie said with a laugh. "They can be kind of stressful and take a lot of hours. Every now and then is fine!"

Zachary sipped his Coke and nodded. "Yeah, you're probably right."

"And yours, MacKenzie?" Walter prompted.

Kenzie looked at Lisa. "Uh… most people prefer that we don't discuss autopsies around dinner time. If they want to know anything about my job at all."

Lisa nodded. "I really don't think we need that kind of thing around the dinner table, Walter."

"We aren't around the dinner table yet."

"But I'd prefer we keep our appetites. Really. It's one thing for MacKenzie to choose such an… unusual line of work. I really don't think we need to discuss any of the details." She cleared her throat. "Ever."

Zachary chuckled. "It's actually one of the things that attracted me to Kenzie, Mrs. Cole Kirsch. The fact that we could discuss forensic and medical stuff over dinner or wherever. Most people don't consider it… polite."

"Oh, call me Lisa, Zachary," she corrected. "Mrs. Cole Kirsch is too much of a mouthful. Much too formal."

Zachary nodded, but didn't immediately say, "Lisa," to show that he would. It would probably take a while before he was comfortable with it, but he called Kenzie's father Walter, and he generally didn't like people calling him Mr. Goldman, so he would adjust to calling Lisa by her first name soon enough.

43

W hy don't you tell us what you're working on?" Zachary suggested, including both parents in his invitation. "You must have some good causes you are working on right now."

Kenzie's parents were always eager to discuss their work, so she was sure that wouldn't be a problem. She smiled her approval at Zachary.

"Well, yes, of course," Lisa agreed. "I'm sure Kenzie probably keeps you updated on what the foundation is doing…"

Zachary glanced over at Kenzie. "Well… I follow a little about what she and Tyrrell discuss…" Tyrrell was Zachary's younger brother, whom they had hired to help Hillary with any administrative work for the Kirsch family foundation. "But I'm afraid I'm not up-to-speed on it other than that."

Lisa arched an eyebrow and looked at Kenzie in reproof. Kenzie wondered just what information Lisa expected her to share with Zachary. She had always worked on the assumption that most of what she had to do with the foundation was confidential.

"She's probably told you we are working more with mental health causes now," Lisa suggested.

"Yes," Zachary agreed rather explosively. "Oh, yeah, I knew that.

I'm really glad to hear it. Not enough people put money into mental health, and it is so important. Despite all we have learned about mental health and resilience, we are still very slow to recognize and treat it, and there is a lot of stigma."

"You don't think we're doing better with the stigma?"

"Better, yes. But it's still there. If you had two good candidates for a job, but you knew one of them had mental health challenges, which would you go with?"

"Well, I suppose it's only natural that I would go with the one who didn't have known mental health challenges," Lisa admitted.

"Hmm."

Lisa pursed her lips. "I'm being honest. That's what you wanted, isn't it?"

"You didn't ask what challenges the other candidate might have."

"Well... no." Lisa's cheeks turned slightly pink. "But I would assume in an example like that, you would give me the challenges on both sides to compare. And then I would decide based on the known factors for both."

"Do your candidates tell you what all of their challenges are? Physical disabilities or disease? Single parenthood? Caring for aging parents? On the verge of divorce? In debt? Mobility or accessibility concerns?"

"No," Lisa admitted. "I guess everybody has some challenges that they are coping with. We don't always know what they are when we hire someone."

"But without knowing what the challenges of both candidates were, you were willing to drop one candidate just because they had a mental illness."

Lisa nodded. "I guess so. I will say we have been very happy with Tyrrell's performance. I knew when we hired him that he had a number of challenges. We were willing to put the time into training him, knowing that he might have certain... attendance or quality issues."

"He really likes the job," Kenzie said. "And I think from what Hillary has said that he's been a good asset. She's been giving him more and more responsibility."

"He has been very helpful," Lisa agreed. "And I think he's more than proven his worth. Even if we do, at some point, have to put money into rehabilitation or a temp to cover him while he gets back on his feet again... hiring him was still the right choice and worth it to the foundation. Not just as a social experiment, but really a beneficial employer-employee relationship."

Kenzie hoped that resolve would hold if Tyrrell did fall off the wagon and had to go back into rehab. It was one thing to say it as a hypothetical. It might be a different story when they faced it in real life. When they had to deal with declining work quality and it cost real money to put him through rehab and get someone to fill in for him. Then, they would see how Lisa really felt about the cost of addiction and mental health issues and the ability of employers to handle them in a constructive, supportive way.

"How is your young friend?" Walter asked, leaning forward. "The boy."

"You know his name," Kenzie said in irritation. "Why can't you call him by his name like a real person instead of calling him our young friend?"

"Oh, of course," Walter said quickly. "How is Rhys? He continues to show improvement?"

"I assume you know as well as I do, since you are still involved in funding his care."

Walter didn't look like he appreciated Kenzie's tone.

"Well, dear." He cleared his throat. "You sound upset that we are providing him financial support. I thought you would appreciate it."

"I thought you were getting out of his case and leaving him alone. Letting Vera and Rhys make the decisions about what he needed."

"We are," Lisa protested. "He isn't in Persons or in that drug therapy anymore. We told his grandmother she could put him into whatever program she thought would work best for him. It's totally her decision, not ours. We're just writing the checks."

"That's good. I just..." Kenzie shook her head. "I don't know. I don't like the foundation being involved after what happened."

"You think it would be better for us to drop our support when he needs it the most? Say that we made a mistake and he didn't respond the way we had hoped to the therapy we chose, so now we're going to dump him and they're on their own again."

"No," Kenzie admitted. "I don't want that. I know I'm being ridiculous. I don't know what it is that I expect. Of course I still want him to be funded and get treatment. Just not from the family foundation. Not after what they—we—did."

Lisa and Walter exchanged glances. "Well…" Lisa considered this. "We could look at some of our partners and the causes that we have funded and see if any of them would take on Rhys's case. There wouldn't be any change from Vera's perspective, but you would not have to worry about us being involved or you having any conflict."

"Or you knowing what was going on with him. I think it's… I don't think it's appropriate for me or my family to know anything about Rhys's mental health or treatment. Other than what he decides to tell us directly."

Zachary had another drink of his Coke. "I hadn't really thought about it like that. It makes sense, though. I see where you're coming from."

"I guess… we'll look at transitioning his funding to someone else," Lisa agreed. "If that's really what you want."

"That's how it should have been done in the first place."

44

Zachary was quiet on the way home, as was Kenzie. It had been a long day and they had worked through a lot of emotional stuff with Emily and then had the aggravation of dealing with Kenzie's parents. Not that Walter or Lisa had done anything wrong; Kenzie just found them challenging to deal with. They made her feel awkward and immature. The rest of the time—or most of the rest of the time—she felt like a competent adult. But with her parents, she always felt like she had to fight to prove herself.

She wasn't even sure what made her feel that way. Looking at her parents' behavior objectively, she couldn't identify anything they did wrong, any tone or nuance or hint that they didn't think of her as a grown-up. But she still felt small and unsure around them.

"Are *you* okay?" she asked Zachary, when they were almost home.

He startled in his seat, surprised by her sudden query.

"Yeah, yeah, I'm fine," Zachary assured her.

"Good."

Kenzie returned to her own thoughts. But after a few more miles, an alarm started to ring in her head.

"Fine?" she repeated. "Did you just tell me you're *fine?*"

It was one of their rules from therapy. No social brush-off. No saying that they were fine. Or good. The answer to "How are you feeling?" or "Are you okay?" or any similar question needed to be thought out, heartfelt, and honest.

"Uh… yeah, I guess I did."

She waited for him to amend his answer and come up with something more real. He said nothing.

"So how are you really?" Kenzie pressed. "I'm pretty tired. Feeling… kind of mentally wrung out." She hoped that her honest assessment would help him on the way.

After a few minutes of silence, Zachary spoke up. "I'm… feeling down. Nothing serious. Just… post-party crash, I think. I need time and space to process. Get out of my own head. A movie or a job or something. I'm just…" He sighed. "I don't know. Feeling a bit low."

"Did we do too much today? It was probably too much, wasn't it? I should have had dinner with my parents another day. Told them that we couldn't make it this week. It was too much to do after the meeting with Emily, and we stayed there for hours."

Kenzie looked at the time on the dashboard clock and tried to calculate how many hours they had been at her mother's house. Unlike dinners at home, which were usually a quick affair, leaving time for other evening activities, the dinner with her parents had dragged out to fill the entire evening, with pre-dinner drinks and conversation, courses served separately for dinner, and postprandial coffee and more conversation. Kenzie had felt the lack of discussion topics halfway through the pre-dinner drinks. After that, it had all been Lisa and Walter feeding her conversational topics that ranged from personal to political.

"It was all too much for one day," Kenzie repeated.

"It's fine. When we visit Mr. Peterson, it takes half a day with the driving and visiting too. And I'm happy to stay there over a weekend. We can spend a few hours with your parents. It's only fair."

"But they're not comfortable like Lorne and Pat. It's more of… an ordeal."

She thought Zachary would chuckle at this, but he just sighed. "It's fine, Kenzie. I told you, it's just my post-party crash. I would feel the same way no matter who it was. It just takes a lot of energy to stay turned on for something like that, and I feel it afterward, even when it's been a really good visit. And it was nice to see your parents. It's good for you to do things with them."

Kenzie looked for a way to argue. She wanted to protect him and his mental health. To do whatever was the best for him. She didn't like his feeling bad after a dinner that she had set up.

But then, she knew that even after a meeting with Lorne or with Joss or Tyrrell, he tended to have that low-energy dip as well. It was hard for her to understand. She did feel emotionally spent after the emotional interview with Emily and spending all night trying to please her parents and stay engaged with them. But she didn't feel that way after every interaction. She was fine after a day with the Petersons, a work meeting, or a lunch with a friend. She felt energized and up, a pleasant afterglow. For Zachary, the more excited and energized he was by a social gathering, the worse he felt in the hours following it.

"Well," she tried to keep a logical, positive tone in her response. "It's good that we could spend the time with my parents. And you just need a little recovery time. That's not the end of the world."

"No," Zachary agreed. "I'm used to it. Just need a little time."

Kenzie was still anxious about his mental state the rest of the night, but she tried to keep it to herself and to give him the space he needed to recover. He didn't need her hanging over him, nagging him to tell her how he was feeling and if he needed to take anything or arrange an additional visit with Dr. Boyle.

And even though she wanted him to take something that would help, she was still concerned when she saw him taking a sleep aid before bed, which he usually resisted. She couldn't help but be concerned that things were really bad if he was taking extra meds to get through the night.

But she forced herself to paste a smile on her face and keep her mood light and pleasant as she got ready for bed. The sleep aid would ensure he had a good night's sleep, so important to maintaining his mental health, and he would feel better in the morning.

45

K enzie called Sergeant Campbell as soon as she got into the office the next day, hoping to catch him before he got involved in meetings. But there was no answer. She considered whether to go upstairs to find him, but it would probably just be a waste of time. He wasn't likely sitting at his desk declining her call. If he didn't answer, he was already engaged with something else. She left him a brief message to get back to her ASAP.

She was eager to share the information she had gleaned from the meeting with Emily Cross. Maybe eager was not quite the right word, since she dreaded having to tell him that a dirty cop was involved in the killing and whatever other crimes he had committed in his interactions with the gang over the past few months. But he needed to know, and the case could not be solved until he had all the details.

There would still have to be an investigation. They wouldn't just take Emily at her word. She could be lying. Accusing a cop because they wanted him off the street. Because she wanted to cover for whoever had really killed Mercer. Because she had done it herself. She couldn't assume that everything Emily had said had been true. She had lied or hidden other things. She had her own agenda.

But Kenzie believed the story Emily had told. It rang true. The emotions were genuine, or else Emily was a *very* good actor.

After leaving a message for Campbell, she hung up the phone and got on with her other work. It wasn't like she didn't have anything else to do. She would leave the police case to the police and take care of her work at the medical examiner's office. The work she had been hired to do.

She had been working for a couple of hours, trying to sort out a slew of reports that had all come back from the lab at the same time. There had been a backlog of weeks on tox results, and everything had suddenly come through simultaneously. A piece of equipment that hadn't been working must have just been brought back online. Or a lab tech who had been on vacation had returned and had started to run the backlog of waiting tests.

The desk phone rang, and Kenzie picked it up without looking at it. "Medical Examiner's Office, Kenzie speaking."

"Ah, Kenzie," it was a familiar voice. "You sound like you're very busy today."

Kenzie looked away from her computer screen. "Dr. Wiltshire. How are you?"

"Well, I wish I could say I was one hundred percent and coming back in next week, but I'm afraid it will still take more time to get rehabilitated."

"It is never as quick as you want it to be, is it?" Kenzie sympathized. "I hope it will heal quickly, but you shouldn't push it too much. Make sure that you're really ready and that you're not going to set your healing back by trying to do too much too soon."

"I know. I will take care of myself and will listen to the doctors and physiotherapist."

"Good."

"I wonder if you would be free for lunch today. I know you work through lunch a lot of days, but could I convince you to take a break and eat at a table today?"

"Uh, yeah, of course. Did you want to come here?"

"I'll come to you, and then we can walk together from there."

Kenzie wondered if he suggested walking her because of what had happened the last time she had ventured out from the medical examiner's office for lunch and had been pushed into traffic. She had, luckily, not been badly injured. It could have been much worse. But that wouldn't happen again if someone were with her.

It seemed like no time had passed before Dr. Wiltshire approached her desk. She looked at the clock and saw that it was nearly noon. And she was still trying to get all the toxicology reports printed and filed.

"Oh, doctor! Good to see you." Kenzie looked for a way to take care of all the printouts quickly so she could go with him.

"You look snowed under! Are you not getting the assistance you need while I'm away?"

"No, it's just the lab. They were backed up. And now… I guess they aren't. They sent everything we've been waiting for through last night."

"Well, that's good news. Glad to hear it."

Kenzie nodded. "I'll get it cleared up today. It's just a lot of paper to deal with all at once."

He waited patiently while she cleared her desk and locked her drawers. It was a pain to do in the middle of the day, but she couldn't just leave work out on her desk.

"All right, that's it." Kenzie grabbed her jacket and they headed up to street level, discussing what restaurant to go to.

She had no idea why he wanted to have lunch with her. Was there a purpose behind it or was he just restless? When he had been working, they had rarely eaten together. Unless he brought donuts.

Maybe he was lonely and wanted to be brought in on any interesting cases she'd had recently. But she didn't think so. He must have other people that he saw socially.

He wanted a sit-down restaurant, not just a fast-food joint. They picked out an Indian restaurant with a buffet so they could serve themselves immediately, and both sat down with plates heaped with curry, fragrant rice, chutneys, and naan bread. They tasted and exclaimed over the various dishes.

"So, I'm sure you're wondering why I wanted to meet," Dr. Wiltshire said eventually.

Kenzie nodded. She hoped it was not to announce that his hand was not going to recover fully and he had to retire. If he left, would

Dr. Cook take over? Or would he only stay for the interim, and there would be yet another doctor to get used to? Another boss who would have different procedures and expectations?

"No need to look so concerned," Dr. Wiltshire quickly reassured her.

Maybe he had decided to tell her the real story behind how he had hurt his hand. There had been a lot of rumors about it. She didn't want to believe that he had been involved in anything shady or fooling around on his wife. He'd hinted that it was a golfing accident, and she was willing to believe that, as unlikely as it seemed. People could break bones in all kinds of improbable ways. He might have slammed it in a car door, or tripped over a cat, or punched a wall when he was angry. Though she didn't think it was that. From what she had seen of his bruised hand and the bits that were pinned in place by the external fixator, he hadn't sustained boxer's fractures. It looked more like a crush injury.

Dr. Wiltshire caught her eyes on his hand and the space-age-looking fixator cage around it. He raised his brows and shook his head. "It's looking better, don't you think? Now that the bruising has faded?"

"Much better," Kenzie agreed. "Is there still a lot of pain?"

"Not much, as long as it doesn't get jarred. Sleeping is getting easier. The first little while there... unless I was heavily medicated, I wasn't getting any rest at all."

She remembered how scattered, foggy, and irritable he had been whenever he had come in to review and sign documents. Between the pain, the painkillers, and no sleep, it was no wonder he'd been in such bad shape.

"But this isn't about me," Wiltshire went on. He leaned back in his chair and dabbled a piece of naan bread in his curry. "I wanted to talk to you about your position in the office."

"Oh." Kenzie's stomach plummeted. She wished she hadn't eaten so much curry already, as it threatened to make a reappearance. She gripped the table, took a deep, calming breath, and did her best to keep her voice steady. "What about it?"

46

I told you," Dr. Wiltshire touched her arm lightly. "There's no need to look so grim. Everything is fine, Kenzie."

"But you need to talk to me about my position."

He stared at her. His concerned expression changed to a twinkle. "You're not getting fired," he said with a laugh.

Kenzie took another deep breath and held it. "Suspended?" she suggested. "Flayed?"

"None of the above. Your work has been exemplary, Kenzie, especially how you have stepped up while I have been gone. I know it hasn't been easy. You've had to deal with a couple of very big, very public cases, as well as taking on new responsibilities and coping with a bigger workload. I know you have Dr. Cook now, and he is able to take up some of the slack, but that has still left you in charge of making sure that everything runs smoothly."

Kenzie nodded. She didn't demur and say that it had been nothing. It had been difficult. It was great to get the additional experience to put on her curriculum vitae, but she'd had a few sleepless nights herself and still had to be able to function during the day and to get the work done, despite any additional challenges. Dr. Cook was a professional and was willing to do whatever work Kenzie pointed him at, which was a big help once he had signed on. But there were things that she didn't want to turn over to him, and he approached his work differently from Dr. Wiltshire, causing a number of friction points.

"I have been talking to my superiors, and they are aware of… your handling of the Wade case and the exposure of what was going on at Persons, and agree that you are a professional and deserve to be recognized for your work. The work that you are doing, since it isn't going away anywhere."

"Okay. Well, that sounds good."

"It is. I told you. This isn't anything negative. You can relax."

He waited, while Kenzie demonstrated her level of relaxation by taking a deep breath and leaning back in her seat. He smiled.

"Up until now, you have been my administrative assistant, taking on an increasing role in the medical practice, learning more about performing postmortem procedures, getting as much practical experience as I could give you. You have been an assistant in the medical examiner's office, but you have not carried the title of Assistant Medical Examiner."

Kenzie held her breath. She had hoped that this would come sooner or later. Still, advancement opportunities were few and far between in a small town, and when they would come was unpredictable. They didn't follow the more regular models in the bigger cities, where one could expect a particular title or recognition after a certain length of time, provided they didn't screw things up too much.

"The Health Commissioner will announce your appointment as an Assistant Medical Examiner tomorrow." Dr. Wiltshire beamed at her.

Kenzie couldn't suppress the grin that nearly split her face in half. "That's great! Thank you. I had no idea that you were thinking of making any changes."

"Well, I know better than to promise anything the bureaucracy hasn't yet approved. It's a surefire way to get yourself in hot water when people don't get what they have been promised."

"I guess so," Kenzie agreed. She had learned more about bureaucracy and red tape in the years that she had been working at the medical examiner's office than in all the years listening to her father talking about politics and everything involved in getting a bill passed. When Walter talked about it, it was just her dad complaining about problems at the office. It was different when it was her own office that was affected.

Kenzie's phone buzzed. She glanced down at it briefly and saw that it was Sergeant Campbell. She wanted to talk to him, but their conversation would be more than a three-second exchange. She would need time and attention to cover everything with him. She sent the call to voicemail and slid the phone away again.

"Is that Zachary?" Dr. Wiltshire asked. "You'll want to tell him right away."

"I will. That was just something else. A call that is going to take quite a while, and I don't want to interrupt our conversation with it. If I'm on my lunch break, then I should enforce those boundaries, right?"

"See? You're already sounding more like an entitled professional."

They both laughed.

"Thank you for doing this, doctor. I really appreciate it. Thank you so much for your confidence and for pushing that through."

"Everybody but me will be glad that I broke my hand. Good things will come of this! I appreciate all the help you have given me since you took on this position. You have always been willing to jump in and do what needed to be done, even if it was something beneath you, like making coffee, straightening out someone else's mess, or staying late to ensure that a postmortem got done so the family could claim the body. You've been willing to take on more and more responsibility, and you have learned and progressed a lot in the time you have been with me."

Kenzie's face burned with Dr. Wiltshire's praise, but she lapped it up. She really needed to hear everything he had to say. She had been diligent, a hard worker, always pushing to be everything that Dr. Wiltshire expected her to be. And it was paying off.

"Does the change in title come with… improved compensation?" she asked tentatively.

Not that she needed the money. Even if her salary had not been enough to support her modest lifestyle, she still had a trust fund she could draw on as well. Usually, she only drew from the trust to divert money to worthy causes, not herself, but she didn't have to. She could have lived on it quite well.

"Yes," Dr. Wiltshire confirmed. "There will be an appropriate increase in compensation to go with the title. You are doing the work of two or three people, including that of the medical examiner. We can pay you the appropriate salary and still make out like bandits."

"Awesome." Kenzie was glad that not only did she get the salary she deserved for the job, but that the Department of Health did not resent the promotion and think that she should still be paid little more than a receptionist for the medical work she was doing. "That's great."

"Zachary will be proud."

"Yes, he will," she agreed. "And my parents. Though they still aren't sure what to think of me working at the medical examiner's office."

He chuckled. "Most people find it quite morbid. They don't see it like you and I do. All of our good work, the people we help, and the interesting mysteries we are involved in unraveling. What more could you want from a job?"

"Live patients, maybe. Not me; don't get me wrong, I'm not saying I want live patients. Especially not on the autopsy table. I'm saying other people think it's not really medical work if it isn't done on live patients. And that I would be happier with live patients than with dead ones."

He shook his head slowly. "Do you know how aggravating live patients are? You think it's difficult working with the next of kin around here. Just imagine what it would be like if you had to listen to the patients' complaints too. This is the quietest medical facility you will ever work at."

"I've always found our patients to be fairly easy to get along with," Kenzie agreed with a chuckle.

"We've got the best job in the world, I'm telling you."

Kenzie nodded. She decided she could afford to eat a few more bites of her curry. Her stomach was much happier now that she had heard Dr. Wiltshire's news. She was very pleased not to be fired and have to look for a new job. Especially since she would be lucky to find another medical examiner job in the state, let alone in Roxboro. The opportunities were few and far between.

47

K enzie returned to the office feeling light and buoyant rather than weighed down by her heavy meal. She and Dr. Wiltshire said their goodbyes outside the building and then she headed back down to the morgue to pick up where she left off on her filing.

She saw Dr. Cook hanging around her desk as she returned, and quickly looked at her phone to see how late she was getting back. She hadn't really been thinking about the time while she was with Dr. Wiltshire, her actual boss, and he was controlling the schedule. She could afford to take a nice leisurely lunch with her boss, who had just given her a plum promotion.

"Sorry," she said. "You were looking for me?"

Dr. Cook smiled. With his movie star good looks, he looked like an ad for dental work. "Oh, that's all right," he told her. "Did you... get any good news?"

"Oh, you knew about this, did you?" Kenzie asked with a laugh. "I thought you were going to be upset I took so long to get back."

"No, no. Honestly, you can take a long lunch whenever you want. It's your office, and I know you put in the hours, whether you take a lunch break or not. You're here late, on weekends, answering call-outs in the middle of the night. You don't need to punch the clock."

That was the way that Kenzie felt about it. Still, she hadn't been sure whether Dr. Cook would see her as lazy or trying to take advantage of Dr. Wiltshire's good graces when she took a long lunch, an afternoon off for couple's therapy, or came in late in the morning after working a call out in the middle of the night.

"Okay. Well, I'm back if you need anything." She looked at him expectantly.

"Honestly, I was only here to see if you were back yet so I could congratulate you."

Kenzie grinned. "Thank you! That's very nice."

"Now, what do you need *me* to work on this afternoon? I saw there was a whole stack of stuff that came in from the lab."

"I've got that under control for now. Speaking of tox screens, though…"

She gave him a few instructions before sitting at her desk and pulling out the lab reports to finish collating.

Kenzie tried to reach Sergeant Campbell, with no answer again, so she left him a message and went back to work. She was searching through slides in the fridge for a misfiled sample when her cell phone rang. She pulled it out to see Campbell's name.

"Hey! I've been trying to reach you."

"And I've been trying to reach you. But I've been foiled all day by meetings. You're free now?"

"Yes," Kenzie confirmed, though she continued to look through the fridge for the sample she was looking for. "Do you want to come down here, or do you want me to come up there?"

"I guess it depends on whether you have anything to show me down there."

"No. I don't have any evidence. Just… information."

"Why don't you come upstairs, then. I'll get a fresh pot of coffee going."

He wouldn't be the one to put it on; someone on his team would. Kenzie suspected that whatever coffee brewing technology they now had in the break room had outstripped the sergeant's skills.

"I'll be right up."

She checked the fridge once more, then left it. She left a note for George that she was looking for the sample, left it stuck to the fridge door, and then went upstairs to talk to Sergeant Campbell.

"Hey, I hear congratulations are in order," he said as he shook her hand in greeting.

"Did everyone know except me?"

"Probably. A promotion like this has to go through a lot of channels, to make sure everyone is on the same page. But I don't think there were too many roadblocks along the way."

Kenzie hoped not. But she thought about her suspension and a couple of warnings about conflicts of interest or other issues and had to wonder. Did all those things get wiped out now that she was being promoted?

"You don't think my... family connections are a problem?" she asked Campbell.

"I don't think so. In fact, I think your family connections were a bonus, not a deterrent."

"They're not concerned about conflicts of interest or political pressure? That I'll cave because my mother or father want me to rule a certain way?"

"That certainly hasn't been our experience in the past." Campbell chuckled. "You've been pretty determined to keep your family and your family name out of all of the medical examiner's office business."

Kenzie had. But she thought that people still perceived that she could be swayed by family pressures.

Campbell led her to an interview room where coffee service had been set up. One of the more comfortable rooms.

"All right, let's get to it. You said that you had some information to pass on to me. About the Mercer case?"

"Yes."

"You haven't found any other physical evidence on the case? Nothing else showed up in the autopsy?"

"No. But there are some tests still pending. I'm not going to change my mind about the cause and manner of death, but I might have more information to add about the state of his health before his death."

Campbell nodded and took a long sip of his coffee. "Yes. Of course. That makes sense."

"The big thing is that I managed to get into contact with Emily."

48

Sergeant Campbell raised his brows. "Emily? And she is…?"

"She was Mercer's girlfriend inside the gang."

"Ah, right. The gang girl. Wearing colors like he was. You managed to talk to her? I'm surprised she would say anything at all to you."

"Rhys managed to talk her into it."

"For someone who can't speak, that boy is awfully persuasive."

Kenzie laughed. "Yeah, you're right about that. I didn't know if he'd be able to talk her into it, but it didn't take him that long. And probably a lot fewer words than it would have taken me."

"Probably. So tell me what you managed to find out from her."

"Well…" Kenzie shifted in her seat and took a sip of the coffee. She tried to think of the best place to start. "She had some interesting things to say. The thing that I'm most concerned about is that she said the guy that shot Mercer… was a dirty cop."

Campbell scowled and shook his head. "It's not that surprising that she would suggest such a thing. She's trying to get the pressure off of herself and the other members of the gang. We knew from our investigation and your confirmation of Emily and the suspect wearing colors that he was from a gang. Being killed execution-style with a bullet to the head is not an uncommon method for some of these gangs. We're looking at the gangs as suspects, trying to figure out whether he was shot by someone in his own gang by a rival or maybe for a double-cross, or whether it was someone from the other gang. So along comes…"

"Emily."

"Along comes Emily to say that, oh no, it wasn't one of the gangs. It was a cop."

Kenzie nodded slowly. "I can see why you might be suspicious of the source, but Emily was very emotional. I know she is afraid of the killer and that he could come after her. She was very close to Mercer. She took his death pretty hard. All of this felt very… raw and real. Not made up."

Campbell sighed. He wrote down a few notes in his notepad. "Of course we will follow up on every lead, this one as well as any others we have come across. Just don't set your heart on her being right. It might have just been a story to throw the police off the trail."

"She is afraid of the police because he was the one who did it. That was why she would only agree to talk to me, not to you."

"That may be. Or it might just be because gang kids don't like to talk to cops. Does this girl have the name of the cop who is supposed to have done it?"

"No. She said that they all just called him by a nickname. So she never knew what his real name was."

"And he didn't wear a uniform. How did she know he was a cop? Did she see his ID? Did he arrest her?"

"No, she was just told by other members of the gang that he was."

"That's not particularly convincing. No name. No reliable source. That's how these investigations go, unfortunately. Everyone has plenty of gossip and speculation about what happened, but no evidence. We hear a hundred different versions of what happened, each one a little different, but no one has the evidence to go with it, and a hundred people who didn't actually see what happened, who are not witnesses…"

"But Emily saw what happened. She took the picture and sent it to her friends. We know that she saw it happen."

"We know that she was in possession of a single picture. And that she circulated it to friends for no particular reason. That doesn't mean she saw the murder take place or that she knows who did it."

"Right," Kenzie agreed. "I'm sorry. That's true. I'm assuming that she is the one who took the pictures. And the reason she circulated them to her friends was that if the killer made her disappear too, her friends would know that she and Mercer hadn't just run away together. They would at least know what had happened to him."

Campbell considered this for a minute before nodding. "That's the first explanation with the ring of truth. I really couldn't find anything else that fit, other than that kids like to circulate pictures to each other and she didn't really understand the difference between a cute meme from Facebook and an actual murder in the impact that they would have on people. She was just looking for a lot of views."

"I don't think that was it at all."

"Neither do I. Every kid understands the difference between circulating something real and circulating something funny or clever. They probably understand it better than we do. Society is changing, but they are the ones who are on the cutting edge and understand what is now socially acceptable."

"So you believe that she saw Mercer killed and thought that her own life might be in danger."

"I believe she might have forwarded the picture because she was afraid of what might happen to her. That's not quite the same thing."

"I asked her whether she would look at some photos and help us to identify the killer. There can't be that many cops who are involved with the gang. It should be pretty quick to identify him, shouldn't it?"

"Do you know what kind of crap I would get from the patrolmen's association if I showed a gang kid a lineup of cops and asked her which one killed her boyfriend? I'd be lynched. I can't do that."

"Oh." Kenzie nodded slowly. She hadn't thought about an anti-cop bias and how it would look in court if it came out that the witness had only been shown photographs of cops when trying to identify the killer. The union wasn't the only organization that would have a problem with that. "But she is willing to help."

Campbell shrugged. "We'll see what kind of help she is when push comes to shove. You think she'll come in if I call her?"

"Well, not call in here... but maybe meet with you somewhere more public. And I don't know if she has a way to get from Burlington to Roxboro reliably."

"From Burlington?"

"That's where she is right now. Or where she was yesterday when I talked to her. I think she will stay there for a while, but I can't be sure. She wasn't giving me any details about her living arrangements."

"You'd better give me her details. You have her phone number?"

Kenzie opened her phone to find the information and gave it to him.

"How about Rhys's phone?" she asked Campbell. "Was there anything else useful on it? I asked Detective Saul, and he said that your forensic IT guys were still looking at it."

"Who?"

"Detective Saul."

"And who is he?"

"He's the homicide detective that you put on the case..." Kenzie's voice faltered as she realized she had never talked to the two of them together and Campbell had never referred to Saul's part in the investigation. She had relayed the same information to each of them separately.

Sergeant Campbell shook his head, frowning. "No. There is no Detective Saul on the case."

49

Kenzie realized she was sitting with her mouth open, and closed it. She shook her head.

"How could Detective Saul not be a part of your investigative team?" she asked. "He's a homicide detective."

"No, he's not. I know of one Detective Saul, but he doesn't have anything to do with this case. I've worked with him a couple of times on other cases." Campbell pressed his lips together, thinking about it. "He's in the narcotics unit."

"Narcotics. What would he be doing on the case?"

"I've talked briefly with narcotics, following up on the gang connection, but they weren't aware of anything unusual happening. They couldn't identify Mercer from his photo. Not an active enough player. Maybe he was new to the gang."

"So maybe that's how he knew about the case. I was sure he said that you had put him on it, and he was working on finding out who Mercer was and who had started circulating the picture to the kids at the school. You put him on it."

"I didn't. He might have heard about it at a briefing, just because we put the word out about the picture and the phone, trying to get some traction on it, to see if we could identify the players involved."

"Maybe that's what he meant. But I did get the impression that he was working with you..."

"Maybe you misunderstood. Maybe he just said I was the one who had opened the case. I wouldn't necessarily be talking to him directly unless he found something worth reporting."

That soothed Kenzie's anxieties. It explained the whole setup. She had gone to Sergeant Campbell with the picture of the dead man. He had opened the phone harassment case. But since he couldn't identify the players, it was only natural that he spread the news to various other departments to see if anyone knew them. Detective Saul had figured it might be gang- or drug-related. It looked like an execution, so gangs were the obvious suspects. Of course the narcotics division, the acting anti-gang unit, would be in on it. Saul had come to Kenzie for more details, had mentioned that it was Campbell's case, and she had assumed that Saul was on Campbell's team.

An easy misunderstanding.

"Yeah, that must be it," she agreed. "So, were the forensic IT guys able to find anything on the phone that might be helpful? Rhys had other pictures of Emily. Conversations that he'd had with her. I know he deleted them, but sometimes that stuff can be restored, right? I know that Rhys wasn't telling me everything he knew. Maybe he thought that it wasn't relevant, or that he could hold it back without it affecting the investigation. Personal stuff, maybe."

Campbell shook his head. "I want to hear more about Detective Saul and his involvement."

"I've just been keeping him apprised of the investigation. He wanted to know the players, when I talked to anyone, that kind of thing. I've tried to keep both of you as up-to-date as I can on developments."

"So does he know that Emily is in Burlington?"

"Uh, no. I know he was going to try to talk to her, but her mom had said that she hadn't been home, so I warned him that he might not be able to find her."

"But you didn't tell him that you had found her."

"No," Kenzie agreed. "Not yet."

Campbell pulled out his phone and made a call, asking for Saul's phone number. Kenzie waited while he tried to reach Saul. He disconnected the call without leaving a message when he got to voicemail. He looked at Kenzie.

"Do you have a description of the cop that Emily said was involved?"

"No, it's pretty generic. White guy. Middle-aged. Dark hair and eyes." Kenzie considered the description. "But it couldn't be Saul. He's pretty young."

"Yeah, but your 'middle-aged' is coming from a teenager. Our perspectives change. That just means he was older than twenty."

"Saul couldn't have been much more than that."

Campbell chuckled. "He was thirty if he was a day. He could pass for twenty, yes. That comes in handy in narco. To you and me, he seems young. But to a kid Emily's age? She can tell he's no teenager."

"You think he's the dirty cop?" Kenzie shook her head in confusion. "I thought you didn't believe there was a dirty cop."

"I said we would have to follow up on all leads. It was probably an internal gang dispute or a rival gang, but… it bothers me that Saul would talk to you and not at least mention to me and my team that he was pursuing leads. Why didn't he keep us looped in on it?"

"Because he couldn't find Emily? He hadn't talked to her yet, so he didn't have anything to report?"

"But it would have been common courtesy for his team and mine to talk to each other. Coordinate talking to witnesses, instead of both calling the same person independently."

"He's young. Maybe he was just being a…" Kenzie searched for an appropriate moniker. "An eager beaver. A hot dog. Thinking that he had what it took to solve the case himself and be the hero."

"I won't deny that we have our fair share of hot dogs in the department," Campbell admitted. "It's possible. I just want to make sure that he is on a leash." He looked down at his phone, picked it up, and made another call. This time, it sounded like he was talking to an equal. He shot the breeze with his colleague for a few minutes before turning to the question he wanted answered.

"Your young Detective Saul. Is he around?"

Campbell was silent while he waited for the answer.

"Yeah, I already tried his number. No answer. I was hoping you knew where he was."

Another silence. "Yeah. Tell me, was he interested in this homicide that we picked up? The dead guy on the phone. You know, the one I opened up." Campbell frowned at the reply. "No? He didn't mention anything about it to you? He's been talking to the medical examiner's office about it. Implied that he knew some of the players."

It was difficult to follow everything that was being said from only hearing Campbell's side of the conversation. But the gist was clear. Saul's sergeant hadn't known of his interest in the case.

"You guys know the players in the gangs. You didn't recognize the guy in the phone picture? We identified him as Trevor Mercer." He listened for a moment. "Yeah. Small time, just moved here recently. Foot soldier, if he had any responsibility. He had a girlfriend in the gang too…"

Kenzie shook her head. "He was the one who brought her in, so she had even less experience with them."

"Oh." Campbell relayed this information to the other cop. "Never mind, she was an even smaller fish than he was. Totally inexperienced."

Campbell hit the speaker button and laid his phone on the table.

"So, what's the deal?" the sergeant on the other end inquired. "Have you got a beef with Saul? If he's been trying to help with the case, I'm not sure what you're calling about. Leave him a message and coordinate with him."

"Our witness says that there was a cop involved in the death," Campbell explained reluctantly. "I don't have any evidence that is true. But Saul talking to the medical examiner and being involved in this without me knowing about it is a little unusual. And without telling you about it, either. I'd understand if he just wanted the limelight, wanted to be a big hero here. But he's not even talking to you about it?"

"What do you mean there was a cop involved in the death?" the gravelly voice of the other sergeant was cautious.

"Mercer was supposedly killed by a dirty cop."

"Where are you getting this?"

"It's the first I've heard of it, so I'm making inquiries. I'm not accusing Saul or anyone else. The witness could be covering up her own guilt here. But Saul has been making inquiries and getting information from the medical examiner and elsewhere. I would like to talk to him."

"Well, I would too," the narcotics sergeant answered. "I don't want my men going rogue or pursuing other cases without me knowing about it. I'll get ahold of him and get back to you."

"Okay. Appreciate that. Thanks."

Kenzie sat back in her chair, thinking this all through. It was a lot to take in at once. She had come up to talk to Campbell, believing that she had some additional information that would need to be investigated, not sure whether to believe Emily's story of there being a cop involved or not. She wanted to believe that, if it was a cop, it was someone from a state or federal agency, not one of the locals.

Zachary had been involved in a couple of cases in the past that included police corruption, and it was difficult to know how to proceed. It wouldn't help anyone for Kenzie to withhold all of the information she had from the local police department. That gave them no chance of solving Mercer's death. But if there was police corruption involved, then she needed to be careful not only of officers whose behavior was suspect—like Saul, who had professed to be investigating the case under Campbell's auspices— but also those who might be aware of what was going on and had looked the other direction. Or who had profited from the corruption. Or who had gotten involved themselves. Being able to identify one dirty cop was not the end of it. The corruption could run deep.

Or it might be just one rogue cop.

50

So, where do we go from here?" Kenzie asked Sergeant Campbell. "I mean... I don't have anything else to tell you, but now I'm really worried. Saul knows who I am. What if he comes back to me for more information? What if he follows me to see if I'm in contact with Emily? Or follows Rhys?"

"Don't jump to conclusions, first of all. There is no proof that he has done anything illegal or inappropriate. He might just have been interested in what he heard on the case and looked into it on his own time. And if he was the cop who killed Mercer... there is still no reason to believe he is a danger to you or anyone else. You don't know what might have transpired between him and Mercer. But he hasn't shown any inclination to harm you or Emily or anyone else in the case. You haven't felt threatened by him in any way before this?"

"No, not at all." He had come down to see her in the morgue, but had not given her any reason to fear him. He had acted like a cop. Like any other cop she had met. Just gathering evidence, finding out what the autopsy had shown, listening to what witnesses had to say. Nothing had seemed the slightest bit out of character.

"Take the usual precautions. Keep your car in the parking garage. Make sure you aren't followed home. Vary your routes, keep an eye on the rearview mirror and spot-check what cars are visible throughout your trip. Don't go anywhere you wouldn't want him to follow you."

"What about when I'm at home? We have a security system, but..."

"You're usually with Zachary. Two sets of eyes plus a robust electronic system hardwired to a professional security company are pretty good measures. Keep it armed and stay aware."

Kenzie nodded. She thought about getting out of her car and walking to the house and her heart started pounding hard and fast. That was a weak point. When she was in her car, she had a layer of protection between herself and any outside parties. She could keep the doors locked. She could drive away. She could ram her way through human obstacles. And once in the house, she had several layers of protection. She knew it took the security company only two or three minutes to get armed guards to the house. The system had been tested before.

But when she got out of the car, she was vulnerable. Anyone could drive up, jump out of a van, grab her, and carry her off.

"Kenzie, are you okay?" Campbell asked in concern. "Can I get you something...? A glass of water...?"

She breathed heavily, feeling again the hands closing around her, throwing her in the back of the van. She felt her head hitting the floor, pain blossoming from the impact point.

The terror of not knowing what was going to happen to her. They had her under their complete control. They could take her anywhere, do anything.

Sergeant Campbell got up from the table and returned a moment later with a cold glass of water, which he put on the table in front of Kenzie.

"Put your head between your knees," he suggested to Kenzie, placing a hand on her back. "Are you feeling faint?"

"No... no, just..." Kenzie puffed, unable to find the words to even begin to describe what she was feeling.

"You're hyperventilating. You'll make yourself pass out. Have a drink. Count out your breaths."

Kenzie grasped the cold glass, but couldn't drink. She was too nauseated. Breathing too fast. She wasn't in control of her own body anymore.

"Zachary."

Campbell reached out and pushed the button on Kenzie's phone and held it down. "Call Zachary," he instructed.

The computer voice answered and the ringing tone sounded. After a couple of rings, Zachary picked it up.

"Hey, Kenzie."

"This is Campbell," the sergeant announced. "I'm with Kenzie and she's having a little trouble. Can you talk her through this? Tell me what to do?"

"Kenzie?" Zachary's voice was worried. "What's going on?"

Kenzie breathed hard, unable to answer coherently. Campbell's other hand was still on her back, pressing firmly as if trying to hold her in place.

"She's hyperventilating," Campbell relayed. "Does she have panic attacks?"

"She was kidnapped," Zachary told him. "Kenz, how about anchoring? Can you tell me five things you see?"

Kenzie tried to slow her breathing down enough to speak. "Campbell... table... chairs..." She gulped and hiccuped. "Coffee. Water."

"Good. Five things you hear."

"You. Phone." Kenzie tilted her head and tried to interpret the outside noises she could make out through the closed conference room door. "Voices. Ringing phone. Photocopier."

"You said phone twice," Zachary said in a slightly teasing tone.

"I think she meant two different phones," Campbell said helpfully.

"What can you smell?" Zachary prompted.

Each prompt got progressively harder to answer, but they slowed things down and made Kenzie concentrate on something other than the thoughts that had originally triggered her, which she didn't want to return to.

"Deodorant," Kenzie said, her body's rising heat and sweat triggering the scent of her own protection. "Sweat. Laundry soap. Dust."

"How are you doing?"

She took a deeper breath. "Okay."

"Okay?" he repeated. "You don't sound okay. What happened?"

"Don't really want to think about it," Kenzie said, "and trigger another reaction."

"Okay. You and Campbell are together? How's it going, Joshua?"

"Kenzie and I have just been discussing this Mercer case," Campbell informed him. "You're aware of the broad strokes?"

"Yeah."

"You know that Kenzie's witness, Emily, says that there was a dirty cop involved?"

"Yeah. I was going to look into that some more. See if I could help identify who it was if there really was a cop. She could be covering for herself or someone else she knows."

"There's a slight possibility that it might be Detective Saul, a cop who has been talking with Kenzie about the case."

"Detective Saul. Really? I thought he was one of yours."

"He is *not* one of mine. I have talked to his commanding officer, and they will have him in to try to sort this whole thing out. Why he was investigating, what he knows, if he has an alibi for the night Mercer was killed."

"Okay. Good. Sounds like you're on top of it."

"But there are security concerns. Kenzie has concerns."

"Yeah. Of course," Zachary agreed. "How are you doing, Kenzie? Still breathing?"

Kenzie forced herself to keep her breathing slow and steady. "Yeah."

"Uh… why don't I invite Mario over for dinner and to watch the game tonight?" Zachary suggested. "He can tail you home. We'll all be watching. Three sets of eyes. We'll keep you safe."

Kenzie concentrated on the image of Zachary and tubby Mario Bowman walking her up the sidewalk from her car to the house.

Only she wouldn't be parked at the curb. That was silly. She would be parked in her own garage. Safe from the view of any outside parties. A big garage door to keep them out. A locked door between the garage and the house to keep everything secure. All doors monitored and alarmed. She wouldn't be in parked at the curb like before.

"Yeah," she agreed. "That sounds good."

"Okay. I'll give him a call. Are you going to stay with Campbell for now? When are you going to come home?"

Kenzie ran her hands over her face, massaging tension points that were suddenly pulsing with pain. She was exhausted. "I don't know. Give me a while to decide."

"Sure. If you're not up to driving, I can Uber over and drive you home in your car. Or I can pick you up in mine and just leave yours in the parking garage for the night."

"Don't know yet."

"Or you could leave yours in the garage and drive home with Mario."

"Maybe."

"Okay. Do you want to stay on the line, or do you want to call me later when you've had some time?"

"I'll call."

"I always want to sleep after a panic attack," Zachary told her. "It's okay if you want to go to sleep. Grab the couch there or come home early."

"Thanks. Okay. Yeah."

Zachary made a kissing noise. "Call me, Kenz, when you're ready."

"Okay." Kenzie tapped the red button to end the call. She sat there looking at the phone, breathing, counting her breaths, in and out, slowly.

Campbell removed his warm hand from her back and sat down close to her.

"You were kidnapped? No wonder you're panicking. I'm sorry, I didn't know that."

"No. Didn't tell anyone. Even Zachary." She blew out her breath. "For months."

"Good grief. How did he not know?"

"He was in the hospital. It was only for a few hours."

"Well, you've got every right to be concerned about your security.

I'll talk to the patrols in your area about rolling by your house regularly."

"You don't need to… especially if Mario is going to come by."

"I'll see what I can do. You stay here while I make a few calls."

"I could go back downstairs. Do some work."

"You could," he admitted. "But you'd just end up having to redo it again later."

Kenzie gave a short laugh. He was probably right about that.

She felt guilty about not going straight back down to the morgue to continue her work. She had already taken time out for lunch.

"I'm getting a promotion," she told Campbell.

"Yeah. I know."

"Did we already talk about it?"

"Briefly."

"Oh, yeah."

51

Maybe it should have bothered Kenzie that Zachary and Mario Bowman seemed to be taking it in turns to walk around the interior of the house, looking out through all of the windows, checking the settings on the security system and making sure that the outdoor cameras were still functioning as they should. It should have made her anxious to have them acting so restless and wary.

But she wasn't anxious. She felt like an animal tucked safely in its den. Warm and cozy and well-protected. No predators could get in. She could rest easy. She looked back at her panic attack of earlier in the day, rolled her eyes, and laughed at herself for breaking down. Yes, she had been through something awful. One time. It had been over in a few hours, and she had not been mistreated while they had held her. The injury to her head had been accidental. They didn't hit her or even put her in handcuffs. They shut her in a room with a bed, didn't abuse or threaten her, and fed her delicious, nourishing soup.

She had refused therapy for the trauma, but she had discussed the incident in couple's therapy a few times as the experience had impacted her relationship with Zachary. She felt that she had put it behind her now. It had just been a fluke that thinking about her security when she got home had triggered panic. Normally, she was just fine with it.

As fine as she could be.

That didn't mean that she was totally over the nightmares. Or that she could talk about kidnapping as if it weren't something that struck her deeply. But she could function on a day-to-day basis and not spend all of her time thinking about it. She wasn't disabled by it. Zachary's experiences had been much worse and he had been able to get through being triggered by fire. Exposure was the key. Not avoidance.

But that didn't mean she needed to talk and think about it all the time. Kenzie pushed the thoughts away and tried to concentrate on the show that Zachary had put on. A silly heist movie, filled with spy gear and car chases, witty repartee, and double entendres. Just the kind of thing they all needed to put the kidnapping and Mercer's murder out of their minds for a while.

It wasn't Saul. Kenzie was sure it wasn't Saul.

He wouldn't have been so bold, coming to talk to her repeatedly, getting all the details he could about the investigation. Getting Emily Chase's name and information about what she had done. Kenzie telling him about Rhys and his disabilities. If he had been the one who had killed Mercer, he would have left town immediately. Or at least as soon as they started to gather more information about what had happened. When Mercer's body was discovered. If he had been the killer, he would have left town at that point.

He wouldn't have just kept visiting Kenzie and pretending to be on the case.

Kenzie wasn't sure when she fell asleep. It wasn't a typical night. She was tired from the panic attack. Zachary had been right about that. He had said that he just wanted to sleep after an attack, and Kenzie felt the same way, but she resisted it. She wanted to show someone— herself or Zachary, or maybe Mario, she wasn't sure which—that she was stronger than that. That she could just bounce back.

Even if she was weak enough to succumb to a panic attack, she was strong enough to carry on afterward. Like Superwoman.

Zachary had promised Mario that they would watch the game together. However, Zachary had probably had to look up what game was playing, since he wasn't at all into sports. So after the heist movie, they had put the game—football—on the TV, and had watched it together, between shifts pacing around the house and looking out the windows. Kenzie sat on the couch and pretended to read a book, turning the page every now and then. But she really had no idea of the words on the page. She was just glad to be there, safe and sound, protected by the security system on the outside and the units that would respond to it, and her partner and a cop on the inside.

She didn't think that she had fallen asleep on the couch. Zachary wouldn't have been able to carry her to her bed. Mario, though a bigger man, was considerably out of shape and probably wouldn't carry anything bigger than a pizza to bed. So she must have gotten there under her own power, but she couldn't remember doing so.

"Zachary?"

"I'm here."

She heard the rustle of sheets as he stirred beside her, the soft click of his putting his computer or phone on the bedside table. Then he was cuddling up against her, putting his arms around her.

"Are you okay?" he murmured in her ear. "You're safe here."

"I know. I just wondered where you were."

"I'm not going anywhere."

"What time is it? You should go to bed."

"I am in bed," he pointed out.

"You should go to sleep," Kenzie clarified. Though of course, he knew exactly what she meant. "You need to get your sleep, too."

"Too early for me to go to sleep."

She couldn't stir herself enough to check the time. She must have dropped off early. Nine o'clock, maybe. It was dark outside, but Zachary would never go to bed that early.

"Soon," she told him. "Don't stay up too late."

"Okay."

He stayed there like that, with his arms around her, just breathing in her ear, until she fell asleep again.

Kenzie didn't know how much later it was when she heard Zachary moving around and distant voices again. She rubbed her eyes and looked at the window to verify that it was still nighttime, and no light was creeping in around the blinds. Her body told her that it was late at night. Or very early in the morning. Maybe Zachary was seeing Mario off. She had thought that he would spend the night on the couch, just to reassure Kenzie that everything was okay, but maybe he had decided that it wasn't worth wrecking his back over.

They had a spare room. He could sleep in there. But then he wouldn't be near any of the ingress or egress points, which made it a silly place to station a guard.

"Zachary?" Kenzie called softly. "Is Mario leaving?"

She would tell him to tell Mario goodbye for her. And thank you for coming when she called him, regardless of how ridiculous it was to need an out-of-shape policeman eating chips in front of the TV while she slept.

A dark form paused in the bedroom doorway. Zachary.

"No, Mario is staying the night."

"Aren't you going to sleep? I thought you were coming to bed with me."

"I was just answering the phone. Go back to sleep."

"Is everything okay?" Kenzie rubbed her eyes. Who was calling in the middle of the night? Sergeant Campbell checking in on her? The security company providing a report that they had driven by and everything looked clear? Someone else that Zachary had touched base with in an effort to improve the security of the house?

"Go back to sleep. We can talk in the morning."

But something told Kenzie that everything was not well.

"What is it? What's wrong?"

Zachary didn't answer for a moment. Kenzie's body wanted to go back to sleep, but her brain kicked into high gear at Zachary's silence.

She reached over and turned on the bedside lamp to illuminate him and keep herself from falling back asleep again before he could tell her.

"Zachary?"

She could see, squinting at him in the warm lamplight, that his expression was grave.

"It's Rhys."

52

"Rhys?" Kenzie's heart raced.

She had been so worried about protecting herself, making sure that Saul couldn't come back after her, that she hadn't thought about the others who might need protection.

Rhys.

He didn't have a state-of-the-art home security system protecting him, with armed guards just minutes away. He didn't have Zachary. Or Mario with his gun. All Rhys had was an aging grandmother who took sleeping pills at night and didn't even notice when he decided to take off on his own.

Kenzie slid her feet over the side of the bed. She was still wearing the yoga pants she had put on to relax before bed and hadn't changed into her jammies. Not that there was any difference other than the appropriateness of each in Kenzie's mind for their utility.

"What happened to Rhys? Is he okay?"

"We don't know." Zachary licked his lips and swallowed. "Nobody knows anything yet, except that he isn't home."

"Vera called?"

"Yes."

"He might just be out for a walk. Taking off to visit with someone, like he's done before."

"Exactly. We know he doesn't always stay home in bed like he is supposed to."

The last time, he had been in a fugue state, wandering near Stanley Green's house. Not a good place for a young, vulnerable teen.

"Has she called Stanley?"

"Yeah. He's gone out to drive around, see if he can see Rhys anywhere. I turned the lights on outside," Zachary nodded to the front of the house. "And I called Tyrrell to give him a heads-up."

Tyrrell lived in Zachary's old apartment, which Rhys had been to before and could conceivably show up at if he were in a confused state.

"What else? Has she called the police?"

"Yes. They know that he is a vulnerable individual and have opened a file. They're starting with the basics. Searching the neighborhood in case he's just wandered off. Asking about acquaintances, if they'd had a fight, all that kind of thing."

"Asking whether he's a witness in a murder case?" Kenzie asked.

"They've been filled in on what we know. Campbell's already been contacted."

"What about the other cop he called? Saul's commanding officer? Have they found Saul?"

"No. He's still not answering. He's not at home. Hasn't reported in for his shift at work."

"He was supposed to be there?"

Zachary nodded. "But he just didn't show up."

Kenzie's heart was pounding. "What if he has Rhys?"

Zachary swallowed strenuously and nodded. "That is being considered."

"Why didn't you wake me up? You should have!"

"There wasn't anything you could do that we weren't already doing. You might as well get your sleep. Be well-rested in the morning. See if you can notice anything with fresh eyes that we might have missed."

"What about tracing Rhys's cell phone?"

"It's turned off."

"Then he didn't just wander away."

"I don't think so. It's possible that he took it with him and he just ran out of juice. Forgot to plug it in at the end of the day, or it wasn't properly connected. I've had a time or two when I plugged my phone in before going to bed and then woke up in the morning and it was dead. Because it wasn't plugged in the right way or the cord was faulty."

"Well, yes. It could happen. But most of us are pretty careful to make sure that it doesn't. And Rhys relies on his phone for communication. He's going to make sure that it doesn't run out of juice."

"Mistakes happen. Technology fails."

But it was a brand-new phone.

Kenzie stood up. "Is there anyone else here? Is it just you and Mario?"

"Yes. Just us. Campbell stopped by for a few minutes to check in on things, but he's gone over to Vera's."

"I should go over there. Sit with her."

"Are you sure you want to go out? I thought... you would want to stick around here."

"Because I'm afraid? It's obvious that Saul decided Rhys was the most vulnerable and went after him. He's in the wind now. He's not coming after me. He got everything he could from me before I realized what was happening. He's not coming over here."

Zachary looked at her for a minute, then nodded.

"Let me grab my purse and splash some water on my face, and then we can go," Kenzie told him.

53

R hys kept his head down, chin to chest, pretending he had fallen asleep. People thought that he was stupid. That he couldn't understand what was going on. He learned a lot by just keeping his head down and pretending not to hear anything.

The bad cop drove into the darkness, his headlights dim on the country road. Just his running lights on. Hardly enough to make out the shape of the road ahead. Because he didn't want to attract the attention of anyone who might live nearby, Rhys assumed. Though it was hard to believe that anyone lived out there in the trees. Maybe some farmers or hunters.

Rhys shifted, flexing his wrists, pushing outward on the bonds that held him. He looked up at the sky and wondered if, had he known his constellations better, he would be able to tell where he was by the stars in the sky. As it was, he only knew the big and little dipper and the north star, though he was never actually sure which one was the north star. Venus was brighter, and he always thought he should be able to follow the morning star instead of the north star to get where he wanted to go.

But being a city kid, he wasn't navigating anything by the stars.

They pulled off of the gravel that wasn't really a road anymore, into the trees. Rhys thought they were going to run directly into one of the trees. Maybe the bad cop had fallen asleep and gone off the road by accident. But he stopped before he hit the trees. He punched Rhys in the arm.

"Wake up, kid."

Rhys raised his head. The bad cop shoved him into the door. "Get out."

He felt for the door handle, but it wasn't in the same place as in Grandma's car, and he couldn't find it in the dark. The cop reached across him and found it, clicked it open, and pushed the door, giving Rhys another shove to encourage him to get out of the car.

He considered running into the trees. It was the one time he was out of the cop's reach. He could probably outrun the cop in a few minutes. He was a fast runner and the cop looked soft and slow. Em said he took drugs, which meant his body was in bad shape. Maybe he even had heart damage.

It would serve him right if he had a heart attack chasing Rhys.

But Rhys was still in handcuffs, and he didn't know where he was or where to find people or to run to. He could run into a river or off a cliff. Or just into a nest of poisonous snakes. There could be other people out there that were working with the bad cop. And the cop was armed. Rhys couldn't outrun a bullet. If the cop got a good shot at him… Rhys knew how it turned out on TV. Down he would go, and no one would ever find him out here in the wilderness. Grandma would never even know what had happened to him. Maybe she would think that he had run away. That he didn't love her and want to stay with her anymore.

He didn't want her to die thinking he had run away from her.

As much as he wanted to be grown up and have a place of his own and be independent of all of the people who told him what to do or thought they knew what was best for him better than he did himself, he didn't want that.

By the time he had finished thinking through whether or not to run, it was too late. The moment had passed. The bad cop was around the car and grabbed him by the arm. Rhys resisted initially, but the cop was strong despite his drug use, and Rhys knew that he wouldn't win anything in a fight. Especially not against an armed man. He just wanted the cop to know that he wasn't going easily. He wasn't beaten.

Rhys couldn't see ahead of him as the cop led him into the trees. Was this it? The cop had brought him out here just to kill him and leave his body there to rot? Was the only reason he had left Rhys alive because it was easier to get Rhys somewhere walking under his own power than it was to transport a dead body?

"Keep walking," the cop growled, holding on to him, but forcing Rhys to walk a little ahead of himself. Rhys stumbled, unable to see where to put his feet. The ground was uneven with rocks, roots, and branches under his feet that threatened to trip him and make him fall on his face.

But the cop didn't push him faster than he could go. As Rhys's eyes adjusted to the dark, he saw a building through the trees. Not a big house, but bigger than the fishing shack Rhys and his mother had gone to when she had been on the run. Rhys assumed that was where the bad cop wanted him to go, and aimed his steps toward the front door of the cabin. This seemed to suit bad cop, since he didn't growl at him again, and was patient as Rhys's feet found their way through the invisible obstacles.

"Nice to have a hostage who doesn't talk back, for once," the bad cop said, and laughed. The noise was harsh in the silence of the woods. Rhys wondered. How many other people had he brought out here? And what had happened to them? Had they left under their own power, or were their bodies still out here, buried in shallow graves somewhere beyond the house?

He wished he had the power to say something smart to bad cop, like an action movie hero. They always had something quick and clever on their lips. They didn't struggle to put together language like Rhys did, and then to push the words out of his mouth and throat.

A mute action hero. Now that would be something.

It would never work. How would anyone know how smart he was? How he felt about things? How would they know the difference between when he was being quiet because he didn't want to give away his thoughts and when he was being quiet because he couldn't get out the thoughts he wanted to share? How would they know whether his smile was genuine or hiding pain? He wouldn't be able to get the girl. He wouldn't even be able to finish training with whatever law enforcement agency initially hired him. He couldn't go rogue if he were never hired in the first place.

The cabin loomed up ahead of him. It was actually bigger than he had thought. It was hard to tell at night from a distance. He stopped walking, and the cop pushed him forward again, one hand still firmly on his arm. Right up to the door, where Rhys stopped again. Was someone going to let them in? How many people did bad cop have helping him?

But the cop didn't knock or ring the doorbell. He jingled keys as he juggled them out of his pocket and found the one he needed, then pushed Rhys to the side slightly in order to unlock two locks. He opened the door and pushed Rhys ahead of him into the pitch-black room. Rhys's toe caught on the lip of the doorframe and he yelped a little as he tripped and then recovered his balance.

The cop reached around the doorframe and found a switch. He flipped it on, and the room was suddenly flooded with light. Rhys squinted and his eyes teared up before they adjusted to the new environment.

There were not a lot of lights, but it still seemed painfully bright. And it would be visible to neighbors or anyone traveling down the road they had driven in on. Did the cop want to give away their location? Did he not care? Maybe there were no neighbors close enough to care about it. Maybe no one else used the road.

How was anyone going to find Rhys? He was still trying to figure out how he would get in touch with Zachary or Kenzie to tell them where he was. His phone had GPS on it. He could send them coordinates. But to do that, he had to be able to get his phone out and find a way to send them a message without the cop knowing about it. It wasn't going to be as easy as it had been when he was with his mother.

And it had almost been too late by the time he had managed to communicate his location then.

54

The trip to Vera's house had never taken so long. Kenzie refused to look at the speedometer as Zachary drove. She knew that he would speed. And he wouldn't get caught; he never did. He would have made a good race car driver, and at night there was little traffic on the roads.

So how could it take so long to get there?

Kenzie resisted the urge to look at the time on the radio or on her phone. It didn't take long to get to Vera's house. Roxboro was not the big city.

Finally, they pulled up to the Salter house. Or a few houses down from it, as there were police vehicles and other dark, nondescript vehicles parked in front of it. It wasn't like the scene when Bridget's twins had been kidnapped. That had happened out in the open and the police knew from the start that it had been an abduction rather than just a kid sneaking out at night. In Rhys's case, they were probably still trying to keep it from attracting too much attention. No point in attracting the attention of all of the neighbors if Rhys had just left on his own, without any coercion, and not as the result of a psychological break. The lights on the police vehicles had been turned off, and there was not a crowd of cops and technicians outside, setting up bright lights and stringing crime scene tape.

Zachary and Kenzie both got out of the car quickly. There was no waiting for Zachary to open the car door for her today. They didn't exactly sprint up the sidewalk, but it was definitely a fast walk.

There was a cop just inside the front door trying to keep control of the scene. He put a hand out to stop Zachary and Kenzie.

"Hold on. Names and roles, please."

"Zachary Goldman and Kenzie Kirsch," Zachary informed him. "Friends of the family. We're here to help."

"Sorry, you're going to have to talk to the family later. It's vital that we get the police investigation off the ground as quickly as possible."

"Ask Sergeant Campbell."

The cop looked surprised at Zachary knowing the name of one of the ranking officials there. "Wait here, please."

He motioned to another cop across the living room to keep an eye on them, and retreated to the hallway that led to the bedrooms, where Vera and Campbell apparently were.

Zachary jiggled impatiently and Kenzie found it difficult not to do the same. She wanted to talk to Campbell. To give Vera a hug and reassure her that everything would work out okay. She wanted to reassure herself that everything would be okay. When Rhys had disappeared the last time, he had been in very bad shape mentally. Had something else happened to trigger him? Had he been released from the hospital too early? Or was it actually an abduction? She hated not knowing.

After what seemed like a long time, the cop returned and motioned for Zachary and Kenzie to enter.

"Sorry. We don't want the place to be overrun," he explained.

"Of course not," Zachary agreed. "Do you want us to wait out here or can we go back and see the bedroom?" His eyes were bright as he looked around the room, taking everything in.

Kenzie imagined that if she were looking over a body or deeply involved in an autopsy, Zachary would see the same kind of calculation in her eyes as she saw in his. While she could see everything he could see around the room, she wasn't thinking everything through the same way he was. His brain was working through all of the scenarios, he was looking for every little thing that was out of place or might give him some clue as to what had happened that night. A voluntary disappearance? Rhys going out to meet another teen? That was the best-case scenario. If he were somewhere nearby, at a friend's house or some meeting place.

"Come on back," Campbell told Zachary, appearing in the hallway behind the officer.

Zachary and Kenzie headed for the bedroom. Kenzie hung back. There were already too many people in the room. It was crowded with Vera, Campbell, Zachary, and a couple of crime scene investigators looking for any evidence that would help them figure out what had happened.

"Zachary! Thank you for coming," Vera told him, moving forward for a hug.

Zachary nodded, giving her a squeeze and letting her go. Kenzie remembered how it had been when Gloria had disappeared with Rhys. Vera had been on the wrong medications and had been confused and muddled, not sure what was happening. It might have been kinder when she didn't know what was going on. The fear and anxiety in her eyes now was painful to see.

"I'm so sorry," Kenzie told her. Vera left the bedroom to hug Kenzie in the hallway. Her grip was tight.

"We will find him," Vera said fiercely. "I know we will find him! After all that boy has been through in his life, this will not be the end."

Kenzie tried to swallow a lump in her throat. Vera's strength made her feel weak and vulnerable. "What do you think happened?"

"I don't know." Vera's eyes were dry. Her gaze was direct and unwavering. "We are going to find out."

"What do you know so far?" Zachary asked, seemingly of the room in general.

"Not much yet," Campbell said. "Vera got up to check on Rhys and make sure that he was settled for the night. He wasn't there. When she checked the rest of the house, she found that his shoes, coat, and phone are gone. The front door was left unlocked. He did not take keys or a wallet with him."

Kenzie frowned, trying to puzzle that through. "Well, that doesn't sound like a kid who's taken off to meet friends or go to a party somewhere. If he was going out to something he didn't want Vera to know about, he would have taken keys with him to lock up and let himself back in again."

Vera was still holding on to Kenzie's arm tightly. "Yes, I agree," she confirmed.

"Why did you get up to check on him?" Zachary asked.

"He hasn't been sleeping soundly since his breakdown. I like to look in and make sure that he's okay. If he's restless or having nightmares, I'll sit up with him for a while. And of course... he just left that night without me knowing it, and I didn't want that to happen again. I wanted to know if he left the house, even if it was just because he didn't want me to know he was sneaking out."

She released Kenzie's arm and massaged the knuckles on each hand. Kenzie didn't know if that was because they were hurting her or if it was a nervous gesture.

"Sometimes kids sneak out," Vera went on. "If that's what he needed to do... then fine. He could sneak out, as long as I knew about it."

Kenzie smiled and shook her head at this. "Then it's not exactly sneaking, is it?"

"If he doesn't tell me, it's still sneaking. If I don't tell him that I know about it, then he thinks he's gotten away with something and he feels stronger and more independent. And..." Vera gave Kenzie a sly look out of the corner of her eye, "I can use his guilt over sneaking out to make him do other things for me."

Kenzie couldn't help laughing, despite the seriousness of the situation. "You are very devious," she told Vera.

"I've raised two girls. Now, girls and boys may not be the same, but they all need a chance to spread their wings. And to have rules and structure the rest of the time."

Kenzie nodded at her wisdom. "I wonder if my parents knew about things I was doing and just never told me."

"You can be sure they did. Not everything, maybe, but parents know. It's best to just keep quiet about it until you need to use it. And even then… you don't mention it directly. Just say that you're so glad that they are willing to help you and don't sneak around like your friend's child or grandchild."

"That sounds very well-thought-out."

"If he didn't take his keys and wallet with him, then he didn't leave of his own free will," Zachary said, bringing them back to the important point.

"But that doesn't mean he was forced," Kenzie said. "If he was sleepwalking or in a fugue, then he could easily have left things that he would need at home."

"What about video?" Zachary asked. "You don't have a doorbell camera. Do any of your neighbors?"

Vera motioned to Campbell. "I think he is already looking into that."

Sergeant Campbell nodded. "Yes. We are canvassing. Just eyeballing each house right now, we'll start ringing doorbells on houses that have cameras at a more decent hour."

"You're putting neighbors' sleep above Rhys's safety?" Zachary challenged.

"It doesn't help us if people are angry at being woken up and tell us that the video is not recorded anywhere, and it is. Then we've just shot ourselves in the foot and lost a potentially rich source of information because we didn't respect the neighbors' sleep."

Zachary frowned. He didn't like this answer, but didn't seem to have an argument against it. If people told the police that they didn't have a recording, they couldn't exactly demand it. They couldn't say anyone was impeding an investigation. There would be no way to prove whether or not they were telling the truth. The cops would just be out the footage that they could have offered. Having to wait a few hours was a risk, but Campbell was trying to weigh each risk carefully.

"Of course, if people are looking out their windows to see what is going on, we can politely ask them if they have any footage," Campbell said. "We just can't go around indiscriminately ringing doorbells at this time of night. I can tell you from experience that it will backfire."

"What else?" Kenzie asked. "Zachary said that Rhys's phone is off?"

"Yes," Campbell admitted. "We're watching for it to come back online, but at the moment, all we know is that it was here when it went offline. No chance of following it for a few blocks so that we at least know what direction he left in."

"And it could just be a faulty battery," Kenzie suggested.

Campbell shrugged. "At this point, I am assuming that is not true. I think the chances that his phone would accidentally run out of juice in the middle of the night, at the same time as he goes sleepwalking or wanders off in a fugue are pretty slim. I don't think that's what happened."

Kenzie had to admit that it didn't sound too likely. "What about an Amber alert? Have you put one out?"

"It will be going out shortly. First, we had to satisfy ourselves that it was a likely abduction. And that the situation would be helped by an Amber alert. Because of course... if it was Saul or a dirty cop who took him, then he gets the Amber alerts, and it will tip him off to the fact that we know Rhys is missing. When otherwise, he wouldn't know that until much later. Keeping him in the dark might give us an advantage."

"But you decided to go ahead. so you don't think it gives you any advantage."

"Having weighed both sides, we decided to go ahead with the alert. If he is somewhere people might see him... it will help us more than hinder us."

55

K enzie's phone buzzed. At first, she just ignored it. What she was doing was far more important than what anyone could be messaging her about. But gradually, as the follow-up reminders to check her message buzzed, she realized that it was still the middle of the night. Who would be texting her at this hour?

She pulled the phone out of her pocket and looked at it. Zachary glanced at her with an irritated look that quickly switched to the same realization.

"Who is it?" he asked.

"Just a second…" Kenzie had to unlock her screen in order to see her messages. For the sake of privacy, her own and others', she did not allow text messages to display on her lock screen. It was a number she did not recognize and, for a moment, Kenzie's heart fell. Just some spammer from some country on the other side of the world where it was daytime. But she glanced at the message, and it was not spam. "It's Emily."

Campbell and Zachary both waited for more information. Vera raised an eyebrow and shook her head slightly. "Who?"

"The girl who sent Rhys the picture of the dead man. She's the one who witnessed his death. The one who… started all of this."

"She didn't start it," Zachary pointed out sensibly. "She was caught in the middle of it. She was recruited into a gang. She witnessed a murder. Neither thing was something she had planned to do."

Kenzie looked at Vera and saw her lips tighten. They were both thinking the same thing. That Emily could still have made different decisions. Decisions that wouldn't have negatively affected Rhys, and possibly other students and people in Emily's community.

But Emily was a kid. And the choices that she had made could not be changed now. It was best to just forget about the past and any part of the blame that might be hers and move on.

Kenzie looked at the message. "She said that Rhys started messaging her." She looked at Campbell. "I thought you said you were watching for his phone to come back online."

"We are." Campbell pulled out his own phone to see if he'd missed any messages from the team. "Hang on."

They waited while he called to check with his IT guys, and shook his head.

"Rhys's phone has not come back online."

Kenzie looked down at her phone. "And this is not the same number that she was sending me messages from before. It might not be Emily. And she might not be getting anything from Rhys. So what is this?"

"What does she say?" Zachary asked.

"She said that Rhys started messaging her. She initially ignored it because she didn't know who it was, but it was Rhys, and he was asking her to meet with him."

"Where is he?"

Kenzie tried to think of the best reply to send to Emily. Was it Emily? And if so, how had she gotten a message from Rhys when his phone wasn't online? Maybe it was a message from the kidnapper. From Deputy Donut, as Emily had referred to him.

How do I know who this is? she finally texted, hoping the direct approach would work best. Emily must know that she would need proof. That she couldn't just assume that anyone who messaged her was telling the truth and was who they claimed to be.

There was no immediate response from Emily. Kenzie waited impatiently. How long could it take to type a message that somehow verified who Emily was?

DD only knew me as M, was the not-so-lengthy reply that Kenzie finally received.

And then another piece of the puzzle.

til you told DD my name

Kenzie read both replies aloud to Campbell and Zachary, even though they made her wince.

"Who is DD?" Vera asked plaintively, upset about being out of the loop and not knowing what they were talking about.

"Deputy Donut," Kenzie said. "A nickname for the dirty cop."

She didn't say Detective Saul. Not until that was proven.

"Okay. So it is Emily," Zachary said, ignoring the sender's accusation. "She got a new phone or is using a burner she already had stashed. But is it really Rhys she is messaging with?"

Kenzie nodded. She texted back to Emily. *How u know it is Rhys?*

They again had to wait for Emily to figure out what to say or to compose it on her keyboard.

Eventually, the answer came through. Not words this time. Instead, it was a picture of a pug with a Sherlock Holmes deerstalker hat on its head and a pipe in its mouth. Kenzie sighed. She showed it to Vera, who was still standing beside her, and then stepped into the bedroom to show it to each of Zachary and Campbell.

"I guess she recognizes Rhys's communication style," Zachary confirmed.

"Give me the number she's texting from," Campbell ordered. Kenzie tapped it on her screen so that she could see the full number and then read it out to him.

"We'll get a trace on it and see where she is," Campbell advised. "And then we can see who she is exchanging texts with too."

"I can just ask her what number he is texting from."

"Don't trust witnesses to tell you the truth," Campbell advised. "Then you won't be disappointed when they lie."

"Trust but verify," Kenzie said, repeating something she had heard on TV.

Campbell shook his head. "Don't trust." He cleared his throat and shrugged. "We're going to take a two-pronged approach. You need to keep messaging with Emily. Get everything you can out of her. She already trusts you, so you just have to make sure not to do anything that will make her back off. Don't ask too many questions. I will get the tech guys on to it, but it will take time to track the number Rhys is texting from and to trace his phone."

"He might not be using text messaging. It might be an app."

Campbell grimaced. If Rhys and Emily were using another app instead of straight text messaging, then it would be that much harder to find the phone they needed to trace.

"Right. Maybe ask her that, but not right away. Like I said, not too many questions."

Kenzie nodded. "Okay." She worked on breathing slowly and regularly.

They were making progress. They would find Rhys. They would bring him back safe.

Kenzie went back out to the living room and sat down where she would be able to text more comfortably with Emily. She didn't want to be looking at Rhys's room, reminded of his absence there. And standing in the hallway was awkward and made her anxious for Emily's answers to come faster than they did.

She sat down with the phone on her knee.

Where is Rhys? Did he say?

Emily's reply was quicker to this question. *wont say DD there probly wont let him*

Kenzie was sure that Emily had probably asked. Had probably wanted to know all of the details. But Rhys's communications were being monitored by Saul, if he was the kidnapper. He couldn't say anything the man didn't first approve.

Is DD Detective Saul? Kenzie typed.

dont know

Kenzie looked around her. People were coming and going, but none of them were of any help to her. "Zachary?"

He was at her side in a minute, looking at the phone expectantly.

"Not anything from Emily," Kenzie said, waving her hand at it. "Can you get a picture of Detective Saul that I can send to Emily? To find out if that's her Deputy Donut?"

"Sure," Zachary agreed. He returned to the hallway, to ask Campbell for a picture, Kenzie assumed.

Why did Rhys send you a message? Kenzie asked Emily.

DD wants to talk to me.

Kenzie wasn't surprised. Of course the dirty cop wanted to talk to her. He wanted to see how much of a threat she was. Or he wanted to take her out so that she was no longer a threat. Since Emily was the person who could identify him as the killer, he probably wanted her to disappear permanently. So that she could never cause any trouble for him again.

Don't agree to it, Kenzie warned.

u think im stupid?

Sorry. Just worried about you. Are you still in Burlington?

There was a long pause during which Kenzie watched the flashing dots and tried not to be too impatient. She tried to think of other things instead of how they were going to get Rhys out of the situation he was in. What work she had to do at the office. What her priorities were. When would her promotion be announced to the public? She hadn't seen any paperwork on it yet. Didn't have anything but Dr. Wiltshire's assurance that she was being promoted.

Her phone vibrated. She looked back down at it.

worried bout Rhys. DD is crazy

I know. We're worried too. Do you have any idea where they are?

trying 2 figure out. something with stars?

Kenzie had no idea what that meant. *What?*

he keeps *starring* words

Like for emphasis? Bolding?

R never does that

"Okay," Kenzie murmured to herself. What was Rhys trying to communicate by starring words? If he didn't usually do it, he was trying to communicate something. Highlighting words that would combine to form a separate, hidden message?

Tell me the words he starred.

no must today do it

All words that someone might normally emphasize in a conversation. Kenzie shook her head. That wasn't it.

What else has he said to you about where he is or what he wants?

What DD says. Meet or Ill hurt people. Rhys mom kids from school all of them

They must still be in Roxboro, then. All of those are people who live here.

More dots. They kept starting and then stopping and Kenzie didn't know if she was writing and deleting her responses or just couldn't think of what to write.

Are you in Burlington or Roxboro? Kenzie tried again to get an idea of where the girl was. Was she in the same city as the killer? Several hours away? Did Saul know that she had gone to Burlington? Did Rhys? The kids kept things from the adults, Kenzie was sure, and she didn't know how much Emily had told Rhys about what had happened with Mercer and the gang and the dirty cop, and how much she had kept a secret.

How much she still might be keeping a secret from all of them even now. The way she told the story, she was innocent of any responsibility in Mercer's death and had only been afraid for her life.

u dont need 2 know

56

Kenzie had to admire the girl. She knew how to protect her privacy. Emily had reached out to Kenzie for help but, apparently, her trust did not extend to telling Kenzie where to find her. But Campbell would soon know.

Kenzie got another message, but when she looked down at her screen, it was not there. There wasn't anything since Emily's last comment. She tapped out of the screen and saw that the OS said she did have another message but, when she tapped that, she saw the new message wasn't in her conversation with Emily, but under Zachary's name. She pulled up the message and saw Detective Saul's picture. It looked like maybe it was his police academy graduation photo. Kenzie texted Zachary back a thank you, then she copied and pasted the picture into her conversation with Emily.

Is that DD?

The response from Emily was a string of expletives.

Does that mean yes?

Another long string of expletives combined with Emily's reply, which boiled down to a "yes."

Kenzie sent a text back to Zachary, confirming that Emily had identified Saul as the cop who killed Mercer. She felt numb. She had been hoping that Emily would say no. That they'd been all suspicious of the cop for no reason. It was just an innocent mistake. Kenzie wanted the dirty cop to belong to another law enforcement organization. Or to not actually be a cop at all, just someone who had pretended to be one to scam everybody.

How could a cop she had known and not suspected of anything be guilty of murder? Not an accidental shooting or a shooting in the line of duty. He had, from Emily's description, killed Mercer in cold blood.

If Emily were telling the truth. But right now, that was all that they had to go on.

Kenzie could hear Campbell's raised voice in the back hallway. He was not happy about something. Obviously, he wasn't fighting with Vera. He wouldn't do that. One of his own crime scene investigators? Kenzie knew them, and they were well-trained. She would have deferred to them on any procedure to be followed or evidence to be collected.

That left Zachary.

Kenzie was right. Within a minute, Campbell and Zachary were both back in the living room. Zachary positioned himself between Campbell and Kenzie, his face intent and body language tense.

"What's the matter?"

"You sent Emily Chase a photo of Detective Saul and asked her if he was the killer?" Campbell demanded.

"Uh…" Kenzie couldn't very well deny it. She looked at Zachary and back at Campbell. "Yeah. I figured that was the best way to find out who we were dealing with. She said she didn't know his real name. We were at a disadvantage, not knowing whether it was Detective Saul or if she was talking about someone else."

"I told you I wouldn't let her look through pictures of cops."

Kenzie cleared her throat. Yes, he had been very clear about that point. Kenzie couldn't say that she had somehow misunderstood. Campbell had not wanted to throw a bunch of cops under the bus. Hadn't wanted her to pick out someone who was completely innocent and identify him as a killer.

But they'd already had reason to suspect Saul. It wasn't just blindly choosing a bunch of police officers and letting her pick anyone she pleased to say that it was the dirty cop.

"I thought since we already figured it was Saul, it wouldn't hurt to get a confirmation." Kenzie looked at Zachary. "You told him that was why I needed the picture, didn't you?"

Zachary didn't answer.

Campbell looked at Zachary. "Oh, this is on you too, is it? You're the one who found the picture for her."

"Yes."

Kenzie was just getting caught up on what had happened. She had thought that Sergeant Campbell had given the picture of Saul to Zachary, but he had not. Zachary had done what he did best—searched out the needed information—and had given it to Kenzie without checking with Campbell first. And Campbell would not have approved Kenzie using it for that purpose.

"Oh... I'm sorry. I thought that you had given it to Zachary when I asked for a picture to send to Emily. I... should have known you wouldn't want me to send it to her."

"You've tainted this witness. You've shown her a picture of one person, and named that person as a suspect, and it will now be firmly entrenched in her mind as the person she saw kill Mercer. If that was actually what happened and not just something she made up."

Kenzie rubbed her forehead. "I didn't realize."

"You know we have rules about showing pictures to witnesses. Photo lineups. Not tipping off a witness that you are looking at a certain person."

"Yes." Kenzie looked down at her phone. She couldn't very well take it back now. Emily had seen what she had seen. If she testified against Saul in court, if they could arrest him for the murder and get her up on the stand, she would be forced to say that she had been shown a single picture. And the identification would get thrown out. "She was pretty vehement."

She turned the phone and showed it to Zachary, but not to Campbell. Campbell wouldn't care. It wouldn't convince him that Kenzie had done the right thing. And she hadn't. Not if she had screwed up that identification so badly. And she was supposed to be a professional, the person getting promoted to assistant medical examiner.

Or maybe she wouldn't. Maybe she would just be fired.

Zachary looked at Emily's message and chuckled. He swiped down the rest of the conversation, his eyes going quickly over their words.

"Stars?" he asked.

"I don't know what it means. I thought maybe the starred words in their conversation would make a message, but it doesn't make sense."

"What's that?" Campbell asked.

"Emily says that Rhys keeps putting stars in his messages. But she doesn't know why. It isn't something he usually does."

"Maybe it means that he is not the one sending the messages. Or that he is not the one with the phone in his hands."

Kenzie shook her head slowly. "Emily was sure that it was Rhys she was messaging with. He was sending her the kind of messages that Rhys does. He has a… unique messaging style."

"So I recall," Campbell agreed. He thought about it. "But Rhys could be telling Saul what to write in the messages, but the punctuation, the starred words, are Saul's own additions."

"How would Rhys tell him what to put?"

"He could…" Campbell's forehead wrinkled as he thought it through. "He could be writing it down. Or he could have another phone and is typing his own messages, and then Saul is retyping them on the phone he controls. Making sure that Rhys can't send a secret message."

"Why would he do that? And if he did, then why would he add something that might tip Emily off to the fact that it isn't Rhys typing?"

"That doesn't seem very likely, does it? Unless he copied the stars from what Rhys typed on his own phone."

"And then we're back to why are the stars there?"

"And we know that Rhys isn't typing on his own phone," Zachary said, "since it is turned off. So Saul would have had to get two new phones, one for Rhys to type to him on and one for him to contact

Emily with. More money, more complications, and the possibility that Rhys could be doing something with one phone while Saul is doing something with the other. He'd have to have eyes on Rhys's phone all the time to make sure he wasn't sending any secret messages. He'd have to be looking at his own phone and Rhys's all the time."

Kenzie nodded at this. It made sense. She didn't think that there were two phones. And even if there were, Rhys was the one who had put the stars into the messages. They had to mean something.

"You remember when Gloria took him?" Zachary asked Kenzie. "He sent me messages to give us information about his location. Even when he could have just said, 'the fishing cabin Grandpa took us to,' he didn't. His problem isn't just with being unable to say things out loud. I don't believe that he even thinks in words. He thinks in images. Or in concepts. And the more stressed he is, the harder it will be to convert those concepts into words."

"And this time, it is even harder, because he's got someone looking over his shoulder and reading all of those messages to make sure that he doesn't say anything that would tip us off."

Zachary nodded his agreement.

"So this is a picture," Kenzie said, closing her eyes. "He's sending two messages at once. What Saul tells him to, and a picture."

57

Rhys watched bad cop out of the corner of his eye as the man paced back and forth across the cold, spare room like a tiger in a cage at the zoo. Back and forth, back and forth, getting more and more agitated. Rhys had thought that he would settle down once he was in contact with Emily but, rather than being reassured that she was no longer in Roxboro and hadn't talked to anyone, he was acting like everything was falling apart.

He watched Rhys like a hawk. There was no opportunity for him to send an extra message to Emily, turn on location sharing, or install another app. All he could do was to send the messages bad cop told him to write and to try to keep everything from blowing up. He didn't want bad cop going after Emily. He wanted to keep them apart and to try to calm things down. If Emily was still in Burlington, that was good.

He thought that she would message Kenzie. They had been in contact, and Rhys figured that once Emily knew he was in trouble, she would reach out to Kenzie and maybe to Zachary.

"Tell her she has to meet me," bad cop growled at Rhys.

He shrugged and spread his hands out a little, as much as the handcuffs would allow him to. He had already sent that message to Emily more than once. Sending it again would not help anything.

"Do it!" the cop snapped, smacking Rhys across the back of the neck and head.

Rhys jumped. It didn't hurt that much, but his heart raced even faster, and it was all he could do not to jump up from the table and find someplace to hide.

There was nowhere to hide. But that's what his body and brain wanted him to do. His instincts were so strong that it was hard to keep himself pasted to the chair. He tried to look calm, like he wasn't bothered at all by the cop or anything he did, but he was sure that every thought was probably written on his face. He wasn't good at hiding his emotions. Not when that was often the only tool he had to communicate.

He popped up the gifs and jumped from one category to another, looking through the app's frequently used gifs to try to home in on related ones that would express what he wanted. He wished he had his own phone and photo stream. But they weren't available. The only thing the cop would let him install was his messaging app, so that he would be able to send Emily the messages the cop insisted he send.

"Come on," bad cop growled, watching over Rhys's shoulder. "Tell her she has to meet. She doesn't have any choice. The only way I will let you go is if she meets with me. Shows me her phone. Shows me that she's gotten rid of all of the pictures. Then she can run away wherever she wants to."

Rhys doubted that the cop would let Emily go anywhere. He already knew he had made a mistake letting her go the first time. Not realizing that she had taken a picture and would send it out to others. She had been in shock. All she could do was go home and go to bed. That was what Emily had told him. She had been too panicked to do anything but snap a couple of pictures of the man she had seen killed and get out of there. It wasn't until she awoke from her first hibernation that she'd sent them out to friends. And then she'd gone back to sleep again, staying in bed for days like she had the flu.

Rhys understood. He knew that mind-numbing feeling that had pressed against his consciousness. That desire to withdraw. The letting go. It was easier to be gone than to face the pain and the panic. Even now, as he searched for a gif to send to Emily, he was fighting hard to stay present. He worked through the exercise Kenzie had suggested. *Five things you see. Five things you hear. Five things you smell.*

He finally found a gif that he thought worked, a meme from one of the TV shows he used to watch as a kid, with text across it. "Meet me halfway."

"Not 'halfway,' " bad cop growled, slapping Rhys's hand back before he could press Send. He grabbed the phone to delete the image and went back to the gifs Rhys had been looking at.

"This one," he pointed.

Rhys wrinkled his nose. A dancing black girl from some talent show franchise Rhys had never watched, with "Meet me" across the bottom. The band name? The song name?

Emily would know that Rhys hadn't picked it out.

He went ahead and sent it anyway. It wasn't like she didn't know the cop was there, reading every message, telling him what to send.

No meeting, Emily texted back.

"She meets with you or I'm going to start cutting off fingers," bad cop threatened, his voice going high and strained, like someone had run over his foot. "Or better yet, I'm going to shoot your kneecaps off!" He raised his gun and pointed it first at one of Rhys's knees and then the other. "Tell her!"

Rhys pointed at the pile of guns and boxes of ammunition that bad cop had stacked on one of the kitchen counters.

"What?" the cop demanded.

Rhys raised the phone with both hands, pointing it at the guns and miming taking a picture.

"You want to send her a picture of my artillery? Go ahead. Send it to her. Tell her I'll use whatever I have to. She *is* going to come to me, one way or the other."

Rhys frowned. Palms up, he moved his hands back and forth. *Here?*

Bad cop scowled and didn't come up with an answer. Rhys didn't know how he thought Emily would get out there to meet with him. She would need a map. And a car. She couldn't just take the bus out into the middle of nowhere. She couldn't get a ride share that would take her all the way out there, where she might have an accomplice lying in wait to rob the guy. She would need a car she had control of and the GPS coordinates.

While the cop thought about that, Rhys composed a message, snapping a photo first of the pile of weapons, and then of his own knees, showing through frayed holes in his blue jeans. Grandma hated that he wore jeans with holes in them. Rhys hated that his knees were so thin and knobby. He wanted to be big and strong like Stanley Green. Like the wrestlers he saw on TV. Massive bodies. No one would push him around then. No one would grab him by the arm and drag him off like he was a little kid.

He tried not to think about how Emily would feel when she saw the threat. How she already felt knowing that the guy she had liked in the gang had been killed. Sick with guilt. Horrified that such a thing had happened while she looked on.

He knew that feeling. That sick, gut-wrenching, mind-numbing feeling. A sinking, heavy, crushing feeling. He felt it all the time when he thought about Grandpa Clarence and what had happened that day, something that he had been unable to stop. Something that could happen again to someone else he loved.

Predators lurked everywhere. Not just outside the house in the shadows, like on TV. But inside. Inside the house. Inside the family. People he knew and loved could do terrible things to each other and to him. People could die while he stood by and watched and did nothing to stop it.

He hoped that Emily would not break down and agree to meet. Unless he and Emily could work out a way between them to set bad cop up. To keep him from being able to hurt Emily. Or anyone else. If they could do that, it was worth whatever pain Rhys had to suffer to get there. If he could just prevent anyone else from getting hurt.

He scrolled through the gifs, trying to think of how they could do it.

58

Kenzie's phone started buzzing and buzzing, several messages coming in right on top of each other. She pulled herself away from the argument with Campbell and Zachary to look at her phone. Her heart beat fast, worried about what was going on. Why had Emily suddenly ramped up the messages? Kenzie half expected her phone to ring with a call from the girl before she had a chance to read the messages. She could see as she checked her notifications screen and switched to the texting app that a couple of the messages were graphics.

Campbell and Zachary went quiet, waiting to find out what Kenzie had received.

The last message from Emily was a shrieking line of OMGs, big and bold and repeated all the way across the screen. Kenzie swallowed hard and scrolled up to see the earlier messages.

The first message was calm. *DD keeps saying he wants to meet and I say no.*

Then, a scream emoji, followed by the pictures. They were photographs rather than popular gifs.

A counter stacked with guns and ammunition boxes.

Two skinny brown knees protruding through frayed holes in blue jeans. A selfie. Someone seated at a kitchen table. Apparently, the same semi-rustic room as the guns were in. Both showed matching furnishings.

DD gonna kneecap R if I dont meet!

Kenzie felt ill. She was glad she was already sitting down, because she didn't think she could have remained on her feet. She felt the blood drain from her face, leaving her dizzy, white sparkles obscuring her vision here and there.

"Kenzie?" Zachary rushed to her side. He sat beside her and put his arm around her, leaning over to look at her phone. Kenzie held it toward him, not looking him in the face.

Zachary swore. "He's got guns. Plenty of guns, and he's threatening to harm Rhys if Emily won't meet."

Campbell leaned over for a look. He raised his voice to speak to one of the other cops. "How close are we to getting the location of that phone?"

A detective across the room, with his phone to his ear, covered the front mic and shook his head at Campbell.

"That's not her phone number. It's part of a block of numbers reserved by an app for people who want to send messages anonymously. We're trying to find out from the company who has purchased it, and to get their information, but they won't comply without a subpoena. Same song from Ms. Kirsch's phone provider. We're working on it from both directions."

"They know that there is a minor in danger?"

"They don't care."

Campbell growled. "Forward me those pictures," he told Kenzie. "We'll see if we can get any information from them."

"Most messaging apps strip the EXIF data," Zachary told him.

Campbell shook his head. "Not all of them. Some of the most popular ones are still unprotected. If they have location data embedded, we can find out in two minutes."

Much faster than they could get the information from the phone or app companies. Kenzie forwarded the two pictures to Campbell, hoping that it would help. She enlarged them on her screen.

"Does that look like somewhere in town to you? Or in Burlington?" she asked Zachary.

He studied it, frowning. "Outdated finishings and fixtures. If it's in town, it's in a very old area." He zoomed in on the corner of the window, caught in the picture of the guns. It blurred before Kenzie could see anything significant, but she wasn't sure what he was looking at. Zachary panned over the ugly tile backsplash with orange bunches of flowers on it, along the wall to the edge of the fridge.

"What do you see?" Kenzie asked impatiently.

He zoomed out more and pointed to the plugin. "There's a two-pronged plugin. No ground."

"That's old. How long has it been since you could wire a house like that?"

"In the city?" Zachary shook his head. "I'd have to look it up. It's been decades."

"In the city?" Kenzie repeated. "Then they're *not* in the city."

"Maybe not," Zachary agreed.

"The stars. The stars he keeps throwing into his messages."

"You can't see stars like that in the city!" Zachary instantly saw where Kenzie was going. "It's incredible when you get out of the city, away from all the streetlights, and can see the stars. Rhys is a city boy. Other than those fishing trips with his grandpa, when was the last time he was out of the city like that?"

Kenzie laughed, shaking her head. "He couldn't very well put pictures of trees or a cabin in his messages. Saul would have known he was trying to give hints about his location."

"Campbell," Zachary interrupted Campbell, who was talking to one of the tech guys. About whether there was any location metadata attached to the pictures, Kenzie assumed. "He's in a rural area. Away from the city. Do you know if he owns any land outside the city? A grandparent's place? Something way out in the sticks?"

Campbell glared at him, still angry about their sending the picture of Saul to Emily.

"How do you know that?"

"Look at the pictures. Old finishings and fixtures. The wall around the windows looks like plaster, not drywall. The plugin is a two-prong. The fridge has rounded corners, and it's not because it's retro. It's original. Maybe even gas-powered."

Campbell blinked, looking at it. "I was only looking at the guns. I can see the finishings are old, but... to be that old and still in use... you're right. It's probably rural. I've already got them looking for any city properties in Saul's name. I'll have it expanded... to the whole state, and any parent's or grandparent's name that we can find."

"Look for obituaries for grandparent names. Any grandparents on Facebook are probably too dialed in to modern technology not to have replaced the wiring by now."

Campbell nodded. "Yeah. Probably right. If we can get this guy before he hurts anyone..."

Kenzie's heart felt like ice. Saul was a dangerous person. Someone who had already killed and was trying to cover up his first mistake. And the second mistake—letting Emily go. He had misjudged her, thought that she wasn't a threat to him, when the truth was that she wasn't prepared to stay quiet and just let him murder. She knew that her safety hinged on her exposing him rather than pretending that she hadn't seen what she had.

He had killed one man already and was threatening to kill another—one Kenzie knew.

Kenzie's phone buzzed, and she looked down at it. She had taken far too long to follow up on Emily's last message. Emily would think that Kenzie had abandoned her.

But the buzz wasn't a notification of a message from Emily. It was an email from Dr. Cook, following up on a toxicology test she had asked him to order from the lab the previous day. Kenzie looked at the living room window. It was starting to get light out. She hadn't realized that so much time had passed. Cook was at the medical examiner's office even earlier than Kenzie would have guessed. It was no wonder she could never get there before he did.

She messaged Emily, trying to think of words that might comfort her. To let her know that they weren't just ignoring what she had sent and her concerns about Rhys being tortured to convince her to meet with him.

Following up on leads, she promised Emily. *Hang on. Stay where you are.*

Wherever she was. Kenzie wished she knew. But Emily wasn't

about to tell anyone, and had already shown herself to be more resourceful than they had expected. Kenzie was afraid that when they managed to trace Emily's phone to a location, they would find out that was spoofed too. Fake phone number. Fake location. She was worried about a corrupt cop. So she wasn't about to give the police any information that might lead them to her.

After sending the message to Emily, she switched over to the email received from Dr. Cook. She opened the attached report to see what they had found.

Zachary was looking at her a few minutes later, craning his neck and getting closer to her to try to see what she was reading. But the type was too small for him to be able to see it clearly, and she knew that, even if it was large enough, he would have had a difficult time reading it. The paragraphs were densely written and full of measurements and figures. Not dyslexia-friendly.

"What is it?" Zachary asked when he realized Kenzie was looking at him.

"It's a tox screen on Mercer."

Zachary laughed and shook his head. "Why would you do a tox screen on Mercer? You already know how he was killed. Bullet to the brain."

"That's what killed him," Kenzie agreed. "But he would be dead now even if he hadn't been shot in the head."

"What?"

Campbell turned around and looked at Kenzie as well, obviously having overheard this little tidbit and echoed Zachary's inquiry. "What?"

Kenzie nodded, looking from one to the other. "He was too impatient. Couldn't wait. If he had, he could have saved himself a bullet."

"From the looks of things, he doesn't need to have any concerns about running out of ammunition," Campbell said dryly. "I wouldn't want to jump to any conclusions, but it looks like the reports of Saul taking weapons and other contraband from the gang members and keeping it for himself were true."

That made sense. And he had stashed them in the cabin to

prevent anyone from stumbling across them too easily. If there were accusations from the gang members that led to his apartment being searched, no one would find anything.

Except for at least one of the guns, which he had used to shoot Mercer. So that the weapon could only be traced back to the gang and street violence rather than back to him.

"What would have killed him if he hadn't been shot?" Zachary pressed.

"Methanol."

He frowned. "Isn't that just alcohol?"

"It's alcohol, but not the right kind. It's very toxic."

"So… who poisoned him?"

"Probably the same person who killed him, since most people don't have several murderers out to get them."

"From the sounds of it, this guy could have."

Kenzie shrugged. "Maybe. That will have to be investigated. The police will have to look into it."

"Was he poisoned, or could it have been accidental?" Campbell asked.

"Accidental is possible, but rare. Then again, murder by methanol is pretty rare too. But it is possible, and you do hear about it every now and then. Or at least, medical examiners do." Kenzie smiled. "Not everyone spends as much time reading interesting postmortems as we do."

"So what did he do? Spike Mercer's drink?" Zachary asked.

"Probably. Emily said that he was acting drunker than he should be. So he was drinking booze. Which actually helps the body to metabolize methanol. Ethanol is an antidote to methanol poisoning."

"So maybe Saul didn't give him enough methanol. Or didn't realize that the stuff would be counteracted by regular alcohol. What made you check?" Zachary cocked his head to the side slightly.

"Emily. It just sounded… like more than a simple drink. Staggering, blind drunk… sweating, dilated pupils. Or rather, she said his eyes were funny."

"Good catch," Campbell told her. "I would never have guessed that there was another contributing factor. The photo itself looked pretty conclusive."

Kenzie nodded.

"And I wouldn't have thought there was… enough of him left to test for toxins."

"Well, luckily, there was enough in his system that we were still able to test for methanol and formate, one of its metabolites. It wasn't cause of death, but if we want a full picture… we want to find those things. One thing we notice with poisoners is that they often don't kill the first time they try. They might go through several different poisons or increasing doses over a period of time. Humans can be remarkably resilient, and many poisoners don't give enough of the poison, or the body… er, expels it before it can take full effect."

"I've heard of that a few times before," Campbell admitted. "Spouses especially. They have access to their partner's food, so they mix a little in, thinking it will just take a little, and then they'll be gone, all neat and quiet. But they get sick and end up in the hospital or are over it after a couple of days. And then the spouse has to move to another poison or more direct action."

"Like shooting the guy in the head."

"Not as many people survive that," Campbell said dryly.

"No. Not nearly as many."

59

Kenzie exited the email report without replying to Dr. Cook. He wouldn't expect her to be at the office for several hours yet, so she didn't need to give away that she was already awake and explain to him that... what? That she wouldn't be in because she was dealing with Rhys's abduction? It wasn't exactly her job, but she couldn't see herself being able to go to the office and do anything else while they were trying to find Rhys and negotiate with Saul.

She reopened the message thread with Emily. She wasn't going to think about anything else yet. She was just going to deal with Emily and figure out how they would make sure Rhys got home safe and sound.

It wasn't like a TV series, where you knew that everyone would get home safely in the end. In real life, there were no such assurances. He was in the hands of a killer. A murderous cop intent on clearing the board so that there wasn't anyone left to testify against him.

Without Emily, they didn't have any proof that Saul was the one who had killed Mercer. They couldn't connect the gun with him. It was doubtful that they would get anyone in the gang to talk about Saul and how he had been harassing and taking advantage of the members of the gang. It didn't look good for them. They wouldn't want to sully their reputations.

We think Rhys is in a remote location, Kenzie texted Emily. *Did DD ever talk about owning a place in the woods? Going there for a vacation or a party?*

It was a while before Kenzie saw the dancing dots pop up. Was Emily busy texting with Rhys? She wondered if Rhys would be able to think of more reasons to take pictures that might help them pin down the location of the cabin.

Never talked to him, Emily texted back. *Not friends.*

What about when he talked to Mercer? Or someone else in the gang?

dont know

There were more dots, so Kenzie waited to see what else Emily had to share.

Hes gonna hurt Rhys

Kenzie swallowed. There was a lump in her throat. All of those guns. Rhys, a gangly teenager, there all by himself with no one to protect him.

dont know what to do, Emily confessed.

You need to talk to the police, Kenzie typed back. *Call me and you can talk to cop in charge.*

no

Leaning with her elbow on her knee, Kenzie ground her fist into her forehead. As if massaging her aching muscles would get her brain working better.

You want me to help, but you won't give me anything to work with.

Kenzie received several files all at once. She tapped the first, which was another photo. This one, she thought, Rhys had taken covertly. Not a message from his captor. He caught a back view of Saul, and part of a facial profile as he bent down close to the kitchen counter. Not to inspect the guns and ammunition but, Kenzie thought, to snort coke.

She hadn't thought she could feel any worse about the situation. She swore and looked at Zachary, who was studying his phone, working whatever magic he could to figure out where Rhys was being held.

"He's doing coke."

After a moment, Zachary looked up from his phone, pulling himself away from whatever he had been focused on. His expression was bleak. "Tell me you're kidding."

"You know I wouldn't joke about something like that, even if it wasn't a dire situation like this."

Zachary nodded. "He might be tired. Looking for an energy boost."

"Well, he won't be going to sleep now."

She had been hoping, in the back of her mind, that sooner or later, Saul would have to sleep. And that would give them some time to chase him down and give Rhys a break. Rhys must be terrified. Kenzie remembered how afraid she herself had been when...

Kenzie pushed the thought out of her mind, scrolling down from the picture to look at the other file Emily had sent. This one was a video. Kenzie couldn't make sense of the screen to begin with. The camera was pointed at the table or floor rather than being held up where Rhys would be able to film his captor or something else in the room that would give them clues as to where the cabin was.

Then she realized that it was the audio Rhys had been trying to capture. She pressed the up-volume control to get it as loud as possible. She could hear Saul in the background, muttering and growling, talking to himself. She couldn't make out the whole thing as he moved around the room.

"Thinks she's smarter than anyone else... can't get away with it... not going to this time, I know better this time, and there's no way she's not going down. She thinks she can control this?" He swore, cussing out whoever he was talking about. A partner? Emily? Kenzie herself? Who was he going after next? Was he giving up on Emily and going to a new part of his plan, or was he trying a new approach to get her?

Had Rhys broken down and given Saul what he needed in order to find Emily? Maybe he had switched to the friends app on Rhys's phone and found Emily's phone location through that? Kenzie believed she herself was safe. But who would Saul go after next? Emily had said that he had threatened her mother and the other kids at school. Maybe one of them was next. Maybe he would just keep grabbing and torturing people close to Emily until he found the key needed to get her to meet with him?

"You'll see," Saul snarled on the recording, "no stupid female is going to get the better of me."

Campbell had been out of the room talking to one of the numerous law enforcement officers who had overrun the house. He returned, looking even more tired and frustrated than he had, if that were possible. He looked at Zachary and then at Kenzie.

"No luck on the photos. No geolocation tags."

Kenzie nodded her understanding. "And property ownership?"

"Going to take a while to find everything we need, especially if it is in a family member's name." Campbell looked around the living room. "Someone needs to do a coffee run."

A younger officer near the door put up his hand. A rookie who had probably been relegated to the fringes of the investigation, appointed to watch the door and the property outside to make sure that no one unauthorized walked in, and he was now eager to get out and do something. Anything. "I'll do that. What do you want?" He pulled out a notebook to start a list.

"Don't get individual orders. You can get it by the box at the place up the street. It's twenty cups or something. Get that."

The young man nodded, put his notebook back away, and walked out of the house. Campbell looked at Kenzie. "You look about as bad as I feel."

Kenzie held her phone up. "Umm… Emily sent a couple more files."

"Forward them to me."

Kenzie did so. Campbell's phone dinged, and he looked at the picture and then opened the video file. He looked confused, then did the same thing as Kenzie had, turning the volume up so that he could hear what had been recorded. He shook his head slowly. "This guy is a walking time bomb. We're doing our best to find him…"

He glanced around the room, probably looking for Vera, but she was not in the room. Maybe she had gone to her own room to lie down or cry in privacy.

Campbell just continued to shake his head. "We're doing our best," he repeated, but Kenzie heard the resignation in his voice. He was worried they wouldn't be able to do anything before Saul had a meltdown or took the next step in his plan.

Kenzie wasn't ready to give up yet. She tapped a message to Emily.

Where are you? We will come to you.

Staying at Vera's house wasn't getting them anywhere. That wasn't where the action was. Kenzie could receive messages nearly anywhere. But Saul had gotten himself far away from the Salter house before he had started messaging Emily; they weren't going to find anything useful at the house. If Emily were still in Burlington, or Rhys thought she was still in Burlington, that might be where Saul was headed next. If Kenzie could do anything to get closer to them and possibly prevent Saul from being able to reach her...

She waited for a reply from Emily, rubbing the muscles around her eyes. She had not gotten enough sleep and, now that the adrenaline was starting to fade, she was really feeling the strain. It was a good thing that Campbell had ordered some caffeine. They were all going to need it.

She continued to wait, but there were no further messages from Emily. She looked at Zachary.

"She's gone silent."

"Check your bars."

Kenzie looked at the top of the screen. "They look fine."

Kenzie sent another text to Emily, but received no response.

"I don't know if it is going through."

"Try sending me something."

She sent a brief test message to Zachary, and his phone immediately lit up.

"That worked," Kenzie mused. "What's going on with Emily all of a sudden?"

Zachary took a deep breath and let it out. "Emily has turned off her phone."

60

Kenzie knew immediately that Zachary was right. Emily didn't like being pushed to talk to the police. Texting with Kenzie wasn't getting her any closer to helping Rhys out. The messages Rhys kept sending her just confirmed that Saul was escalating, that he was working his way up to torturing Rhys to convince Emily to meet with him. And he had other people on his hit list if Emily didn't respond to the torture and death of Rhys. Her mother. Her friends. Saul would just keep going until she listened to what he said.

And did they really think that a fifteen-year-old girl was going to stand up to such intense pressure? Saul was a cop. He had guns. He had Rhys. He had all the power. The only way for Emily to stop it was to give in.

"We have to find them," she said urgently. "We need to know where Saul and Rhys are."

Zachary shook his head. "No. We're too late now. By the time we figure it out, he'll be gone. He needed somewhere to take Rhys where people wouldn't see him, and to access his weapons and coke. But he's not going to meet Emily there. Even if she has a car, he's not going to want to give her directions to drive to his hideout. She could call the police and send them to him. He won't want her to come to his safe ground."

"Okay." All of that made sense. "But Emily has shut off her phone, so she is going somewhere and doesn't want the police to be able to track her or for me to be able to reach her. She's given up on us."

Kenzie couldn't accept that she had failed. Emily had reached out to her. They'd had a connection. Why hadn't she been more careful not to push Emily too far? Why hadn't Kenzie said something to give her hope that they would be able to save Rhys before anything happened to him?

"So where would they meet?" Kenzie asked. "Where is Saul going to set up a meeting?"

It was an impossible question to answer, and they both knew it.

"I think we need to go," Zachary said, looking around.

Kenzie knew that look. If she didn't get on board, he would end up leaving without her, off chasing a possible lead.

"Okay," she agreed. She looked at Campbell. "There's no point in us sticking around here. I don't think there's anything to find."

"No," he agreed. "I don't know how much longer I'll be here. Probably just long enough to get a couple of cups of coffee onboard. Maybe then I'll know what to do next." He rubbed his forehead, undoubtedly feeling the same fatigue that Kenzie herself felt after being woken up in the middle of the night and thrown into an emergency situation. "Might call in the feds. They have more resources. Might be able to do some things with technology that we can't."

"On TV, they can turn someone's phone back on remotely," Kenzie contributed.

"Yea. Maybe they'll be able to do that," Campbell said tiredly. But he didn't sound very hopeful. Maybe, like so many of the other things that law enforcement was seen doing on TV, that was just another wave of the magic wand, like always being able to identify the origin of the trace soil left in the tread of someone's shoes. "Thanks for coming by. And for what you were able to squeeze out of Emily." Campbell nodded to Kenzie. "Hopefully, it will turn out to be useful in the long run."

He had, apparently, given up on the short run. When Kenzie thought about Rhys, she wanted to cry. He had been so brave, finding ways to bury clues in his messages to Emily and sneak additional ones to her, despite his challenges and a murderer hanging over him, rapidly going off the rails.

They said goodbye to Campbell and left before the coffee arrived. Kenzie regretted that part. She really could use a boost. But she knew that if she didn't leave with Zachary, he would go rogue. And she didn't want to be left behind trying to catch up with him while he ran off trying to save the world by himself.

Again.

They walked out to the car in silence. Zachary took the wheel, looking aside at Kenzie.

"Are you okay?"

"No, not really. You?"

He shrugged and grunted. No words were really needed. Kenzie understood. He pulled away from the curb. Kenzie had no idea where they were going. Maybe just to drive around aimlessly while they spit-balled ideas.

"Do you think she's still in Burlington?" Zachary asked.

Kenzie thought about it. She had asked more than once, but Emily had never answered, other than to tell her that she didn't need to know. Kenzie closed her eyes, but that didn't help. She reviewed the string of texts on her phone.

"No."

"No, you don't think she's in Burlington?"

"No. If she was in Burlington, she probably would have been okay with telling me that. She was far enough away that even if I wanted to get to her, it would take a couple of hours to get there. Even if we could get a location on her phone and knew where she was, she had a cushion of a couple of hours."

"But here, she doesn't," Zachary pointed out the obvious.

"Exactly. If she's in Roxboro and we go looking for her... we could get there in a few minutes."

"Especially if we have her phone location."

"But we don't, and she knows that," Kenzie tried to follow all of the clues to their conclusion. "So she must be somewhere we could find her just by what we know about her."

Zachary nodded. He had apparently followed this chain of logic as well, and that was why he'd wanted to get away from the Salter house. Emily wasn't there. But she was somewhere close by. And she was getting ready to act. That was why she had shut off her phone. She was no longer looking for help.

"She is somewhere we know about." Kenzie considered it. "Home or the school. Or wherever the gang hangs out. But I never got where that is from Campbell or Emily. Is it like in the old books and movies? Do they have a specific territory? A clubhouse or home base?"

"I don't think it would be with the gang. Emily already knows that the other gang members will listen to Saul and let him get away with whatever he wants. They've let him get away with ripping them off; why would she trust them to protect her interests when they haven't protected their own?"

"Maybe now that people know what he's been doing, they'll stand up to him. Or Emily thinks they will."

Zachary shook his head again. And Kenzie trusted him. He had good instincts. If Zachary didn't think that Emily would go to the gang, if he was that sure of himself, he was probably right. He knew human behavior. He could read people.

"So, home or the school. Or somewhere else?" Kenzie asked.

"I think home is too dangerous. I don't think she would agree to meet him there. Not where he could get close to her mother. Home is *her* safe space. Her den. Her cocoon. When she witnessed Mercer's murder and was in shock, she went home to sleep. Not the place you would take someone who was a threat to you and your family."

"So the school." Kenzie looked at the time. "Her friends won't be there yet. But if he is an hour or two away at his cabin then, by the time he gets here, some of the early birds will be starting to show up at the school. Not her friends, maybe, but some of the staff. Early morning clubs. Orchestra practice."

"He'll want to meet somewhere away from people. She'll want to meet somewhere close to people."

Kenzie nodded, thinking about it. The only place they had met with Emily had been at the bus stop across from the school, next to the convenience store. But Emily couldn't meet with Saul there. It was out in the open, where everyone would see. He couldn't bring Rhys there at gunpoint. He would never agree.

Would he have Rhys with him? Or would he leave Rhys stashed somewhere?

"Behind the school?" Kenzie suggested. "In the parking lot?"

"Not bad," Zachary admitted. "But still out in the open. Even in an isolated corner, he won't be able to ensure that no one sees them. As a cop, he'll want to make sure there is a way in and a way out, and that they can't be observed while he is there."

"Somewhere inside the school."

"Yeah."

"It won't be unlocked yet," Kenzie objected.

"It will be soon. At least a couple of the doors. And Saul has ways of opening locked doors, so that isn't a limitation. He knows how vulnerable a door is, even if it is locked. Pick it or kick it."

"Right. Okay. Inside, then. Where does Emily feel safe inside the school?"

They drove in silence for a while, both of them considering the matter.

61

By the time they got to the highway, the stars had faded and the sky was brightening. Rhys was rarely up in time to see the sunrise. Would it be the last one he ever saw?

The bad cop concerned him even more now. He had been worried during the drive to the cabin, wondering how he would survive the ordeal. The cop had grabbed him and handled him like he was just a doll and not a real person. He was rough and wanted to show Rhys he was in charge. The least little thing that Rhys did that didn't comply with his instructions or expectations resulted in a smack or a threat. But it wasn't like he'd gotten beaten up. He'd still been okay when he got to the cabin. Scared, but in one piece.

He wasn't sure how far they were going to make it in the car. The coke affected bad cop's driving. He was fast and reckless, and honking horns followed them everywhere they went. A couple of times, he even tapped someone's bumper when they didn't get out of the way fast enough, and they took one guy's side mirror off when bad cop skimmed past with only inches between the two cars. Rhys hung on to the door and the emergency brake and tried not to cry out every time it looked like they would end up in an accident.

The whole time, the cop kept up a running monologue, like he had been doing while pacing at the cabin. Rhys didn't know whether he was talking to Rhys, to himself, or to someone else he saw or heard in his head. He railed at the drivers, about Em, about Mercer, the gangbanger he had killed. He yelled about his boss and the other cops he worked with. And Kenzie, too. How she was wrong about everything and didn't have any idea what was going on and he'd heard that she had made mistakes on other autopsies.

They were headed back into Roxboro. Rhys still had the phone. The cop hadn't thought to take it away from him when they had started back toward the city. Rhys had casually slid it into his pants pocket, and bad cop had been so amped up, angry, and distracted that his eyes had slid right over Rhys without any indication that he had seen Rhys pocket it.

The cop had been mad when Emily had shut off her phone. He wanted to be in control, and the fact that he could no longer communicate with Emily at all had him frantic. He threw things across the cabin, making Rhys duck and flinch. As much as he tried to show no reaction to anything that bad cop did, he couldn't control his body. The cop kept insisting that Rhys message Emily again to make her turn the phone on, and Rhys kept showing him the *User Offline* message on the screen. He thought the cop was going to throw the phone across the room. Then he would have no way to communicate if Emily decided to turn her phone back on or if he were somewhere the cop couldn't see him for a minute. He could message someone else for help.

Then they had to go outside to see if they could get a better signal and get a message to send from there.

Rhys knew what had happened. He knew that Emily had shut off her phone after her last message. But the cop didn't want to listen to anything Rhys had to say or to take the time to figure it out. Rhys knew that more messages and going outside or even to the highway would not make any difference.

Em was so strong. Tiring of the cop's threats, she had just told him where she would be, and then turned off her phone. There were no more negotiations. Emily was done. The cop could curse and complain as much as he liked, throw as many things as he wanted, but none of that would change anything. He could crash the car, flip it over, and wreck half a dozen cars on the highway, and it wouldn't change anything. Emily was out of touch and the only way to talk to her was to go where she was. That was what bad cop had wanted all along anyway, wasn't it?

They nearly sideswiped a semi, making Rhys let out an inadvertent yelp. The cop swore and swerved and gave the other driver the finger and kept driving with his pedal to the metal like he was some Indy racer. Rhys knew they were never going to make it. The stupid, stoned cop would kill them both before they could even make it back to Roxboro.

***

But somehow, they did it. They got back into the city, and the cop even slowed down once he hit the city streets and did not swear and gesture as much. Maybe the initial kick of the cocaine was wearing off, or he had exhausted enough of his fury, or was now thinking about meeting Emily and what he would say and do to her when that happened.

Rhys touched the phone in his pocket. He wanted to look at their messages again, to see whether Emily had understood everything he had told her. But he already had the whole conversation in his head. He was sure they had understood each other, despite bad cop's determination to control everything.

There were a few cars in the parking lot at the school. Not a lot, but people were starting to arrive to prep for classes, have a coffee, or attend one of the early-morning clubs. Emily had enjoyed her early-morning activities before she and Mercer had become friends. She'd been part of a different crowd then, and Rhys had seen her more often. He didn't like the kids she hung out with now, staying on the outskirts of school society when she wasn't hanging out with Mercer and the gang.

She used to get up early in the morning. Now, she was rarely up by the time school started. Sometimes, she got there in the morning and sometimes not before noon. He missed the way things used to be. It was Mercer's fault that she had changed so much. And now Mercer was gone, but things wouldn't go back to how they used to be.

Bad cop pulled his car into one of the slots that was supposed to be reserved for staff members. Rhys didn't suppose it mattered. Was someone going to give him a ticket? Have it towed? What difference would that make now?

62

Z achary and Kenzie didn't find Emily so much as a result of careful deduction and logic, narrowing down where she would be based on everything they knew about her and what the chances were that she would make certain choices. Instead, they walked through the school, avoiding anyone else and trying doors to see what was unlocked. They stuck to the quieter areas of the school, especially the basement, assuming that for a clandestine meeting, they would prefer a location away from the busy hallways. The early-morning enrichment clubs had started up, and they tried to avoid the kids who were there early and to look like they belonged there and knew where they were going.

Kenzie found a door unlocked and swung it open, only to find a small group of students gathered in a circle, talking.

"Oh, sorry," Kenzie said, ready to close it again. Then she stopped.

A couple of faces looked familiar. She gave herself another second or two to remember them before withdrawing. She jerked her head to invite Zachary to follow her, and when they were both in the room, they shut the door again.

"Um, this is the drama club," a high-pitched, nasally voice told them. "I don't know who *you* are, but this is our room. Talk to Mr. Jefferson."

Kenzie looked carefully at each one of them. Then she returned her gaze to Graham. The one who had told her that he could produce a much more realistic picture of a corpse than the one Emily had taken. Even though the one that Emily had taken had, in fact, been an actual corpse.

"Hey," she said. "You remember me?"

Graham's eyes slid toward a closed door on the other side of the room before looking back at Kenzie.

"You can't be here," he said. "Like Chantelle said, we have the room booked."

The girl who had told them that already nodded, a superior, challenging look on her face.

"Is she here?" Kenzie asked.

"I'm right here," Chantelle said in a huff.

"Not you." Kenzie looked back at Graham. "Emily."

"You know where it is," bad cop growled at Rhys, giving him a shove forward with the barrel of the gun.

Rhys didn't think it was a good idea for him to still have the gun out when he was in the middle of the school. There weren't a lot of kids there yet, but it wouldn't be long before the hallways were full and they were in danger of being accidentally shot by the jumped-up cop.

"Hurry it up," the cop told him. "Don't make this difficult. The more trouble you cause me, the worse things are going to be for your friend."

Rhys looked back at the cop, nodding, letting him see that Rhys was complying with his instructions. But rather than speeding up, he slowed very slightly. The cop might think he could force Emily and Rhys to do whatever he wanted to, but Rhys still had some control over the situation. The cop couldn't force him to go any faster, even if he did have a gun. How would shooting Rhys help him at this point?

He would lose his guide and have to find his way to Emily's meeting place. While dealing with a school on lockdown.

"The theater," bad cop repeated. "You know where it is. And if you try to lead me in another direction, I can look it up on the floor plan or ask someone else. I don't need you."

If he didn't need Rhys, then why didn't he let him go?

He continued to walk slowly along, looking in the other open classroom doors. Wondering if he would run into any teachers along the way or anyone else he knew. He didn't like walking through the school when it was so quiet. It was creepy.

They reached the stairs and Rhys indicated that they had to go down. The cop didn't seem to like the idea, but he looked at the signs and saw a placard for the theater, so he nodded and Rhys started down the stairs ahead of him.

They could hear other activity. The orchestra was practicing. There were shouted instructions and grunts from the direction of the gymnasium. The early-morning programming was in full swing.

The phone in Rhys's pocket started chirping. He pulled it out to check to see what was happening, then remembered that the cop was watching. He might not want the man to see the message or messages on the phone and tried to shove it back down before the cop could realize what was going on.

"What is it?" bad cop said sharply.

Rhys shrugged and kept going. Bad cop closed in on him when he reached the bottom of the stairs, grabbing him by the shoulder and shoving the barrel of the gun into his ribs with a smack that was bound to leave a bruise. Rhys gasped and held his side.

"Let me see. Give it to me."

The phone had been silent since Emily had shut off her phone. The incoming messages could only mean one thing… she was back online again. And if she was online, she could see his location. She had requested to track his live location through the messaging app in one of the last messages they had exchanged. Bad cop, pacing and arguing with himself, breaking down and going off the rails, had not seen the message request, and Rhys had quickly deleted it from the message thread as soon as he had granted permission.

So Emily knew that he was in the school now.

Rhys wrapped his hand around the phone and didn't give it to the cop.

Bad cop didn't spend any time arguing about it. He grabbed Rhys's arm and then pried Rhys's fingers away. He was strong. As tightly as Rhys tried to hold on to it, he couldn't prevent the cop from stealing it. Bad cop looked at the screen and gave a bark of laughter. He handed it back to Rhys.

"Tell her good riddance!"

Rhys looked down at the message on the screen.

Im so sorry Rhys its the only way I can end it

Rhys didn't send a response, and the cop didn't force it. Rhys walked a little more quickly toward the theater. They wanted to get the timing just right.

They were almost there when the report echoed from the theater.

Bad cop swore under his breath and shoved Rhys again, hurrying him toward the theater and what they would find there.

Rhys pushed his way through the side door that led into one of the wings of the theater. It was silent as a tomb. Rhys hurried across the empty wing toward the stage.

A couple of spotlights were turned on so that the scene on the stage was brightly lit. Rhys let out a howl.

"Emily!"

Bad cop had been reaching for him again, whether to slow him down or to push him forward, Rhys didn't know, but he fumbled and fell back slightly in surprise at Rhys using his voice. Rhys ignored his reaction and rushed up to Emily.

63

E mily sat slumped in one of the stage chairs. An upholstered chair with wings and arms. Maybe even the one used in *Arsenic and Old Lace*, the classic murder mystery performed by the school almost every year. The gun that Emily had held in her hand had dropped to the floor.

In the side of her forehead was a bullet hole every bit as vivid as the one Emily had caught in her pictures of Mercer. Every bit as gruesome as the one Rhys had first seen in his grandfather's forehead, repeated in his head thousands upon thousands of times since.

The pink flush was gone from her cheeks as her blood ceased to circulate, already taking on the gray pallor of death. There was a trail of blood down her cheek and a fine spatter on the chair. They wouldn't be able to use it as a stage prop again. Not unless they re-covered it. Rhys grasped Emily's hands, still warm, but limp. Rhys felt her wrist and then her throat for a pulse. He turned to the cop and tried to get out the words he had practiced in his head.

She's dead!

His lips formed the words, but no voice came to his aid.

The cop's eyes were wide with surprise. He stared at Rhys and could clearly understand the words without needing to hear them.

Besides, he could see for himself. He had seen enough bodies to know the difference between living and dead at a glance.

"Saves me a bullet," he snapped.

He considered Rhys for a moment, and Rhys thought that he was going to grab him by the arm again and drag him off, as he had before. Then the cop just turned and walked out, sliding his gun into a concealed holster as he went.

Rhys watched him walk back through the curtain and listened carefully for the noise of the door as he left the same way they had come in. He squeezed Emily's hands and waited.

64

Saul moved quickly through the hallway, mapping out his escape plan. With Emily out of the way, there was no longer anyone who could tie him directly to Mercer's killing, but he still didn't plan to stick around town. His cover had been blown and, whether or not they could officially accuse him of anything, he knew he wouldn't ever have a responsible position with the police department again. Even if they couldn't fire him with cause, because they couldn't prove what he had done, they could sit him in front of a computer all day. Or at the public-facing desk at the precinct, dealing with civilian complaints all day. That would drive him away faster than any criminal investigation.

He had plenty of guns, money, and drugs. He had criminal contacts who would help him to disappear. He could get away cleanly and they could never put anything on him. He could start life somewhere else.

A school bell rang, and Saul could hear doors closing. It seemed odd to be closing doors instead of opening them as the students arrived for classes.

He was moving much more quickly toward his car than he and Rhys had walked when they entered the school to find the theater. Of course the boy had not wanted to move very fast. He knew that things would not turn out well when Saul and Em had their face-to-face discussion.

As it had turned out, things had gone much better than Saul had expected. He laughed to himself. Nice of her to do the dirty work for him. She had known what was coming and had taken the coward's way out rather than to have to face him.

He hit the crash bar on the exit door and got three steps out in the parking lot toward his car before realizing anything was wrong.

"Freeze! Hands in the air, Saul!"

Saul looked around, taking in the guns pointed at him from several directions. Cops sheltering behind cars, over roofs, around corners. It must have been all the active officers on duty, and maybe a few who should have been home, too.

He searched for a way out, his mind racing. The coke made him think faster, but even this juiced-up version of his brain was not coming up with any great solutions. He could pull his gun and shoot it out but, with so many weapons aimed at him, he didn't stand a chance, and suicide by cop was not an honorable way to go out.

They didn't have enough to arrest him for Mercer's death. He was sure about it. The boy's kidnapping? Maybe. But he couldn't testify. And Saul hadn't been the one to pull the trigger on Emily. He could find a way to plead extreme emotional distress or confusion from the drugs. He could get bail and then run for it. He knew how to foil an ankle monitor.

He turned around, looking in all directions. He already knew there was no physical escape. He raised his hands to shoulder level.

"Take a picture."

Kenzie looked down at Emily, who was still slumped in the chair, eyes closed, her mouth barely moving when she spoke.

"What?"

"Before I move or take any of this off. You need to take a picture for me."

Rhys finally moved from his position, holding Emily's hand and looking stricken. He rose to his feet and looked for the best angles to take some pictures from. He still looked upset, and Kenzie wanted to get him to his grandma and maybe to the hospital as quickly as possible. The two kids seemed to be too occupied with the staged scene and makeup to worry about real life just yet.

Rhys got the pictures he wanted and tapped Emily on the shoulder. She opened her eyes and looked at him.

"Got them?"

Rhys nodded.

Emily stretched and yawned widely, displaying her tonsils for all to see. She looked at Kenzie, not at all embarrassed. "I don't think I got a wink of sleep last night. I'm gonna go home and sleep for a week."

"You're going to need to talk to the police first. And maybe get checked out by a doctor."

"A doctor? What for?"

Kenzie looked at the bullet wound in the side of Emily's head, which she knew wasn't real, and tried to come up with an answer. "I know you haven't been physically hurt, but you've been through a lot of traumatic stuff the last couple of weeks. You should talk to someone."

"I don't need to. Not right now. What I need is sleep. And knowing my boy is back!" Emily grabbed Rhys and gave him a hug, making him laugh. Kenzie was sure that if his skin were lighter, they would have been able to see him blushing. Emily rubbed Rhys's tight black curls roughly. "Rhys is the one who needs to see a doctor." She pulled back from him a little to look him in the face. "I was so scared he was going to hurt you. When he said he was going to shoot you in the knees, and you sent the video with him sounding so whacked out…"

Rhys nodded. He wiped his forehead dramatically with the back of his hand.

Kenzie studied Rhys, looking for any signs of injury. "Did he hurt you? Did he touch you at all?"

Rhys waved her question away as inconsequential. Kenzie shook her head. "Rhys. He was acting crazy. He was threatening you. He killed that other young man. I didn't know if... I didn't know how we were going to get you back safely." Her voice cracked a little, and she let it. It wouldn't hurt him to know how emotional she was about it. How much she and Zachary cared.

He nodded and looked down for a minute, and she thought he was probably thinking about how close he had come and how he himself had wondered if he would make it. He must have been terrified, no matter how casual he was trying to act about it now.

"We did it. Everybody is safe," Emily said, pulling Rhys to her again, to hug him sideways and then keep her arm wrapped around his shoulders. "But I don't know how you got here," she told Kenzie, "Did Rhys share his location?"

Emily knew that she hadn't shared hers. Kenzie shook her head. "No. And it would have been nice if one of you had thought to do that. You could share with each other, but not with us?"

Emily rolled her eyes and looked away. "Didn't want you tracking me. Didn't need more cops showing up to wreck everything. All you wanted to do was sic the cops on me."

"That's not true. We were trying to help you and Rhys."

"By bringing the cops in," Emily reasserted. Kenzie wasn't going to be able to talk her out of her opinion that the cops would have just ruined everything and gotten Emily or Rhys killed.

But then, it had been a cop who had killed Mercer. Did Kenzie really think that she could talk Emily out of how she felt about that? That, okay, there was one corrupt cop, but there were no more and they would all behave just exactly how they had been trained? It was a hard sell.

As they spoke, cops were starting to drift into the theater. There hadn't been time to get them in place before Saul arrived with Rhys. They'd barely had enough time to get the stage set before Saul had gotten there. Emily had been watching their location on her phone, so they had known how close they were and there had not been time to get the police there before his arrival.

Campbell climbed the stairs to the stage and walked up casually. Though he was obviously tired, he looked much better than the last time Kenzie had seen him, when he had been worried that they had lost Rhys. That the boy was about to be tortured and killed by a coked-up dirty cop. Now that both teens were safe and Saul was in custody, Campbell's limbs were loose and his face unlined. Back to the cool, friendly cop that Kenzie knew. He looked Emily over, studying the makeup.

"Well, that's convincing. I guess it helps to have a coroner doing your makeup."

"It wasn't me," Kenzie said. She looked around for the drama club kids, who were still hanging back. "Graham told me he could do a better job of making up a dead person than the photo I had." She grinned at Campbell, sharing the joke that her picture *had* been of a dead person. "And I gotta say, he came through. I just helped with a few small adjustments."

Graham stood back from them, blushing.

"You did it," Kenzie told him again. "Saul never had a doubt that Emily was really dead."

"It was the blood spatter," Graham said. "That was you."

"No. That zombie skin tone…" Kenzie disagreed.

Emily fingered the fake bullet wound. She caught Rhys staring at it. For an instant, Kenzie saw concern flash across her face. Then she was swaggering and making faces at Rhys. "You gonna have nightmares about zombie girl now? This is the stuff of your worst nightmares, isn't it?" And it probably *was*, but Emily was trying to make it comic now, to erase anything serious or scary from the experience. She moved her lips in weird, exaggerated shapes, threatening to kiss Rhys, making him laugh and pull back from her, holding his hands up to stop her. He opened his mouth to say something, but no words came out, and he just shook his head and mouthed "no, no, no," as Emily fooled around, trying to make him laugh harder.

Emily had good instincts. Kenzie thought that maybe a bullet wound in the head would be less traumatic for Rhys to remember, with the addition of Emily and her silly faces and teasing. Maybe now, when the images of Grandpa Clarence came up, he would be able to push them away instead of obsessing over them.

65

Things moved slowly, as they always did when there was a crime scene to be processed and witnesses to be interviewed. And Kenzie herself was one of the witnesses this time, trying to describe the thought processes that had brought them to the school and how they had helped to stage the scene before Saul had arrived. *And* had called the police. Kenzie emphasized that they had promptly contacted the authorities as soon as they became aware of the situation.

Principal Lakes came to talk to the police and to Zachary and Kenzie. And she gave Emily and Rhys both quick, tight hugs to let them know that she had been concerned about them and was glad that things had worked out so they were safe. Rhys ducked his head and looked embarrassed, and Emily returned the hug with a big one of her own. Kenzie couldn't believe how different Emily looked with a smile on her face. The sullen, withdrawn girl that she had met earlier was gone. She was back to that chipper, happy girl her mother had missed.

"Things are going to change around here," Principal Lakes warned, putting a hand on either side of Emily's face and looking her in the eyes. "I want to see you back in the drama club and stirring things up around here. I don't like the way that girl disappeared."

Emily nodded, swallowing a couple of times. "I miss it too. It's been…" She trailed off, not sure what to say.

"Don't let yourself get swallowed up by someone else's personality. You're special just the way you are."

"Special," Emily repeated mockingly.

"You are," Principal Lakes told her. "I don't care what anybody has to say about it."

"Okay." Emily gave a little laugh. She was stuck being "special" but seemed to be okay with that.

"And you…" Lakes looked at Rhys. "You're always getting mixed up in things."

He shrugged and looked away.

"He hears things," Kenzie said. "He's quiet and people forget that he's there, but he sees and hears things no one else does."

Rhys nodded his agreement.

"I don't know why you won't hang with the drama club," Emily told Rhys. "You're a really good actor."

He shrugged.

"I mean it," Emily said. "Do you think just anyone could have sold that performance? What would have happened if he hadn't believed I was dead?"

Kenzie had a hard time believing how smoothly it had gone. Saul had not even hesitated. He had believed that Emily was dead one hundred percent and, with that task taken care of, had been prepared to just disappear. If only the police hadn't been stationed outside to nab him as soon as he left the school.

"Let's get these kids to their parents," Campbell said. Principal Lakes had decided to keep the school open for the day, even though the students who were there were too distracted to focus on their studies. The school was the only form of childcare and supervision that a lot of those families had. But Rhys and Emily were going home. To catch up on their sleep, if nothing else.

Kenzie joined hands with Zachary, and they walked out of the school to the designated area in the parking lot where the parents and several medical professionals were waiting. Vera held out her arms for Rhys, crying as she approached. He swallowed and smoothed the expression on his face to keep from giving away how emotional he was and walked into her arms. Vera held him close, eyes closed, squeezing him hard.

Emily's mother was there too. Standing beside Vera, She looked uncertain, watching Emily approaching, not sure how to act. Their hug was more awkward. They appeared to be less emotional than Vera, but Kenzie saw each of them wipe a tear away.

"Hey," Emily's mom said. She sniffled. "You know where my hair dryer is? I haven't been able to find it."

Emily laughed. She hooked a thumb back toward the school. "Art room. I was using it to dry papier mache."

"Don't take my stuff without asking," Mrs. Cross told her sternly. She tightened her grip. "Especially don't take *you* away. I hate that."

"Okay," Emily laughed and sobbed, holding on to her. "I'll ask first next time."

EPILOGUE

Kenzie was glad to be at the Petersons'. Somewhere she always felt welcomed and cared for and could just relax and be herself. There were no expectations like when dining with her parents. No need to be perfect or "switched on" the whole time.

"So, it sounds like you've had a pretty eventful few weeks," Lorne commented, as everyone dished up Pat's homemade gnocchi. "A promotion, a gangland murder, and a kidnapping?"

Kenzie sipped her drink, then took a few long breaths, waiting for her heart to slow down. She wanted to be able to talk about what had happened calmly, without having to relive her own abduction. She paid attention to the coldness of the glass, the sweetness of the peach spritzer, and the hearty, spicy smell of the marinara sauce, trying to dwell on the moment and not to let herself slide back.

"Yes, it's been kind of crazy," she admitted. "I'm really glad that everything turned out okay. I wasn't sure that it would." She swallowed. "Things were looking pretty grim there for a while when Saul was holding Rhys and threatening to hurt him and anyone else Emily knew." She looked at Zachary, passing the question off to him.

"It was pretty intense," Zachary agreed. "Trying to figure out where he had Rhys, where he was going to meet Emily, and trying to figure out how to stop him and get Emily and Rhys somewhere safe." He shook his head. "Emily and Rhys had already concocted this whole thing. I'm not sure how, when they had to hide their messages in plain sight."

"They must be on the same wavelength," Pat commented.

Zachary and Kenzie nodded. "It can be challenging to communicate with Rhys at the best of times," Kenzie agreed. "They practically had to be telepathic to set Saul up like that. But they did it. A picture here, a word there. Emily, at least, was able to write whatever she wanted to. Rhys was more limited."

"But he still did things like typing the stars around words in his messages," Zachary agreed. "I think the two of them know each other a lot better than either of them is willing to tell."

"And the gang member who was killed? Was her romance with him just a sham?" Lorne asked.

"No. Definitely not," Kenzie shook her head. "Probably nothing good would ever have come from it even if she and Mercer had run away together somewhere they could be safe, but Emily really did have feelings for him. It's hard as a teenager... those relationships don't last, but that doesn't make them less real. I think that Emily and Rhys are just good friends."

"Hopefully, Emily will turn her life back around now that Mercer is gone," Zachary offered. He rubbed the bridge of his nose. "Principal Lakes is going to make an effort to keep her in school and away from the gang."

"And Rhys too," Kenzie contributed. At Zachary's confused look, she clarified. "I think that Emily is going to be his special project too."

"And maybe he'll be Emily's. She wanted him to get into the drama club."

"Is there a funeral for the young man who was killed?" Lorne asked. "A chance to say goodbye and get some closure around his death? It must have been difficult for her to deal with his death the way things happened."

"No, his cremains are being shipped back to Ohio. Where he

originally came from. I guess that's where his parents are. I hope Emily gets some therapy to help her to work through it."

"And Rhys? I hope someone is working with him," Lorne said. "That's a lot of trauma to work through."

Kenzie swallowed and just nodded.

"We'll make sure he gets some help," Zachary supplied. "He's already in therapy. But so far… the last few days, he's seemed stable. Better than he was before."

"As long as he's not just masking." Lorne raised one brow speculatively. "It could all come tumbling down later."

"I think that the thing that bothered him the most was the picture," Kenzie said. "It made the memories of Clarence's death that much more real. Now that justice has been served, and he had a part in it, maybe he feels like he got his power back. That he isn't trapped anymore, forever a five-year-old with the adults making all of the decisions."

And maybe Kenzie had gotten a bit of her power back too, helping to get Rhys away from his kidnapper after she had been powerless to escape her own.

Maybe now they could both feel a measure of peace.

Did you enjoy this book? Reviews and recommendations are vital to making a book successful.

Please leave a review at your favorite book store or review site and share it with your friends.

Don't miss the following bonus material:
Sign up for mailing list to get a free ebook
Read a sneak preview chapter
Other books by P.D. Workman
Learn more about the author

DON'T MISS A THING! GET THE LATEST NEWS AND A FREE EBOOK

PDWORKMAN.COM/SIGNUP

PREVIEW OF SHE WAS OUT OF REACH

She Was Out of Reach

is the next book in the Kenzie Kirsch/Zachary Goldman timeline

PREVIEW CHAPTER 1

Zachary had been surprised that Rose Bircher wanted to meet him in her lab rather than at home. Most women in her circumstances would have been at home, unable to focus on work. They would take a leave of absence until things could get straightened out.

But maybe that was an unjust judgment. He hadn't known many parents in her circumstances and supposed that a mother could want to bury herself in her work just as much as a father.

He only waited in the reception area for a couple of minutes. There was a lot of white. White walls, white tiled floors, a sign on the wall with the lab's name in silver letters mounted on a shiny white surface. It made him think of a school or hospital. Not a restful place. Somewhere important work was being done and people were all focused on their projects.

The door into the inner workspace opened and Zachary got his first glimpse at the woman who wanted to hire him.

Rose Bircher was casually dressed. No white lab jacket. She was a thirty-something woman, on the thin side, with straight brown hair and a pleasant face. She wore dark-rimmed glasses and an aqua polo shirt with the company logo. She looked at Zachary, giving him a quick once-over, then held out her hand.

"Mr. Goldman?"

"Just Zachary."

"Rose. Thanks for coming. Follow me." She turned away from him, back toward the door. "You want coffee?"

"Sure."

"Good." She led him first to a breakroom with a coffee machine, stacks of mugs, and a couple of vending machines. The smell of freshly brewed coffee filled the air. "We go through the stuff like water around here. And it's pretty good."

She poured them each a mug and handed one to Zachary. He followed her further down the hall, through a bullpen with lots of cubicles and young people pounding away at keyboards, their eyes intent on their screens. Few looked up to see who was walking by as Zachary followed Rose to the meeting room.

Rose poked her head into one of the meeting rooms to make sure it was vacant and then motioned Zachary in. There was nothing special about the room. He'd seen a hundred like it before: a table, chairs, and a small side cabinet with supplies. A whiteboard on the wall. There was a projector and screen controlled by a remote and currently recessed out of view.

Rose sat down and motioned for Zachary to do the same.

"I really appreciate you coming."

Zachary nodded.

Studying her, he could see the signs of stress on Rose's face. Puffy skin under her eyes testified that she hadn't slept well, though a layer of concealer kept the dark shadows from being visible. Faint lines across her forehead. Her hand shook as she raised the coffee mug to her mouth.

"I was told that you have investigated missing children before."

Zachary nodded. He'd had a little experience in that area. Usually teenagers, though he had also rescued his ex-wife Bridget's twin babies.

"I have some experience in that area, though I don't do a lot of missing persons," he told her honestly. "It is your daughter who is missing?" He asked it tentatively. She was too young to be the mother of a teenager. But she was not frantic like he expected the parent of a missing baby to be. But Rose had already surprised him in several respects.

"Yes." she swallowed and stared past Zachary at the wall. "My daughter Claire. She is five."

"Did you report her missing to the police?"

He had learned not to take this for granted. Not because it was like on TV where kidnappers for ransom told the parents not to call the police or FBI *or else*. Many parents did not report their children missing to the police because they knew who had taken the child. Often a family member. And they just wanted the child found and returned with the least disruption possible. Without making family business public or making a parent or grandparent look bad in front of their friends. People preferred to keep personal business quiet, even when it involved a child being taken.

"Yes. I talked to the police. They think that it was Claire's father."

That explained why he hadn't seen anything about it on the TV or internet news. Parental abductions were routine, of little interest to the public unless there were some unique, attention-grabbing details.

"Are you married? Or were you?"

"No. I met him in school. We lived together for a while. But we weren't really compatible. It didn't work out."

"Does he have shared custody? Visitation?"

"No. He didn't want anything to do with Claire, and I respected that. He has never been involved in her life."

"And that hasn't changed lately? He hasn't come to you asking if he could see her? Talk to her? Maybe he offered to pay something for child support?"

"No. We have some mutual friends, so I've kept track of him from a distance for the last few years. Occasionally, we've ended up at a party together or something like that. He asked for a picture once."

"Recently?"

"How long ago is *recent?*" She held her palms up questioningly. "It was... maybe a couple of months ago."

Zachary pulled out his notepad. He made sure that the date was filled in at the top of the page and wrote down Claire's name and the fact that her birth father had asked for her photo a couple of months before. That could be significant. He *had* shown some interest in her recently. Depending on what kind of a picture it was, he might have been able to repurpose it for a passport photograph or other identification. Or maybe just a phone picture flashed at someone to prove that yes, he was Claire's dad, or he wouldn't have her picture on his phone, would he?

Rose watched him and didn't make any comment about his messy, nearly unreadable handwriting.

"Does that mean you're taking the case?"

"Let's get a few more details first. Why do the police think Claire's father has her? Have they talked to him? Where did she disappear from?"

"Such a high percentage of kidnappings are non-custodial parents or family members; that's just what they assume from the beginning unless you have eyewitnesses who saw her being taken. And no one did. We were at a kids' play place at the mall. I was... on my phone. You can't keep an eye on your kid the whole time; there are all kinds of tunnels, slides, climbers, and ball pits. Your kid just gets swallowed up by this place with all of the other kids..."

Zachary nodded. He had seen places like that. A great adventure for kids. Playing tag or dare with their friends, running off excess energy, exploring.

"How did he get her out of there? Don't they have ID to make sure you can only take the kid you arrived with?"

"Yes. I don't know how anyone could get her out of there. Some of their security cameras were down. I always thought they had really good security: guards, monitors, sign in logs, all that kind of thing. But someone got in there and got my daughter out without anyone noticing. I called her and looked for her. I got frantic. They thought I was just being a helicopter parent and freaking out because she was out of sight. But when they made announcements and had their staff members walk around looking for her, no one could find her."

Rose swallowed hard and sipped her coffee. Zachary wasn't sure why she felt it necessary to mask her emotions, to make it look like this hadn't affected her. Most mothers cried. They weren't afraid to show him just how upset they were.

"How long has she been missing?"

Rose looked at her watch. "Three days." She put her palms over her eyes, warming them. After three days with minimal sleep, she was undoubtedly feeling the strain. Scratchy, sticky, swollen eyes. A fatigue headache. Brain fog.

"Have the police talked to her father?"

"No. They tried to track him down to talk to him. But he's out of the country. They haven't been able to talk to him or to get other authorities to talk to him." Her tone was flat.

"Out of the country? Where?"

She stared down at the surface of her coffee. Her eyes glittered with unshed tears, but she didn't let them fall. She just stared as if mesmerized by the reflection of the light on the surface of her drink.

"Saudi Arabia."

PREVIEW CHAPTER 2

Z achary's heart sank. He wasn't going to be able to do anything for Rose Bircher. *Saudi Arabia?* If Claire's father had taken her there, there wasn't much that Zachary—or anyone else—could do about it. That was one of the countries where non-custodial fathers liked to take kidnapped children—a country where he had all of the rights, and Rose had virtually none. The authorities there would not cooperate with US authorities. They would not deal with the child's mother.

"I'm not sure there is anything I can do to help you," he told Rose gently.

She didn't look surprised, her expression unchanging.

"I was told that you were unconventional. And stubborn. That you could get results where the police couldn't."

"Well... sometimes that has been true. But I can't always find something helpful. The police are your best bet. I just... sometimes I can find something else that they missed or follow up on a hunch. But... Saudi Arabia is a long way away."

"I know it is. But the police will only follow their specific proto-col. And if they think that the child is out of the country and in a place where they can't reach her... they just issue whatever paper they do to tell the government that they believe she is over there and object to them not helping with the kidnapping case… and that's it. Then they just put a flag on his passport so that if he ever comes back into the country, they can pull him aside and talk to him."

He wasn't going to bring her back. If he had taken his daughter to Saudi Arabia, he intended to keep her there. He wasn't going to bring her back to the US.

"What is his name? Claire's father?"

Rose looked at him for a moment before answering, considering his response. Zachary examined it himself. If he couldn't do anything for Rose and didn't intend to take the case, then why ask for his name?

"Amir Osman."

"Is he from there?"

"No. He was born in America. But I guess… with his family name he could get a visa or whatever you need to immigrate there." She rubbed her temples. "I don't know all the details of that kind of thing."

"So he had been planning this for a while. He asked for her picture. He had to apply for whatever paperwork he needed to take her there."

"I suppose."

"Do the police have confirmation as to whether she was traveling with him?"

"He had a child with him. But a different name. Not Claire Bircher. He was also traveling with a woman. The child is supposed to be hers, not his."

Zachary nodded. Just enough obfuscating to make it effective. If an Amber alert had been issued under the name Claire Bircher, no one would have connected her with a child of another name. Until it was too late.

And because Amir hadn't had anything to do with his biological daughter before that and had never said he even wanted a visit with her, there was no reason for her mother to mention him when Claire went missing from the mall. It wasn't a case of a non-custodial parent not returning her on time after a visit. There had been no reason to suspect that her biological father had any interest in her until it was too late. And getting a child back from a country like Saudi Arabia... Zachary had heard stories.

"I'm not sure what you're hoping I can do for you," he told Rose. "The police have done everything they can, and I assume you've talked to experts in this kind of case. I don't have a lot of familiarity with international kidnapping and certainly have no experience flying to another country to try to get her back."

Rose took off her glasses and rubbed the bridge of her nose.

"There hasn't been much of an investigation into this case," she said slowly. "I mean, on the surface, they've done everything they should. They locked down the mall and made sure that no one could get her out, but obviously she was gone by the time that happened, because there was no sign of her. They set up roadblocks. They did a search with K9's. They talked about an Amber Alert, but it didn't go out until quite a bit later because they didn't have a description of the kidnapper or the vehicle. But once all of that preliminary stuff was done and they found out that I am... estranged from Claire's biological father, they decided that it was him. They put out all those travel alerts and searched to see if he had left the country during the window from the last time I saw Claire until they stopped him from traveling outside the United States."

"And that was when they found he had already fled with his daughter."

"With his girlfriend's daughter. They don't have any evidence that it was Claire."

Zachary was starting to get a feeling for what Rose was getting at. "Do they have any footage of Amir with Claire?"

"No. They have a few fuzzy airport surveillance pictures of him... but there's no way to tell if the girl with him is Claire or someone else. The girl in the picture is dark-haired."

At Zachary's look, she pulled out her phone and, after finding a picture, turned the screen around to face him. A little girl with long, blond hair and an impish smile.

"He might have dyed her hair."

Rose nodded. "Of course. And that is what the police are assuming. They all assume that the girl Amir had with him when he left the country was Claire."

"No full facial views"

"No. I thought all the airports had those check-in terminals that take a picture of you. But I guess they don't. Or they don't take pictures of kids who are too small to reach it, just their parents."

Zachary nodded slowly. There were holes in airport security procedures, despite what the officials would have people believe. People still traveled under forged documents. And the holes for children were even bigger than those for adults. Children weren't terrorists. They were vulnerable, but they were not a danger. It was a different mindset.

Zachary scratched a few more notes into his notepad and turned his eyes back to Rose.

"So there have been no confirmed sightings of Claire since you last saw her at the play place."

"Yeah. Exactly."

So, was she taken by a stranger? Or had she been taken by her birthfather, passed off as another child, and flown out of the country? Without putting eyes on her, they couldn't be sure. The police might be right. They probably were. The ex-spouse or the child's non-custodial parent was the number one suspect in any child abduction case. It was far more likely to have been committed by a parent or other family member than by a stranger.

But Amir had not been part of Claire's life. He would only know where to find them if he had been following them.

"How many times have you seen Amir in the last six months?"

Rose shook her head. "Not at all. Well, maybe once, I guess. When he asked about a picture."

"You said that you sometimes run into him at events. You have mutual friends? Or are you in the same profession?" Zachary looked around him. "What exactly do you do here?"

"Like I said, I met him in college. We were both in computer science together. He went into industrial applications and I went into research, so we didn't exactly follow the same path. But we were both techies. And… yeah… some mutual friends."

"Have you talked to any of those friends about him? About Claire being missing?"

She shook her head. "No. Do you think I should?"

"If you could give me names and contact numbers, it might be better if I reach out to them. An unbiased third party rather than the mother accusing her ex of doing something."

"Okay." Rose didn't argue about it or say Zachary wouldn't find anything out talking to them. But if she'd been told by whoever referred her to Zachary that he was unconventional and dogged and might be able to find something out, then Rose would be more open to giving him whatever he needed without question. She looked at her phone. "Do you want me to read them out to you?"

"Why don't you just share the contacts with me from your phone? Then I won't get any digits reversed."

She nodded her agreement and spent a few minutes reviewing her contacts list and texting some of them to Zachary.

"Maybe Amir would have talked to one of these people about Claire," Zachary said. "If we can even get confirmation that he has been talking about her in the last few months, that would be a start. And if he has been saying that he wants to be a part of her life..."

Rose shook her head. "If he wanted to be a part of her life, then why wouldn't he come to me and ask me about seeing her?"

"That would be the logical approach," Zachary agreed. "But people make choices that aren't logical. Maybe he figured you would say no, and he didn't want to tip his hand. Easier to get away with it if he never let on that he wants to be in her life."

"I guess," Rose agreed. "If he'd been trying to get visitation or custody and then she disappeared from the mall or anywhere else, then he is the first one I would have thought of. It wouldn't have been hours before the police put a stop on Amir leaving the country."

Zachary nodded his agreement. "Who was the first person?"

"What?"

"You said he would have been the first person you thought of. As being her abductor. Who was the first person you thought of?"

"Oh... well, I just thought of someone who had been hanging around the play place. Some perv who went to watch the kids and was watching for a little girl to be by herself. A stranger, like on TV. I know parental abductions are more common, but I never thought of Amir as being her parent. I'm the only parent she's ever had in her life."

"What about your parents? Is there anyone else who helps to take care of her?"

"They're in New York. They only see her now and then when they come for a visit. And they don't babysit."

"Do you have a caregiver? Who looks after her while you're at work?"

"She's in school now. I have a woman who does after-school care until I can get there. But it's only an hour or so. A woman in the neighborhood who looks after a bunch of kids."

"A day home."

"Like that, yes. But just for after school."

"Can you give me her information?"

Rose shrugged and conceded.

"Did you see anyone at the play place you were suspicious of? Uncomfortable around?"

"Well, like any other mother, I kept a pretty close eye on any men who were there without a wife or girlfriend. The play place isn't supposed to let people without kids of their own in. You know, it's supposed to be a safe place where pedophiles can't hang around watching kids. It's just kids and their parents."

"I don't imagine it's too hard to get around that. Tell them that your wife and kid are already there. Point someone out and say you're with them. Or go with your sister or best friend and her kid."

Rose sighed and nodded. "It's great if everyone is honest and follows the rules, but the people who really want to get around the rules will."

"Like gun registration," Zachary suggested. "The people who follow the rules are the ones who are not planning to break the laws. Those who are planning to use their guns for illegal purposes are the ones who *don't* register them."

"Right."

"Was there anyone at the play place that day that stuck out to you?" Zachary waited a few seconds to see if she would answer before prompting her further. "Anyone you felt was watching Claire? Or watching you?"

She hesitated, then shook her head. Zachary raised his brows. "Who did you just think of?"

"No one. I didn't think anyone was watching Claire."

"Someone watching you?"

There was another instant of hesitation before Rose shook her head. "No."

"Did the police get any surveillance video from the play place?"

"Some. But they said that only a few of the cameras were recording." She pressed her lips together and shook her head. "I always thought they were much more secure than they really are. There are lots of cameras around and signs saying that you are on camera. I don't know if they were even all real cameras. But only a couple were maintained."

"Did they show you any of the surveillance videos? Show you any pictures of men who had been hanging around that might have been suspicious? What did you tell them when they first arrived?"

"They didn't show me anything. I guess they must not have found anyone suspicious."

"I'll see if I can get copies of them. You never know. The police might have missed something." He'd been able to spot tiny details on videos before. Details the police had missed or not thought important.

"What did you tell the police when they first arrived? That Claire had disappeared? That she was gone? That she had been taken? What did you think had happened?"

"I said... that someone must have taken her."

"You'd never had any episodes with Claire before? When you lost track of her for a few minutes, thought something had happened, and then found her again?"

"No... maybe when I lost sight of her for a minute, but I always found her again. She stayed close by. She'd be on the other side of the clothes rack at the department store. Or looking at a toy or snack she wanted to buy. Something like that."

"And at the park? School? The play place? What did she like to do? Did she ever play hide-and-seek? Play a prank on you?"

"No. She was a pretty easy kid. Lots of energy, but she was a good girl. Mostly, she followed the rules. She was never far away."

"So when you couldn't find her, she didn't come back to you, didn't come when you called, you believed that someone had abducted her."

Rose nodded. "Yes."

"A stranger. You never thought that someone you knew might have come and… taken her out for ice cream or taken her because they didn't think you were a good parent. Or Amir because he wanted her to be a part of your life and didn't think you would allow it."

Rose shook her head slowly. "None of those things ever occurred to me."

Zachary looked at the notes he had written down while they talked. The girl was missing. The police thought the case was solved, but the girl was out of their reach.

But there was no proof that Claire was with Amir. He understood why Rose felt so unsettled about the case. Not angry because Amir had come and stolen Claire away, but full of questions and not sure the police were right about what had happened to her little girl.

"Okay." Zachary dug a card out of his pocket and laid it before her. "Those are my rates. I'll need a small retainer to get started. I will see what I can dig up."

She let out her breath in a long sigh. "Thank you. I needed somebody in my court. I really don't think Amir took her to Saudi Arabia."

She Was Out of Reach, Book #17 of the *Zachary Goldman Mysteries* series by P.D. Workman can be purchased at pdworkman.com

ABOUT THE AUTHOR

P.D. Workman is a USA Today Bestselling author, winner of several awards from Library Services for Youth in Custody and the InD'tale Magazine's Crowned Heart award, and has published over 100 mystery/suspense/thriller and young adult books, including stand alones and these series: Auntie Clem's Bakery cozy mysteries, Reg Rawlins Psychic Investigator paranormal mysteries, Zachary Goldman Mysteries (PI), Kenzie Kirsch Medical Thrillers, Parks Pat Mysteries (police procedural), and YA series: Tamara's Teardrops, Between the Cracks, and Breaking the Pattern.

Workman loves writing about the underdog, who the reader may love or hate. She has been praised for her realistic details, deep characterization, and sensitive handling of the serious social issues that appear in all of her stories, from light cozy mysteries through to darker, grittier young adult and mystery/suspense books.

> P. D. Workman, does not shy from probing the deep psychological scars of childhood trauma, mental illness, and addiction. Also characteristic of this author, these extremely sensitive issues are explored with extensive empathy, described with incredible clarity, and portrayed with profound insight.
>
> — —KIM, GOODREADS REVIEWER

Some of Workman's titles have been translated into Spanish, French, Portuguese, German, and Italian.

Workman began writing at an early age and is a prolific reader as well as writer. She is also passionate about teaching and learning, expresses her creativity through art and cooking, and loves exploring the Calgary parks and green spaces where the Parks Pat Mysteries are set. She was a legal assistant for many years and has done extensive charitable work.

Workman was born and raised in Alberta, Canada, and is married with one adult son.

Please visit P.D. Workman at pdworkman.com to see what else she is working on, to join her mailing list, and to link to her social networks.

If you enjoyed this book, please take the time to recommend it to other purchasers with a review or star rating and share it with your friends!

tiktok.com/@pdworkmanauthor

facebook.com/pdworkmanauthor

x.com/pdworkmanauthor

instagram.com/pdworkmanauthor

amazon.com/author/pdworkman

bookbub.com/authors/p-d-workman

goodreads.com/pdworkman

linkedin.com/in/pdworkman

pinterest.com/pdworkmanauthor

youtube.com/pdworkman

Find P.D. Workman's books at

PDWORKMAN.COM

Scan the QR code below

www.ingramcontent.com/pod-product-compliance
Lightning Source LLC
Chambersburg PA
CBHW031104030726
47496CB00002BA/366